"Twelve thousand miles west of the Hollywood Bowl, it was already the morning of the next day...."

Colonel Smith had counseled Henderson back at what passed for their Officer's Club at the US Embassy compound in Phu-Lama, "The names are different here than in Vietnam, but it's the same fucking clusterfuck, son. So just do the usual fuckin' things — keep yer map coordinates straight and carry extra ammo and water when yer in the chabongas.

And, as it's Phuland, stick to yer cover, keep yer mouth shut in bars, avoid the press like the fuckin' plague, and don't even think about gettin' captured. Do all that an' you'll be fine. But in any case don't sweat it too much — it's nothin' you haven't dealt with before."

Amazon Publishing Inc.

for

PNG-RDC(BVBA)

Copyright © 2020 P.N.Gwynne

All Rights Reserved

ISBN-13: 978-0-578-73050-9

Library of Congress Control Number: 2020913331

Cover design by Matthew Morse at HeyMatthew.com

Other novels by P. N. Gwynne:

Firmly by the Tail
Pushkin Shove
The Bronx Bombing

ACKNOWLEDGMENT

Other than the fictional characters' names (and in some cases their deaths) and the Kingdom of Phuland itself, everything in this novel is faithfully reconstituted as I remember it.

I'm indebted to the estimable Civil War veteran on the Union side Ambrose Bierce (1842-1914), the written and filmed versions of whose extraordinary "An Occurrence At Owl Creek Bridge" (1890 and 1962 respectively) made lasting impressions on me as a young man.

And bookoo thanks to Annie for the splendid "Beast".

"It's customary to say that we lost
the Vietnam war, but who's 'we'?"

— DINESH D'SOUZA

"The Vietnam War was fought all over the world."

— A. A. GILL *(in the LONDON SUNDAY TIMES, 1996)*

"We will win the Vietnam War not in Vietnam,
not at the Paris talks, but in the streets of America."

— YURI ANDROPOV

*(He said this when he was still head of the KGB, addressing the Soviet Politburo
in 1972, as quoted by the Soviet defector Arkady Schevchenko. Note the "We".)*

"Nobody goes through life undefeated."

— DON IMUS

"IMPERIALIST WARMONGER PIG"

OR

AN OCCURRENCE AT LANDING SITE-ECHO

A NOVEL BY

P.N. GWYNNE

1/ 0800 HOURS (LOCAL TIME)

"Wars are not fought in grassy meadows on sunny afternoons."

— THE DUKE OF WELLINGTON

It was 26 April 1972 in what the protesters called Amerika.

George McGovern was inflicting his Dakota whine upon the nation's screens and airwaves, enjoining his "peace children" as well as the bemused rest of the country to "Come Home".

The Watergate wouldn't be broken into for another three months, and President Tricky wouldn't end the draft for another nine.

In Washington D.C., the fact that it was getting late — 9 P.M. already — was not deterring *in the slightest* a semi-huge mob of goofy "counter-culturists" from cheering on a smirking Norman Mailer, a doddering Dr. Spock and an excruciatingly self-conscious Joan Baez, along with other fashionably scruffy "Resist The War" luminaries, as they attempted, in the artificial light brought on by the eerie bluish televisual glare — to do something surreal to the Pentagon. There was much, if loose, talk of levitation — and some there were who actually believed it.

Jane Fonda's notorious picture, the one of her seated at a North Vietnamese anti-aircraft gun with an NVA helmet on her head, still took pride of place, alongside Che Guevara and Eldridge Cleaver, in college dorms throughout the parts of the country where "concerned" folk held sway... in this recently and suddenly and, it had to be said, mysteriously re-fashioned "Republik".

Meanwhile, it was still 6 p.m. out on what one of the Smothers Brothers liked to call "the Specific Coast", where Leonard Bernstein and Country Joe and The Fish were headlining a sold-out concert at the Hollywood Bowl, a benefit for the Prisoners Of Conscience International ("POCI"), which included appearances by the Berrigan Brothers, Angela Davis, an assortment of lesser Greek, South African and Central American Marxist-Leninist celebrities, and Mr. Thich Van Dzu, the dotty *chou-chou* of the international Left, who could normally be found holding forth in Saigon's An Quang Buddhist pagoda, thumbing his nose at the "Thieu-Ky Puppet Clique" that was still running things in South Vietnam.

And as this vast bi-coastal extravaganza of collective wishful-thinking, self-delusion, communal infantilization and, er, aspirational elevation, if not actual levitation, was going down....

+ + + + + +

Twelve thousand miles west of the Hollywood Bowl, it was already the morning of the next day, the 27th of April. And US Army (Special Forces) Captain Jerome J. "Bush Pig" Henderson, 25 years old but looking older than that, of Houston (specifically its Sugar Land suburb), Texas, was sitting on a stack of USAID rice sacks, in a remote corner of dusty, ramshackle and already-hot Phu-Lama International Airport, Kingdom of Phuland, ("KOP" as it was known in US Government parlance.)

He was managing to fitfully doze through a throbbing hangover. A tangle of military equipment and web-gear was piled at his feet. He wore his Vietnam canvas/leather jungle boots, faded blue Levis, a black T-shirt with a small breast pocket, and a tiger-stripe camouflaged field jacket with no insignia on it, but with four pockets large enough to hold, say, cantaloupes. It was the black-dominated pattern favored by the US, ARVN and Thai Special Forces.

Actually, the jacket *did* have a sort of insignia: On his right shoulder, Henderson wore the flag of the Kingdom of Phuland, a white 3-headed griffin-like creature on a purple field. (For what it was worth, Henderson thought it a damned handsome bit of vexillology, a term which was, oddly, one of the few things he retained from his recently-concluded what could only laughably be called "studies" at the University of Texas).

Indeed, every man in the Royal Phu Armed Forces (RPAF - "Are-PAF") wore the flag on his uniform, a reflection of official Phu-Lama's brave if shaky determination — more like aspiration — to "solidify its presence in the provinces". A practice that was emulated, in "solidarity", by Henderson and his handful of fellow US advisors, implementers of the Top Secret "Operation Roundhouse", who very carefully were not, strictly speaking, in uniform. This no-uniform technicality was a result of the firm adherence to the Phu Neutrality Codicil to the Lao Neutrality Treaty of 1962 by the U.S., who was the only one of the seven signatories to that (literally) fantastic document confected in Paris, that even *pretended* to observe its provisions.

There had been a surprisingly heated debate over the equally surprisingly vexed question of whether the US advisors should wear the flag, with Colonel Smith, the Defense Attaché at the US Embassy in Phu-Lama and the CO of Operation Roundhouse, arguing that to do so was fairly begging for unfavorable and, worse, unnecessary media exposure at the hands of the ever-intrusive and inevitably-hostile press. But the Phu Minister of Defense insisted that it would help the Americans to carry out their mission if they were associated directly and visually with the Royal Government, and the US Ambassador — a career State Department mandarin whose ideological DNA caused him to regard the very presence of the paramilitary advisors with distaste — had reluctantly agreed with his host government.

Henderson also wore the dark green baseball cap of the Dallas Commanders, the latest American League expansion team. The cap had a white military-stenciled D on it, and on its bill it sported some white military-style "scrambled eggs" — "Commanders", get it? — a martial touch that might well have been axed by protest-weary PR "suits" in any American city other than Dallas. On the back of this cap, Henderson had sewn an olive-drab US Army name-tag with the words BUSH PIG on it. "Bush Pig" had been Henderson's radio name when he'd been an A-Team Executive Officer first, then Team Leader, at the Dak Phuoc Special Forces camp in South Vietnam's II Corps during his '70-'71 tour there.

(For reasons now lost in the mists of time, all the members of the Phuoc Long Province Special Forces radio net had adopted porcine call signs for themselves. There had been Pigpen, Hog, Swine, Pork Chop, Sooey, Sow, Porky, Razorback, Chitlin and even others, so that when instructed to equip himself with a call sign, Henderson had been hard-put to come up with anything. Bush Pig had been the best he could do and, like many other things in his short life that he'd originally viewed with trepidation, he'd grown rather fond of the tag as time passed. He'd even been known to end notes and even the odd letter with "...hoping this finds you, I beg to remain, B. Pig". Not exactly Henry Jamesian, perhaps, but, well... what the fuck....)

Henderson's cap had been a present from his younger brother Jeremy. "Junior" as he was known to everyone. Junior Henderson was a pitcher, a "long reliever", for the Commanders, in his second year in the Bigs. He'd spent most of his rookie year learning how to spit tobacco juice in the Chicago White Sox bullpen, but he'd been sent to Dallas as the "player to be named later" ass-end of a complicated trade, which had ended up being fortuitous for young Junior, for not only had his pitching improved in Dallas, but he'd developed into something of a minor home town hero, being the only native Texan on the entire Dallas squad. Moreover, Junior had been exempt from the non-sporting draft, the *real* one — the military draft — thanks to, rather incredibly, an occasional bleeding ulcer, a most bizarre condition for a 22-year old relief pitcher, and one which Junior proudly attributed to his fondness for cream soda-and-wine-and-vodka cocktails.

If such a thing were possible, Junior was even less (allegedly) "serious-minded" and more (supposedly) "irresponsible" than his older brother. And, if the Bush Pig had been described as a guy of few words, usually by girls whose gruntlement he'd managed to seriously deplete by his verbal unresponsiveness, Junior was a guy of virtually no words at all. Three words was usually his sentence-limit... or four/five if he really *really* wanted to make a point. But regardless of all this, and despite what those who didn't know them well might think, the Bush Pig and Junior were both great enjoyers of life and, incidentally, immense pals.

To understand why Jerome Henderson should have a young brother called Jeremy required an understanding of their father, J. D. (Jervis Danforth) Henderson:

J. D. was what you'd get if you asked the editors of MOTHER JONES magazine to conjure up an image of a typical rich "Anglo" Texan. A wildly successful Houston corporate lawyer, he could've been a proto-type for someone's caricature out of TV's "Dallas". J. D. Henderson was a huge, cigar-chomping, back-slapping, Stetson-doffing, big-tipping, 55-year-old, Marlboro Man Good Ol' Boy and, in the bargain, a pretty sharp elbow-shover as well. He was also a golf partner of the Governor's and even an hombre that LBJ himself was... *aware* of.

Before he and Mrs. Henderson had divorced — with Mrs. H. taking herself off to marry a Nevada ski resort promoter/tycoon — they had produced three kids: Jerome, Jeremy and a daughter called Jeraldine, a pretty little thing who was now sixteen and off at The Stoneleigh-Burn-ham School, in Massachussets. As it happened, Jeraldine, who to Bush Pig's happy surprise was turning into an actually really good kid, *hated* the spelling of her name — "Fer cryin' out loud, Daddy, people see that and'll think I'm *black*, for God's sakes!" — and insisted on spelling it with a G.

J. D. had done the name-picking, and had not Mrs. Henderson one day woken to find herself sick and tired of both J. D. *and* Houston, there's no telling how far the ludicrous name situation might have gone. But the two brothers never seemed to mind being both basically Jerrys. Hell, when he'd "prepped" at Andover, Jerome-The-Future-Bush-Pig had run into Cape Cod and Fairfield County richies — *guys* — with names like Cubby, Trig, Chase and even Flipper who had sisters called such things as Rain, Arrow, Misty and Bambi, affectations besides which old J. D.'s whimsies paled.

2/ 0805 HOURS

"There are no worthwhile occupations other than farming and fighting."

— SHANG YANG (4ᵗʰ century B.C.)

His ass still comfortably parked on this USAID rice sack, Henderson the Bush Pig opened his eyes, blinked and picked some crud out of the corner of one of them.

Wow, that had the makings of a truly fucking crazy dream, short and sweet — that castle, those girls, phew... good thing I woke up before it got really going — this sure as hell isn't the time for any a that heavy dream shit... Since joining the Army Henderson had developed the ability to fall asleep — on a dime, like *that* — and his propensity to dream had also notably increased — accompanied by an uncanny and most welcome ability to *direct* his dreams, like a movie director. *But now's not the time for fucking dreaming, man, jeez, come on, get a grip, here....*

He heaved himself erect and walked around behind the rice sacks, where he committed a small piss. Which he peered at in mild interest.

Hmm, at least it's the right color — after a night like last night, you never know, it's been known to be some fucking funky colors in the past...

He checked his watch — a hand-wound Timex with a luminous dial that only lit up when you pushed a little button. *Yeah, it's time.*

He hoisted his ganglion of web-gear to one shoulder and looked across the chopper pad at the ancient Sikorsky helicopter, into which a 2-man crew had climbed while Henderson was dozing, and whose rotor blades had just begun turning.

The cobalt blue-and-gray-painted chopper belonged to America Tropic Air Services, Inc., (ATAS), a Miami-based outfit which did exclusively US Government (i.e., CIA) contract work. In addition to the rather creaky old H-34 "Choctaw" warhorses like the one Henderson had been assigned this morning, the company could also crank up a fleet of considerably more expensive and up-to-date "Vietnam"-type Bell UH-1 "Huey"s, about twenty Swiss-made STOL Pilatus PC-6 "Porter"s, a handful of Pipers and Beechcrafts, a half-dozen-each C-46s and C-47s, even a couple of C-119 "Flying Boxcar"s and C-123 "Provider"s, and one C-130 "Hercules" that flew out of Udorn Thani AFB in Thailand. (One of its two C-7 DeHavilland "Caribou"s had been hit in the tail by a lucky NVA RPG and forced down onto a Laotian mountain over a year ago; both the pilot and crew chief had been wounded but managed to get hauled out by an ATAS Huey that had luckily been in the neighborhood.)

Except for the usual "No Step"s, "Ground Here"s and "Hand Hold"s written in both English and Phu, all of America Tropic's aircraft were "unmarked" in the conventionally-understood sense. Which in reality meant un-numbered — their fuselage numbers had been taken off. But Henderson knew that if the old bird before him had been able to show off its "licence plate" it would have read YW-317N — he could recognize it by the three patched bullet holes in the ship's right flank. Not to mention the fact that McElmore, the lightbulb-nosed beery leathery old fart of an ATAS four-striper was grinning at him from up in the pilot's perch and, with a hand adorned by a massive solid gold ID bracelet, was flashing him the bird.

Henderson wasn't too much in the mood to play grab-ass games with McElmore just now. Truth be told, he wasn't in the mood for much of *anything* except for going back to his rack and head-downing:

For he, Henderson, McElmore and a few others in the wider "Advisor Contingent" had gotten monumentally drunk last night at the White Rose "restaurant", (Phu-Lama's finest blow-job emporium, "hands down"), until 2 a.m. Henderson and an Air Force Buzzard (a FAC — a Forward Air Controller; in Laos they were known as "Ravens" and here in Phuland as "Buzzards") called Rinaldi had watched — Rinaldi excited, Henderson embarrassed — more at Rinaldi's excitement than anything else — as an uncharacteristically bumbling McElmore had endeavored, ultimately unsuccessfully, to transfer a mercifully unlit Winston from the business end of an undressed-where-it-mattered young Phu lady to his own lips, undropped.

Henderson had ended the night — not so many hours ago, actually — practically catatonic, drinking directly out of a bottle of White Horse scotch as he plopped Phu 100-penny coins into the White Rose's juke box which extraordinarily contained "The Thrill Is Gone" by B. B. King and which Henderson kept playing over and over until McElmore had clotured proceedings by pulling the plug on the machine as they'd stumbled out... "C'mon, kid — bed time...."

Normally Henderson didn't do all that much socializing with the America Tropic pilots. They were, of course, the bravest and most competent (though the press — if they'd known about them — would undoubtedly have called them reckless and unscrupulous) pilots anywhere in the world, most of them being retired — or resigned — US military flyers. They would unhesitatingly fly through walls of ground-fire to save the hash of stranded Americans or allies of Americans — military or civilian — not just in Phuland, but all over Southeast Asia.

On the other hand, they were a surprisingly parochial and blinkered bunch. Their conversation seemed, to the necessarily more widely-focused non-flying Advisors, almost exclusively confined to shop talk, about such riveting stuff as the down-draft at the saddle near Bravo Lima Lima, or how Porter Fox Papa Niner could only coax eleven thousand pounds of torque at anything above thirty-five hundred feet — or to speculate about their sometimes substantial investments back in the States. They were brave, but, unlike the Customers (which was their term for the Advisors) they were handsomely paid to be brave. (As it happened, Henderson and his fellow "Customers" didn't think much about money, one way or the other. Which was probably just as well.) All in all, the humor of the America Tropic pilots, such as it was, tended to the "Hey Hambone — do you eat pussy?" variety... good guys all, but hardly likely to show up on Rowan and Martin's Laugh-In.

No, by and large Henderson preferred the company of his fellow Advisors, the case officers of Operation Roundhouse, an anonymous posse of out-of-uniform Army Green Berets, Navy UDTs, USMC Recons, USAF "Palace Dogs" and Air Rescue-types, CIA paramilitaries from their Special Activities Division ("SAD"), and various other experts, bounty-hunters, hired guns and loose cannons culled — and contracted — from the farthest recesses and bureaucratic cubbyholes of the Federal Government. There was even one shaved-headed maniac who called himself "Lex", (after Lex Luthor), who swore (to general skepticism, it had to be said), to be on loan from the Customs and Immigration Service.

Collectively, then, this was the mob that the America Tropic jocks knew as "The Customer", and their double anonymity (no real names and no real uniforms) allowed these profane, cynical, weatherbeaten and not entirely housebroken characters to indulge in a level of tomfoolery which was to some extent denied the perforce slightly less anarchic America Tropic pilots.

But anyway, all that said, McElmore himself was a kind of cross between John Wayne and the Creature That Ate Cleveland, and was something of an exception to the other pilots. And he and Henderson had pulled this humongous bar-troll of little Phu-Lama last night, culminating at the ultimate oasis, the White Rose, and it was now just passing 0800 and Henderson was still half-shitfaced and the other half about half-sick. The sun had only been up about an hour, and already things were beginning to shimmer in the heat.

With an audible moan, Henderson hoisted up his web gear and appendages that hung thereupon, bowed his head from the weight of it all not to mention from the sun, and stared at his boots as he walked to the chopper. He waded gratefully into the refreshing turbulence of the rotor prop wash, and chucked his gear inside the open door, just forward of the patched bullet holes.

He pulled out a bit of paper from his T-shirt pocket upon which he'd pre-scribbled:

GOOD MORNING, SHITBIRD.

KINDLY TAKE ME AND THIS AMMO AND ALL THIS OTHER SHIT UP TO LS-ECHO, RB 770016. DROP ME OFF AND COME BACK FOR ME AT 1500. I HOPE YOU FUCKING FEEL BETTER THAN I DO. IN FACT I FEEL FUCKING DEAD ALREADY SO I'D GREATLY APPRECIATE IT IF YOU CAN MANAGE NOT TO CRASH. FUCK YOU VERY MUCH, B. PIG.

Standing on the landing gear, he handed this through the open window to the grinning McElmore, who read it, nodded and slid his window shut. Henderson, still with physical and audible effort (that pleased him to exaggerate) climbed into the belly of the bird and strapped himself into one of the canvas slings that served as a seat.

In a series of restorative maneuvers, he: blew his nose (head pointed aft) in the traditional finger-against-nostril manner, sneezed, coughed, wiped the beading alcoholic sweat off his forehead with his T-shirt and reached for his pistol-belt from one of whose pouches he extracted four aspirins that he washed down with canteen water.

Strapped to the forward bulkhead of the chopper's cargo/passenger space was the sawn-off bottom of a 50-gallon drum, that was known by ATAS and Customer alike as the "Toys For Tots" Bin. This contained sundry articles such as rope, a flashlight, rags, flares, toilet paper, first-aid kit, the odd used paperback novel, etc., as well as random items of food and drink that previous Customer/passengers might have donated and/or left behind. This amenity was sometimes, *in extremis*, removed and left on the tarmac when weight was a factor, but today it had been judged acceptable by McElmore, and Henderson now fished around in there for a can of Lucky Lager beer. Which he drained. Then he belched and stowed the crushed empty in an empty rice sack jammed up behind the drum that served as the helicopter's rubbish bin. *Gotta remember to put in a coupla fresh ones when we get back... for the next guy... hell, who might well be* me *again....*

The helicopter's relative darkness was most welcome, though he could have done without all the goddamn vibration and noise.

He settled his ass down into a makeshift seat he fashioned in the netting that lined the fuselage wall, folded his arms and eyeballed all the supplies he'd managed to scrounge for today's mission, and which took up most of the H-34's interior:

- 4 cases of M-16 ammo
- 6 cases of .30 caliber ammo (for M-1 Carbines)
- 2 cases of frag grenades
- 1 case of Claymore "mines"
- 1 case of smoke grenades (yellow)
- 30 rounds (6 crates of 5 rounds each) for 60mm mortar
- 50 US Army ponchos
- 1 large cardboard box full of odd fatigues, black rubber jungle sneakers, fatigue hats, entrenching tools and plastic canteens
- 10 x 50-kilo sacks of USAID rice (with the US-handshake logo stamped on the burlap)

All of this stuff, except the rice, had been collected yesterday by way of a judicious trip Henderson had paid to Are-PAF headquarters in Phu-La-ma. It had only cost him one USMC K-Bar knife and a couple of old Playboys to that fat little colonel who was the acting RPAF S-4 (Supply). (K-Bar knives were easy to get from the Marine guards at the Embassy, who had them up the ass, so to speak. Not to mention old Playboys.)

RPAF Captain Che Kak had asked for a good deal more than this when he'd contacted Henderson on the radio several days earlier:

"... awso nee' mawtah, big wan, etty-wan. Awso nee' radio, talkie-walkie sty' radio like you hab. Awso nee' machee gon, fipty cariber...." And still more besides....

Well, tough tittie. A lot of what Che Kak had asked for he either didn't really need, or neither the Are-PAF S-4's shop or the Attaché Logistics Warehouse had at the moment, or had been vetoed by Colonel Smith, the US Defense Attaché and the generalissimo of this whole secret, para-military Operation Roundhouse roadshow:

"Goddammit, son! Give 'em anything weighs more'n fifteen pounds an' they'll leave it behind when they get overrun — an' supplyin' the fuck-ing NVA is the Ivans' job, not ours."

A harsh verdict, perhaps, but one which had unfortunately too often proved to be true in the eighteen months since open warfare had broken out with the North Vietnamese in the mountains of eastern Phuland.

So this was all Che Kak was gonna get this time around, and, anyway, what the shit, it was just about all McElmore's sixteen year-old heap, which was already lugging the extra weight of its own custom-installed supplementary fuel supply, could hoist (without dumping the Toys For

Tots Bin) up to LS-Echo — which was *way* the fuck up at a semi-unbelievable altitude of some 9,800 feet. Up in the goddamn clouds, most of the time, this God-forsaken little clearing on top of a karst cliff, which they chose to flatter with the name of "Landing Site", around which Che Kak's company of irregular RPAFs, (who came complete with wives, kids, old mama-*sans* and papa-*sans* and bony pye-dogs), hunkered. Wishing that the cursed North Vietnamese would just leave them alone....

Normally Henderson would have been accompanied by his officially-assigned interpreter, young Corporal Mekki, who, as a half-Phu/half Meu Jong, was an RPAF rarity — and for whom Henderson would've gladly jettisoned the "Toys For Tots" tub to make the weight. But the kid had sent him a message at the Advisors' Hooch the night before — and despite himself Henderson had to smile as he thought back on the effort...

MISTER JERRY. I SICK HAVE HEAD-AIK, THROW UP TOO MUCH, I THINK MABY BE OK IN 1 MABY 2 DAY. SORRY THANK YOU GOOD BY, MEKKI CORP. RPAF

Welcome to the club, Mekki, you little shitbird.... But a pity, nonetheless. Henderson had, over time, gotten quite fond of little Mekki, whose father was Something-Or-Other at Phu-Lama's little National University, and his English was passably fluent, if annoyingly slangy (he'd mislearned a lot of stupid crap from American movies, not to mention from successive Roundhouse guys). Mekki had proved himself damn useful in handling the misunderstandings, complications, and sundry non-senses which invariably arose when the American advisors dealt with the troops of the Royal Phu Armed Forces.

Mind you, the Meu Jong ("Mountain People" in their lingo) fighters — such as those Henderson would be visiting today — were a bit more disciplined and tractable, not to mention brave, than the more decadent lowland "regular" Phu Army troops. So he ought to be able to muddle through without Mekki the Terp today — and hell, he had no choice, anyway, as he'd promised Che Kak he'd bring at least the ammo, and not to do so would be to grievously lose face — not to mention maybe allow Che Kak to be overrun... *Aaah, fuck it, I should be OK... Still, ya never know.... there's always some goddamn thing....*

3/ 0810 HOURS

"If we weren't in the shit in the first place, we wouldn't be here. In the first place."

— *PAUL KEATING (ex-PM of Australia)*

As the old H-34 prepared to hit the Pang Phu Meu ("Great Phu Mountains"), as the northeastern part of Phuland was called, Henderson pondered and adjusted his mentality and even his intended vocabulary, preparatory to dealing directly, *sans* go-between, with Captain Che Kak. He'd done it once before, and Henderson now remembered that the experience had been intellectually, well... *invigorating*.

And, indeed, he was lucky to even *have* Che Kak, who was one of the few local commanders in Henderson's AO who actually spoke a sort of semi-comprehensible English. "Phungrish", Phu-Lama wags called it.

Yeah, Che Kak was, all things considered, a pretty squared-away dude — about the best Phu officer that Henderson had worked with in the three-odd months since he'd arrived in Phuland. Which, in fact, had been why he'd recommended that Che Kak be given the command of the brand-new 200-man "Special Mountain Security Battalion" (SMSB), a supposedly elite (*Yeah, they're "elite" alright — compared to what? Hey, everything's relative, man*) hand-picked (which meant volunteer, which meant volunteered-by-their-families) unit, but one whose members, Henderson knew, were actually the greenest of kids — most of whom, in fact, a mere month ago had either been tending their family's opium patches or else making great nuisances of themselves riding their noisy, smokey, obnoxious little Honda motorbikes on the country's dusty, mostly unpaved arteries.

Well, one thing's for sure, Henderson thought, *Che Kak's gonna have to straighten 'em out pretty goddamn quick....* Because for the past two weeks, both USAF Intelligence and CIA reports had pointed, with rare unanimity, to a serious North Vietnamese attempt at seizing the Pang Phu Meu before the rainy season came, which gave them... *us...* barely thirty days... *to get fucking squared away....*

Xuam Long Province, as the Pang Phu Meu was administratively known and which "belonged" to Henderson, was all mountains. But not mountains like the Alps or Rockies — rather something quite different but equally stark known as "karst topography"... which, instead of snow, involved rather *bookoo* cliffs. A vast vista of jutting, jagged, *impossible* cliffs. Upon which grew thick, double- and even, in places, triple-canopy jungle. Which made it some of the most impenetrable terrain in the world, and one which Henderson, along with the virtual unanimity of all other foreigners who'd ever set foot in it, heartily felt merited nothing but neglect.

But, unhappily, this forbidding chunk of topography happened to be the literal as well as proverbial focal point of North Vietnam's strategic plan for all of Southeast Asia. And the moment the NVA's tactics turned from indirect fire/harassment, selective ambushes and hit-snatch-and-run attacks on villages, to large-scale ground-gaining assaults — as they soon surely would — Henderson knew that Landing Site-Echo would be one of the first Royal Phu Army-held targets to receive the full brunt of a bugle-blowing NVA regimental charge, complete with sappers plastered with satchel charges who went off like human nukes. Henderson knew the ghastly choreography all too well — *Jesus Christ, what a fucking horror show.*

And all Henderson had to counter this inevitable shitstorm was Che Kak. And the *worst* thing was that it could have been worse. For the truth was that while Che Kak might be by way of being one's standard-issue, garden-variety slanty-eyed Southeast Asian gangster, he *did*, as previously noted, speak what could pass for English... and he certainly did hate the communists:

"Gah-dam comoonits — !" he'd once cried to Henderson over too many Singha beers in the White Rose, " — they aw rike fockin' ants! No hab hots! — " (*"Hots"*? It had taken the sodden Henderson some little time to register that the agitated Phu captain had to be referring to *hearts*) "— no... no... no happiness! Impossiber be lich, hab goo' rife wi' fockin' comoonits!" *Hey, what can I say — right on, Che Kak.*

And on top of all that, Che Kak had already, in Henderson's few months with him, demonstrated, in several exceedingly hairy ambushes and counter-ambushes, that he owned a pretty hefty pair of *huevos,* as his old Basic Training pal Rojo called them. In combat, the man didn't just, as too many did, follow his instinct to hunker — rather, he *moved.*

To defend Xuam Long Province and its 250,000 civilian population of ethnically un-Phu, semi-neo-Tibeto-Mongol mountain folk (known as the "Meu-Jong" both among themselves *and* by the Phu lowlanders), Captain Che Kak had at his disposal — in addition, through the Roundhouse guys, to the all-important USAF — the aforementioned untried SMSB and also, scattered around a half-dozen Landing Sites, a little over a thousand (the number varied daily, even hourly) "indigenous", i.e., Meu-Jong, "Irregular Local Forces" ("ILF"s).

ILFs were utterly independent, undisciplined, unreliable, squad-to-platoon-sized mini-mobs of Meu Jong sub-clan cousins and other relations whose national allegiance depended largely on whether the monthly payroll from Phu-Lama was on time or late. Not to mention awarding themselves extended unauthorized "leaves of absence" whenever they got the urge. They *could* be ferocious fighters when they wanted to be — when they were "happy" — and they had a certain advantage over the much better-equipped and -organized enemy, the interloping North Vietnamese, by knowing the Pang Phu Meu like their own back yard. Which it was.

But Henderson had already learned that there were scores of hopelessly complicated factors which determined whether a unit of ILFs was "happy" or "unhappy". It was all an ultimately indecipherable bucket of worms, involving "face"-saving, relative number of wives (?) (!), how the *juju*-dispensers were getting along with the various "Buddhas" and "spirits" at any given time, whether or not their officers and NCOs were of the same (or competing) sub-clans, how a particular group was equipped compared to the neighboring unit, the amount of USAID rice allotted to the Meu-Jong generally — and to this or that village in particular — by the central Phu Government, and, (certainly not least), the fluctuating international price of opium. And even *other* things as well....

As Colonel Smith had counseled Henderson back at what passed for their Officer's Club at the US Embassy compound in Phu-Lama,

"The names are different here than in Vietnam, but it's the same fucking clusterfuck, son. So just do the usual fuckin' things — keep yer map coordinates straight and carry extra ammo and water when yer in the chabongas. And, as it's Phuland, stick to yer cover, keep yer mouth shut in bars, avoid the press like the fuckin' plague, and don't even *think* about gettin' captured. Do all that an' you'll be fine. But in any case don't sweat it too much — it's nothin' you haven't dealt with before."

After only three months of trying to sort this all out, Henderson had begun harboring the subversive doubt whether the monumental task of whipping the ILFs into something resembling combat effectiveness was worth all the effort.

Certainly, however you looked at it, it was a hell of a messy situation: The lowland Phu didn't like the Meu-Jong and were never likely to allow themselves to be tricked into risking their lives for those "savages". And the same was true in reverse, with *at least* the same level of intensity. The only positive aspect of the whole mess was that the Meu-Jong liked the Vietnamese (for whom they had a special name, which translated roughly to "venal sneaky yellow scum from the east") even less than the Phu.

And anyway, shit... there isn't much choice, is there.

So. Until the day that the King's be-ribboned ministers and cousins and other poncing, sponging hangers-on, who constituted the RPAF Maximum Muckamuck High Command, agreed to swallow a bit of face and deploy some of the fat and happy RPAF units from the Phu-Lama Capital Region up to the Pang Phu Meu — *if* that day ever came — Xuam Long Province was going to have to somehow depend on the brand-new SMSB (whose 200 members were currently finishing-up parachute training in Thailand, without their already-Airborne-qualified CO, Che Kak), and the dicey ILFs. It was a serious headache, no doubt about it.

But there was only so much Henderson could do about the precarious military situation in the Pang Phu Meu, so, as Col. Smith had counseled, he didn't worry about it overly much. In fact, since Dak Phuoc in Vietnam, he'd grown, if not downright cynical, at least phlegmatic about such things, and wouldn't have sweated this particular "hopeless" situation even if ol' Smithy hadn't advised him against it — or about the Byzantine intrigue, elaborate diplomatic posturing and absurd Ruritarian politicking that ran rampant throughout the sweltering offices, decaying corridors and gekko-strewn patios of official Phu-Lama. The squabbling between the Phu and the Meu-Jong was a problem for, if anybody, the Ambassador and the "Country Team" that surrounded him. All Henderson had to do was to try to keep Xuam Long Province out of North Vietnamese hands. *Hmmm... "All"....*

If they could just hold on until the rainy season, the whole region might stand a chance. Fucking slim one, that was for sure — but still, a chance. Next-door Laos at least appeared to still be hanging in there. Again, it pretty much all depended on Captain Che Kak, who fortunately (and unusually) actually had some Meu-Jong blood in him: He'd once tried to explain his convoluted lineage to Henderson, over sticky rice and beakers of rice "wine", after which Henderson had responded,

"Shit, Che Kak, you sure a complicated bowl a gumbo, you know that? — you sure you ain't got no Jewish in you? Or Apache?"

"Soor, soor! Hapashi is OK!" (Che Kak had seen American movies too.)

And so, as a result of his fortuitous ethnic anomalies, Che Kak enjoyed a measure of authority over the ILFs (as well as the SMSB) that he otherwise might not have. Unfortunately, Che Kak could only be at one Landing Site at a time.... *For that matter, me too,* thought Henderson....

All of this — none of it new — flicked through Henderson's still-soggy mind, there inside McElmore's clapped-out H-34.... *Ah, fuck it....*

4/ 0815 HOURS

"Whatever you do, don't miss your war."

— PETE HEGSETH

Satisfied that all, or at least almost all, of the supplies he'd requisitioned had found their way on board, Henderson turned and nodded to Sandoval, the Filipino kicker.

(A "kicker", the job description whose name was derived from the act of kicking out supplies and sometimes even people during a drop, was also a chopper pilot's combination mechanic/impromptu door-gunner/whipping boy and general-purpose one-man Air Crew. America Tropic, at the prodding of its chief customer, the US Government — for whom a "low profile" had become a politically-necessitated obsession — had been laying off US kickers and replacing them with Asian ones. And, for some reason — most likely because they were ethnically "neutral" and most of them spoke good English — a high proportion of the new kickers had turned out to be Filipino. *Fine by me,* had thought Henderson when he'd learned of this phenomenon, *I can keep up my Espanisse with 'em....)*

The upper part of Sandoval's pock-marked brown moon face was masked by his huge fly-like gray crew helmet, on the front of which was painted America Tropic's eye-catching, if incongruous, logo: a stars-and-stripes palm tree standing, swaying, atop a stars-and-strips cloud... *pu-leez* — it was more redolent of Waikiki than the free-fire zones in which it proliferated. But the bottom bit of Sandoval's face grinned and then mouthed soundlessly (well, soundlessly to Henderson) into the tiny plastic mic pressed against his lips. Immediately, McElmore torqued up power in the old Sikorsky and it started its ungainly roll out of the America Tropic corner towards the main chopper pad at the northern edge of Phu-Lama International Airport.

As they bumped unsteadily along, Henderson offered Sandoval a Salem and lit one himself. Before putting his Zippo back in his front jean pocket, he looked at it for the millionth time: On one side was engraved

To 1LT Bush Pig, from the men of A132-C, Dak Phuoc RVN '70-'71

while on the back was written, in tiny script,

The Team that drinks together, kills dinks together.

Even now, he managed a kind of smile. As he thought about That Time: That party in Georgetown soon after his return from Vietnam... He'd been assigned TDY to the "Office Of Special Requirements" (OSR) in the surreally-named "South East Asia Current Tactical And Operational Joint Integrated Intelligence Command Task Force" (SEACTAO-JIICTF) in the Pentagon, and had been living in rather spartan circumstances in a studio apartment up at 17th and Corcoran — and had somehow been invited to this boisterously liquid reception in someone rich's spacious back yard in that someone rich's Georgetown townhouse. And he'd been making what he hoped were not (but suspected probably were) overly crude and perhaps even untoward advances upon a nubile and, really, astonishingly large-breasted "politically concerned" female person who turned out to be an administrative assistant for some equally "politically concerned" congressman from Maryland called Leah. The girl, that is, not the congressman.

Leah had certainly been friendly... almost certainly of the Joosh persuasion... all *helpful*... feeding him these little cheese thingies, saying "eat eat, you're too skinny"... *Hey, Leah, it's called "in shape", but yeah, ok, sister, for you I'll try one a those smelly little things....*

All had seemed to be going swimmingly until Henderson had gone and ruined everything by lighting up a Salem with this here lighter, which she'd taken out of his hand and read — both sides. And just about had a goddamn exploding cow right then and there. Jesus H. Humphrey, the recriminations — compounded by the inexcusable fact that the Bush Pig had been trying, despite his tell-tail Army haircut, to pass himself off to Leah as "a graduate student" (and when she'd asked "of what?" and "where?" he'd answered vaguely "oh — transfer, actually" and "sociology" which he reckoned was pretty much what attending this party *qualified* as....)

Well. Oh dear oh dear. Not only had he not "scored" that night, he'd been goddamn lucky not to get his face smacked. He, Henderson a dreadful *dreadful*, nasty man. And disgusting liar to boot. Had she *actually* called him an "imperialist warmonger pig"? It was extraordinary to think that there were breathing, presumably sentient, beings out there on the loose who actually *used* such words... and worse, were respected citizens entrusted with respectable jobs in the Federal Government... As he obeyed Leah's orders that night to "get away from me, you creep", Henderson remembered having thought *Jeez, honey, you think* I'm *bad — I should introduce you to a* real *sociologist, my main man Private E-Zero Rojo....*

+ + + + + +

Henderson stared out of the gaping open door of the H-34. Sandoval had fastened a cargo strap across the two-meter wide aperture.

They taxied by a few Royal Phu Airways C-47s, rather handsome in their purple-and-white livery. Past an Air Vietnam DC-6 (at which Henderson bestirred himself to crane his neck out the door to see if he could catch a glimpse of one of their inevitably stunning stews in their turquoise *ao-dai*s — ah, there was one, standing under a wing... Henderson sighed appreciatively and sat back. You couldn't count on much from Air Vietnam, but a fucking piece of ass stew, yes. You could. Every time. Just ask Air Vice Marshal Nguyen Cao Ky...). Past a really sad-looking Royal Air Lao C-46 which was having one of its tires changed. Past a squadron of Royal Phu Air Force T-28 trainers-transformed-into-dive bombers, to which crew chiefs were attaching great bulbous 500-lb bombs as well as some definitely more demure, though no less nasty, white phosphorous rockets. Past an Air France Caravelle, just in from the Saigon-Vientiane-Phu-Lama-Bangkok-Phnom Penh run.... Taken as a whole, this wasn't so much an International Airport as a real-time aviation museum — in fact, they even passed a USAF EC-121 Lockheed "Warning Star" Super-Constellation, a weird enough-looking thing even with*out* the great goiterous AWACS mushroom-thingie sticking out its top.

McElmore reined in the straining, juddering old H-34 while a mysterious (to others than McElmore and Henderson) unmarked America Tropic C-119 "Flying Boxcar" gently put down, and then the OK came in from the tower.

It had been a hell of a long time since Henderson had managed to get worked up about flying in a helicopter, unless the damn thing was taking rounds or losing fuel or some other such diversion. In Vietnam he'd once fallen asleep in a re-supply slick and had fucking well nearly fallen out the side of the damn thing when the pilot had banked extremely sharply to get away from some unexpected ground-fire, which probably still ranked as Henderson's most memorable helicopter ride. But, *naaah*, normally they were about as exciting as excursions in elevators. Sandoval offered him an extra set of earphones so that he might tune into the aviation chatter, but Henderson declined them. Even with*out* a hangover, he found all that racket to be an ear-splitting electric crackle of meaningless (at least to Henderson) drivel. So instead he just sat there, arms, for want of anything else to do, hugging himself.

The internal noise and vibration increased to such a point that it seemed that the old bird was on the verge of popping all its rivets. The interior of the apparatus morphed into a cross between a gigantic clothes dryer running on one cylinder and the Great Piñata From Hell. Its tail lifted, as the craft lurched forward. For a second, there, it seemed as if the whole contraption might fall over onto its great broad nose, but then it *just* managed to jerk itself into the air, wheels still spinning.

Gathering up as much dignity as it could muster, McElmore's ship gained altitude, cleared the stacked concertina-wire perimeter of Phu-Lama International Airport, skirted a corner of the sun-scorched pastel city, and headed out on a north-easterly vector across the plains and rice paddies of Phuland, towards a tiny chopper pad on top of one of the nameless mountain ridges in the Pang Phu Meu, a hundred and thirty miles away. No, check that, not nameless — Landing Site-Echo.

5/ 0820 HOURS

"History isn't something over and done, you know. It's now, too."

— JOHN UPDIKE

At 75 knots (*75 knots?* Jesus Christ — there were *animals* that could go 75 knots....) and with the big side-door open, the interior of the helicopter became quite breezy and almost pleasant. Henderson felt *slightly* better now — and definitely better now than when he'd staggered out of his bunk this morning in the "Combined Logistics Group"//"Roundhouse" (euphemistic names proliferated like mildew in these official purlieus) barracks/hooch in its shady corner of the sprawling US Embassy compound on the outskirts of Phu-Lama. Three months ago, Henderson might have been hanging out the H-34's door to check out this weird and new country, but all that was long *fini* — not any more. *Now, just relax. Move the face a bit, just so, to catch that jet of air, ah, that's the thing... ooof... bit of go back to ti-ti sleep now... leave the driving to McElmore....*

So he closed his eyes, but he didn't properly sleep — rather, it was instead the 3/4s gaga state of almost-colloidal daydreaming which is the soldier's version of playing possum. Sleep standing up. Sleep with your eyes open. Henderson had once read that Napoleon would sleep while riding his horse, and he believed it. In fact, Henderson had once been feeding ammo to a guy firing an M-60 machine gun on a range at Dix, and the bozo had stone fallen asleep in the middle of *that* — fucking half burned his stupid nose off. (Rojo claimed that he could even bring a fuck to a successful conclusion while fast asleep — "...out like you maw-fockeen ligh', baby!" — and Henderson certainly didn't doubt *that*, either.)

Henderson had been in the Army a little over three years now, and he was still struck by a peculiar paradox about the life of a soldier, which people who'd never been "in" would never be able to understand. Namely, that the military life was a very contemplative one. Indeed, despite (or perhaps because of) the communal living and forced collectivization, every troop — every swinging dick — regardless of rank or branch, was alone with his thoughts a good deal more than was the lot of most civilians, (with the possible exception of hermits, shepherds and lighthouse-keepers working the midnight-to-0800 shift).

Indeed, from the endless hours of standing, waiting, marching, waiting, crawling, more waiting, still waiting, "hurry-up-and-wait"ing and general "mill-around–mill"-ing of training, and then later, during the long, unhappy and nervous nights of enforced silence on perimeters, or beyond the perimeter, manning Observation Posts, or to the monotony of duty on all-night Listening Posts — or to any and all the other soul-crushingly tedious mundanities which were a part, (a *large* part), of what they called, sometimes with absurd incongruity, "active duty", much of one's military experience — from the lowest grunt on up to company-grade officers as well — turned out to consist of *loooong* lonely hours with nothing to do but ruminate, meditate, dream, regret, retrospect and introspect.

This had certainly been true for Henderson, and he was confident that the same went for the three and a half million other souls who at that moment wore a uniform of the United States. (Or those vanishingly few that *should* have been wearing, but conspicuously *didn't* wear — as he currently didn't....)

Not only was it strange that this should be so, in a profession that was so widely supposed to be brutish, impersonal, violent and (not to put too fine a point on it) virtually non-cerebral, but Henderson also considered it amazing that he, of all people, for whom active mental activity had heretofore been merely a means to attaining some end, should have turned into, (since becoming, for all intents and purposes, a "lifer"), such an accomplished dreamer — a conjurer of mental abstractions — a daydreamer whose thoughts often served no purpose whatever other than providing himself with his own private, personal entertainment system. This gift, if that was what it was, was one of the things for which Henderson was grateful to the Army... though he ruefully reckoned that prisoners in solitary were also recipients of the same "gift"....

So, as he hovered between dozing and actual sleep, he let his mind wander. And it wandered first into the fantastic quagmire that the Kingdom of Phuland had become. Or maybe had always been....

Phuland. *Phuland,* for Christ's sakes, even the name seemed to fit the faintly, to be frank about it, pitiful and even ridiculous country. Yah, yah, *Phu* in the local parlance meant something having to do with Reverential Spirit of Ancestors or some such bilge, but in French it sounded like "crazy" which was certainly closer to the truth. *Phuland! — for fucks sakes, it sounds like something outta Dr. Seuss.*

Then there was the unbelievable *shape* of the goddamn place. For it was an undeniably obvious fact that Phuland's outline very much resembled the female sexual, um... *area*. Crammed in between Burma and Laos on each side, with China to the north, it was shaped like the good old erotic triangle, and to complete God's little dirty joke, its only major river, the Phumia, began in the northern mountains and ran right down the center of the country (to disappear into Thailand, to the south), virtually splitting the country in half and looking *exactly* like you-know-what.

Certainly Henderson could never look at a map of Phuland without thinking of Leon Russell's then-popular song "Delta Lady", and, indeed, the whole rather unseemly phenomenon was lost on few of the few people in the world who were even aware of little Phuland's existence... and you could *certainly* rest assured that it was most emphatically not lost on the happy misfits who made up Operation Roundhouse and the larger "Combined Logistics Group". For instance, the Phumia River would every year during the rainy season rise and flood every damn thing for miles on either side of it, and this occurrence was invariably described by the incorrigible Roundhouses as "the river's on the rag again". It was all rather sophomoric ... but not inaccurate.

More seriously, Phuland's peculiar shape merely symbolized the fact that throughout her long and inconspicuous history, she had usually been getting screwed by *someone* — by others as well, of course, but historically mostly by China. As far back as the 12th century, the Chinese had looked upon the Phu Kingdom as little more than one of their own private opium patches. (And disbelieve anyone who ever tells you that opium was first "forced" onto the pristine and unsuspecting Chinese by the unscrupulous Brits — the former were onto the stuff *long* before the latter horned in on the action in the 19th century). Indeed, only the extremely painful inaccessibility of the karst topography of the Pang Phu Meu mountains, plus the fact that the Chinese were more interested in even lusher opium patches in Laos to the east, had prevented the sleepy and unobtrusive little Kingdom of Phuland from being annexed outright and becoming a province of China.

But still, China kept pecking and gnawing away, and whenever they'd overdo it and become *seriously* threatening, the succeeding kings of the Phu Vathak Dynasty had been able to rally enough support from the "Mongol" Meu-Jong mountain people and bribe them to successfully mount guerrilla hits-and-run against those for whom they, the Meu-Jong, had a special name which could be translated as"The Great Yellow Pains In The Arse From The North".

These short, sharp and stinging Meu-Jong counter-strikes, although each by themselves relatively minor, had proved painful enough to re-teach the intruding Chinese the lesson that the wretched backwater of the Pang Phu Meu was probably more trouble than it was worth, and the invaders would invariably lumber off to make trouble elsewhere. Thus, for many generations, whoever was at any given time the Phu King (of *all* Phuland, of course, but specifically of the lowland ethnic Phu), would "reward" the Meu-Jong by buying up all their opium and raw silver, the only two cash resources of the Meu-Jong.

This mutual back-scratching *modus vivendi* between Phu and Meu-Jong permitted Phuland to limp through History practically unnoticed until 1861, when England decided to... to... well, to *appropriate* it. To, as a Minister in the Colonial Office had put it at the time, "to take it on board, don't you know". This one *really was* colonized, in Disraeli's amusing phrase, "as an afterthought" — inasmuch as the Crown already had more silver and opium than it knew what to do with (or even where to put). No, in the end, what really swung the decision in London was nothing more inspired than a mulish unwillingness to concede the place to the sodding *Froggies*, who, after their successes in *l'Indochine*, gave every evidence of wanting to get *their* bloody *pattes* on *Le Phoulande* as well.

But despite these rather haphazard and (it had to be said) less-than-enthusiastic beginnings, the colonization of Phuland had proved to be not only totally bloodless, but even, as these things went, rather amicable — thanks to the fact that the then-reigning Phu monarch, King Solong Vathak, had himself benefited from a quite enjoyable three year *séjour* at Balliol College, Oxford, and had returned therefrom convinced that, all things considered, it was a very much better thing indeed to be protected by Her Britannic Majesty — and particularly Her Britannic Majesty's *Forces* — than to be left to deal incessantly with the Chinese dogs oneself. *And,* as he cheerfully declared, he was too old and lazy to learn "Frence". (Although the kindly old fellow, even unto his deathbed, had never been able to fathom *why* the British lords should want to do such a manifestly daft thing as to come all this way just to sit, in their buttoned-up khaki, white, or red get-ups, in the sweltering Phu-Lama sun and drink gin and endeavor to govern this so-called country which, even by Asian standards, was pretty comprehensively, and manifestly, ungovernable... *Weeeell,* maybe he *could* get the gin part, but as for the other....)

For their part, the Meu-Jong, up in their mountain redoubt, had voiced no complaints over the colonization of the country they were nominally a part of. (Of course, it also had to be said that no one ever bother to ask them). In fact, the entire process had been completed before even the most modern and worldly-wise (relative concepts up there, to be sure)

Meu-Jong chieftain had even been aware that some white people from who-knows-where were interested in their pile of mountains. And the bottom line of it was that it didn't matter to the eternally pragmatic Meu-Jong one dead lizard whether their silver and opium went to Phu-Lama, Siam, "Ing-Rand" or wherever, so long as *some*one bought it.

When the Japanese came tearing through the place in '40, two steps behind the outnumbered, fleeing "Ingrish", the poor Phu (much more than the isolated Meu-Jong) suffered a great deal of rape pillage and plunder. King Matak Vathak II, unlike his badminton partner to the south, the King of Siam, decided not to make any deals with these cursed Japs, and in a move that would later become known in Phu schoolbooks (such as these were) as "The Great Salvation Trek" (in reality more "schlep" than "trek"), bundled up his court and ministries and hightailed it across Burma into India, where he sat out World War II in a largely-ignored-by-the-rest-of-the-world huff.

Then one day the Americans dropped the Great Bomb which ended it all for these Nips From Hell. This event filled King Matak Vathak with such awe and respect for the Americans that, years later, in Phu-Lama, he would tell his young son, Pom,

"These people, the Americans, will often appear to be confused and foolish — indeed, sometimes they will act like crass, blundering idiots — but never believe the Chinese or the Russians or anyone else who tells you that they will not do what is absolutely necessary to look after what they see as their vital interests... so it is not a bad idea to become an American 'vital interest'." Prince Pom had been seven years old at the time and had had no earthly idea what his father was talking about.

After VJ-Day in 1945 and up to more or less the present, the Kingdom of Phuland had continued to bask in its natural state of anonymous torpor.

Oh, yes, alright — here and there a few things happened. Such as... such as... such as, well, such as in '48, the Labour Government in London sent out orders to bring down the Union Jack from Government House in Phu-Lama, and the outgoing Governor had told old King Matak, "Thanks very much for everything, Your Maj, the whole experience has been utterly spiffing, best of luck, old chap — that's alright, we'll see ourselves out — ", and had disappeared. The King had summoned his Prime Minister and, in his best residual Oxford vernacular, announced to him, "Right, well, we're on our own, now — we'll be needing pretty sharply to re-design the flag and print up some new stamps — see to it, will you? There's a good fellow...."

In the 1956 Olympics, a stubby little RPAF sergeant, of all people, had copped a gold medal in the 25 kilometer speed-walk event. This was in Melbourne, and the poor half-pissed (as they say there) Metropolitan Brass Band had had a hell of a time with the National Anthem... Couldn't find it in the bloody folder... *Phuland?* Yeah, you bloody berk, there, there, behind bleeding Philippines... Oh, too right... Thanks, mate... Right, here goes... *toot toot...* the damn thing had sounded like a cross between Brahms' Tenth Bassoon Concerto and Happy Birthday. Still, the little sergeant had been happy enough — in fact, he's stayed there, Down Under... married an Abo girl called Dandelion... opened up a bar in Moonee Valley called "The Mountain Way Café" which did surprisingly well... Strewth....

In 1962, a month before US President Kennedy went to Paris to sign that fantastic (in the original sense of the word) Laos Neutrality Treaty, which contained the equally fantastic "Phuland Codicil", a meteor — a *meteor* — about the size of a Fruehauf semi-articulated 36-wheeler slammed into, and utterly vaporized, a whole Meu-Jong village called Trach Yip, high up in the Pang Phu Meu, a catastrophe that actually made the pages of both PARIS MATCH and LIFE magazines.

But otherwise, however, nobody save for people like the UN's U Thant and Eleanor Roosevelt (who, as it happened, died shortly after that meteor did its hideous thing) paid the slightest attention to Phuland. Lucky Phuland — not many people or institutions had been known to survive the poisoned ministrations of such as U Thant and Eleanor Roosevelt, and being ignored by the rest of the world for so long had been a boon worth more than all the gold or oil one could ask for.

But eventually, history (as it tends to do) caught up with little Phuland: Hanoi's apologists on American campuses, TV screens, pulpits and airwaves notwithstanding, dominoes are real enough and can, if properly shoved, knock over their neighbors with tolerable efficiency.

The closest domino to Phuland, and the one that would push it reluctantly into the world's spotlight, was its neighboring Kingdom, Laos.

Poor old Laos, at the beginning of 1972 was definitely wobbling. The Hmong "secret army" of battered (if hardened) irregulars and its avuncular generalissimo Vang Pao — that "army" that THE NEW YORK TIMES had chosen to characterize, quite wrongly of course, as "The secret CIA-led army of Hmong mercenaries" was being, for all THE NEW YORK TIMES' sinister implications, systematically ground down by the three regular North Vietnamese divisions in its area, and its component bits forced increasingly to hunker down in their own little mountain villages. All was not lost over there — yet — and the Hmongs' own handful of paramilitary CIA advisors were desperately trying to buy themselves, and the Hmong, time — to regroup. But nevertheless, the Hmong's weakened situation...

...had freed-up some *other* 40,000 North Vietnamese regulars to threaten to take Vientiane itself. And Hanoi was demanding that the "neutralist" Souvana Phouma negotiate. *Negotiate.* At least that's what Hanoi and its claque in the international media chose to call it. But Hanoi's idea of "negotiation" was in fact a "plan" for Laos to be divided in half, with the eastern bit being ceded to North Vietnam outright as a, you should pardon the expression, "protectorate", with the rump western part still being called something like "Laos", but under a "coalition" government headed by Souvana Phouma's communist half-brother, Comrade Souphanouvong and his Pathet Lao.

Meanwhile, as all this was being bruited about in Hanoi and Vientiane, nobody back in America who "mattered", that is to say, none of America's "opinion-makers" seemed to give much of a damn. All their attention was trained — and outrage expended — on Tricky's "aggression" in bombing those North Vietnamese soldiers who were at that time camped out in, and traveling through, Cambodia. Thus Cambodia was the focus of the angry American media, leaving no one to notice the devouring of Laos by Uncle Ho's regular, mechanized, uniformed, uh,... agrarian reformers. (Not, to be honest, that any of those American opinion-makers would have bothered to object if they *had* noticed.)

But despite the deteriorating situation in Laos, things in the rest of Southeast Asia were, well, mixed: Phuland and Cambodia continued, at best, shaky, but South Vietnam had definitely pulled back from the brink and the big prize, Thailand, was feeling positively robust.

The Thai government, alarmed that Laos was in danger of disappearing down Hanoi's gaping maw, decided not to passively wait around for any of that nonsense, but rather to preempt things. And, without so much as even asking Senator Fulbright's permission, the Thais dispatched two infantry divisions to Cambodia, and so far, those creditable elements had been able to help keep the government of poor old Lon Nol and his army of scared, too-lightly-armed little-more than boys and girls... afloat.

(Although already, rumblings were being heard in Democrat corners of the grumpy U.S. Senate about "Uncle Sap" footing bills for what Eugene McCarthy was calling Thailand's "illegal military adventures".)

Happily, regardless of the foreign policy fulminations of certain Democrat senators, the US economy was improving by early 1972 and to the extent that anyone was making a stink about the Southeast Asia War in the presidential and congressional elections, that attention had concentrated on America's happily dwindling presence in Vietnam. So the Thais, with quiet US help, had sort of surreptitiously managed to... Get On With It, unimpeded. And thus, (with a further bit of help from certain ARVN Ranger units which, such was the improving situation in South Vietnam, could be spared to go over to lend a hand), the Thais were keeping the NVA busy and uncomfortable in Cambodia. And, as a result, Phnom Penh was still secure. Weeell, maybe "secure" was overstating it a bit, but at least it remained un-communist. For now.

A drop of sweat fell from Henderson's nose onto his hands, which he wiped on his T-shirt. He turned his face towards the draft again...

Politics... jeez...

6/ 0825 HOURS

"Never allow yourselves to be separated from the Americans."

— WINSTON CHURCHILL

...yeah, politics... what a crock, huh?

On those extremely rare occasions when he thought of his own congressman, a bar of soap-shaped little segregationist Democrat dingbat called T. D. Longfellow (who seemed to believe his nickname was the nice, folksy "Peckerwood" but which was, in reality, the rather earthier "Peckerhead", an entirely different kettle of fish), Henderson *fils,* who'd actually never met the fellow, was sort of neutral: The guy was clearly something of an ignorant jerkoff, but at the same time, given the temper of the times, the chances of his being replaced by an even *more* ignorant, *bigger* jerkoff were definitely greater than 50-50.

Certainly that was the opinion of Henderson *père,* who, although a Republican, was naturally an old pal of the august Democrat statesman, Representative Peckerhead, of whom he said,

"There's worse than ole Peckerhead, lemme tell you, son. When you bribe 'im, he damn well *stays* bribed, and in any case he don't steal more'n his fair share — an' as a bonus, he's with General LeMay, he'd nuke them Veetmanese into the goddamn Gobi damn *Desert* if he had his way — "

"Viet-nam-ese, Pop, not goddamn *'Veetmanese'* — jeez — "

"Yeah, and them too."

Not like Rojo…. Not at *all* like poor old Rojo: Isidro. Private Last-Class Isidro Jésus-Maria Rojo-Rosario, from "New York, New York, so nice they name it twice!", Henderson's great pal and bunk-mate back at Basic Training and, following that, at Advanced Infantry Training (AIT) as well.

Henderson smiled as he thought now of Rojo, and That Time — That Time he'd gotten his spic ass into *all* kindsa shit with the pitch-black Sergeant First Class (five stripes) Reggie D. T. Philips, their training platoon's chief Drill Sergeant: The fucking business had wildly metastasized out of a semi-disastrous initial incident that Rojo had caused, in which his crashing the squad-bay's beguilingly-lethal floor-buffing contraption into — and actually dislodging — a crapper in the large, communal latrine, had figured rather more prominently than the hapless young *señor don Privato* Rojo might have wished. A minor catastrophe that had been almost immediately followed by a fit of what, even for Sergeant Philips, was a blast of semi-deranged hyperbole, as this starched and quivering-with-rage Guardian of the Republic had proceeded to unambiguously inform "Private Limp-Dick No-Class Roe-joe", at the speed of about 185 decibles-per-spittle, that this latter "Third-World Reekin' No-Count" had just destroyed US Government Property, for which Rojo would have to reimburse the Government "with fuckin' interest and penalties!", which, given "Private E-Zero" Rojo's derisory "pay" would take him "till you dies a ole age, which in *your* case, Roe-joe, ain't never gonna happen 'cause if *any*damnbody's gonna get his dumb ass greased by Charlie, it fuckin' *you,* dipshit!"

The indignant Rojo had gamely squeeked back, "*Hépa,* Saryent, ee é-no fair, nobody tell me how you drive thees theeng, mang — thees fockeen' boffer theeng, mang, Saryent — "

To which Sergeant Philips had found it useful to roar, "*Oh yeah? Well then why don' you jess write yer fuckin'congressman, trainee Roe-joe!*"

Poor old Rojo, never one to leave well enough alone, had almost suicidally riposted "My *congressman? Puta, coño,* Saryent, my fockin' Congressman is fockin'*Bella Abzug,* mang! — an' she a *commoonista* — she a cross between a fockin VC an' a fockin' grizzly bear wid *tits,* mang, no *way* I can gonna write to *her,* mang, I mean — be fockin' *real,* mang... Saryent... sir.... "

But Smokey Bear Drill Sergeants have nothing if not the last word which, in this case, consisted of Sergeant First Class Reggie D. T. Philips spinning on his spit-shined heel and emitting a disgusted,

"Dat sound like a *per*sonal problem, Roe-Joe! — drop down an' gimme fifty!"

Politics....

Henderson figured his kid brother Junior was more right than he knew — Junior Henderson had once memorably declared, when being nagged about his disinclination to go to college,

"The three most important things in life — no, check that — the *only* three important things in life are, in no partic'lar order: Drinkin' beer, chasin' pussy, an' throwin' fastballs... And my only ambition in life is to be the first person ever to do all three sime-simo-simontaneously.... An' yeah, thanks for askin', I'm gettin' there... I'm workin' on it.... " And then he'd gone and passed out ("took a nap") on the pool table.

Ah yes, Junior....

The Bush Pig thought he might try out "The Junior Henderson Philosophy" on the next NVA "cadre" his guys brought him in... see how it flew, across cultures.... *Yeah, the NVA... fucking fuck... now there's a buncha guys who're a barrel a laughs, alright, Jesus H. Humphrey... But still... politics....*

It couldn't be denied that Nixon's program of "Vietnamization"*was*, just as its critics had feared, proving to be something of a success. By the dawn of 1972, there were exactly only 24,200 US servicemen still stationed in South Vietnam (down from the high of 536,100 at the end of 1968) — mostly Special Forces, Artillery, Signal, Intelligence and Air Force guys. Weekly US combat and "combat-related" deaths were down to the low single digits, and the last US combat unit, the 196th Brigade of the 23rd Infantry "American" Division, had left Vietnam (I Corps) in January of that year.

Furthermore and as previously noted, by the beginning of 1972 the ARVN pretty much had things under control throughout the South; countrywide, things were winding down. The Delta (IV Corps), except for an occasional mined road or somesuch, was pacified — you couldn't beg, borrow or steal a VC down there. (In fact, by 1972 there were, in California alone, a great many more people who believed themselves to be "Viet Cong"*than in all of South Vietnam.*) Only in I Corps, where the NVA could still use the trusty old Ho Chi Minh Trail through "liberated" corridors in Laos like some kind of Southeast Asian New Jersey Turnpike, was some semi-serious fighting still occurring. But fortunately for the Good Guys, the ARVNs had their best (and their best weren't half-bad) units up there — Ranger regiments and Airborne battalions.

So all in all, then, at that moment in time — about three months prior to the very moment when Henderson's ass would be bouncing along on a northeasterly vector in a slow helicopter in Phuland — South Vietnam was a more peaceful place than at any time since that day way back in December 1946 when an ex-Parisian hotel dish-washer called Ho Chi Minh had kicked off armed hostilities. And the "Theu-Ky Clique of Puppet Running Dogs", as Ho's minions on their Liberation Radio liked to call it, was more firmly in charge in Saigon than ever before.

Right. So up in Hanoi, Ho's Boys had said, "Alright, fuck this," ("*Được rồi, địa ngục với cái này*"for those taking notes) "what we're going to have around here is a change in strategy." And they'd picked up a red phone and called a number that rang at #2 Dzerzhinsky Street, in Moscow .

And a Big Meeting had been organized in Russia. Big and Secret. Soviet Politburo guys in charge. It was convened in a sumptuous KGB safe-*dacha* located a bit outside of Moscow, hidden away in the fancy Zhukovka suburb, to the west.

High-ranking "observers" from the "Forward Defense Department" of the Red Chinese Ministry of State Security were in attendance, no matter what the outside world thought it imagined about a "Sino-Soviet rift". And of course, from Southeast Asia, the whole "Liberation"-*sma-*

la was also there: Le Duan, Giap and four other generals from Hanoi; the head of "COSVN" (the technical name of what was affectionately known on US campuses as "the Viet Cong"); The "People's Prime Minister" from "liberated" Laos, Souphanouvong; that hysterical little creampuff of a fraudulent "Prince" from Cambodia, Norodom Sihanouk, accompanied by a nervous and sinister slug of a guy called Pol Pot whom Sihanouk had recently elevated to head the "Khmer Rouge", and finally, Patom Matak.

Patom Matak was the Secretary-Colonel (*"Secretary-Colonel"*? Yes, don't ask — it was an old Trotskyite thing, very abstruse) of the "Phu Istakat" ("Free Phu"), a gang of about 3,000 (maybe 3,500 if you added their dogs, mothers and the sympathetic international media people who regularly sought them out) communist insurgents, holed up, some in the suburbs of Phu-Lama and the rest up in the Pang Phu Meu — a motley agglomeration made up of about half deserters from the Royal Phu Army, and the other half students — in fact, its "officers" (more "political" officers that combat officers, really) had been students who'd gotten indoctrinated at such places as both Cambridges (the one in England and the one in Boston), Berkeley, NYU, the Sorbonne, "Patrice Lumumba Friendship University" in Moscow and — surprisingly, far from least — the University of Bologna.

Prior to this Big Meeting in Moscow, the closest thing to either a military or political success ever achieved by the Phu Istakat, since the day in 1960 when it had been created in Hanoi, had occurred in the fall of 1970, when Patom Matak had been included among the invitees to an "International Symposium on US War Crimes" organized by the 3/4s decrepit and totally bananas Bertrand Russell, in Toronto. The hapless "Secretary-Colonel", who'd never previously been out of Asia in his life, had contracted a terrible case of the shits on his Aeroflot flight (*not*, to put it mildly, the ideal venue for experiencing such an attack) to Canada, and for the entire three days of this bewildering blatherfest of an "international symposium", he'd sat, worried and uncomortable, behind his little purple, red and yellow Phu Istakat flag, in embarrassed pain and silence.

So that was Patom Matak — something less than a towering statesman of Global Import.... But still, Moscow had Big Plans, and these plans included Phuland. Over a million communist soldiers might be dead so far in this gory and more-difficult-than-originally-planned communization of Southeast Asia, but still Moscow had Big Plans:

The Chief Commie In Charge, KGB boss Yuri Andropov, (*I Comi di Tutti Comi,* as he was irreverently known by the two observers from the Italian CP), explained it thus:

- Thailand must fall, of course, but only later;
- South Vietnam is still the main brass ring, but that can't be won until we get Cambodia, because what the Imperialists call the Ho Chi Minh Trail for the time being only functions through eastern Laos; it is blocked in its Cambodian arteries, which are potentionally closer and therefore more useful;
- But we can't be assured of liberating *anything* until and unless Thailand is, if not defeated, *at least neutralized.*
- Now. We all know that sooner or later our comrades, here, from Vietnam are going to be belly to belly with the Thai lackeys. But lackeys or not, the Thais are no damned pushovers, and even as we speak, they're certainly not getting any weaker. In fact, they've just completed the process of equipping their *entire* military with the M-16 and have been given 60 new F-4 Phantoms by the Im-

perialists, to boot. So, the sooner we deal with them, the better — agreed?

Everyone at the meeting agreed, *You betcha, comrade, numbah wan!*

- Very well then. Now, we've drawn up a two-pronged plan to divide the Thai forces, inasmuch as we deem them too dangerous to fight on only one front: Our comrades already inside Thailand will help, naturally, but they may not be ready to play a central role for some time still. For now they are far too weak and since we must act with alacrity we can't wait for their struggle to mature. So we'll hit the Thais in two places: in their northeast, coming from Laos, and in their northwest, down through the Pang Phu Meu — there, the old woman they call a king, Matak Vathak II, even if he had the will, has not the means to do much to hinder us.

- Now, that northwestern front has already been satisfactorily prepared but, as you know, there are now close to a hundred thousand Thai troops massed near the Lao border. We must therefore move quickly through Phuland and developed that western front. Overall, the Vietnamese comrades have consecrated and assigned 150,000 newly-retrained troops to the liberation of Thailand, and one third of them will constitute the Vanguard of this latest Front in the Great Struggle, emanating in Phuland. (Le Duan smiled as the KGB boss laid this out — it would cost that old viper Andropov another cool $1 billion {1972 dollar$}per year to continue to support this latest Vanguard of the Front of *whatever-the-fuck it is we're calling it now....)*

And Andropov the Chief-Commie-In-Charge ended his own contribution to the meeting with this exhortation:

As for the Americans, (pause, here, for the drama that was in it), *they will do nothing but look helplessly on from their golfing courses and supermarkets in Honolulu!* (And at this, the meeting took a brief Mirth Break).

The Meeting had gone on for another week, during which the details of the above Grand Strategy had been hashed out. But that had been basically the Big Commie Plan for Southeast Asia at the dawn of 1972.

And shortly thereafter, US intelligence (NSA) implantations here and there in the Eastern Hemisphere began detecting a marked increase in suspicious radio traffic and, worse, *actual* traffic — traffic on the ground. This last was, in fact, none other than the 301B and the 210th NVA divisions humping westwards, across northern Laos, (waving hello to the the 338th and 360th NVA divisions, who were resting briefly at the NVA's legendary "Group 579" mobile logistics center, as they passed), and spreading out into the Pang Phu Meu. So the Great Plan was moving right along....

+ + + + + + +

But about that time something happened which not even the best-laid of Soviet 5-Year Plans, or Little Red Books of Chairman Mao's Thoughts, could have foreseen:

One day in early-November 1971, old King Matak Vathak II, 78 years old, caught pneumonia while cruising on his royal barge on the Phumia River, and thirty six hours later expired with a splendidly regal gasp in his palace outside Phoo-Lama.

Now, the Phu people, and even the non-Phu Meu-Jong, had traditionally — and genuinely — been quite fond of their monarchy (to the disapproving bewilderment of progressive sociologists worldwide), but they were especially fond of *this* monarch, who they called "The Gentle Leader", who'd led that "Great Salvation Trek" back in '40, and who had conducted the Affairs of State with more justice and dignity than anyone in this little corner of the world had ever been accustomed to. And as a result of this feeling of goodwill, when his death was announced the whole country went into an extended period of heartfelt mourning which had produced what was for Phuland a quite novel experience — a feeling of nationhood and oneness among its people. A kind of astonished patriotism. Even the most hard-bitten and cynical Phu-Lama politicos and power (such as it was)-brokers were a bit taken by surprise at the novel phenomenon.

Crown Prince Pom, a near-hairless and (so far) heirless gangly youth of 24 had just been finishing up his last weeks of his three years at Sandhurst Military College, on the Berkshire/Surrey border, in England, at the time, and the death of his papa had been announced to him by the Regimental Sergeant-Major just after Retreat. It had to be said, the unsentimentally-delivered — virtually barked — words from that hard-bitten source had taken the poor young devil utterly unprepared. (As it does to us all.)

For a few days after learning the news, Prince Pom felt rather... bereft. In fact, initially he'd weighed the option of Panic, and had only discarded it because he wasn't sure how to go about even *that*.

His father, of course, had tutored him reasonably well in the requisites of Kingship, but nevertheless, he felt quite adrift as he now kind of sleep-walked through the formalities of packing-up and checking-out of Sandhurst, and then on that afternoon, as he sat in Heathrow Terminal 4's VIP Lounge, waiting for the Royal Phu Air Force DC-7C to arrive with his uncle, the Minister of Defence (*sic*), to take him back to Phu-Lama — well, at that moment, he actually considered going into the Gents', shedding his RPAF Colonel's uniform (with Brit jump wings pinned above the left breast pocket), and bloody *chucking* this whole Kingdom thing. Just get back into his purple Jaguar E-Type (which had been arranged to be shipped to Phu-Lama later on) and drive back out to grassy Berkhamsted and ask the young and lubricious Miss Fiona Ponson-by-Lyons (actually, *Lady* Fiona P-L, a lovely deb he'd met at a Sandhurst "do" and with whom he'd being "going" ever since — rather too chastely in his opinion but promisingly-enough nevertheless — and in any case steadily-enough to have made the gossip-columns) to go away with him. To anywhere: Mexico. Greenland. Timbuktu. *A*nywhere, sod it, other than home to Phuland. Well, he'd considered it, but in the end he fretted that she'd think him Drunk With Grief or something similarly girly, and anyway — *I know her*— *she's certain to be booked-up this weekend...* Posh and pretty English society girls seemed genetically able to effortlessly contrive to cause themselves to become "booked-up"*poof!*, just like *that,* with astonishing spontaneity....

Sitting dejectedly in that VIP lounge, half-consumed glass of gin-and-tonic threatening to fall out of his uncaring hand, his chin sunk into his as-yet unjustified medals, the new young King of Phuland had been roused by his somewhat glassy-eyed, just-arrived Uncle Minister of Defence, and after said uncle had forced the remaining g+t down the young royal gullet — and indeed had produced and administered a couple more, for each of them, for the road, as it were — the two Phu dignitaries had stood, thanked the nice ladies who kept the VIP lounge so splendidly toodle-pip, and regained the purple-and-white Royal Aeroplane.

And thus the worried young King had been whisked back to the turmoil and, probably, peril of the beloved, if anxious, Kingdom.

Once arrived in Phu-Lama, however, Prince Pom very soon — indeed, almost magically — began to "evolve". He quickly surmised that not only in the capital but also (from his visits up there) up-country, the people somehow, for reasons that were not immediately obvious to him, looked up to him as something resembling a worthy king — "The Gentle Leader's Son". *Imagine that.* Goodwill seemingly everywhere. Well, *almost* everywhere. *Mostly* everywhere. People smiling and bowing. At *him,* for God's sakes....

And more and more, as he saw wide-eyed children staring at him in what might, by the mal-intentioned, have been mistaken for imbecility but was more probably awe, the strange thought began to infiltrate his consciousness that he, King Pom was in some weird (but no less real for that) sense, the Father of His Country. That's right — *He,* whose only previous brush with actual paternity had been a lamentable and thoroughly shameful episode involving some £300 out of his own pocket and an aborted fetus being dumped with criminal indignity into a Bayswater Road rubbish "skip" — He, Pom, had suddenly become a kind of symbolic, surrogate father of all these children. Also, of course, of all these helpless women, opium-racked old men, malaria-ridden soldiers, veterans without limbs, not to mention all the other hawking, spitting, fractious, squawling, intractable souls that made up the population of Phuland. They were all his children now and all, in one way or another, looked to him for protection, for their daily rice bowl, for spiritual guidance, and for all those other things that people looked to their fathers for.

Rather less grandly and more mundanely, Pom's understanding of governance, though undoubtedly benign, was not very deep — indeed, it didn't extend far beyond a vaguely-assumed paternalism. And as for his understanding of economics, well, sadly, neither Friedrich Hayek nor Milton Friedman were included in the curriculum at Sandhurst. So in these, more practical aspects of Kingship, Pom sensed — and feared — that he might be a bit adrift.

Now this was one heavy (as his young, non-royal, Sandhurst peers would have put it) set of changes that Pom went through. For weeks, he was nervous and preoccupied. By day he fiddled with his gilded and bejeweled sword (upon which he once badly cut his hand when he wasn't paying attention — *useless bloody thing….*). At night he sweated, felt nauseous and had difficulty sleeping. He paced his private quarters in monotonous laps, as though he were in a human zoo. *What to do? Heh, wat to do?*

In this state of mental turmoil, he went — precisely thirty days after leaving London — and knelt for seven hours (*seven hours!*) before his father's tomb at the Great Wat, not far from the Royal Palace. For the first few hours his knees had given him great pain, but eventually they'd gone completely numb, so that was alright. Finally, with the sky growing pink at six in the morning, he'd creaked painfully to his feet and, regaining purpose in his stride, had marched with a new confidence into his Palace:

Henceforth he would be a proper king to his people. *His* people. The Phu people. And also not forgetting his at-times troublesome but ultimately faithful cousins, the Meu-Jong. They were all his people. The whole business might well end up costing him his life, but that night young King Pom had decided that as long as he was King, his people would look to *him*. Not to Hanoi or Moscow or Bangkok or Tokyo or London or Peking or even Washington. They'd look to *him*.

And the first thing this "new", revitalized King Pom did was to take the Minister of Finances, the part-Chinese Dr. Ho Tou Fat, and ship him off to New York as Phuland's first-ever (the old King had never though it worth the money or the bother) Ambassador to the United Nations. Before old King Matak Vathak's death, the worldly, not to say devious, Ho Tou Fat had been advising him that Phuland had to "learn to live with" the neighboring — and threatening — communist regimes, "like the Burmese do". In addition to this (in Pom's view) crappy advice, Pom knew that at least one of Ho Tou Fat's sons was surreptitiously at least an associate member of the Phu Istakat. Well, now that he was King, Pom reckoned he didn't need any of *that* bloody nonsense here in the Royal Palace, so he decided to let Ho Tou Fat go and flatulate harmlessly in New York. Whenever he'd been pressed on the matter of the UN, his father had answered that the United Nations were a bunch of useless left-wing fussbudgets — that even included a couple of regicides — who cordially deserved each other. *And if that's the case, it'll be perfect,* now thought Pom, *for Dr. Ho Tou Fat.... "Doctor" my arse — what's he a "doctor" of, anyway? Intrigue, I wouldn't doubt....*

The next thing Pom did was to have a long talk with his Senior Uncle, the Minister of Defence. They discussed the Phu Istakat and agreed that, *taken alone,* they were really not up to causing any serious alarm. For one thing, although Phuland was hardly a rich country, no one starved in it or, come to that, even went hungry in it. In fact, ironically enough, the only ones who had trouble finding their daily bowl of rice were the Marxist-Leninist Phoo Istakat — Mao might prattle about communist guerrillas swimming "among the population like fish in the sea", but the reality was that the earnest losers of the Phu Istakat were closer to starving flounders flapping on rocks; and Karl Marx and Vlad Lenin meant no more to most of the Phu people than did Groucho Marx and Charlie Chaplin — rather less, in fact. Neither, for that matter, did Mao Tse-tung....

In this last respect, the Meu-Jong mountain people were more sophisticated than the lowland Phu. For the Meu-Jong *did* know, as a result of past encounters, *all about* the Chinese from the north... and the Vietnamese from the east. Painful nuisances, the "neighbors". And as a result, the Meu-Jong didn't much like *any* foreigners — hell, it was all they could do to stomach their co-nationals, the Phu in the south. In fact, truth be known, the only foreigners they'd ever dealt with who'd ever treated them decently were, of all people, the Americans. Which was the reason the Meu-Jong had been quite happy to enter into an Odd Couple-like paramilitary relationship with the "Big Noses", who they regarded, among themselves, more as a species of largely incomprehensible, if unaccountably sympathetic and generous, well... *extra-terrestrials* — than mere "foreigners".

However, although the Phu Istakat were pretty much a manageable matter, the forty-to-fifty thousand North Vietnamese Army regulars currently marching into the Pang Phu Meu were definitely less so. True, their eventual aim might be Thailand, to the south, but King Pom and his Senior Uncle realized unhappily that for this to be achieved, Phuland would first have to be emasculated, à la Laos.

This, then, was the salient *res.,* the bloody big headache that was the most immediately pressing concern of young King Pom. He and the Senior Uncle considered their options:

The Conservative government in London had sent a ten-man military training mission to Phu-Lama a year ago, and those chaps were still around somewhere, presumed to be supervising weapons training. Or something. Nice fellows, certainly, but their value against the NVA was negligible. To put it mildly.

The Senior Uncle had not minced his words:

"Our only hope is America. We must point out our situation to Washington and show them quite frankly how our demise will be their loss. But it must be done secretly. Well, as secretly as possible. If we indulge in the publicity and, indeed, what amounted to public blackmail like the Cambodians — that stupid she-clown Sihanouk — did, we will be turned down. They cannot do otherwise, for they have a, a ... *difficult* situation at home — many influential Americans would like to turn their backs on us here in southeast Asia altogether... it's all a bit like the story of the monkey and the centipede that His Highness your father used to tell... remember?"

Pom vaguely remembered the parable but didn't immediately have the slightest clue what the hell it might have had with their currently dangerous military situation.... "Yes, I remember. But how can this be done? Talk to the Americans? Their president? *In secret?* I can't do *anything* in secret — I mean to say, Phuland may be merely Phuland, but dammit, a King is still a King."

"True, Pom. Therefore, *I* will arrange, through the American Ambassador, for a trip to Hawaii, (which, as you know, is American — it's a proper American state), to coincide with a large meeting there next month of what they call their 'Pacific Security Group'. Many top generals and ministers — in fact, what is most important to us is that their

Ministers of Foreign Affairs and Defence will be there. And *I* can meet with them. Do you give me full powers, Your Highness?"

"Of course, Uncle. What a question."

And so, Uncle Minister of (Phu) Defence had done precisely that and, in a series of meetings in Honolulu and Guam with, variously, Secretary of Defense Melvin Laird, Chairman of the Joint Chiefs of Staff General Earle Wheeler, COMUSMACV General Creighton Abrams, CINCPAC Admiral John McCain, CIA Station Chief "Ambassador" William Colby and, on one brief occasion on a conference telephone call, with Le Grand Tricky himself — a limited and highly confidential — in fact, Top Secret — US-Phu Emergency Cooperation Annex (UP-ECA) had been drawn up, whereby:

A/ The US would provide $25 million dollars' worth of military equipment for the year 1972, (NB, these were of course 1972 dollars) subject to "re-negotiation" (re-adjustment) on a yearly basis;

B/ 100 company-grade Phu Army officers would receive "advanced counterinsurgency" training at Fort Bragg; 10 Phu Navy (its little "brown- water" squadron of "riverine" patrol boats) would receive something similar at Subic Bay Naval Base in the Philippines; and 15 Phu Air Force pilots would get qualified on old T-28 trainers that had been converted into dive-bombing aircraft at Travis AFB in Oakland.

C/ Eight of those "obsolete" (well, "obsolete" to the American "Big Noses", not to the Rest Of The World — which those "Big Noses" called the "ROW") North American T-28 "Trojans" would be de-mothballed and sold to the Royal Phu Air Force, such as it was, for $1 a piece, and would be fitted for — and supplied with — machine guns and 500-lb bombs, to be used in close ground-support operations.

D/ More importantly, the US would expand its Military Attaché staff by 30 "combat advisor" paramilitary officers who would operate directly with RPAF (and RPAF-ILF) units "in the field" (although "mountains" would have been more accurate than "field"), along with 20 further "general and air support" personnel. Thus was born "Operation Roundhouse", named after the bar-restaurant outside Schofield Baracks in Oahu where Laird and Colby had met separately from the others and, after hours, originally sketched out this particular program.

E/ Lastly, and most importantly of all, it was agreed that the "combat advisors" provided in D/ would have the discretionary power (that could be exercised independently of the Ambassador and that was subject only to the veto of the Defense Attaché) to divert tactical F-4 "Phantom" and even strategic B-52 air support from US bases in Thailand and elsewhere, if the ground situation in Phooland so warranted.

Uncle Minister of Defence had gone through the ritual motion of also requesting regular US Army units to confront "his" NVA, but he'd of course been turned down — with Melvin Laird, smoothing back his non-existing hair and saying to Pom's uncle, "Hell, Your uh, Your uh, Excellent, what is it — Highness? No? OK, well, whatever, Your Honor then — I hear what you're saying, but *you*'ve gotta understand that even *me* — hell, even *I*, the American Secretary of Defense — can't hardly get into my own dang *office* for all the... well, for all the... gosh-darn protesters as it is *now*, so if we tried to implement an expansion of our, you know, our conventional military operations into your, uh, uh, your Phuland AO, there, well the shi— the, uh, the, uh, the you-know-what would *really* hit the gosh-darn fan...."

In all honesty, King Pom's uncle hadn't even expected to get as much as he *had* done, and he flew back to Phu-Lama well pleased with himself.

The first of the US "advisors" (Henderson's immediate predecessors) had arrived in December '71, all in mufti — indeed, except for their individual weapons, which they brought with them on their unmarked flights from Thailand, they could have passed for a particularly rough-looking softball team.

And along with the advisors — in fact, as part of the whole UPECA deal — had arrived a whole mini-fleet of airplanes and helicopters belonging to something called America Tropic Air Services, Inc. (ATAS). The King and his Court (his Cabinet, actually) had chosen not to monitor this development too closely: air support was air support, after all — probably the single most precious military asset there was at that time in the whole world. The Royal Phu inner circle of decision-making-*wallahs* was grateful for any and all of it, and furthermore, it was Oriental enough to know better than to delve too deeply into whatever face-saving arrangements the Yankee Big Noses had had to make with themselves in order to provide this help.

In any case, fifty American paramilitary advisors were not likely to exactly turn Phu-Lama into another Saigon. They *might*, however, be of some crucial help in halting, or at least slowing, the advance of the fearsome North Vietnamese Army. After all, although they were few in number, they brought with them upgrades to, and significantly increased numbers of, M-16s, ammunition, radios, helicopters — and, above all, they had that direct line to the mighty US Air Force. So, although it was wise to keep an eye on the Americans, it was best not to interfere too much. In the turbulent world of 1972, Phuland did not dispose of a limitless supply of allies.... *Best to bear in mind the story of the monkey and the centipede....*

For his part, it had not been without a certain amount of trepidation that the battle-scarred Nixon had put his John Hancock to the (Top Secret) US-Phu Emergency Cooperation Annex: He was fully cognizant of how apoplectic — even *more* apoplectic — the virtual entirety of America's "chattering classes" would be if the paramilitary project, even a *hint* of it, got blown. He shuddered (a rare occurrence indeed, for him) just at the thought of it.

But, as he'd commented to his pal Bebe Rebozo, *Fuck it, anyway. You know?*

Because Tricky also knew of that Big Meeting in Moscow, and the Big Plan that had resulted from it. He'd had virtual real-time intel on their bull session and, well, goddammit, "Vietnamization"*was* working — had *already* worked — and America had come too far — too goddamn painfully far — to have it all reversed now just because the commies had decided to shift gears. Even though his pussy Secretary of State had (of course) argued against the signing of the UPECA Annex — the Chiefs of Staff, and those other members of his cabinet who mattered, had been (even if somewhat hesitantly, it had to be said — except for Mel Laird) in favor of it. But it hadn't been any of their counsel that the President had listened to; only his own. America was still the Leader Of The Free World. And so it would remain while he was President. Simple as that. Southeast Asia might one day, after all this blood, sweat, piss and misery, fall to the Reds... but fucking not while *he* was President.

And Tricky hadn't needed to kneel before his father's tomb for seven hours to come to that conclusion, either....

7/ 0850 HOURS

"It is one thing to face the music, it is another thing to dance to it."

— SAKI

As McElmore's helicopter overflew the foothills of the Pang Phu Meu, it hit a spot of turbulence. Thinking about the whole wretched Big Picture had finally pushed Henderson over the brink to sleep, but he was now rudely jolted awake. His tongue tasted as though the entire Soviet Red Army had walked across it in its socks, and he unscrewed himself a shot of canteen water.

Sandoval appeared to be asleep. *Hard to tell in that science-fiction helmet of his if he's even* alive — *fucker could probably sleep through a shoot-down....*

Henderson checked out the scene below. Some scene. Big green nothing. Although he was mildly gratified that by now, after a few months, he could begin to recognize some of the streams, valleys and karst ridges. It was about forty minutes to Che Kak's position, up there in that shithole of an LS-Echo.

He bent over, untangled, and deliberately — plenty of time, nothing else to do in this rattletrap — put on his web gear. *Good to have this crap handy — never know when you'll need it:*

On his pistol belt were fastened:

- Two canteens of water;
- A USMC "K-Bar" knife in a canvas sheath;
- A pouch containing a Swedish "Silva" compass, an SDU-5/E strobe-light device, and a 33-function Swiss Army knife;
- Another pouch containing a small pair of Zeiss "self-focusing" binoculars;
- Two specially-modified US Army first-aid kits, with 6 morphine syrettes in each;
- A Special Forces survival kit (into which he'd jammed extra aspirins and bouillon cubes);

and

- A loaded Browning 9mm automatic with an extra 13-round magazine attached to the holster. (When he'd first arrived at the Combined Logistics Group in Phu-Lama he'd been given the choice of the Browning, a Smith & Wesson "Police .38", and a captured Russian Tokarev 9mm — but the fucking Tokarev came with no safety on it — typically Russian, and he couldn't hit shit with the .38, so he'd gone for the Browning. Damn fine bit of ordnance, in any case....)

He further placed his two bandoleers of M-16 magazines across himself, Pancho Villa-style. Each bandoleer contained seven 20-round magazines, so he carried 280 rounds across his chest — which, when added to the 30-round magazine in his rifle, gave him a total of 310... hardly excessive, if things got hairy for longer than a brief-to-medium-length firefight, but it was all he could reasonably hump, along with his other shit — after all, even though it was 5.56, his extra ammo alone weighed over sixteen pounds.

And at his feet sat his rucksack, which he'd sling onto his back as soon as he de-assed the old H-34. Inside *that* he had:

- Four M-26 frag grenades, still in their individual black cardboard containers — the America Tropic jocks would refuse to let the Customer on board if he had frags hanging off him like Christmas tree ornaments;
- Two red, and one green, M-18 smoke grenades;
- A Navy MK-31 flare "pen" (launcher) with three green and three red flares;
- Two extra batteries for his HT-2A radio;
- Two cans of C-Ration "Boned Chicken": Much-prized as it was everyone's favorite — or least reviled; (most reviled: "Ham & Eggs");
- A tightly-folded Army green nylon poncho;
- Two extra packs of Salems;
- A set of acetate-covered maps of Xuam Long Province (the Pang Phu Meu);
- A leather-and-sterling silver pint flask from Neiman-Marcus that had been given to him as a going-away present when he'd shipped out to Vietnam by good ol' Junior, that was currently filled, more or less, with White Horse Scotch whiskey;
- A hundred-foot coiled piece of nylon cord. This bit of gear might, in some conceivable circumstance, be the most crucial of all, but when he'd signed for it at the supply hooch down at the CLG and

the Airman-clerk had asked "What you aim to do with this here piece a string, Cap?" Henderson had answered "Hell, whaddya think — hang myself — ";

- A much dog-eared paperback copy of a novel called "The Ginger Man" by a guy called J.P. Donleavy that one of Henderson's fraternity brothers had once passed on to him and which had become his "bible";

- And finally, what Henderson consciously did *not* carry, either anywhere in or on his gear, or even in his battered wallet (that he had in his jeans' ass pocket and which only contained a modest supply of Phoo currency and a couple of condoms) was any ID. Of any kind. Not even that ridiculous laminated Department of Agriculture ID card, that was safely stashed by his bunk in the hooch back in Phoo-Lama.

(Mothers, wives, girlfriends and perhaps even sisters might have wondered why he carried no spare socks or underwear — underpants. U-trou. And the answer would have been, obviously, that Henderson didn't expect to be gone nearly long enough to warrant a change of clothes, but also that in any case, Henderson never wore any of these in the field — old habit from a hard-learned lesson in the Nam: Gross it might sound, but in the perpetually damp not to mention rancid living conditions of Southeast-Boondock-Grunt-Asia, socks and skivvies were far more trouble — *painful* trouble — than they were worth. They just were. And hey, not carrying spares of those allowed him to carry a bit of whiskey and a paperback book instead....)

His M-16 automatic rifle and HT-2A "Village" radio, a device that was about the size, shape and weight of a quart bottle of White Horse, also lay on the helicopter's floor, between his rucksack and his feet. One of the Supreme Things you had to learn (and soon) in the Army was to "keep your fucking shit in a High State"… or, failing that, at least to "keep your fucking s. *together*". Otherwise, your were in Deep *Kimchee*. Or Dog Meat — which was even worse.

So Henderson checked it all out again, and strapped it all together… one more time. Then he pulled his Commanders cap low over his eyes, perhaps perchance to get a little more zonk time in…. That was another thing he'd learned from "Sam": sleep. *Sleep, m'boy, sleep.* Sleep — it was as though America Tropic had had sleep in mind when they'd come up with their motto: *Anytime, Anywhere, Anyhow. Phhhh…* Phuland… Henderson… Phuland… Henderson… *Sheee-it… zzzz….*

+ + + + + + +

At twenty-five, Henderson had become rather a strange-looking bird. Well, at least strange-looking for a Henderson. The rest of the family was large and blonde. But he was 5' 10", weighed 146 pounds, (the smallest male Henderson anyone knew of) and had jet black hair which, even in his college days when it had been worn long, had hung close to his noggin. In other words, he more closely resembled a young Geronimo or a young Napoleon than, say, Art Garfunkel. His mouth was wide, thin, and usually closed. All his features were sharp: you got the impression that you could slice bread off the bridge of his nose. His skin verged on the olive and his eyes were so dark they might as well have been black. He wasn't *bad*-looking — if anything, he was actually OK-looking — but he was just definitely a little… *odd*-looking; It was hard to imagine wanting to *cuddle* the fucker, but you certainly *noticed* the fucker….

In Houston, whenever he'd felt like it, Henderson had been able to frequent the wetback bars and pass for a Mexican. His Spanish wasn't flawless, but then again neither was most of the Mexicans', *y de todo modo tenia bastante huevos para que nadie me los rompieron* and well, the general effect had been good enough for him to get by mostly untroubled. (Until, of course, ubiquitous, nation-wide arguments over "Vietnam" had intruded, and fucked up everyone's social equilibrium.)

Right *now*, of course, his face was even darker because of the shadow of Junior's lowered cap... but also because of the seemingly ineradicable grit, dust, sun, death and general generic dirt that, in Southeast Asian combat zones, sooner or later became part of one's facial topography.

Henderson's near-black eyes were huge. Originally, they'd been about normal-size, but guys' eyes somehow either actually grew, or certainly *seemed* to grow, bigger the longer they beheld a combat zone. Maybe it was a, pardon the pun, a *trompe l'oeil,* and it wasn't the eyes that were growing but the face that was shrinking — it didn't really matter, except that as a result he, like just about every other veteran grunt, looked seriously *zoned*.

Henderson currently hadn't shaved in about forty hours, and the overall aura he radiated, quite deliberately, was that of a slightly mad, cynical, dangerous semi-maniac. A camouflaged, 1972-model compact Bush Pig, equipped with all the options. And that was alright, because looking like a mean motherfucker was half the battle in the endless "face" game one had to play with the locals.

But in actuality, Jerry Henderson wasn't quite that easily pegged:

Although a shy-ish boy — not shy to a fault, you understand, more polite, really, than anything else — he'd enjoyed a basically "normal" '50s American childhood.

But whenever he'd been out at his Uncle Morton's colossal ranch, with gaggles of cousins and attendant snot-nosed pals, Henderson would often organize war-games and hikes and the building of forts and dividing everybody into "feuding clans" (whatever the hell those actually were — little Jerry had never seen any actual such things as "feuding clans" in real life but he'd heard about 'em on TV and they'd struck him as great pretexts for contests... if not actual fights) with the aim, of course, to kidnap or otherwise visit mayhem upon the other guys. Young Jerome loved concocting wily and what would much later be known as "outside the box" plans and stratagems, and often his side would win as their youthful opponents would, quite understandably, be less than enthusiastic at getting soaked or waiting immobile for hours or jumping down from walls and trees — all tactics which Jerome's side employed with relish — to beat that "other mob".

And speaking of mobs, the motley factions comprising the Henderson family, when assembled, were full of noise, laughter and anarchy.

But Henderson's childhood, though largely idyllic, had not been *all* fun and games:

Once, when he was eight, Jerome was caught lifting a dollar bill from J.D.'s wallet which he'd come across, one Sunday in the master bedroom where he'd gone to get something.... He certainly didn't need a dollar, and afterwards had wondered why he'd been such an almighty asshole (a word he'd only recently learned and was now shocked to find himself applying to himself) to do such a thing. His enduring memory of the dreadful episode had been his fear of being thrashed by J.D. but then being even *more* horrified when his father had just looked down sadly at him and said, "Now son, you don't want to go around doin' something like that, do ya." If he lived to be two hundred he'd never forget a single detail of that awful mistake.

And another time, he'd been caught red-handed, you should pardon the expression, together with his school pal Petey Hatfield, with some raunchy (and quite bewildering — *"wait, d'ya put it there, or there?" "I dunno... I thought it was there, but maybe not...." "and what's with THAT?"*) pornography that was being passed around during recess. They'd been so engrossed by the black-and-white photos that they hadn't noticed the approach of their 6th-grade teacher Mr. Glass. Young Jerome had been sent home with a shameful note requiring parental autographs... the whole unseemly (Jerome's ears had reddened with embarrassment) episode had been regrettable, to be sure, but not *quite* as traumatic as when his pop had caught him lifting that stupid stupid damn dollar bill....

Still... Life, he was constantly informed by his elders, was all Ups and Downs, and for the youthful Jerome Henderson the ups greatly outnumbered the downs; which is perhaps why he would now remember the latter so much more vividly.

Had he been a little bigger and maybe with blonde or, better yet, red hair, Jerome might have been a Norman Rockwell-esque prototype of the All-American Boy: He even had to attend goddamn Sunday School, where he once, while the matron-in-charge was droning on about loaves and fishes, distinguished himself by winning a surreptitious gum-chewing contest: he'd managed to cram nine and a half sticks of horrible Black Jack cinnamon gum into his gob... his jaw had ached until the next day, but it had been worth it! — in life, you had to be able to distinguish — and choose — between what was important and what was not....

For high school, he was shipped off to Phillips-Andover Academy, an expensive and snooty prep school off in Massafuckingchussetts, where J.D. maintained some rather mysterious business ties with a guy who was a Trustee there.

To Jerome Andover was like a foreign country and he was bemused, though not all that surprised (and not necessarily displeased) to find himself considered mildly exotic because he was from Texas, a mythic land that was equally foreign to most of his schoolmates as his schoolmasters — who were more familiar with Paris, London and Switzerland than points west-by-southwest. His grades were nothing to write home about, but he did well in history, a subject which somehow all made sense to him. He also became a pugnacious midfielder on the varsity lacrosse team and in his senior year scored two (2), by God, goals against their most hated rival, Deerfield.

Thanksgiving vacations were usually pissed away in Boston, always with school buddies who, although of that *milieu,* were just as socially Out Of It as Henderson was. The lot of them making great flapping fools of themselves as they tried expensively and almost always unsuccessfully to "score whores" (*"They can teach you stuff, man"*), and instead settling for sweaty, half-assed and ultimately pointless and unsatisfactory make-out sessions with girls from nearby female versions of Andover such as Abbott or Miss Hall's, episodes that in truth more resembled wresting bouts than anything remotely amorous... on a wide variety of porches, back seats of sedans (sedans if they were lucky — of Volkswagen Beetles if they weren't) and, worst of all, on cold, nocturnal beaches with their painfully intrusive and smelly seaweed, rocks and sticky sand. *Hey, you win some, you lose some...* (mostly the latter....)

During the summer vacation of his junior year, back in Houston, Henderson was deemed fit and approved by the grownups to work with the terse, uncompromising, tobacco-chewing cowboys on his Uncle Morton's 5,000-acre ranch, a spread that was considered small, by the way, by other, neighboring cowboys.

Although there were plenty of laughs during that gig, the hours were punishing and the work was hot, uncomfortable, tiring and, when not difficult and dangerous, often boring. But over the weeks of that summer it occurred to Henderson, in a fleeting glimmer of self-awareness, that He Was Becoming A Man. *Imagine that.* This transition was symbolized by his witnessing, and even, in a fumbling way, assisting in his first live birth — of a calf — a semi-shockingly rough and bloody spectacle that would stick with him for a good long time. He also saw, and helped carry, his first dead body — one of the cowboys, a funny, leathery older guy called Veto (*not*, the fellow had been anxious to assure others while he was still alive, "Vito"), had been killed by a falling branch when the tree he'd been standing under in a thunderstorm had been hit by lightning.

Then on to the University of Texas. Henderson hadn't cared much of a damn where he went to college — or even *if* he went. But J.D., class of '37, had been something of a Big Man On Campus there and, with a somewhat envious eye to his pal back east in Andover, was a recurring — though as yet unsuccessful — candidate to its Board of Trustees.

As indifferent as Jerome had been to the whole college business — *Rah rah, Hook 'em Horns* — once he got to Austin he found himself quite enjoying himself. "Quite" enjoying himself, hell — *greatly* enjoying himself....

As soon as he could, he pledged up with Pop's old fraternity, a gang of amiable layabouts who would eventually take advantage of Henderson's manifestly devious mind, with its clear affinity for strategy, game theory and counterinsurgency, by electing him, twice — simultaneously as their Rush Chairman and their Pledgemaster.

Jerome Henderson's college interregnum was, not to put too fine a point on it, essentially four years of happy sunny insouciant drunkenness. He achieved as near as one could to a sustained level of Nirvana, if of a somewhat cut-rate, inelegant and threadbare sort, without actually landing oneself in the slammer. Not that he hadn't, at times, seemed to be trying his hardest to accomplish just this very thing — and, upon a few semi-spectacular occasions, (one of them, for example, involving two other frat brothers, three almost-naked Tri-Delts, a case of vile Mount Gay rum, a temporarily-stolen VW bus, a kidnapped St. Bernard puppy and a near-disastrously, it turned out, *not*-deserted moonlit lake), had damn near succeeding in doing so.

Indeed, one most unexpected (though certainly no less welcome for that) development that manifested itself early on during his spell in Austin, and one which only grew throughout his identification with Pop's old "house with the 5 white columns", was that girls suddenly got easier to score with — "scoring" being a whole fraught process which hitherto had been, at best, confusing and complicated — but which was now becoming, to tell the truth, almost... *routine*. And even more amazingly, at times it involved good-looking — *really* good-looking — specimens of the blonde and long-legged variety that Henderson wouldn't have thought were in his league. But no, he realized to his own occasional astonishment, it seemed that he *had* been magically moved up into a new, and superior, league.... *Hey, I can live with that....*

The only fly in this Austin ointment, it seemed, was that all the hugely enjoyable alcohol-sodden tomfoolery tended to diminish in direct proportion that he physically strayed from the actual hedonistic cocoon of the old fratty house: For if the U. of Texas was not, perhaps, the *most* fevered cauldron of drugs and "revolution", it *was*, nevertheless and after all, a large American campus in 1968, and, as such, it had its requisite supply of SDS'ers, Black Panthers (real and wannabe), Kosmic Karma Space Kadets of every ideological stripe from Left to Lefter, as well as Maoists and Che Guevara enthusiasts on the faculty — all of which resulted in a near-permanent succession of sit-ins, "teach-ins", "die-ins", "encounter sessions" "workshops", demonstrations of every flavor, womensliblesbian whateverthefuck "performance art" occurrences, building takeovers, and near-(and occasionally real-) riots — in short, the full panoply of the grim insanity that had attached itself to what passed for America's culture in the late 1960s like a great collective dementia.

And finally, the U. of Texas even managed to distinguish itself from all the *other* roiled campuses in America, (no easy feat, given the anarchic excesses which had become the norm), when one particularly loopy energumen climbed up to the observation deck of the Main Building Tower and started potting random students with a high-powered Remington 700 hunting rifle. *Sheesh.* Even the bemused Henderson, as he stood with a boozy eye propping up one of his fraternity house's famous white columns, listening to the lunatic episode being frantically reported on the campus radio station that one of the brothers had going nearby, and cursing himself for not having brought his own rifle to school with him from home, otherwise he would have gone over there to lend a hand in taking the guy out, had to admit that, much as he disdained his fellow (non-fratty brother) students on campus, this was really an enormity too far. *Way* too far. *I mean, what the fuck, man — can't be having this shit, man....*

Throughout the country, buildings were being blown up and state troopers were being gunned down with decreasing infrequency and, arguably worse, drinking buddies began defecting to the Great Relevance Crusade. And some of his aforementioned beloved and reliable long-legged lovelies were now beginning to affect purple or orange Gloria Steinem-style "grannie glasses" and accusing him of being a Philistine and admonishing him that If You're Not Part Of The Solution You're Part Of The Problem.... to which Henderson would reply with a gentle *shee-it* and a smile — but latterly that *shee-it* was sounding more and more inadequate and the smile was becoming a tad more forced.

As his contemporary America increasingly appeared to sit around "organizing", screaming, preening, posturing, "freaking", mimeographing, chanting, drumming, and "rapping", the more Henderson would roll his eyes (figuratively but often literally as well) and hop into his red Alpha Romeo Giulietta Sprint convertible, which the previous owner, the head-mechanic at his local Sunoco station, had equipped with a Ford "Boss" 302 engine (causing the little Wop job to go, if Henderson said so himself, like a fucking *bomb. La Bomba!*) and take off for aimless "road shows" to New Orleans, Mobile, San Antonio, even sometimes to southern Oklahoma (Durant, Hugo and Idabel), and all the hell over northeastern Mexico. Usually alone, though sometimes with some hijacked buddy — either a fratty brother or a schoolboy friend of his and Junior's. Hours of night-driving. Top permanently down, even in the rain — Henderson had long ago determined that 43 mph was the speed which needed to be maintained in order to stay dry. His body was like a kind of human solar battery, kept charged-up by cold coffee, warm beer and cheap Scotch. Listening to Tony Joe White, The Steve Miller Band and The Sir Douglas Quintet on the car's elaborate music system, loud. *Had* to be loud, what with the top down and the Boss 302 engine and all.... Squinting dazedly into orange sunrises. Occasionally eating, and doing his business and occasionally even washing in a MacDonald's or, better yet, at a Whataburger. Once or twice even making the odd pit-stop at the roadshow-mate-of-the-moment's house, if the guy thought his parents were out, and he had a key.

By midway through his Senior year at the old U. of Texas, Henderson felt that he'd acquired an intimate knowledge of virtually every truck stop, diner, road-house, whorehouse, bar, topless "lounge" and mile of paved and even unpaved road in east Texas, southern Oklahoma, western Louisiana and the hazardous Tamaulipas State of Mexico. Along the way there were casual lays and definitely less casual legal skirmishes with the variously-uniformed but uniformly un-humorous armed and mobile constabularies of the relevant states. Sometimes scuffles and even the odd punch-up with hippies, who were often far less pacific than they made out to be, and a surprisingly wide variety of other miscellaneous, obnoxious assholes.

By and large, Henderson thoroughly enjoyed this motorized vagrancy, but semi-consciously he realized that old J.D., although far from uptight about such things and really quite indulgent of his sons, was bound to stop bankrolling him after a reasonable amount of post-graduation time had been frittered away. But in any case, while it never would have occurred to him to have anything as dorky as a "life plan", it had never been

Jerome's intention to be a drag on the family pecunity. On the contrary, he vaguely felt that he had places to go, people to see, and things to do.

And so, one day in June 1969, Jerome Henderson found his college days over, and — rather to his genuine surprise — himself in possession of a BA degree in History. For what *that* was worth, (which wasn't, Henderson suspected, a tremendous lot.) Indeed, Henderson's academic energies, never rising much above anemic, had deteriorated to the laughable extent that he'd barely managed to successfully scrape by his final semester without ever being *exactly* certain which courses he was actually signed up for. And he'd had to visit a highly bemused lady in the Registrar's office to "check" what, precisely, those courses were — so that he'd know which final exams to attend.

A week after his last final exam, he attended a monster "Summer Splash" party at the monster Evinrude "estate" (ranch to you and me) in a snooty corner of River Oaks, itself a snooty corner of Houston, thrown by — and in "honor", if that was the word — of Sally Evinrude.

Now, God knows, Sally Evinrude was a good-looking piece of work. But she also was — or could be, when she put what passed for her mind to it — a highly irritating airhead. She was reputedly worth about twenty million buckaroonies, and Henderson had initially felt quite pleased with himself that time of the big A & M Weekend, thrashing around in the fratty house's "solarium", while everyone else was making drunken asses of themselves over at Memorial Stadium. The dreaded Beast With Two Backs. They'd done it *standing up*, for God's sakes, *wow, big stud, Jerome*.... At the time, nailing Sally Evinrude had struck Henderson as a Big Deal. Well, big-*ish*, anyway... except that even as he was triumphantly claiming his prize, so to speak, he'd had an intimation that he was far from alone in this accomplishment and that about half of Houston, including about two-thirds of those lunkheads on the football team currently losing up there to A & M, had *also* enjoyed, or soon would enjoy, the same Big Deal with Sally Evinrude. And thus, in the cold light of the next Monday, upon sober pondering and everything considered, he'd reluctantly come to the sad conclusion that *La* Evinrude was probably more trouble than she was worth — as considerable as that worth — and as long as those legs — might be....

So he and Sally Evinrude were no longer an "item", but he'd accepted the invitation to her "Summer Splash" anyway — to not have gone would have drawn needless attention to himself, and anyway, why the hell not? A party was always a party. And certainly the evening had begun splendiferously enough, all black tie and fancy gowns... but it had quickly become a semi-catastrophic bummer: Henderson's date, his sister Geraldine's "modern-dance coach", a soft-spoken dark-haired beauty called Leann, for reasons best known to herself had recklessly consumed too many whiskey-sours too soon, and had abruptly puked all over Henderson's white tux front and shoulder. She'd then run off crying somewhere, leaving Henderson standing there like a stinking pile of shit.

But that wasn't even the worst:

At some point, after washing himself off as best he could and not being able to find Leann anywhere, (and in any case thinking that if he never clapped eyes on Leann again it would be too soon), he'd found himself, inexplicably, sitting in his Alpha, with the top down. Even at the time he'd had no idea where he thought he wanted to go, (and he certainly couldn't remember later), but what was undeniable was that at that moment he'd unaccountably and impulsively jammed the car into reverse and roared straight back into a ditch, at a speed of about thirty-five miles an hour, snapping the rear axle in half like a fucking Italian bread-stick.

Appropriately enough, the one vivid memory he retained from that fateful moment was that, once his beloved Alpha had achieved sudden, rude and full incapacitation, Doug Sahm and Augie Meyers were loudly, if plaintively — and rather ungrammatically — singing, on the car's radio, "...*wasted days and wasted nights, I have left for you behind...*"

Chinga, mierda, y me cago en la leche... as they liked to say in his wetback bars over on Westpark Drive.... *Fffffftt....*

Somehow, later that night, the very drunk and by-now thoroughly soul-weary Henderson had transferred his sorry self from his marooned Alpha Romeo to a turquoise aluminum-and-vinyl lawn chair, and downed a half-empty glass of some goddawful something he'd found under a table, possibly even ingesting a cigarette butt in the process. Emotionless. Numb. *Tired, boy.* His unseeing eyes looking right through whatever odd human body moved through their unfocused field of vision.

At that precise moment — 0409 hours — he decided to join up. The Marines or the Army, he didn't care which.

Three reasons:

1/ There wasn't anything else he even remotely felt like doing;

2/ He'd always kind of wondered how he'd shape up in combat, getting shot at and shooting at people and all the rest of it;

and 3/ To find out fucking once and for fucking all about this whole fucking Vietnam business, which had been busting everybody's aching asses for so fucking long — he'd really had it up to *here* with all the radical loonies raving about The Beast Amerika.

Thus satisfied at having finally determined his immediate future, he passed out in the lawn chair.

By about eleven-thirty later that morning, the wraith-like team of Mexican servants that was gliding about silently cleaning up the grounds, was finally forced to prod — and then shake — Henderson awake.

Hoping against hope that what he feared had happened a few hours previously was a horrible figment of his overstimulated imagination, he glanced around him. But no, there it was: the underside of his cantilevered, stricken Alpha Romeo, looking, in truth, from this angle, like a sinking ship. *Oh fuck. Fucking fuck. Alright, deal with that later....*

He stole away and hitched a ride back to the Henderson family compound in an electrician's pickup truck. There he pissed, crapped, washed, shaved, and changed clothes before draining another quick beer for the "hair of the dog", made himself a cup of coffee and sat down to make some phone calls to the 'rents.

First he called his mother in Nevada and told her that he was, that day, going off to enlist.

"Oh? *Really?* Well, that's nice I suppose, dear... what does that mean? — when will we be seeing you again?"

Jesus Christ, what the hell kind of question is that?

"Uh, I really dunno, mom. Huh — I hadn't even thought of that — it'll be... you know, whenever. Some considerable while, I'd guess. But not to worry. Bye."

J.D.'s secretary told Henderson that his dad was in New Orleans, that week, on business, but when she offered to do so Henderson thanked her and told her, no, not to bother to "patch him in". Instead he just wrote and left J.D. a note on the living room mantelpiece.

He also wrote a note for his sister Geraldine, which he left upstairs on her bed. It said "Gone to enlist, kiddo — tell Leann I hope she feels better. Love, Jerry".

Then he took a bus to their local Post Office, where he first approached the booth of the USMC recruiter. But a hand-written sign propped up on the desk there said BACK IN 20 MINUTES, so he turned and walked fifteen yards over to another booth which advertized US ARMY: CHOICE NOT CHANCE and presented his ready willing and able, if grossly hungover, ass to an unsmiling Staff Sergeant Timberlake — a white guy with a blue Combat Infantryman's Badge on his chest, a Big Red One patch on his right shoulder, and the complexion and personality of ancient parchment:

"Don't call me 'sir', kid — I work for a living. You say you ready ta join up *right away*? OK, well we can probably live with that — here, fill out this-here form...."

Enlistments were rather perfunctory affairs in those days, and so the next night — which suddenly loomed as his last night of civilianhood — he and Junior (who, despite a splendid 2.14 Earned Run Average had gone and done something mysterious to one of his ankles and was currently on something called the "10-Day Disabled List", and therefore fucking off at home too) had taken the Jeep Wagoneer that was sort of generically part of the Henderson Compound and had gone drinking at one of their old haunts, the Encantada Café, off of the aforementioned Westpark Drive.

"So Jay Are, listen up. You can take the Alpha. In fact, *please* take the Alpha. Here, here the keys — "

"Hey, thanks, Jerome — that's damn white a you." Junior, not being an "ex" of Sally Evinrude's, hadn't been invited to her "Summer Splash" and thus wasn't *au fait* with recent Alpha Romeo-related developments....

"Don't be too quick to thank me — 'cause the fact is, the damn thing's stuck in a ditch by the Evinrude driveway, with what looks very much like a busted rear axle, and Sally's fucking old man wants it the fuck outta there like *yesterday*." He paused to put away about half of his current Lone Star long-neck, "Though mind you, between you an' me I wouldn't be surprised Sally wasn't busy in the back seat a the thing with some poor asshole right now, as we speak, ... but *anyway*... thing is, I couldn't get the garage to go get it 'cause it's the weekend, but *some-body's* gonna need to get it the fuck outta there, and maybe fixed, first thing this week — if you take care a that for me, kid, it's yours."

"Don't worry about it, man — I'll deal with it. An' the car'll be yours when you get back, whenever that is. So when you leavin', zackly? To-morrow?"

"Yeah. Afternoon, 2:30 — or, I guess, 14:30, as those guys say. From the post office, bus to Fort Bliss. Basic fuckin' Training."

"Oh shit — *Bliss?*" Even as "medically unfit" for the military — and as otherwise generally insensate — as he was, Junior had heard things about the place. None of them pleasant.

"Yeah, heh. What the fuck. Though ya gotta admit — it's a great name, ain't it?"

"Huh. Hey, listen — you take care out there, Jerome, heah? Bound to be some weird shit...."

"Sure. What the fuck. Here, you want another — ?"

8/ 0900 HOURS

"One of the things I shall always associate with Army training is the exertion and indignity of carrying large, heavy objects."

— DAVID LODGE

Sandoval, his boots now propped on a can of 7.62mm ammo by the now-closed H-34's door, had lit a cigarette and the smoke had wafted towards Henderson's nose, which had caused him to open his eyes. *Now why should the smoke from a fucking Marlboro wake me the fuck up? It doesn't make any* sense....

...cigarettes... smokes... "smoke 'em if you got 'em!"... Smokeys... Basic... seemed like a lifetime ago....

About sixteen hours after Jerome and Junior had wrapped it up at the Encantada Café, Henderson, carrying a gym bag containing, as instructed, only a toilet kit and his set of "orders", alighted from a city bus and approached the Post Office building on nearby Grants Lake Boulevard — and discovered that it was littered out front with about two dozen "anti-war" demonstrators who were lying on their backs loudly performing a "die-in". One of them wanly waved a Viet Cong flag on a stick. They covered the sidewalk in front of the Post Office and even spilled out into the street. A starched five-stripe black "Smokey Bear" drill sergeant (Henderson would go on to discover that over half the Army's drill sergeants were black) intercepted Henderson and a few fellow recruits who were converging on the building from various directions, and directed him — them — towards a waiting BlueBird school bus, trying to conceal his amusement as he barked:

"Fort Bliss inductees on that bus! — an' pay no mind to the prone bodies, step aroun' 'em, try *not* step *on* 'em! — 'less of course you absolutely *have* to — but I am instructed to advise you to try *not* to — Fort Bliss inductees that way, on that bus — !"

And about four hours after *that,* Henderson and a hundred and fifty other, even more (than he) raggedy-assed, scared, smelly, ungainly, tired, raw, confused, stupid — and some still pimply — recruits were lined up outside the Fort Bliss Induction Center Classroom Building, the evening gloom somewhat alleviated by a single light-bulb of perhaps a thousand watts attached to the top of a very high nearby telephone pole. Freshly shaved-headed and wearing brandy-new, ill-fitting, stiff, itchy and strange-smelling green fatigues made of a material that felt very much like sail-canvas, they resembled nothing quite so much as a batch of youthful candidates for the furnaces of Dachau.

The were being addressed by a short, brick-shaped brown-skinned three-stripe Smokey Bear sergeant of indeterminate ethnic extraction who bore the embroidered name tag PINGO above his right breast pocket. This troll-like little human dynamo bawled at them:

"STAN' UP STRAIGHT AN' DON' MOVE YOU UGLY GARBAGE! DE GODDAMN PICNIC BE OVER! YOU IN DE ARMY NOW AN' DON' FORGET IT! ON BEHALF GENERAL THOMP-

SON COMMANDING, I WANNA WELCOME YOU PERSON-
AL TO DE US ARMY AN' FORT BLISS! FROM NOW ON YOU
ASS DEY BELONG TO SAM! SAM HE OWN YOU ASS AN' HE
CAN BEND FOLD AND/OR MUTILATE IT AN' YOU GONNA
LEARN TO LOVE IT! AN', ALSO, TOO, SAM HE GONNA GIVE
EACH ONE A YOU SORRY FUCKERS THREE HOTS AN' A
COT FOR EV'Y DAY DAT YOU CONSTRIVE TO STAY ALIVE
WHICH IS A SHITLOAD BETTER DAN MOST A YOU USE-
LESS BASTARDS CAN MANAGE ONNA OUTSIDE! DE ARMY
BE GOOD TO YOU! YOU KEEP YOU NOSE CLEAN, DE ARMY
TAKE CARE A DEY OWN!

NOW DEN! I WAN' YOU ALL PUT ALL YOU MARIJUANA AN'
ALL UDDER DRUGS AN' PILLS — DAT'S PILLS TO INCLUDE
ASPIRINS AN' ASPIRIN-BASED AN' ASPIRIN-RELATED PRO-
DUCKS — AN' ALL WEAPONS TO INCLUDE ZIP GUNS AN'
KNIVES OB ANY LENTH — AN' ALL PHOTOGRAPHS BOOKS
AN' FILM OF A PORNOPH, PORNOG, POR-GODDAMMIT I
MEAN PUSSY PITCHERS IS WHAT I MEAN AN' YOU FUCKIN'
KNOWS IT — AN' YOU STOP LAFFIN' DERE — *YEAH, YOU!*
— OR I PERSONAL GONNA RUN YOU TILL YOU ASS FALL
OFF! — AN' ALSO ALL BOOZE AN' ANY UDDER UNAUTHO-
RIZE ITEMS — RIGHT HERE INTO DIS HERE HEFTY BAG
I PASSIN' 'ROUN', AN' NO QUESTIONS GONNA BE AST! —
AN' BELIEVE ME, PEOPLE, DIS DE ONLIEST TIME YOU GON-
NA BE IN DIS MAN'S ARMY AN' BE IN POSSESSING ILLEGAL
SHIT AN' NO QUESTIONS GONNA BE AST!

NOW DEN, AN' FURTHESTMOST, I AM INSTRUCTED BY
DE SECRETARY OB DEFENSE TO INFORM EACH A YOU

SWINGIN' DICKS DAT HENCEFORT' AN' FROM DIS MOMENT ON NONE A YOU IS BLACK, WHITE, BROWN, YELLA, PINK OR ANY OTHER PIG, PIGTA, PIGMA — AH FUCK IT, ANY UDDER FUCKIN' COLOR! NO, FROM NOW ON EACH AN' EV'Y ONE A YOU POOR ESCUSES FOR A HUMAN BEAN IS GREEN — ARMY FUCKIN' GREEN! — AN' YOU GONNA *STAY* ARMY FUCKIN' GREEN UNTIL YOU HAS FULLY FULFILLED YOU'S ENGAGEMENT TO UNCLE SAM OR YOU'S ZAPPED BY CHARLEY CONG, WHICHEVER COME FIRS'!

NOW DEN — YOU GONNA FILL OUT SOME EMERYENCY INFORMATION CARDS SO WE KNOW WHERE TO SEND YOU BODIES IN CASE YOU FUCK UP — AN' AFTER DAT YOU ALL GONNA GET SOME SHOTS, AN I DON' WANT NONE A YOU PUSSIES COMPLAIN OR FAINT OR ANY A DAT SHIT WHEN DEY GIB YOU DE SHOTS, GOT DAT? YOU FUCKIN' STAN' AN' TAKE YOU SHOTS LIKE A MAN AN' GOD HELP ANY PUSSY WHO CRIES CAUSE HE GONNA GET MY BOOT SO FAR UP HIS ASS IT GONNA COME OUT HIS FUCKIN' NOSE.

OKAY.

WELL, AS I SEE DAT DEY'S NO QUESTIONS LEMME ADD MY OWN PERSONAL WORDS A WELCOME: NOW I KNOW YOU'S ALL NERVOUS, WORRIED, SCARED, MAYBE YOU AWAY FROM YOU HOME FO' DE FIRS' TIME, CONFUSED ABOUT WHAT GONNA HAPPENG TO YOU — WELL LEMME TELL YOU: YOU *RIGHT* TO BE SHIT-NERVOUS WORRIED SCARED AN' CONFUSED ABOUT WHAT GONNA HAPPENG TO YOU! *DAMN* RIGHT! AN' MAY GOD HAB MERCY ON YER USELESS

SHITBIRD SOULS, CAUSE FOR SHIT-SURE NOBODY ELSE
GONNA!

YOU WELCOME!

NOW, LEF' FACE! *LEF'* FACE, YOU GODDAMN DEAF FUCKIN'
CLOWNS, WHAT DE HELL DEY TEACH YOU IN SCHOOL?
YOU AND YOU — YEAH, *YOU,* SHITBIRD — I WAN' YOU ACT
AS ROAD GUARDS — *ROAD* GUARDS, YOU SORRY BRAIN-
DEAD SHITBIRDS, DAT MEAN YOU RUN OUT AHEAD AN'
KEEP TRAFFIC FROM RUNNIN' DOWN YOU BUDDIES —
GOT DAT?

NOW, *MOVE OUT!* HUT TWO, HUT TWO, HUT TWO, LESS
TRY A SOUND-OFF, YOU SACKS A SHIT KNOW HOW TO
SOUND OFF? *A CORSE* YOU DON', YOU DON' KNOW FUCKIN'
NOTHIN', SO I GONNA SHOW YOU NOW...!"

Ah, Basic. Basic Training at Fort Bliss, 1969. Henderson learned all
kinds of things in those eight intense weeks: Among them, how to disas-
semble, reassemble and fire an M-16 automatic rifle accurately, by day or
night. In fact, Henderson surprised himself, rather, be turning out to be
a pretty decent shot. Fucking Deadeye Dick — for which they gave him
a Sharpshooter's badge. How to shine combat boots using, among other
arcane aids, "5-Day Deodorant Pads". How surprisingly many perfectly
fine guys there were in the United States with IQs of under 80 — simply
amazing. He learned how to open and eat cold food out of cans and
then stow the empty containers upon his person while tramping in the
woods with fifty to sixty-five pounds of shit on his back — and *in the
rain,* to boot, which would invariably delight the Smokeys and brighten
their moods even *more.*

All kinds of great stuff: Grenade-chucking was his favorite: While it was nowhere near the level of Junior's, Henderson had a pretty handy arm — though the skill involved with grenades was more akin to football than baseball. And the obstacle courses were pretty good fun, too.

The daily three-mile run in combat boots (that their main Smokey, the fearsome horse-faced pitch-black Sgt. Phillips insisted on calling "comboot bats"), steel pots upon noggins (*sans* liners), and rifles at port arms had undoubtedly been his *least* favorite activity.

During his second week, a captain from the Training Brigade S-1 (Personnel) Staff — a body which, for all Henderson and his fellow trainees were concerned, might as well have been Mount Olympus — pulled him out of the ranks during morning formation and ordered him to follow him to an empty office in a nearby Admin building. Henderson searched his mind for any particularly egregious infraction he might have committed and wondered What The Fuck? The Captain looked at — or pretended to look at — papers on his desk. After what seemed like a very long period of silence, he eventually looked up and actually addressed these words at Henderson:

"Trainee Henderson. Lieutenants are in short supply in Vietnam — they keep getting knocked off. You interested?"

Henderson had blinked and stammered, "Eh? Sorry? I'm, uh, sorry... *what?* Sir?"

"O.C.S. You wanna take the test? It says here you know how to read and write, which is always good. College, an' all. What about it, Trainee Henderson — you up for it?"

So Henderson had taken the O.C.S. test. Or rather test*s*. And apparently scored the highest aggregate grade ever racked up at Fort Bliss. This, he was assured by the superannuated major from the Adjutant General Corps who'd overseen the testing and given him the results, said less about Henderson than it said about Fort Bliss. *Ooooookay, sir.*

After that, for the rest of Basic Training, various officers took to pulling Henderson out of formations or off of firing ranges or out of classrooms to join them in their offices for little, usually uncomfortable and, to Henderson, often baffling, chit-chats. About this and that. And once, the Trainee Brigade's Chaplain, a Captain Rizzoto, had invited him, buddy-buddy, *as one Man Of The World to Another, you understand,* to reveal who were the guys in Henderson's platoon who smoked dope.

To which Henderson, hoping he was successfully masking his incredulity, not to mention his indignation, had lied without so much as a nanosecond's hesitation:

"Sir, I don't know anybody who does that." He'd been tempted to add, "And by the way and while we're at it, fuck you, padre", but he'd managed to check his tongue.

Instead of resenting Henderson because he was one of the few among them who'd finished high school, let alone college, the men of his Basic platoon sort of liked him — and Henderson was astonished to discover that many of them would come to him and solicit his help and advice with various concerns. Concerns which, if the Army had known about, it would have lumped under the rubric of "personal problems", and many of which Henderson found to be positively surreal. (Henderson's platoon was almost entirely made up of low-to-no-education kids who'd been drafted under a special Department of Defense "dispensation" program instituted in 1967 and known unofficially by the Smokeys as "MacNamara's Boys" — and how a volunteer with a college degree like Henderson had ended up in a training platoon of virtual illiterates was just another cosmic Feddle Gummint mystery).

For example, one amiable — at least towards Henderson — gigantic black dude in Henderson's squad, who came from Baltimore, apparently had two wives, neither of whom he could stand. Henderson had found it hard to get his head around the first datum, but rather easier to credit the latter one. The guy — big kid, really — was called "Scarface" André Boskins. He'd been a rising young boxer (hence the "Scarface") and had been about to turn pro when he'd been drafted, but could neither read nor write. Moreover, his two wives — one in Baltimore and the other in Washington D.C. — were scarcely less unlettered than he was, and after mail-call he'd bring their pathetic missives to Henderson for deciphering. Then Henderson would be enlisted to pen Boskins' dictated responses. Most of the mutually-reciprocated incoherence that passed for human communication in this correspondence seemed to center around the hotly-anticipated but only haphazardly (if that) actually executed remittance of large chunks of Boskins' already derisory E-zilch "salary" to these unforgiving ladies, and Henderson could only shake his head in disbelief... *Boy, you talk about surreal....*

Boskins would plaintively tell Henderson, "Don' never get muhfuckin' married, Hennerman, they stone *kills* ya, ah swear."

To which Henderson would answer something like, "Yeah, André, I can believe it — which leads a guy to wonder... why the fuck you did the fucking thing *twice*, and *at the same time*!"

"Dat de *fack*," the morose Boskins answered, " — hell, why the shit you think ah so happy when they drafted me? Ah trahd t'en*liss*, t'git the fuck away from *bofe* of 'em, but they wouldn't take me causa the readin' thing — but th'draff done save this nigga's ass — bes' thing evah happen to me!"

"Well... shit," had been all Henderson had managed to reply to all this. Not Shakespearean, to be sure, but these were not un-trying times.

There had also been a skinny bespectacled Jewish kid from St. Louis, who couldn't take a crap "in front of others" which, given the barracks' partition-less latrines, immediately created a huge, not to say existential, problem for him. In addition, he was convinced that everyone hated him, including his fellow trainees which, except for Henderson, who'd sort of felt sorry for the kid, was pretty much true. In any case, the skinny Jewish kid from St. Louis had disappeared early in the third week. The Smokeys vaguely claimed that he'd committed suicide, but nobody ever saw any evidence of this, much less any trace of a body... and there even existed in their particular Trainee Company a small and sinister clique of self-styled "Black Muslims" led by a Newark New Jersey street-punk whose civilian name was Luther "Nightshade" Williams but who styled himself "Ali Hijazi" and who muted it about that the St. Louis kid had been "offed" by "forces of the Third World Power" and, (as if that weren't enough), his dead body had been... *eaten* by these... avenging specimens. Apparently to imbibe some "mystic warrior strength". This all sounded like ludicrous drive-in B-movie-type drivel to Henderson, but when he'd asked Boskins, his personal conduit to his black platoon-mates, about these macabre rumors, he'd been told "Don' aks, Hennerman. An' don' get involve — this ain't nuffin' f'you, truss me."

Then there'd been an overweight white guy from Severance, Ohio, who tried to tell everyone he was dyslexic but he couldn't even pronounce it correctly and in any case, no one — least of all the Smokeys — gave a shit. This poor guy could never finish the 3-mile runs or, for that matter, manage *any* of the physical stuff. Even the biggest T-shirts didn't fully cover his belly, and almost from Day One the Smokeys called him "Fat Stuff", a tag that had cruelly been picked up by his fellow trainees. Like the departed kid from St. Louis (for whom he naggingly regretted not having been able to do anything) Henderson felt kind of sorry for Fat Stuff from Severance Ohio, and he'd sometimes make it a point to talk to the guy when they were on smoke breaks and he'd see the fat boy left standing conspicuously on his own. One Saturday morning, while the platoon had been cleaning their barracks, a close-to-tears Fat Stuff had come up to Henderson and horrified him by blurting out that he didn't think he "believed in God no more". Henderson's first reaction had been to suggest that the kid take the matter up with the Chaplain, but then he'd flashed back to that cunt Capt. Rizzoto and so, instead, had, as soon as he could — after second mess and sacrificing his normal Saturday-afternoon nap-time — dragged Fat Stuff over to the PX. There, over a pitcher of beer, he, Henderson, who was, at best, nothing more religious than a reluctant, grudging "deist", found himself telling the fat kid from Severance Ohio,

"Hey, look, don't worry about it, God's cool. So even if you don't believe in him any more, he's still there. Listen, God didn't organize this whole fucking shitstorm without expecting there might be a few guys who didn't get with the program. He figured there'd be doubters, along the way. Really, He's cool — God's not a ball-buster. So don't sweat it, man."

"Yeah?"

"Yeah."

In the event, the overweight kid from Severance Ohio had been "re-cy-cled", which meant he hadn't graduated from Basic with the others and had been made to take it again. But at least he hadn't been *eaten.*

+ + + + + +

Henderson's best buddy in Basic was the previously-mentioned "Noo Yawkuh", the "Reekin' Rican", Isidro Jésus-Maria Rojo-Rosario, and after their two months of Basic Training wound up, the two of them were among the contingent whose orders instructed them to proceed to a further two months of "Advanced Infantry Training" (AIT) at Fort Dix, NJ.

But first they'd been given a week's leave, during which Henderson had jumped home to Sugar Land — to discover that before being re-activat-ed to pitching duties for the Commanders, Junior had indeed managed to drag the Alpha out of Old Man Evinrude's benighted ditch. And had apparently driven it off to rejoin his team in Dallas; *Well I hope at least those idiot Commanders're payin' the kid enough to cover that fuckin' parking in Dallas....*

Which was fine except that it meant that Henderson now found him-self with no wheels for the duration of his week's leave, a bummer of a crippling situation which caused him to dick around the boring old Sugar Land corner of Houston in increasing frustration for six days, to the point that he found himself, amazingly, by the end actually looking forward to a resumption of the training, at Fort Dix....

On top of which, *weird vibes, man,* as his awful civilian peers liked to say, were otherwise increasingly in the air and these *weird vibes, man* were, as they also liked to say, *like invading his like consciousness, man....*

In fact, a particularly vivid manifestation of this weird vibery followed Henderson, after his wasted week, on his journey back to the Army: In those days the airlines gave the military a 50% discount if they traveled in uniform, and when he arrived at New York's LaGuardia Airport in his Class A "greens", en route to catching a bus to the Port Authority Bus Terminal, to then catch yet another bus to Dix — he'd been accosted by a gang of hippies, (who on this occasion included in their number, it had to be said, some quite cute chicks), and who'd been camped out with the inevitable Viet Cong flag and some sleeping bags in one of the airport concourses. When they saw the uniformed Henderson approach, carrying a big green duffel bag, they'd roused themselves and fell into step beside him, to accompany him and "encourage" him to "... like free yourself, man, and like, desert, man — you're not a robot, man, c'mon, re-join the human race, man...!". Henderson had just walked on, saying nothing but smiling and shaking his head... *Fuuuuck me, I'm pretty sure they don't have scenes like this in fucking Hanoi....*

+ + + + + +

AIT was similar to Basic in duration and organization, although it was noticeably more "serious", which meant that they were introduced to more various and powerful weapons and the training became more frenetically combat-oriented. Vietnam, (Republic of), loomed.

So that now they learned things such as:

How to probe for Soviet land mines. *"Like porcupines fucking — you do it carefully, gentlemen, very carefully".*

And becoming comfortably handy with the venerable but marvelous M-60 machine gun, a miraculous killing machine upon which Henderson *also* qualified as a Sharpshooter and with which he astonished himself by being able to hit targets so far away *that he couldn't even see them.* He'd had the following exchange with his pal Rojo:

"You hit song *siluetas* you cang even *see*, mang?"

"Yeah, it's fuckin' un*can*ny, man — it's like instinctive, like I can tell, from, like, *intuition,* where the target *should be.*"

"Fock, mang. *Cabron*, I got enough trouble wid de ones I can *see*. You spooky — you a fockin' danger, mang."

"Damn right. Stand well back, Roe-joe."

And also map coordinates and topography — "Land Navigation" in Armese.

The placement, use, and safe relief of observation posts and listening posts.

Ambushes of various configurations — the laying and survival thereof.

Traumatic first aid — including fascinating stuff such as if a fellow was so badly wounded that he was incapable of firing it, his own rifle could be used as a splint. *But remember to clear the chamber and retrieve all magazines first.*

And speaking of magazines, when it was a good idea to tape two together, end-to-end, for their M-16s, and when it wasn't.

The care and use of the goddamn Prick-25 radio, as well as the humping, and care for, its batteries.

And the one that was a veritable pleasure: the firing of the popgun-like M-79 grenade launcher, which almost seemed to Henderson and his de-lighted mates like a weapon that had been developed for use in a fun-fair.

All of this, and more, Henderson learned, often wrapped in his never-quite-dry poncho in the miserable freezing rain of the north-west New Jersey swampy chabongas, during this AIT — and he mostly loved it all. He was born for this shit.

Also unlike Basic Training, during AIT they were occasionally granted weekend passes, and thus during his time at Fort Dix and environs, Hen-derson also learned some non-military things:

Such as how to handle himself, sometimes literally, in places like the Pink Flamingo Lounge up on 125th Street in Harlem, this particular "block of instruction" being provided by Rojo, of course, who had a "cossin" who was "a senior dish-washer" up there, (though how dishwashers merited ranks, and what dishes might conceivably need washing in an establish-ment called The Pink Flamingo Lounge, were... interesting metaphys-ical questions that remained unanswered). Anyway, Rojo had located and dragged this *chacho* from somewhere "in back", and the rather ratty and nervous-looking fellow had got them admitted after passing a loud — necessarily so, to be heard above the din of Sly And The Family Stone — yet judicious word in the ear of the Joe Frazier-like bouncer who, up to that point, had been favoring the interloping white-boy Henderson with a hairy fish-eye. *New York fucking City, y'unnerstan'....*

In this same vein, although considerably further downtown, on the Sat-urday night before the Sunday AIT "graduation ceremony", Henderson and Rojo had found themselves trying to pick up "something" — or as Rojo called it, "sonsing" — at the Club 45-A-Go-Go down in the Times Square area;

"Ees égoo' place, Hendysoh, dey got easy *chicas* dere songtime, I bee' many time befo', dey knows me dere — ".

So it was in that venue, then, where, after Henderson and Rojo had contrived between the two of them to put away the equivalent of an imperial quart of cheap generic house "scotch", and to the soothing crashing roar of Steppenwolf blasting out of speakers the size of telephone booths, that Henderson had found himself endeavoring to convince a gum-chewing blonde in a tiny mini-dress that looked like it was made of tin-foil chain-mail and with hair stacked on her head like a giant Carvel ice-cream cone — a professional colleague of the one currently bouncing around with stars on her nipples up there on the platform in the middle of the circular bar — that although his intentions were entirely honorable, she couldn't possible live one more minute without him.

But this girl — name of Sheree, as it happened, from Riverside, California — didn't, apparently, want, as they said in Noo Yawk Noo Yawk So Nice They Named It Twice, to know from Henderson and must have given off some kind of secret signal, or something, to this effect because suddenly, out of seeming nowhere, an unbelievable Dago greaser in a black jumpsuit with boomerang-shaped lapels, black nose-picker "Beatle boots", and about 5 pounds of gold-plated hardware variously adorning his head, neck, ears, hands and wrists, had materialized from behind Henderson and, producing a 4-inch flick-knife from one of the jumpsuit's many pockets, had stabbed the semi-hell out of Henderson's right arm just above the elbow.

OW! Jesus Christ!

¡Puta Coño!

Rojo, who'd been a few yards away, now manifested himself on the spot just as unexpectedly as the Dago stabber had, and clobbered the fucker with a fist to the ear, driving him to the floor. In the sudden pandemonium and eruption of male shouts and female screams, Rojo had then grabbed the stunned Henderson by his still-good left arm and hauled him the fuck out of the Club 45-A-Go-Go and into a vacant yellow cab that happened to be at curbside, having just disgorged a fare.

The cabbie, apparently a black guy, from the sound of him (he was practically invisible in the dark and on the other side of the opaque ad hoc plastic Berlin Wall that separated fore and aft in New York taxis in those days) drove off and made a right on a yellow, damn near getting them all killed because he kept turning around and addressing the two new occupants of his back seat in an alarmed tone,

"Hey, you motherfuckers *ain't bleedin' all over my motherfuckin' cab*, are ya? *Goddammit — !*",

With Rojo yammering right back at him,

"Ees only a scratch, pendejo, ees nothin' — watch whe' you goin', mang, *y no me jodas, coño, pues! — look out!*"

Their taxi ride was rendered even more chaotic by neither of the idiot soldiers being able to decide on a destination to give the aggrieved and agitated driver, until in a spasm of inspiration Henderson remembered the address of the narrow brownstone on 85th Street near 1st Avenue where he'd once dropped a girl off — an address where this said girl, called Robin Hudnut, that he'd met during one of those prep school Thanksgiving or Easter vacations, lived. She was a friend of one of his

Andover pal's sisters and he'd once enjoyed, if that was the word, a brief, sweaty, and drunken "makeout session" with her at a party that had ended... well... inconclusively. He couldn't remember exactly if it was an "executive assistant" or a "trainee executive" — maybe it was both — that she'd since become at the Chemical Bank, and more to the point, he had no idea what sort of reception he and Rojo were likely to get — or even if she was home — but in the tumult of the moment he couldn't think of anywhere else to direct this importuning cabbie.

Well, not only did it turn out that Robin was at home, but — maybe it was all the blood now on Henderson's civilian clothes or Rojo's undeniably dramatic demeanor — despite her initial alarm and befuddlement, the bathrobed and bunny-slippered Robin had, after his third ring and her squinting through the peephole, unchained her door and allowed them in.

"Jerry *Hen*derson? What? What on *earth* — ?"

"Ah, thanks Robin, and hi by the way — wasn't even sure you'd remember me — this is, hah!, kinda a long story, actually — just in from Fort Dix, you know, the army base — yeah that, that's nothing, small unpleasantness downtown — this here's Rojo by the way — it's good, he's OK, he's a friendly — one of us, yeah, in our army, I mean... "

"*Carajo* — sorry, how you doin', miss? — yeah, he'll live, ees no' as bad as it looks..."

Henderson and Rojo stood there in the tiny foyer of her one-bedroom ground-floor apartment, while Robin had padded into her bathroom to fetch "some cotton and Peroxide". While she was away doing this, Rojo — trust the bugger — had leaned over and muttered,

"Hey, Hendysoh, she goo' lookin', mang, you a fockin' dog — you get a stab a somadat?"

Before Henderson had had a chance to hiss back at Rojo to "fer fuck-sakes try an' act housebroken", she'd returned and done her Florence McNightingshades thing with the fizzy Peroxide and what seemed like great gobs of cotton and a vast expanse of gauze and *sparadrap* and whatnot, and eventually his arm was more or less squared away.

It being near one in the morning by now, Robin then invited them to sort themselves out as best they could on the couch and floor in the main room, and excused herself and disappeared into her bedroom, shutting the door behind her. Henderson, exercising a kind of non-sexual, territorial *droit de seigneur*, unceremoniously flopped onto the small sofa, tossing the sort of throw-rug he found there at Rojo, who curled up with it on the floor.

"G'night, Rojo — and keep the farts down — this a nice girl."

"Fuck me, mang. *Puta sagrada, que noche.*"

The next morning, the bedraggled two got their shit together in best field-expedient fashion and prepared to head back to the looming, wretched Fort Dix, from which they were due to officially separate themselves that very afternoon. Henderson had paused at the door on his way out and whispered into Robin's not un-delectable ear that peeked out from her butternut-colored hair, that she was the sweetest girl he'd ever known. She, for her part, had said nothing — just kissing him in an unmistakably friendly manner before closing her apartment door behind them.

+ + + + + +

So that Sunday afternoon, after the AIT "graduation ceremony" (some parents and girlfriends actually attended these things), the Trainee Brigade First Sergeant had given each of them a handshake and a manila envelope that contained their Further Orders. While virtually all the guys were being ordered to infantry units in Vietnam, Rojo, it appeared, was — astoundingly — shipping off to, of all places, Alaska. To a certain Fort Wainwright that nobody seemed to have ever heard of. His MOS (Military Occupational Speciality) remained 11B (Infantryman) like the others, but apparently Uncle Sam required him to exercise these skills in Alaska. "Luck of the draw" all his fellow platoon-mates said, but Rojo had initially reacted with indignation, squawking like a speared parrot that inasmuch as he already couldn't stand the weather of "fockin' New Yerssey, mang", how on earth was he expected to survive in, "can you fockin' believe it, mang, *freekin' Alaska?*" But then, as virtually all of the aforementioned platoon-mates reacted to his words with eager offers to trade their orders for his (and even throw in a bit of financial inducement as well), it quickly sank in to the not-stupid Isidro Jésus-Maria Rojo-Rosario that *many* fewer American peers of his in Green were dying in Alaska than were dying in Vietnam, Republic of, at the moment — so he adopted a more philosophical outlook and resigned himself to the Frozen North.

"Hey, Hendysoh, you fockin' Lifer — if you ever nee' my help again you fine me in some goddamn igloo, mang! Yah, thass righ', a fockin' *igloo*, mang! So take it easy, *hijo*, but take it. An', ah, ... get some Congs for me, *huevo! Cabron!...*"

+ + + + + +

Henderson, of course, alone in his AIT platoon, had been tagged for OCS, so now it was off for six months of (Infantry) Officer Candidate School (OCS) at Fort Benning, Georgia, near the town of Columbus. What a place. Actually, Columbus, what little he ever got to see of it, seemed a nice-enough little burg — it was the Benning that was the ball-buster. *Christ.* Next to Infantry OCS, Basic Training and AIT were mere Cub Scout meetings. In truth, Infantry OCS turned out to be an ingeniously-crafted extended *régime* of unrelenting physical and mental abuse which (mostly) stopped *just* on the kosher side of torture.

(A dozen years after Henderson had submitted his ass to its tender ministrations, a movie would be made of OCS — albeit the Navy version, which barely counted as *real* OCS anyway — called "An Officer And A Gentleman", that starred a guy who was mistakenly reputed to be what the Aussies called a poofter called Richard Gere and that even included *girl* candidates in the program, which, {not surprisingly, coming, as it did, out of Hollywood}, missed the essence of the *real* OCS by a country mile. And a half.)

No, the *real* OCS turned out to be a pretty seriously, awesomely, indeed *existentially* shitty 4,368 long, sometimes seemingly interminable, hours (6 months = 182 days x 24 hours) of human provocation and endurance:

About half the candidates who entered the program either dropped out or got kicked out. And the attrition rate undoubtedly would have been even higher if it had not been the case that, in the memorable words of that captain from Henderson's Basic Brigade's S-1 Staff, "Lieutenants are in short supply in Vietnam. They keep getting knocked off".

But on the other hand, two factors had kicked in to make the hell of OCS more tolerable for Henderson than it otherwise might have been: 1/ He finally found himself, for the first time since joining the Army, among young men who were roughly his "peers", mentally and motivationally; and, 2/ He'd by now cottoned, more or less, to the Army's "game" — its peculiar ethos and thoroughly idiosyncratic way of doing things.

And so, his half-year of OCS had gone by, certainly not painlessly, but at least productively. One thing was for sure: He learned in any one day at Fort Benning more than anyone back at the U. of T., a place that now seemed to Henderson to be a remote island of terminal fantasy and fatuity, was likely to discover in four (or even six!) years. For instance:

- How to kill a chicken not only with your own hands but in such a manner that its demise would make a minimum of noise. And then — the icing on the cake, as it were — eating at least one substantial mouthful of the thing raw (indeed, still warm) having first pulled the feathers off the wretched thing in front of your Tactical Officer (OCS's lieutenant version of the Basic and AIT Drill Sergeant/Smokeys). The whole chicken thing was a truly Sisyphean exercise, the most damnably difficult aspect of which was *catching* the fucking chicken in the first place. As Henderson, in a rare burst of loquacity, would later comment on the experience to Junior, "Hey, jess *you* try it sometime — an' be sure an' give yourself plenty a extra time, 'cause catching a chicken's a *bitch*, trust me — it's close to, though not quite, impossible".
- How many pounds (a surprising lot, it turned out) of C-4 *plastique* it took to knock out the average suspension bridge. And to make this educational point, the Army had installed a half-assed, though near-lifesize, easily-replaced tubes-and-plywood erector-set facsimile of such a bridge over the Chattahoochee River that separated Georgia and Alabama, next to their "model Viet-

namese village", that successive OCS classes took great pleasure in blowing up.

- How to act in ambushes and, arguably more crucially, how to avoid them in the first place. In AIT they'd learned how to *set* the various types of ambushes ("linear", "L-shaped" and, for the really hairy-balled, "counter-"), but now they were drilled in how to overcome the reflexively instinctive human impulse to freeze in such a cataclysmic occurrence. In fact, how best to react if one found oneself in the sudden hell of an ambush turned out to be satisfyingly primal: Scream, shout, fire on full auto, yell like fucking hell and charge *into* the direction of fire. This might be counter-intuitive, perhaps, but at least it was certainly uncomplicated. And it was, after all, the fundamental purpose of all this training to make automatic what had previously been contrary to normal human nature.

- Another subject which was gingerly broached in their training was: What to do if and when one's men refused to move in a combat situation. (They were, after all, being trained to be lieutenants, who were those officers with the most direct contact with NCOs and enlisted men.) This was, not surprisingly, a most sensitive matter indeed, and there was a good deal of dissimulating hemming-and-hawing by the instructors in the course of this vexed "block of instruction". Because the bottom line was there wasn't all that much they could usefully say on this subject, and so they resorted to a lot of rather lame and not-very-helpful references to World War I episodes of desertion and punishments thereof, and even less practical enjoinders "not to get into such fucked situations in the first place." In the end, the closest thing the Candidates received to useful advice was, "Worst comes to worst, defer to the Platoon Sergeant." ("And whaddaya do if yer *platoon sergeant's* part of the mutiny?" "Then you're good and fucked, lieutenant.")

- How to call in air strikes by day, and medevac choppers also by day but even — if one were being overrun, or about to be — *in extremis* and if you were lucky enough to have suicidal chopper pilots attached to your unit, *also* by night. All of this required great care and prudence, as screwed-up map coordinates were a frequent cause of "friendly fire" and other catastrophes. If one was lucky, it involved acetate-covered fragments of local maps, folded so that current coordinates could remain readily to hand, prominently marked, and easily re-marked as one moved about. If one was less lucky, it involved map coordinates hastily scribbled on palms and inner wrists. And as for doing any of this at night, the Candidates soon learned why grunts kept red-lensed flashlights attached to their rigs, at armpit-level, facing out.
- When to shoot a prisoner, and when not to. *Relax, gentlemen — the first eventuality is only in case of attempted escape; otherwise, never.*
- Tricks for staying awake; sometimes for extremely long periods of time; two, even three days straight. This, obviously, was more informal training, i.e., received from one's fellow candidates, rather than anything they got from the instructors: One of Henderson's mates showed him how to prop his eyes open with customized wooden matches. Not ideal. Another guy, Rickard from Trafalgar, Indiana (pop. 457), proudly claimed that he could sleep standing up ("Like a horse, man. Hell, why not?" he maintained, in a glorious *non sequitur*, "Napoleon useta sleep on his fuckin' horse, man — I read that."), but Henderson didn't believe it — Napoleon, maybe, but not the human being able to sleep standing up bit, *nevah hotchee*. And another guy, a farm kid called Bottomley, from North Dakota somewhere, could sleep with his eyes wide open, which all the Candidates thought was pretty nifty, if more than a little scary — but they also agreed that Bottomley's gift didn't

solve their problem of how to stay awake. Regardless of all these attempts, it is no exaggeration to state that throughout OCS, Henderson was dead tired from the first day to the last — Dead Tired, indeed, seemed to have become his default position.

- In short, they learned how to stay alive, how to help keep others alive, and what to do when others died — this last being the particular domain of lieutenants, in all armies, since time immemorial.

In addition to all this military skill and associated arcana, Henderson learned other stuff along the way, some of it clandestinely- or incidentally-obtained, with every experience or morsel of knowledge unexpected and, each in its own way, marvelous:

- Probably the single most surreal thing they were instructed in were the niceties and obligations involved in "paying a social call on the wife of the Post Commander", an apparent anachronism in the Army's "Officer's Code" that dated from, who knew when? *Mexican War* days?, and which, once the disbelief had dissipated, elicited no end of ribaldry from Henderson's fellow Candidates. To their credit, it can't be said that the embarrassed instructors lost too much time on this particular "block of instruction" — in fact, their "lecture" on the subject consisted of little more than mentioning the existence of the notional "requirement" in question, followed by "Alright, at ease, that'll do, at ease...."
- Much more practically: How to cache a smuggled Large Pizza inside a Dempsty Dumpster for up to two days without it going bad — or, let's say without it going *inedibly* bad — while also preventing it from being hauled off by the garbage men or eaten by rats. The technical term for all contraband grub in OCS was "Pogey Bait", and its pursuit and occasional acquisition was a constant

preoccupation of the Candidates, activities to which they applied a disproportionate percentage of their considerable creativity.

- Which "Go-Go Girls" in Columbus Georgia and Phenix (sic) City Alabama had the clap and which didn't. This was intelligence which the Candidates only acquired near the end of their 6-month purgatory, when they finally felt confident/reckless enough to mount forbidden, hence-perilous, sometimes solo but usually 2-man, recon missions to those towns' garish oases of off-limits sin.

In fact, one memorable, fateful and almost fatal Saturday night, Henderson and one of his best Candidate pals, a half-black half-Powhatan Indian from Rising Sun, Maryland, called Carlson Littletree, had taken off their OCS insignia and hitched a ride to Phenix City where they'd picked up two black girls in a semi-topless go-go bar called The DMZ, and the four of them had spent an indescribably tawdry half hour *in the same double bed* in one of the girl's nearby rented dark and tiny apartment. A fumbling and shambolic exchange of, first, "intimacies", and then, currency, had more or less been successfully transacted, but the episode had, thirty-six hours later, resulted disastrously with both Candidates erupting with the clap. Neither Henderson or Littletree had any idea what was suddenly, and horribly, befalling their respective johnsons, but more experienced fellow-Candidates quickly assured them what was what — and took no small pleasure in doing so. There was then no way the two infectees could avoid going on sick call, where they each received, from a bemused Spec-4 medic who couldn't disguise his *schadenfreude* at these pre-2nd Lieutenants' looming ignominy, massive jabs of penicillin which would have sufficed to cure be-clapped rhinoceroses. And of course the OCS Training Command S-1 was notified by the medics of all this, and the next day, magically-clapless but *extremely* apprehensive Candidates Henderson and Littletree were being jacked-up by a seriously pissed-off Training Company Commander, a young captain with Vietnam service ribbons, a Bronze Star, and a Combat Infrantryman's Badge, who muttered at them,

"By all rights you two fucking jokers should be thrown the fuck outta the program, busted to privates E-shit, and shipped to the fuckin' Central Highlands tomorrow. Assholes — what were you fuckin' thinking? Ya couldn't keep yer dicks in yer pants *fer another six fuckin' days?* Jesus fucking Christ. But," he flicked at a paper on his desk in disgust, "they're goin' through 2nd fuckin' johns over there faster'n we can crank 'em out, so I'm sorry to say you two get to skate, this time. So get the fuck out of my sight, both of you, and try for the love a God to act like something that resembles leaders when you get over there in Show Time. Disfuckingmissed."

"Jesus," said Littletree as they scurried, mightily relieved, back to rejoin their platoon, "that's some vote a confidence, huh?"

"Yeah — this 'they're short a lieutenants over there' shit's gettin' kinda old, you ask me — it's a fuckin' broken record...."

+ + + + + + +

Those Candidates that survived OCS and popped out the other end as those unanimous objects of derision in all Armies since the time of the Pharaohs, Second Lieutenants, with in this case gold bars on their shoulders, received Further Orders, along with their commissions.

Henderson, peering at and deciphering the Armese gobbledegook that these documents were written in, was pleased to discover that he'd been assigned to the 5th Special Forces Group, headquartered in Nha Trang,

Republic of Vietnam. Pleased, but also somewhat surprised, because the scuttlebutt around Benning had been that no one in his OC class would be going Special Forces, who were said to be in disfavor by CO-MUSMACV (Commander U.S. Military Assistance Command, Vietnam) General Creighton "Abe" Abrams, an old tanker of Patton's 3rd Army who reportedly thought, not *entirely* without justification, that, admirable as they might be, Green Berets were becoming irrelevant as the Viet Cong were increasingly replaced by massed divisions of regular North Vietnamese troops. But whatever — there it was, in black and white — 5th SFG. The only one in his whole OC company. Don't ask, don't argue. *Fine with me, in any case....*

+ + + + + +

So now it was three weeks of Jump School, *also* at Fort Benning — just a few hundred meters away from the OCS barracks, in fact, right on the other side of Wold Avenue and Marchant Street.

And here the nature of the training once again changed, but — inevitably, this being the Army — it retained its comic, less-comic and even surreal, aspects.

On their second day, after they'd drawn chutes and other airborne stuff, a 5-stripe Jump master was informing them at max decibels,

"... AND WHEN YOU FIRST FEEL AIR UNDER YOUR FEET YOU *WILL* YELL, WITH THE UTMOST VIGOR AND ENTHU-SIASM, 'AIRBORNE! ALL THE WAY! *AAAAAARGH!*' — "

And someone behind Henderson in formation had asked, "Not 'Geronimo!' sergeant?"

"FUCK NO! THASS CARTOON SHIT — THIS HERE'S *REAL* SHIT!"*

Indeed it was. Almost too real. For fucking Jump School really *had* scared the piss out of him. Apparently there are people scattered randomly in the general population who actually enjoy hurling themselves out of moving airplanes — hell there are even, it is rumored, *grandmothers* among them. But Henderson did not figure among those. *Oh, no.* In fact the whole thing went against his grain to the most profound extent, and, bad as the preliminary drops from the 250-foot static towers were, it took all the willpower he could coax from the depths of his very bowels to shuffle out the open door of their lumbering C-130 for their three day, and one night, qualifying jumps.

The whole experience being rendered indescribably even worse, if such was possible, during his second jump, when he'd watched, agog in horror, as the kid behind him in the stick, a young black PFC whose name or even home unit he didn't know, went streaking by him, his defective (or badly folded or packed) parachute flapping behind him like a great mocking umbilical cord. Henderson had yelled '*Hey!*" utterly uselessly, and his mouth went sour as he peered through his risers to see the kid crash — *and bounce!* — to his death in the Georgia scrub a thousand feet below.

This had understandably cast something of a pall on the proceedings. Though it certainly didn't interrupt them, and it seemed almost as if the instructors' chief reaction was... *anger* — that the kid hadn't insured that his chute was packed right.

The most relief Henderson had ever felt thus far in his young life had been when the whole messy, weird, painful, and thoroughly fraught not to mention dangerous and seriously uncomfortable, unpleasant and un-welcome business of Jump School was finally over. Afterwards, in the Officer's Club, with several other 2nd Johns, silver wings safely pinned on their chests, Henderson had unburdened himself,

"I'll tell you one fucking thing for nothing. It ain't gonna break my god-damn heart if I never jump again. I mean *shit*. Damn idiot thing to do in the first place. Nuke the fuckers from your basement — *that*'s the way to play war. Shit."

+ + + + + + +

And even *then* the training wasn't over. There was still fifteen weeks of, uh, "specialized" training at the John F. Kennedy School of Special War-fare at Fort Bragg, North Carolina — outside of Fayetteville.

Back then, in the infancy of the JFK-reinvigorated Green Berets, the fa-bled Special Forces "Q" course hadn't yet grown into the six-to-twelve month marathon it would later become, but its four light months were still plenty long enough to learn more — and to Henderson's amuse-ment, ever-more esoteric — stuff. Such as:

- How, how much, and, often most crucially, *in what currency* to pay informers. For example, for many of the *Montagnard* hill tribes, actual folding money was less useful than in-kind items like salt, for the preservation of meat, and fuel/kerosene. *Jesus, what am I gettin' into, here? Holy cow, need a degree in — what's the one? Anthropology? Yeah, that one....*

- That the liver of a polar bear would kill you if you ate it. *Eh? Say again. In fuckin' Nam? Would someone please give me a break, here?* Although, to be fair, their instruction also addressed more regionally-appropriate sources of sustenance, and, indeed, their week-long "final exam" field exercise included an upgrade of the old AIT catch-and-eat-chicken requirement — the Special Forces version of which involved catching and eating at least one good bite of one of the many species of non-venomous snakes that graced the Carolina scrub. This actually proved easier than catching that fucking chicken, as snakes, both venomous and non-venomous, were so plentiful — and lethargic — thereabouts that the Green Beanie trainees actually speculated on whether SF Training Command had a deal with some local snake farm to artificially stock the training areas. (They didn't.)

- Proficiency training in French, Brit, Swedish, German, Russian/ChiCom and Israeli weapons, and specially with the world-ubiquitous Belgian FN automatic rifle — which Henderson found to be an unbalanced piece of crap, *gimme an M-16 any day.* But those two days of firing all these foreign rifles and pistols had been the high point of their training — the guys were like little boys set free to sample everything in F.A.O. Schwartz's toy emporium — *blam! blam-blam-blam! brrrap!* all day long....

- How to isolate and kidnap ("lift") the *right* bad guys in a village. Quite a tricky business, this, and one that required considerable political/intel savvy. The VC "political cadres" were forever assassinating village chiefs, and it was the Special Forces' job to preemptively take out those murderous, murdering VeeCees first. Snatching them, to turn them over to the ARVNs for interrogation and further "processing" was preferable to killing them — though the latter would certainly do, if and when something went wrong with Plan A.

- Rappelling. Either down actual cliffs, or (in training) walls; it would be limestone karst topography in Vietnam's Central Highlands; or "free fall" from helicopters hovering 200 feet up. Rappelling looked so easy in movies — but was so perilously... *precipitous* in real life. *And doing it while taking fire?* — as Rojo would have said if he wasn't off rubbing noses with Eskimo chicks somewhere, "Wha'?Fahgedda*bah*did, mang!"

- Advanced medic training. Well, more advanced than what they'd had so far, anyway. The 12-man Special Forces "A" Teams contained different occupational specialties, such as weapons, intel, engineering, commo — and, notably, medical. And, moreover, any one member was supposed to be able, at least theoretically, to fill in for any other guy on the team. So they were given information and taught some techniques that went well beyond ordinary first-aid training — such as how to tuck a guy's guts back in more or less where they belonged and, forget sewing, *taping* or even *stapling* him together securely enough for at least a medevac to get him to an aid station more or less in one piece and still breathing. (Yes, medics carried staplers. Unofficially, of course, but yes, they did — just as grunts carried "unofficial" shotguns.)

- He also learned new (well, new to Henderson) and rather esoteric ways of killing someone. Either with his own hands or using, as they quaintly said, "handy everyday civilian items". Their main instructor was a Nepalese 5-striper sergeant-first-class of unknowable age with a CIB (Combat Infantryman's Badge) who told them, in an amusing Brit-accented semi-pidgin "I chose not to join the Gurkhas, cause they too pussy, and also cause they not in Nam. Betta heah; betta Nam. Now, what I teach you is not gonna be boo-shit, not gonna be no pahlah (parlor) game to show off you friends. What I teach you gonna be for you to *use*. And make no mistake." Henderson had been an enthusiastic-enough student,

Heh, I coulda used some a this fancy stuff back with Rojo in that stinkin' Club 45....

- And finally, (though this certainly wasn't part of the official program), how astonishingly and, yes, shockingly easy it was to make it with certain horny wives of NCOs, a surprisingly high proportion of which were German-born and whose Fort Bragg-based hubbies were currently serving in Vietnam. Or at least *one* of them. The episode in question, with a little blonde called Petra, had ignited with a chance exchange in the music section of the PX one Sunday afternoon, had proceeded to flame briefly over a bottle of California Riesling in her little on-base semi-detached house, but had been extinguished at the last minute by Henderson, who'd, in the end, desisted. Pulled back, so to speak. Stammering excuses to Petra, he'd quickly dressed himself and fled — thinking belatedly, and rather horrified at what he'd been on the verge of... *What the fuck am I doing, here? How can I be doin' this? To a brother, who I don't even know? Get a fuckin' grip, man....* So he'd technically remained sinless... well, at least of *this* sin. But the experience sure had been an eye-opener.

+ + + + + +

And then finally one day, all of Uncle Sam's training, both formal and informal, a total of fifty-seven weeks' worth, was done. Well and truly *fini....*

9/ 0915 HOURS

"When you men get home and face an anti-war protester, look him in the eyes and shake his hand. Then, wink at his girlfriend, because she knows she's dating a pussy."

— USMC GEN. JAMES MATTIS

Henderson had an itch on his head that briefly interrupted his snooze. He scratched it, raising Junior's baseball cap in the process. Then, rather than putting it back on his head, he stuck it between his ass and the helicopter's cargo sling on which he dozed. The fact was, and as much as he'd appreciated Junior's original gesture, if it were up to him, he'd have gone hatless. But the military always required headgear of some kind, and he was still notionally, residually, technically still in the military, so....

...headgear...

The truth was, some guys looked a little foolish in a Green Beret, upon whom it might sit like a droopy, green personal-size pizza. But on Henderson it looked pretty good... well, maybe "good" wasn't exactly the *mot juste,* but at least it certainly made him look... *meaningful.* And, as he *de-planed,* (as they'd unaccountably started saying these days),in Houston from his flight from Charlotte to start his 30-days leave prior to his designated departure for Vietnam (what would the masters of the nation's *zeitgeist* be calling *that*, now — "*en-Nam-ing*"?), he couldn't help noticing that a lot of the civilians, of all ages and both sexes, that he passed on his way to, and as he waited at, the baggage claim place, glanced at him rather more pointedly than they needed to. (He wasn't conscious of it himself, but the fact was, he exuded "business". And not the "office" kind of business, either.) And he also noticed that his "antiwar" — *if they're "antiwar" how come they carry Viet Cong flags?* — hippie friends who were so doggedly camped out in the commonly-used corridors and other random locations in public Amerika, and whose currently self-appointed job in life was evidently to nag, harangue, beseech and sometimes screech at other passing soldiers to "like, desert, man", chose, now that he had a Green Beret on his head, to let *him* proceed on his way, pretty much un-harassed.

As after Basic Training, his obvious, default destination had been back to Henderson Family Headquarters in Houston. But once there, his old room up on the second floor, full of his old boyhood stuff, now struck him, as he dumped his duffle bag in there, as a curious, foreign country — or, more precisely, like a set for a sitcom that he vaguely remembered enjoying a long time ago, but could no longer now remember the point of.

All this time spent in various Army training regimens had rendered normal civilian schedules and even the seasons of the year irrelevant to his immediate concerns — only one item on the calendar had any meaning for him, and that was his ODD (Overseas Deployment Date), ex-Travis Air Force Base, in Oakland. For the rest, not only did he have to remind himself what day of the week it was, but even what damn *month* it was.

Thus, he was vaguely surprised, when he finally made his way back to Sugar Land, to find that The Big House was actually empty, save for the trusty Bahamian domestic couple: Brenda the housekeeper and her husband, Winston, the gardener/handyman. Henderson's dad, whose well-paid secretary did a great job of keeping his exact location at any given time practically a state secret, seemed to be more or less semi-permanently away on business trips to Austin, New York and Washington; his mother was off living the high life in Nevada or God-knows-where-else at this point; and his sister was back east at her prep school (or was she in college already? Henderson seemed to remember hearing something vaguely about a place called Wells College in upstate New York...). And Junior, that ass, had sadly, in the meantime, allowed himself to be traded to the fucking California Angels, as a result of which he apparently now maintained some kind of crash pad in Anaheim — and he appeared, from the occasional phone call Henderson managed to have with him, to have become terminally Californian. But at least, either through kindness or, more likely, by coincidentally-convenient good fortune, he'd left the restored and functioning Alpha in the garage — *Jay-Are, I don't give a shit what they say about you, yer OK in my book....*

But it had been over fourteen months since Sally Evinrude's fateful "coming out" shindig, and the crack between Henderson and his old life back here in Houston, a psychological gap that had already begun to manifest itself in the waning days of his college "career" (more, in truth, his *fraternity* "career"), and even more so in his week off between AIT and OCS, seemed by now to have grown into an unbridgeable gulf:

Attempted link-ups with guys who'd previously been pals and even fixtures in what passed for his social orbit — whose hair was now considerably longer and sprouting in new places, while his was practically

Army-nonexistent — now proved awkward and stilted. His old male acquaintances seemed incapable of concentrating on much beyond their individual draft statuses, whether their dope dealers had been busted or not, and current Canadian immigration regulations; their reunions with Henderson had therefore now become cringe-worthy and mutually embarrassing. And as for the girls... well, they just couldn't seem to take their transmogrified gaze away from his GI haircut.

And the result was some kind of squirmy variation on:

"Hey Jerry, hi, yeah, dig it — where ya *been*, man? What? Say *what?* Green Beret? *Green Beret? Green Be— !* — holy shit, man, yeah, like... wow, man... *Green Beret....* heavy, man — definitely *hea-vy...* wow... so, like, look, man, like have fun, you know? Yeah, I gotta split, you know? But, I'll catch ya later, sure, sure... so, like, you take care, now..."

(whew)... (eye-roll) — *Holy shit, Jerry Henderson's really fuckin' flipped, I always* knew *he was one a "them"....*

Which, after a little initial surprised annoyance, Henderson decided was just fucking fine with him. It pretty quickly dawned on him that he had not one damn thing to say to these people anymore, and, judging from their half-embarrassed, half-stoned stutterings that stopped just short of open hostility, neither did they, to him.

So for the first few days of his leave, once it was clear that he'd pretty much been disowned by such of his old crowd who hadn't *themselves* been drafted, he spent several long evening hours drinking with the cowboys on his Uncle Morton (J.D.'s older brother)'s ranch, where he'd worked the summer of his junior year of prep school, and where he was therefore remembered and accepted. Into this group of cynical wise-asses, most of whom were too old for the current conflict — though the foreman, Lucas, had been in Korea (*fuckin' shit-show, man*). But two of the younger guys had actually been to the 'Nam, and had come back and had since left the Army: one, a draftee who'd been a trucker in III Corps and the other, a grunt with the 25th "Tropic Lightning" Division, operating around Pleiku.

"Jerry, when you over there, don't be a prick like them West Point pussies, or you get y'ass fragged," said the ex-trucker.

"Fragged?" Henderson knew what it was, of course, (how could he not? — it was a favorite word of the demonstrators'), but he felt, perversely, like pretending he didn't.

"Nah," the ex-grunt from the 25th assured him, "don't worry about it, you ain't no prick, you be alright,"

"Yeah, but what's 'fragged'?"

"Fragged," persisted the Transportation Corps guy, "my young pal, is when a asshole lieutenant is acting like what they was born to be, which is to say, a asshole, which is not necessarily a capital crime *in itself,* y'understand, but when that asshole lieutenant starts t'get a little excessively gung-ho an' starts t'unnecessarily endanger the lives a his men, he sometimes gets a US-Government-issue M-26 frag grenade shoved up his ass, which usually stops the aforementioned assholeness in a right smart fashion — and is called fragging."

"Ah," said Henderson.

"But not to worry, lil brother, like he says, I reckon you be alright — you ain't West Point."

"Yeah — " said the grunt from the 25th as he reached into the tub for more long-necks, "an' what you bustin' the kid's ass for, anyway? — he's Special Forces, an' they got nuthin' ta do wit' draftees like us an' Black Panthers an' fraggin' an' any a that shit — whole 'nother *world*, man. Shit, if he's gonna buy it over there, at least it'll be at the hands a the fuckin' NVA, like it should be...."

"You guys are all heart," said Henderson, "you know that?"

Even so, even in the fissiparous atmosphere of anomie and social dys-function in which he found himself beyond the confines of the ranch, he *did* get invited to the odd get-together and even party — and some-times he even went. But the people at these things just struck him as irretrievably... not so much foolish, as *irrelevant*.

He slept a lot, usually alone... although he frequently woke up in unusu-al places, including sometimes on the floor, and even floors that turned out to be most emphatically not his. He even got stoned on grass a few times — twice, to be precise — and he discovered that he *hated* the stuff: everyone around him wouldn't stop giggling and he just got increasingly paranoid, convinced that everyone was giggling *at him* — and for all anyone could confirm or deny it, they were. When he told the girl who'd given him the grass, that second time, how disagreeable he found the experience, she enlightened him,

"That's cause you're still drunk. You really shouldn't drink and do grass at the same time — and if you insist on doing dope while drinking, then do coke — *that*'s the drinking guy's drug."

"Oh yeah?" She turned out to be right — he'd tried coke once, too, and quite enjoyed that — but desisted from persisting with it, as he retained enough residual sense to see that nothing good could conceivably come from continued use. Even he intuited that that looked like one bad habit too far.

So Henderson futzed around, spinning his wheels. Junior of course was sadly unavailable for "road shows", as were his other old buddies who now seemed all to have either shacked up in some manner or other with a chick, or become communists, (or both), so even the beloved Alpha was only good for little more than beer runs to the grocery store/*bodega*. He found himself watching a lot of stupid TV, which revealed itself to be an unbroken parade of scarcely conceivable idiot bullshit nonsense. At one point, he got so desperate that, before rejecting it as insane, he even considered flying up to Alaska to try to find fucking Rojo "in some gah-damn fockeen igloo, mang!"

Instead, however, what he finally did was:

One morning he got up, stashed the Alpha back in the house's two-car garage, packed an overnight bag (a green Dallas Commanders sports-bag, inevitably courtesy of Junior) with his best civilian clothes (it occurred to him that the next few weeks could well be the last time in his life he'd ever wear civvies) and a silver flask full of bourbon. He then put his uniform back on, shook Winston's hand and kissed Brenda on the cheek, and splurged on a cab to the airport where he bought a one-way ticket on a Braniff Airlines flight to LaGuardia.

Once in New York, his natural frugality kicked back in and he bused it to the Port Authority Bus Terminal, with which Henderson had gotten so familiar in his Fort Dix days, and near which he now found a Blarney Stone bar and "restaurant", one of the few public accommodations in America that, in those days, not only didn't reject the patronage of uniformed soldiers and Marines, but positively, if decorously, welcomed them.

So at the Blarney Stone at 8th Avenue and 31st Street he right smartly consumed four Rheingold beers and three Scotch whiskey chasers, then proceeded to piss most of all that out in Blarney's stinking *pissoir*, after which he made his bibulous way by taxi crosstown and then uptown to 1st Avenue and 85th Street, to Robin Hudnut's building where, Green Beret in hand, he knocked. Or rather, buzzed. Hers being a ground floor studio apartment, he actually contrived to do both, knocked *and* buzzed — he was, as previously noted, a little light-headed by now. He knocked and buzzed twice again, and nothing continued to happen for two full minutes. He was on the verge of walking away and this time *really* hauling his ass up to Alaska to find goddamn Rojo, when....

He heard the sound of unlockings and the door tentatively opened to the regulation New Yorkian 3-inches' chain-length, from which poked the tip of the nose, part of the chin, and a considerable amount of the streaked-blonde hair of a sleepy (it was somewhere around O-One-Forget-About-It Hours) Robin Hudnut. This partial face whispered/croaked,

"Wha? Who is it?"

"Hi Robin — it's me, Henderson."

"Hen — ? Henderson? Wha — *who*?"

"Jerry Henderson — you know, from Houston."

"What? Jerry? *Jerry? My God,* what are you *doing* here? What d'you want — are you... *stabbed* again?"

"Ha ha, no — look, I just — "

"Aren't you supposed to be at some Army training camp or something?"

"Nah, that's all finished now."

"Well... what do you *want*? It's, like... the middle of the night."

"I just thought I'd say hi."

"Jesus Christ, I don't bel*ieve* this — this is like the *last* time you came crashing through here, when you were bleeding, with your drunken buddy — what the hell *is* it with you, why the hell didn't you call?"

"Yeah, sorry, I probably shoulda." The fact was, he didn't even *have* her phone number — if she'd ever even given it to him, he'd long since mislaid it somewhere....

"I'll say — so, like, what do you *want*?"

And here was where his alcoholic investment back at the Blarney Stone paid off — it was with alcoholically-fueled reckless cheekiness that he asked "Well... can I come in?"

Robin's fragment of a face now hesitated. Then it shifted slightly, and Henderson could see a pair of lovely pursed lips. Muttering what sounded like "I don't believe this", she closed the door, causing Henderson to momentarily think he'd blown it, but that was just so she could unchain the damn thing, and then she opened the door fully.

"So come in, then. Jesus Christ."

And Henderson had gone in. As it were.

The 5'2" Robin had been sleeping in her panties and a long, man's "Woodstock: 3 Days Of Peace, Love And Music" T-shirt that went down to her upper thighs and served as a virtual nightshirt. Still half-asleep, she blinked in further quizzicality at his Commanders bag as she ushered him into her little kitchen.

"I'm damn well not having any coffee at this time a night — morning! — but maybe you could use some..."

"Naa, thanks, but... you got any water?"

She raised her eyebrows as though she thought he might be a little not right in the head, and indicated her sink. She sat in one of the two kitchen chairs and watched as he took a glass from her drying rack, poured in a bit of tap water, and half-filled the rest from a silver flask that he pulled out from his bag.

She lit a cigarette, put an elbow on the Formica table and rested her chin on the palm at the other end of that elbow, and, turning to him, said,

"Well. So. Jerry Henderson. What's the deal, here? What's *your* deal, here?"

+ + + + + + +

Robin Hudnut, of Greenwich Connecticut, was a very recent English Lit graduate from the University of Pennsylvania and was now an apparently up-and-coming Career Trainee at the Chemical Bank and Trust Co.

She'd been unofficially engaged — "engaged" because the Party of the Second Part had given her a not-*huge*-but-not-tiny-either diamond ring from Zales, and "unofficially" because no parents had yet been informed. This last was per Robin's expressed, if unexplained, wish and which itself was a result of the unexpressed (and blissfully unsuspected by the P. of the Second P.) fact that she hadn't yet definitively made up her mind — to one of NEWSWEEK's movie reviewers, a young supposed hot-shot recent graduate from NYU's School of Advanced Exquisitely Pretentious Inanities (as Henderson was later moved to call it), for about nine months, now.

But by a stroke of miraculous good luck for all involved (which even many months later, Henderson couldn't quite bring himself to believe), this sleek and well-connected — and, incidentally, expensively draft-exempted — fellow, originally from the Bronx's snooty Riverdale section, was currently off in Peru, (or was it Bolivia? *some*fuckingwhere down there, anyway), supposedly reporting on the making of an "iconic" movie by the newly-celebrated Dennis Hopper and a mini-constellation of trendy Hollywoodniks, called "The Last Movie".

"I don't get it," Henderson had remonstrated to Robin, when she was endeavoring to explain her domestic situation to him, "He's being paid — I guess big bucks — to go to South fuckin' America to report on a movie that... doesn't exist yet?"

"Yes. 'Fact, he's leading a whole team — it's like they're making a documentary on the making of the movie."

"Fer fuckin' *NEWSWEEK*?"

"Well, they're part of a larger... media consortium, I think they call it."

"Has this kinda thing ever been done before? — is this what people do these days?"

"Yes, no, I don't know. It's supposed to be 'iconic'."

"What, the movie that doesn't exist yet?"

"Yes."

"How can a movie — or *any*thing, for that matter — be 'iconic' when it hasn't even been made yet?"

"I don't know. It just is. Don't ask, you wouldn't unders — look, it's not meant for people like *you,* anyway — it's a whole different world and it's *def*initely not one you want to know about."

"Got *that* right. Come here...."

An that's pretty much how things had gone.

Henderson was only too delighted to allow NEWSWEEK's baffling corporate/creative decision to detour and exile its star young movie re-viewer indefinitely — in fact, the longer the better. He just thanked the Sweet Jesus for whatever wave of temporary insanity was wafting over its editorial offices on Madison Avenue, as, nightly, he and the trendily unfaithful Robin screwed until their eyeballs just about popped out of their besotted heads. And they did this right next to an 8x10 portrait of the — windblown, yet — Boy-Wonder Cinecritic, that sat right on the night-table on "Robin's side" of her big and comfy queen-sized bed. When the mock-irritated Henderson had tried to shitcan the thing, or at least chuck it in a closet, she'd said,

"Don't. He's sweet. Leave him there, it's his place."

"*Sweet?* Holy hell, sweet. Am *I* sweet?"

"No, Henderson, you're most definitely *not* sweet." Ever since her initial, querulous "Jerry?" at the door that first night, she'd reverted to calling him "Henderson". Exclusively.

+ + + + + +

So for the remaining seventeen days of his leave, Henderson spent the vast bulk of his time in and around that little ground-floor studio on 85th Street:

He'd watch Robin rise early, get ready in a most piquantly pleasing flurry of fragrant feminine swishiness, and whisk herself off to ingratiate herself with, and impress, the powers that were at the Chemical Bank (if that really was its name). After she'd gone Henderson would leisurely get his shit together, organize his matutinal coffee-with-a-beer-chaser, and decadently loaf around, listening to her surprisingly-good-for-a-girl music collection while keeping a wary eye on the war in Vietnam as filtered through news bulletins from Robin's Sony Trinitron.

Robin had suggested that if he wanted to exercise and didn't want to go all the way to Central Park, there was the much smaller Carl Schurz Park right around the corner where he could jog and do "all the, like, P.T. stuff" he liked, but Henderson had demurred, figuring that after fourteen months of the most rigorous physical training imaginable (at least imaginable by him), he was in as good shape as he was ever going to be, and two weeks of goofing off wasn't going to noticeably alter that.

So instead, he'd occasionally wander over to the local Gristede's supermarket where he bought the few things Robin had left for him on her daily list, which, when all was said and done, seemed to consist of little more than yogurt, bagels and olive oil — or so it seemed to Henderson, to whom all three of those items had been hitherto pretty much foreign. Then he'd stop off at any of a number of local bars on 1ˢᵗ Avenue where he'd drink further beer and disinterestedly watch sporting events involving unfamiliar teams — hell, even unfamiliar *sports;* at Andover they'd had just about every conceivable sport, but here was some shit out of Australia that was... well, what the hell *was* it? and who the hell were these people in New York fucking City that watched it?

And if the TVs in the bars in New York fucking City weren't showing foreign sports, they'd have game shows going which absolutely floored him with their asininity. There'd also, in these bars, always be lying around somewhere a kind of communal copy of the Daily News, which Henderson would glance at, mainly to pick up where the tube had left off regarding the latest out of Vietnam. Not that the Daily News knew its ass from its elbow about Vietnam, but still, it was all there was.

Lunch would be one of those delicious Sabrett's hot dogs from the corner cart belonging to the guy with the most mysterious ethnicity since good old Screaming Sergeant Pingo, back at Basic. With mustard and kraut — there was nothing better, and sometimes Henderson even had two.

Robin would re-appear at about six each evening, after which she'd change, down a white wine, and then they'd enjoy what they rather unimaginatively called a "quickie", after which they were free to go out and play... the Great Idiot "New York Scene" Game, a routine that usually involved whatever passed for dinner and live music downtown somewhere, at one of those innumerable gathering-grounds-for-parvenus of which the most famous were Max's Kansas City and CBGB's, (Henderson drew the line at "clubs"), invariably linking up or otherwise ending up with some of Robin's seemingly inexhaustible supply of school or work friends — sometimes both. To whom she'd neutrally introduce him as "my friend from Texas", wording to which he'd originally been prepared to take umbrage, but then decided to *ahhh — let it slide.*

This regimen — a movable smorgasbord of conspicuous hedonism and chemical excess — not surprisingly turned out to be even more insufferable horseshit than Henderson's old version of the same game back in Houston, and one in which he, in any case, could never be a proper participant — for even if he'd wanted to, which he emphatically did not, his Army haircut continued to single him out, in a very real sense (and here in Greenwich fucking Village more than anywhere) as an Untouchable... in this rigid socio/political caste system that held sway in early '70s New York fucking City.

But Henderson survived it all insouciantly unscathed and even, as a then-popular song by Traffic had it, "feelin' alright" because ironically, he already happily *considered himself* "untouchable" — in the sense of being cosmically, as they liked to say, removed from this pathetic civilian riff-raff. That attitude, plus staying serenely and constantly half-popped throughout, allowed him to float above "The Scene" largely oblivious to everything but the lubricious Robin and her big soft and beckoning bed.

Of course, always encroaching at the margins of his consciousness was the looming and rapidly-approaching Reality of Vietnam, but that only rendered the piddling concerns of contemporary civilian (civilian to the point of being actively anti-military) New Yorkers, no, *Noo Yawkahs,* even more laughably trivial, as well as gloriously moot.

+ + + + + + +

On one of their two Saturdays Henderson announced that he wanted to take Robin to Coney Island, a legendary destination he'd long heard about and seen in movies. Robin said, "OK, cool — but I've got no idea how to get there." So they ducked down into the 86th St. subway station, where, in the process of buying four of those funky "Y"-perforated tokens that looked like currency from the Ottoman Empire, they'd been informed through the mandatory bullet-proof glass that they needed to go down to Grand Central, Shuttle over to Times Square, and then "take da Q allawayta Coney Ahl'." Well, Henderson remembered Times Square well enough from his Rojo days, so that was all the instruction he needed, and off they went.

The festive vibe of their adventure was enhanced by the subway cars themselves which were so comprehensively graffitied-over that they looked like gaily-decorated rolling circus wagons. And Henderson found it endlessly fascinating to observe the human kaleidoscope of the little individual psychodramas that each of their fellow passengers presented: noticing that only one of whom actually made the whole trip with them to Coney Island — this one being a presumably human bundle of rags whose sex and even race was impossible to definitively identify, who stayed immobile, curled up on the bench at the end of their carriage and was given a wide berth by all the other alighting and departing riders. "I wouldn't bet too much that whoever that is is even alive," commented Henderson, as, at the end of the line, they left the mystery form to resume its return journey back to wherever it had begun.

In the event, Coney Island proved a huge success, an inspired idea — and even Robin's protective carapace of mild cynicism was discarded for the day.

They did the whole bit: the Parachute Drop, which Airborne Henderson had insisted they go on before anything else; the Cyclone roller coaster that was suitably rickety-scary; the Dodgem Cars; the Ferris Wheel; the Crazy Mirrors; chucking beanbaggy softballs at leaden milk bottles; water-zapping the balloons that grew out of the wooden clowns' mouths....

But the two definite high points were:

First, the Ghost Train, a noisy and bumpy little ride in the middle of which their car got derailed and needed to be put right by a couple of black guys who normally played "ghosts" but who'd sheepishly had to emerge from behind the black plywood "scenery" to shut down the ride and lift the little conveyance back onto its tracks — with Henderson stifling any stupid comment about "spooks".

And second, the air-rifle shooting gallery, at which dead-eye Army Sharpshooter Henderson contrived to so comprehensively demolish a series of little lined-up clay pipes that he found himself the winner of an enormous — as big as he was — stuffed purple gorilla. Unfortunately, Robin absolutely refused his bestowal of this chivalric boon: "Where the hell d'you think I've got room for that? Plus, it's hideous" she protested. And so he ended up giving it away to the first recipients he could find who'd accept it: a bemused Spanish-speaking couple pushing a toddler in a stroller.

"Quick, let's vamoose before they give it back — "

"Henderson, you'd make a great Santa Claus."

And, arguably best of all: more — *and even better than the Sabrett guy on your corner* — hot dogs.

Coney Island — Henderson loved the place:

"When I get back from Nam I might move out here. These are my people — I'll get Rojo to come an' join me. He'd be a fucking *king* here. Yo, Robin, whaddaya think 'partments go for, out here?"

"For you? With your accent? They'll see you coming and double the rent."

"Naaa — Rojo'll be king, an' I'll be The fuckin' Prince Of The City."

"Sure you will, Henderson — 'Prince Of The City', that's you alright. C'mon it's time to go back — I want a bath."

+ + + + + + +

Despite all the ambient noise during those couple of weeks in New York, despite the constant contact with at least *some* aspect — whether it be demonstration, plastered poster, noisy protest, provocative mural, sidewalk canvasser, real or threatened riot, or merely casual insult about his haircut — of the prevailing "antiwar"/pro-Ho Chi Minh animus which infected so much of the country but which was *so* particularly centered in New York fucking City, that time in Manhattan with Robin was as happy a period as any Henderson could remember experiencing since his carefree days back at the old fratty house, which now seemed a whole different, vaguely-remembered, universe ago.

Together they spent practically every goddamn penny he had, a good chunk of hers, and at one point he even had to go begging on the telephone to Junior for $500 which, true-blue stand-up dude that he was and to his eternal credit — literally — Junior had coughed-up without the slightest squawk or demurral, arranging with Chemical Robin to wire-transfer and to cause to materialize the requisite cash for him from some unlikely-sounding branch of the Bank of America in a place called Mission Viejo. ("Hey, really, thanks Jay Are, this is extremely white a ya — an' you know you'll get it back." "Acorse I know that, man — meanwhahl jess try not to catch nothin' shameful 'fore you even get over there.")

Robin, for her part, was just about perfect. No fuss, no muss. Ask me no questions, I'll tell you no lies. She looked good, she acted good, she smelled good — hell, she even laughed. As an approving Rojo would have said, "Jew cang beat dat, Hendysoh!" And while her lineage was undoubtedly Old-School (a deceased moneybags dad, mom dividing her time between Greenwich Connecticut and Boca Raton, Florida), in her pastel mini-skirts and pulled-back dangling bouffant hair-do she wouldn't have been out of place as one of the dancing bimbos on the set of Laugh-In. Plus, if she had any disobliging political views of her own, she kept them to herself (which made her just about unique in her national demographic cohort) and she even sympathized with Henderson when he'd curse the demonstrators in the streets and stoutly defended him when bouncers and maitre d's at various establishments would, noting his Army haircut, attempt to turn him away.

Sure, there did intrude the occasional intimation of larger, still-distant perhaps, but nevertheless gathering, Storm-Clouds Ahead: Like wind-blown Mr. Moviecritic, who remained on her bedside table. And one night, when he thought she was asleep and was about to zonk off himself, Henderson heard an odd sound coming from Robin. He frowned in the dark — *damn,* she appeared to be crying. Alarmed, he nudged her and asked what the h–, well, what was the matter, and she, wiping her tears in the dark, had sniffed,

"Henderson, do you — do you think — ?"

"What? Do I think what?"

"Oh... nothing." *Sniff sniff.*

Jesus H. He'd kissed her on the forehead and put his arm around her and murmured, "C'mon, go t'sleep, we can pick it up in the morning...."

But in the morning they hadn't, and Henderson had been only too happy to pretend the baffling little episode had never happened. And they resumed their blissful, if temporary, occupation of what Henry Miller, unbeknownst to either of them, had once described as "The Land Of Fuck". All in all, Henderson reckoned that he was the only happy person in all of New York fucking City. In fact, he'd also hoped that Robin was happy too, but with girls — as that little sniffling weirdness in the night had shown — you could never be completely sure.

+ + + + + + +

Inevitably The Day arrived. He had to get his ass over to Travis Air Force Base. In Oakland. Today. *El pronto* and without fail-o.

0630 hours. His eyes snapped open, courtesy of his internal alarm clock. Robin, naturally, was still lost in innocent, streaked-blonde tousled sleep. Henderson rose soundlessly and eased himself into the bathroom where he quietly got himself ready. He then carefully put on his uniform, and packed away his civvies in his Commanders sports bag, which, as previously agreed with Robin, she'd squash as flat as she could, put in a box, and mail to the Henderson address in Houston, via the slowest and cheapest method available.

Then, although it made him feel a bit like a jerk out of precisely the kind of embarrassing movie he disdained, Henderson allowed himself a moment of what passed for him as sentimentality, and dropped one of his dog-tags (of which he had extras) onto Robin's pillow, next to one of her half-opened hands.

As per his orders, he took with him only his toilet kit and a set of those very orders, both which he now placed in a small plastic bag he'd fished out of Robin's waste-basket. *Right, I'm ready.* It had been his intention to tiptoe to the door and leave the apartment while Robin was still asleep, but when he got there and went to undo the locks to ease it open, he saw that Robin — just as quietly as he'd been — had followed him there. He jumped back in a veritable cartoon version of shocked surprise. And before he could even speak she threw her arms around his neck and buried her face in his uniform buttons.

"Will you at least write?" he heard, muffled from down around his chest.

"Write? Sure. Of *course.* Of course I'll write — what d'ya think? That I wouldn't write?" *Write? Shit, and here I thought I was doing pretty good just to remember her street number. You need a zip code to write — what the fuck's her zip code?* "But you better give me your zip code...."

As she fished out a discarded envelope from a little trash can by the door that had her address on it, to give him, he said "Hey — " and kissed the top of her head.

Now that his plan had been blown to hell and she was awake and even bestirring herself, it occurred to Phipps, in semi-panic, that there was something kind of important that he ought to say to her — or even, strangely for him, that he *wanted* to say to her — but he couldn't untangle and come up with the right thoughts, let alone the right words. And anyway, there wasn't much time and the one thing that *was* clear to him was that it was highly likely that anything he'd say now not only wouldn't make anything better, but almost certainly would make things *worse.*

So instead, after he pocketed the envelope, he cupped her face with his two hands, kissed her softly on the lips, and said,

"See you, Robin. Thanks for everything. I mean that — you have no idea. Thanks. You're the best, kiddo."

"But..."

"It's alright. It's alright. Someday we'll figure all this out. *Bound* to, for sure. Meanwhile, go back to bed. Go back to sleep. You'll be fine. You'll see."

And with that, he disengaged himself from her arms, closed her door behind him, dug out his last subway token that he'd had the foresight to stash with his orders, and stepped out into the early morning sun.

10/ 0930 HOURS

"They were afraid of dying, but they were even more afraid to show it. They found jokes to tell."

— TIM O'BRIEN

Being nominally a civilian outfit, ATAS helicopters did not deploy with door-mounted ordnance, but in combat situations the kickers improvised to make up for this lacuna. Accordingly, Sandoval had used a cargo strap to secure an M-60 machine gun to the hand-grip by the H-34's once-again open door, and was now checking its ammo, in the process of which he slammed down the cover on the feed tray — making a noise that was discrete from the *other* noise in the chopper, and thus briefly waking Henderson.

Seeing Sandoval there, in his helmet with the absurd stars-and-stripes palm-tree logo on the front, for some reason reminded Henderson of the hilariously progressively-worsening stewardess situation on that series of flights that had taken him, along with what would eventually be some three hundred other American servicemen, ranging from Private E-2 to Colonel O-6, from New York to Vietnam, via Oakland and Guam: pert, mini-suited chick stewardesses on the New York to Oakland leg;

guy stewards from Oakland to Guam; and guy stewards *carrying Smith & Wesson Model 10A .38 revolvers on their hips* from Guam to Vietnam.

Huh. That sure had been weird. We were all thinking the same thing when that 2-striper across the aisle from me asked that steward, "Hey sweetheart, what's that thing for — you guys think we're gonna hijack this motherfuck-er? Or jump out of it?" Huh — And those few hours spent at Travis AFB had been some fuckin' trip too, right?....

Oakland's Travis Air Force Base had been the main trans-shipment air-link between the US and Vietnam, both coming and going, and as such, it was a scarcely-imaginable hive of frenetic activity. It was somber and deadly serious in the Departure area, and giddy and semi-hysterically euphoric over in the Arrivals area — all of it overseen by sardonic Air Force people who camouflaged their secret Vietnam-avoidance guilt in a veneer of cynicism.

Into this maelstrom strode Army (Special Forces) 2nd Lieutenant Jerome J. Henderson. Carrying just this little plastic bag that he'd retrieved in the dark from Robin's kitchen, that he only now noticed was from an "Ellen Cosmetics" of Lexington Ave. — *Great, just great —* he first checked in, got his orders duly stamped, and then headed into the huge Officer's Club. In the Departure Area at Travis, they didn't have "loung-es" or eateries or bars, but rather Officer's, NCO's, and Enlisted Men's Clubs.

As a 2nd Lieutenant he was of course regarded by all and sundry, military and civilian alike, with, at best, pity, and at worst, scorn. But the fact that he was also a Green Beret negated all that and caused him to be an object of near-unanimous interest, both professional and even personal. Like it or not, and you could say what you wanted, but whether it was a result of the headgear, or of that stupid song, or of the lingering effects of President Kennedy's blessing and patronage, or whatever it was — Green Berets, of all ranks, were looked upon, by both civilians and even their fellow military, as special specimens, a breed apart.

So heads turned in his direction as Henderson elbowed his way up to that Travis O Club bar. But once there, he doffed his beret, and the rubberneckers re-directed their attentions elsewhere. Henderson ordered his usual — Scotch and beer chaser, hah hah — and found himself chatting with the guy next to him, a red-headed fellow-2nd John with Engineer insignia. It turned out they were on different flights — the engineer's was bound for Cam Ranh Bay, while Henderson's was going to Saigon/Tan Son Nhut. At one point, his new pal nudged Henderson and pointed out at least three pairs of Air Policemen conspicuously positioned near the walls inside the cavernous hall, presumably guarding against any last-minute freak-outs.

"Lookit that — that's something you don't see in yer average departure lounge."

Henderson snorted, "Yeah, encouraging, right? Huh. I can see they might want a few of those in the EM club, the draftees an' all — but in *here?*"

"And what are they gonna do to us, anyway, if we *do* get outta line? Send us to Vietnam?" This was a mildly-amusing-the first-time-he-heard-it catchphrase Henderson would hear untold times — too many times — in the coming year....

+ + + + + + +

Some 23 hours later, after a refueling stop in Guam during which all the military passengers had to stay on board and the unarmed cabin crew got replaced by the aforementioned armed one, the chartered World Airways DC-8 deposited Henderson, along with those other three hundred-odd tired, unshaven, smelly and variously apprehensive troops into the great cavernous green maw of Tan Son Nhut Air Force Base, outside of Saigon. This awesome hive of noisy round-the-clock frenetic bureaucratic organized chaos even eclipsed that show back at Travis.

Following signs and barked orders from airmen in green fatigues, Henderson underwent a good deal of what anyone who's ever been in the American Army will recognize as "Hurry Up And Wait"-ing and "Mill Around, Mill!"-ing, but which was in fact a winnowing process that shunted him in and out of ever-smaller "repo detos" (replacement detachments), his orders being scrutinized and passed around at each station to such an extent that he feared the flimsy paper itself might fall apart, until he'd finally been reduced to a "fuckin' newbie" party... of one. And assigned to report to a remote corner of the vast Tan Son Nhut complex where America Tropic Air Services (ATAS) inconspicuously held sway.

Once there he was told by a pretty Vietnamese lady in a flattering turquoise *ao-dai*, (the first of what would be for Henderson a *long* succession — that never failed to please — of flattering *ao-dais*), to kindly wait as they fueled up a C-46 which would shortly be heading up to the coastal town of Nha Trang, halfway up-country, which is where he was meant to be.

+ + + + + +

Henderson stared agog at fabulous beaches as they bounced to a landing in Nha Trang. Once on the ground it wasn't hard to catch a lift, in this case on a returning deuce-and-a-half, to the sprawling, dusty headquarters of the 5th Special Forces Group (Vietnam).

On their bumpy way, Henderson noticed two things right off the bat: One was the redness of Vietnam's dirt roads, which came from the country's laterite soil and which produced vast amounts of dust in the dry season and mud in the wet season. Henderson had only ever previously seen anything like it on the unpaved roads outside of Nassau, where he'd once gotten drunkenly lost back when he'd gone there at Easter break with some fratty brothers.

And the other thing he immediately noticed was an unmistakable (even if reversed) red swastika on the façade of a passing Buddhist temple. Henderson had been told about this quaint cultural artifact, back in In-Country Orientation at Bragg, but it was still jarring when you saw it, live front and center, in shiny lacquered plaster. *You'd expect a fuckin' hammer-an'-sickle, but* this?....

"Sonovabitch, ain't that something?" he said as he pointed out the swastika to the bemused Spec-4 driver, "Makes ya wonder if you're in the right country, right?"

"Funky place, no doubt." replied the guy, as he beeped and nudged his way around a couple of water buffaloes that a papa-*san* was unsuccessfully trying to control with a long stick. The Spec-4 kid had scrawled "TOO SHORT FOR THIS SHIT" on his boonie-hat with a black magic marker.

Oh, and a third thing Henderson noticed right off the bat: The whole country seemed to smell, not quite *terrible*, but definitely... well, it was... *getting there.*

"And what's that smell?"

"Yeah, that. About one third of it's nook-mahm, one third's flowers, and one third's shit. You get used to it. 'Course, it gets worse when dead bodies get mixed in, specially burning ones..."

Alighting at the main gate of 5th Group Headquarters, before he could even show his orders to the MP at the gate, a passing full-bull stopped to peer at him and told him to get a haircut. *Unfuckingbelievable... Is that the damn CO of this place? Jesus, could be.... I miss Rojo already — "already"? More like "again"....*

He drew equipment and weapons, filled out forms, spoke first to a light colonel, and then to an obviously sleepy major who, once Henderson had had to re-inform him of who he was and why he was there, had in response told Henderson where further he *still* needed to go and what he was supposed to do, more or less, when he got *there.*

And so... before he still quite knew what the shit was going on, and with the aid of a further hitched ride, this time in an ARVN jeep, he found himself dumping his gear at the last stop of this almost laughably long journey from New York's East 85th Street, at a reinforced-company-sized military encampment near the fortified hamlet of Dak Phuoc, Phuoc Long Province, home of 5th Special Forces Team A132-C.

Yes, this was one of those fabled Special Forces "A-Team"s (technically, bureaucratically known as ODAs — Operational Detachments Alpha) that had been so immortalized by the slightly-more-than-a-little embarrassing singing Green Beret Sergeant Barry Sadler, the B-side of whose "The Ballad Of The Green Berets" was a song called "The A Team".

However, inasmuch as "A132-C" didn't trip off the tongue all that trippingly, the denizens of the place referred to it as Camp Happy Holidays. A name which was, in truth, scarcely any shorter than "A-One thirty two-Charley", but it did afford the Americans assigned to it the dubious, childish pleasure of hearing the locals struggle with "Horidays".

This camp — which was really a modern-day fort, actually — was located on a somewhat elevated bit of ground not far from what was marked on the maps as a the Song Canh "river" but was in fact the Song Canh little muddy stream, that flowed out of uncertainly-demarcated Cambodia, a klick or so to the west.

And the job of US Army Special Forces A-Team A132-Charley was, apparently, two-fold:

1/ To observe, report on, and, when necessary and appropriate, to "interdict", as it was put, the People's Army of (North) Vietnam. Or at least such units of it as ventured into A132-Charley's AO.

and

2/ To endeavor to stay alive. And, of course, to keep alive the various indigenous forces who were in their charge.

Now, it had to be said that the efforts the team expended in pursuit of these two missions were not, unfortunately, equal. Indeed, the notion that little A132-Charley — however tight a unit and together its members might be, even with its local appendages — was likely to stop, or even noticeably slow, the inexorable human lava-flow of North Vietnamese regulars pouring into South Vietnam via the "Ho Chi Minh Trail" (which would have much more aptly been called the "Ho Chi Minh Highway") through Laos, Phuland and Cambodia, was more than a little laughable. And thus the stark truth was that mere survival remained A132-Charley's main function, and any North Vietnamese they managed to blow away in the process were a bonus — more icing on their muddy red cake.... As Winston might have said, "Some icing; some cake."

The team itself consisted of one officer — in this case a huge captain who'd played football at West Point (where they'd quietly tweaked their size limitations for him) called Marcellus Gallaway — and eleven other guys, who were all NCOs. Special Forces lower ranks such as Private E-2s and PFCs spent time with B and C headquarters teams before being promoted and being allowed to graduate to A-Teams. And A-Teams sometimes had a Warrant Officer instead of a senior sergeant as an "XO".

Typically, the A-Team roster of NCOs were made up of two medics, two heavy weapons guys, two commo guys, two language/interpreter specialists, and one-each intel guy, an engineer (who doubled as a mechanic/transportation guy, handy with both boats and vehicles), and one "operations"/light weapons specialist, which was just a fancy name for the machine-gunner. And Henderson was, at least for now, the XO, but he was technically there to replace Gallaway, who was about a month "short".

Attached to this 12- (or, temporarily, 13-) man team was a 150-man company (although they called themselves a "battalion") of Cambode "Chan" montagnard "mercenaries", who'd been recruited from the recently-disbanded and quaintly-named Cambodian "KKK" (*Khmer Kampuchea Krom*). Plus a 100-man company of ARVN "Regional

Forces/Popular Forces" — known by the Americans indulgently, if not quite affectionately, as "Ruff-Puffs". An interesting "family", then, that hunkered at Camp Happy Holidays. Motley, certainly, but not-ineffective and even, when conditions were right, quite lethal.

+ + + + + +

A tour in Vietnam was a lot like a fingerprint. Or like a snowflake: Each man's tour had its own trajectory, and was quite unique.

But as it happened, Henderson's hadn't turned out very much differently from what he'd expected: Because beyond the individuality of everyone's experiences, there were many things that pertained in South Vietnam that were constant, immutable, and affected everybody in an American uniform that spent time there. And this was certainly true in the Dak Phuoc AO. Things such as:

The red dirt, of course, but also the ubiquitous red dust or red mud that came from it and found its way everywhere and into every blessed thing, well beyond the roads. And then, next to, above, around and beyond the red roads there was the enveloping green of the vegetation that almost immediately became jungle. (Ask any Vietnam veteran what colors he associates with the place, and he'll answer: green and red. With perhaps brown thrown in, for the shit.)

Nights so dark that black didn't seem to do justice to the word — it was indescribable, really, a brooding, limitless *void* — or lack of presence — like what the men presumed might be meant by the term "black hole", which, for what it was worth, was what Henderson chose to call his own personal foxhole, out there on the Inner Defense Perimeter. He'd even made a little sign to that effect. HENDERSON'S BLACK HOLE. The guys had thought that was semi-funny and had asked the Captain if he was gonna call his position "Gallaway's Black Hole", but he'd just responded with "Fuck you all you idiots" and had put up a little sign on the lip of *his* firing position that said HENDERSON-FREE ZONE. But that was just what passed for yuks out there where, in fact, the two officers got along fine — Captain Gallaway even called Lieutenant Henderson, who he towered over by a good eight inches, "Li'l Buddy", (though *that* was as much an ironic reference to TV's Gilligan as it was to any conventional friendship). Emotions were surprisingly nuanced in combat zones, where it was a big mistake by external observers to suppose that they were stunted or suppressed. On the contrary, emotions were just more primal, distorted and volatile in combat circumstances than in civilian life — but certainly no less "real" and complicated for that.

Sweat every day; sweat even in the rain. Sweaty became the body's Default Condition.

Then there were the people, the people of Dak Phuoc village:

Squawking old crones, squatting there in their dirty black silk pajamas, their betel-bathed mouths looking like someone had popped a small grenade in there.

Naked toddlers and young children, with pot bellies and stick-like limbs, snot-nosed, always either laughing or crying — never, it seemed, anything in between — friendly, imploring, often brazen, sometimes treacherous. Shortly after Henderson arrived in Dak Phuoc they got word that down in Saigon two guys from the 9th ID had gotten blown away, in a "Saigon-tea" bar, and a couple others badly wounded, when a little boy had entered, left a shoeshine box with a grenade in it, and run away. There had been silence in the hooch among the four members of A132-C that night when, over beers, the story had been recounted. Until Spec-5 Daniels, the team's junior medic, had piped up: "*Shoe*shine? The *fuck*?"

Gnarled, toothless old men whose deeply-creased bronze-colored faces were, along with their allegiances, truly questions wrapped in enigmas wrapped in riddles, which themselves were wrapped in tea-leaves. Not to mention opium balls and even, in particularly dire cases, animal entrails. (What one *hoped* were animal entrails.) One reason that old people seemed to figure so prominently was that there concomitantly appeared to be precious few villagers of either sex between the ages of ten and sixty — any males being most likely either in the ARVN or dead, and any females between, say, fifteen and fifty were either working in or running the Saigon Tea establishments of Nha Trang.

And then the endless *pok-pok-pok* of helicopters, which was a kind of "white noise" that soon, for the newly-arrived troop, settled into being somewhere between annoying and reassuring.

The equally ubiquitous static, hisses, squelches and squawks escaping from the half-dozen or so radios of differing sizes and configurations that were permanently turned on in the commo room of every unit's inevitable TOC (Tactical Operations Center).

The spectacular "fireworks" display of rockets, flares, tracers, and other military illumination that went on every night, without fail, that was ass-puckering deadly bad news for *someone, somewhere...* but, if one wasn't that particular someone at any given moment, could be as awesomely beautiful as any civilian fireworks show back in the World. (Although the converse of this was that it would permanently spoil any future anodyne fireworks shows for a lot of these guys in later civilian life. For those that made it back, that is....)

And in Camp Happy Holidays itself, as no doubt in every other semi-permanent American military position in South Vietnam: Ammo boxes, ammo cases, loose ammo, expended ammo brass, empty cans of Hamms, Schlitz and Carling Black Label, empty C-Ration cans and boxes, cigarette butts, empty cigarette packs and other grunt detritus. Despite the A132-C Team's best efforts, which, by Army standards in Vietnam, were better than most, you could never keep the place as policed-up as it was supposed to be.

The permanent stink of the latrine, made worse by the periodic burning of the shit. For real. (Civilians — don't ask.)

And the constant bouquet of *other* stinks — dead fish, rotten fish, sick flesh, dead flesh, rotten flesh, expended ordnance, fuel exhaust, the aforementioned sweat, and... more shit... *different shit*, shit from elsewhere than the latrine, civilian shit. You got used to it. That was one of the problems — you got used to *every* damn thing....

The same green fatigues, long since turned reddish-brown, the color of bricks, from that fucking invasive laterite. The same green jungle boots long since turned into virtual mud themselves *by* the mud, and the same piece of broken mirror to shave into twice a week. The shaving might be haphazard, but the one bit of personal hygiene that the men stubbornly *did* cling to, no matter what, was brushing their teeth; their toothbrushes became like talismans — their irreducible, residual link to their former, more innocent existence — and they carried their toothbrushes *some*where on their persons, at all times.

The camp's inner perimeter with its individual firing positions and sandbagged bunkers, and its outer perimeter festooned with concertina wire and studded with planted Claymore mines — a seemingly-intricate and formidable but in fact rather flimsy and threadbare defensive set-up that only brought home the unnerving realization that "we only hold the ground we lie on, and we're not even so sure about *that*".

The ex-Cambode KKKs, their skin the color of teak, their necks dashingly adorned with scarves made from ripped parachutes — they looked like jaunty little brown Errol Flynns. In contrast to the ARVN Regional Forces "Ruff-Puffs", who were for the most part scared, secretive, bitter about yesterday, uncertain about today, and yearning only to be alive tomorrow.

These things never changed. Day after day. One hundred, two hundred, three hundred days. Days, in fact became meaningless; very soon after arriving in-country you stopped tracking — and the year was punctuated not by fixed, commemorative dates such as birthdays and Back-In-The-World holidays, but by guys' injuries or, occasionally, deaths. Or, more mundanely, guys' in-country arrivals and of course, the Holy Grail, the "DEROS", the date of one's projected departure. Or promotions — around about his fourth month in-country Henderson was informed by the Group 1st Sergeant in Nha Trang that he'd been promoted to 1st Lieutenant, and in filling out the paperwork for this huge, *hah hah,* occasion he realized that at some point his birthday had come and gone some weeks ago without his even noticing and that he was now a year older than when he'd arrived. *Woop de doo, Trung Uy.*

But in addition to the Constants, there were other things that were more fleeting... ephemeral. Like, obviously, his friends, his team-mates of A132-Charley:

This Captain, here, for instance, this Marcellus Gallaway — six-foot-seven, from Greenwood, Mississippi. He'd been a good student and high school football star, but it was his mama, who worked as the resident and traveling nurse at the LeFlore County courthouse, who'd browbeaten the local congressman down there, a white Democrat, to "do de raht thaing fo' once" and appoint her boy to West Point.

Gallaway was indeed an impressive fellow — his looming athletic bulk alone assured that. Although he *did* have the off-putting habit, when pissed off, (which he permitted himself to be more often than most company-grade officers), of calling anyone and everyone — especially the Vietnamese — a "stupid fumb-duck nigger". And on top of everything else, Gallaway (reminiscent to Henderson of his old pal Littletree back at OCS), had some Choctaw in him, which only added to his exotic mystique. In fact, the Vietnamese, who called him "The Giant Bear" (*Con gấu khổng lồ*), weren't even completely convinced that he wasn't some specimen of parallel humanity. He was more feared than liked by these locals, which, as everyone knows, is the better of the two — if you can't have both.

Gallaway was finishing up his second tour in-country, and by now he'd picked up a little usable Viet and even some Chan, so all in all he was a right piece of work, equipped with a damn good idea of what the hell was going on around him and able to project a certain rough young James Earl Jones-ish dignity... even, when he put his considerable heft into it, *gravitas*.

But on the other hand, it had to be said that Gallaway was also, in the end, somewhat... well, lazy, so Henderson, as #2, had had to shoulder a lot of the consequences of that. Which meant assuming responsibilities and humping a little more than he otherwise might have had to — but it did help to "orient" (*orientate* in Armese) Henderson pretty damn quick.

Being the only two officers at Camp Happy Holidays, it would have been understandable if Captain Gallaway and Lieutenant Henderson had become either fast friends or else, though less likely, rancorous rivals. But in reality neither of those two eventualities was the case, during the four weeks or so that their tours overlapped, and instead what evolved between them was a relationship of reserved and respectful cordiality. Although on only two occasions could it be said that true, vulnerable humanity intruded into their smooth working *modus operandi:*

One night they were expecting to be hit by a *serious* assault by what the enemy called a sapper (an old term inherited from the French which originally meant "engineer" but which had come to mean, in commie-talk, "commando") reinforced company that they called a battalion, from the thrice-fucked 105B NVA Division which operated in their AO. They didn't need any intel reports to tell them this, as they could actually *hear* the clanking treads and the diesel whine of, according to one of their Observation Posts, at least four enemy T-54 tanks as they approached in the night from the west, preparing for a dawn attack.

Where the fuck are our *tanks,* wondered Henderson, *and meanwhile what I wouldn't give to have all those assholes in the media and on campus back home who keep yellin' about us bein' up against "poor peasants in black pajamas and flip-flops made outta inner-tubes and carryin' muzzle-loaders"... over* here, *with us,* raht *fuckin' now, tonight....*

While everyone was hustling, Alamo-style, to and from the perimeters throughout the night in preparation for the attack, Gallaway was checking with the Chan and Ruff-Puff commanders to make sure their guys were present, accounted-for and ready to rumble. And Henderson was on the horn to the Air Force F-4s in Tuy Hoa, alerting them to get ready for a bit of sport in this sector very shortly, as well as preparing the dust-off choppers in Nha Trang. After which he switched to another frequency on his radio and checked with his one LP (Listening Post) and two OPs (Observation Posts) that they remembered how and where to get back into the perimeter so they wouldn't get zapped by their own guys. In the middle of this gigantic and tense clusterfuck, Gallaway and Henderson had at one point bumped into each other, and as they passed, Gallaway had turned back and said,

"Yo, Henderston, wait one — do me a favor. It may be the shit *really* gonna hit it tonight, an' if I don' make it an' you do, here," and he scribbled something onto a ripped sheet from his pocket notebook, "here, this where my ma an' grandma are at, in Greenwood. Please, mah man, if I don' make it, I'd like for you t'be the one go see 'em. I don' want some fuckin' leg-ass REMF" (Rear-End Mother-Fucker) "from D.C. bustin' their ass. You'll do."

Even in the middle of all the fear, confusion and adrenaline, Henderson had been taken aback.

"Sure thing, Gallaway. But shit, you'll make it just fine — you the fuckin' Magic Bear, man. *A*nyone doesn't make it, most like it'll be me. So here," and he'd ripped out a page from *his* pocket notebook on which he scribbled *his* coordinates — or rather those of Junior and Geraldine.

A most weird little scene indeed.

In the event, of course, neither of them had been killed by the NVA, though not for lack of trying by those tough little motherfuckers-from-hell. By the time the sun was fully risen they counted 3 Chans and 7 ARVN Ruff-Puffs killed, and a total of about 15 wounded. Oh, and Sgt. (three-stripe) McAdoo, the country boy from Saugerties NY (*"Fuckin' Woodstock, man!"*) who was one of their two heavy weapons specialists, got a 6-stitch cut on his cheek from a random piece of hot flying something.

But they hadn't been overrun. That was the big thing. The withdrawing NVA had dragged their own casualties, including their dead, back with them, so it was impossible to evaluate the *dommage* inflicted on them — except for two of those fucking T-54s, which had been taken out by a couple of direct hits from the team's plentiful supply of little M-72 LAWs (Light Antitank Weapons). Later that day, when the hulks had stopped smoking, the men of A132-Charley had had their group and individual pictures taken posing on the most photogenic of the enemy tanks, the one with blood visible on the turret and even down its sides, with their little Kodak Instamatics.

Yes, that night had certainly been a pisser.

Then there had been another night, a quieter one:

It had been pouring down buckets, but at least the fucking fucks from the NVA 105B Division were off hunkering down in *their* shitholes, or shit-tunnels, or whatever. Gallaway and Henderson were spending some relatively infrequent time together, in the Commo Bunker, monitoring the traffic on the various radio nets — from other SF Teams in their Dak Phuoc/Phuoc Long sector, but also from Nha Trang and even from Danang and Saigon. Listening in on the other freqs was really the only way you got to know what was happening even in your own fucking AO, never mind in the wider fucking war, and one of the two of them was usually attempting to do it, but this was a rare moment when they found themselves doing it together.

In fact they were taking advantage of the situation to do some chilling ("chilling" was hip new Amerikan parlance, back then), sucking down Carling Black Labels and smoking. Cigarettes, that is, not the other. Mentholated Salems, as it happened — Henderson had picked up the menthol habit back in Basic and AIT from his black fellow trainees, one of whom he'd once asked about this apparent black menthol-predilection, and had been answered "Memphol give us bruthas a legal hah, Hennerman, but ah pretty sho' it don' work on you honkies, too bad, yo." And sure enough, Henderson had never detected any "high" — much less "hah" — but he *did* like the hint of peppermint.

Things had definitely been sort of mellow, (*also* hip new parlance back then), that night, even though by the crackling sound of it over the horn, the poor fuckers from the 1st of the 7th (of the 4th Infantry Division) were having a bookoo shitty night of it over in Gia Quac District. Gallaway popped two fresh Black Labels. They were discussing the relative merits of Wilson Pickett, Otis Redding, Ben E. King, Ray Charles, James Brown, Sam and Dave, Joe Tex and Solomon Burke:

"Yeah, but the best of *all* was a guy you never heard of, Henderston, a dude called Chuck Willis. Wore a turban. A *fucking turban*, mah man. Had a hit song called 'Betty And Dupree', I don't think a better blues tune was ever written. Drank himself to death at the age of thirty-two — his last record was called 'What Am I Living For?'."

"I'll check 'im out, if I ever get outta here. You sure know this R & B shit, don't you, Gallaway,"

"Bet y'ass I do. Sheet, I was brought up on it. White folks had wallpaper, we had R & B." He paused. Then, "I tell you what — after I've done my twenty, I'm gonna go ta law school on the GI Bill — "

"They still got that? I thought that was old World War Two-Korea stuff."

"Naaa, it still exists, I checked it out — you jess need to know where ta look. Anyway, my plan is to go ta law school, and become a music lawyer — big bucks in that shit, better believe it. Set myself up, most likely in Memphis. I been checkin' things out, up there, last time I was on leave.... Already written to the U a Tennessee law school — watch my fuckin' smoke, young el tee...."

"Geez, Gallaway, you somethin' else. The Man with the Plan."

"Damn right. What about you, Bush Pig — Bush Pig my ass!, by the way, no offense — what you figure to do when you get outta this shit?"

"I dunno. I'm *here* 'cause I didn't know what the fuck else to do. Maybe I'll follow you to Memphis, but without the law school — I couldn't begin to even *think* about any a that law school crap. Me *bookoo fini* with any fuckin' school, man. Maybe I'll just learn to play the bass — how hard can *that* fucker be? — and join a band. If I hang around you, you can introduce me to whoever needs a bass player. Hell, you can be my lawyer. I'll be like a white Duck Dunn."

"Duck Dunn *is* white."

"Yeah, I knew that — I think. I mean I'll be a*nother* Duck Dunn. In a band like the M.G.'s. You can be my personal lawyer and negotiate between me an' all the groupies."

"Yeah, I like that. Between the groupies. Kinky. Right on, Henderston — you'll do." "You'll do" had turned out to be Gallaway's only term of praise, but he used it generously. When he wasn't calling you a "fumb-duck nigger", that was — which, it had to be said, he'd never called Henderson.

When Gallaway rotated back to The World at the end of Henderson's first month, the Team had a small ceremony for him in the Commo Bunker, enlivened by Gary U.S. Bonds howling loudly on the communal Akai reel-to-reel tape machine from Hong Kong and pushed along by bookoo Johnny Walker Red. The men presented the Cap with the requisite teak plaque that they'd ordered from the shop that made this crap in Nha Trang, which bore the message,

For CPT Marcellus Gallaway from the men of A132-C

Dak Phuoc, RVN '70-'71.

"RESPECT"

and the equally requisite engraved Zippo, from the same shop, that said:

CPT M. GALLAWAY,

Dak Phuoc, RVN

"Numbah 1 Fumb Duck"

And later that night, on his cot under the mosquito net, the Bush Pig was struck with the dawning realization that the war would be a whole different ballgame for him now, with Gallaway gone. He wouldn't feel as safe, for starters. If you could even use that word in the circumstances.

But Gallaway's departure turned out to usher in an even greater sea-change than a mere loss of a feeling of relative safety: At first, the now in-command Henderson had felt somehow a little... bereft. Even though he was surrounded by a dozen of his Green Beret brothers, for a few days there, as the only American officer out in Camp Happy Holidays, he'd felt more personally alone than he ever had in his life.

But that only lasted a couple of days: The very next NVA probe of the perimeter, which was not long in coming, caused him to get his shit together *right* smartly, as it rudely sank in to him that *there's no one fuckin' else, man,* no one to turn to — that he was in charge now, and that if he didn't stop feeling sorry for himself and moping about the loss of the Gallaway crutch, he wouldn't make it the hell out of here in one piece. And a good thing he did, too, because it was almost like the NVA 105B Division was waiting for Gallaway to de-ass the area for them to ramp up their already considerable efforts.

But OK then — he might still have a couple of months to go in his 23rd year, but he was the goddamn Boss around here, now, and no mistake. For the rest of Henderson's tour, there would be a low-level, if permanent, rumor out of 5th Group Hqs that an XO, a brandy new 2nd John fresh out of Ft. Bragg, might be on his way... but, in the event, the poor guy only showed up just days before Henderson himself was rotating the hell out. The Bush Pig had just had the time to introduce him around and give him all the necessary codes and call signs, pat him on the shoulder and tell him "Don't worry, man, you'll be OK...." But that would come later....

In the meantime, there had definitely been some outstanding guys in A-Team 132-Charley, the command of which Henderson now assumed. In fact, they were as damn fine specimens of American male-itude as you could find anywhere, if maybe a little... well, *idiosyncratic.* As Gallaway had liked to say, specially if, heaven forbid, they might be taking stick from "legs", brass, REMFs or whoever — "Hey, we 'special' — it says so right on the package."

The youngest member, Spec-5 Ronnie Newhouser, from Grafton, New Hamphsire, one of the commo specialists. A skinny, likable pothead of a kid who, in about Henderson's 8th month, had somehow managed to get himself the clap in that supremely unromantic rat-hole of a hamlet of Dak Phuoc. The penicillin that Simmons, one of their two medics, had jammed in his ass over his squawking protests ("Hey Doc, don' bother, man, I can cure myself *by sheer willpower,* I done it once before, in Cam Ranh, I got th' ability — save your juice for peo — OUCH! — gah-*damn*, man....") hadn't even started to work when the kid was shot to death by mistake by some anonymous, nervous KKK trooper on the perimeter when he, Newhouser, was returning from a 3-man recon patrol one evening at dusk.

Jesus Humphrey fucking Christ on a fucking crutch, that had been just a *great* fucking scene — the whole fucking camp had opened fire on itself and kept it up for a full fucking minute before a horripilated and frantic Henderson had been able to get the goddamn idiots to stop firing.

And, of course, being the Team CO, he'd caught a huge and embarrassing ration of shit from the pogues, his overseeing Chairborne Rangers, back at Group in Nha Trang — but by now Henderson had progressed long past the stage of giving even a semblance of a rat's ass of what anyone in those air-conditioned offices thought. *If* they thought, which he seriously doubted.

No, the thing that troubled him most about the whole fucking episode, quite apart from losing the kid Newhouser, was writing The Letter to Newhouser's people: He didn't need to think about it overly long before deciding *I'm not gonna bust those poor people's balls with any bullshit about "friendly fire" — you shitting me?* And he'd written them that their boy had died bravely, which of course he had, in an NVA ambush, which was a *little* more problematic, but fuck it, it was Close Enough For Government Work.

And then, of course, he had to get on the horn with Group S-1 to start the seemingly endless bureaucratic haggling for a replacement commo specialist.... a sad, bad business.

Who else?

Staff Sergeant Vincent X. Rogers, from Theodosia, Missouri, whose body was very hairy — he'd laugh at his own story when he told of how a Saigon Tea Girl had once screeched at him, preparatory to Getting Down To Business, "Aaawww! You look like big *maw*nkey, hee hee hee!" — and who was always being told by the brass to shave even when he'd just done so scant hours previously, the senior heavy weapons specialist.

Rogers had been kicked out of OCS for cheating (or *try*ing to cheat) on a written exam — on Military Justice, of all things. The Reassignment Board had noted his Airborne status and "Expert" qualifications with the M-60 machine gun, 81mm mortar and M-67 Recoilless Rifle and in a rare burst of wisdom and prescience, had decided not to bust him to E-1 and send him to a line unit, but rather, as one Board member put it, "let the Green Beanie weirdoes deal with him".

One day, the two of them, Henderson and Rogers, had been standing around, waiting out on Camp Happy Holiday's main LZ for a re-supply slick to come take out a couple of Chan WIAs and maybe also bring them some much-needed radio batteries and maybe even the goddamn mail, and, just to make conversation, Henderson had asked Rogers what had motivated him to enlist in the first place; (there were no draftees in the Special Forces) — "Not, heh heh, that yer not a fuckin' outstanding adjunct to the team, ya understand — jest wondering..." (Henderson was most interested in two things about his fellow troops: Where they were from, and why they'd enlisted.)

"Well, El Tee, everybody's gotta be *some*where. I mean, I guess." Then Rogers started doodling in the red dirt of the LZ — they'd been, for some reason, squatting — and added, in a more pensive tone, "But not to worry, sir, soon, none of us'll be nowhere." Something like a *frisson* had run through Henderson at these words, and he would often thought back on them. *That shit would make someone a fine fucking epitaph*, he remembered thinking at the time....

Sgt. (three stripe) Johnny Ray Twist, from Trafalgar, Indiana, where he'd grown up on a dairy farm and had been an Eagle Scout — the senior commo specialist. And although it wasn't one of an A-Team's official Specialties, Jay-Are (as Henderson had christened him, in honor of Junior) had established himself as A132-Charley's resident expert tracker. He was part Shawnee, on his dad's side, (*Holy cow, seems like there's a lotta Indians and part-Indians in the Army, jeez, fuck me* it had occurred to Henderson) but this skill was not "native". As he put it, one night, to Henderson:

"When I was a boy scout — fuckin' Eagle — as a kid, because I was part-injun everyone figured I had to be some kinda expert in trackin' and wind talkin' and all that s'posedly injun bullshit, like I was fuckin' Tonto or somethin', you know? But instead a fighting it, I figured, why th' fuck not? It might be cool — specifically it might help with pickin' up chicks, ya know? — the hippie ones, anyway. So I taught myself trackin'.

I started with a book I found in the school library. Turns out, it ain't magic — just a matter a payin' attention ta li'l details and knowin' what to look for. Cute tricks to do with acorns an' moss an' pine-cones an' shit like that. Wind and shade and that crap enters into it, too, quite a lot, actually. But it ain't no big deal, really — hell, even Sergeant Kraut could pick it up...."

Did someone mention Sergeant Kraut? Staff Sergeant (four stripe) Hans-Jochen Hübel, from Faytetteville, North Carolina, one of the team's intelligence specialists who, although eight years an American citizen, still managed to sound like Hogan's Colonel Klink when he'd say things like:

"Dere voss zome more Fee-Cee bolitgal shits brobagandizing in das fill-age egaine lest night, Cherry."

Hübel was the most fearless motherfucker Henderson had ever known; he handled enemy booby traps in ways that most normal people wouldn't handle a bar of soap. Fucking Hübel. (When Henderson had first met him, and learned that he made his home in Fayetteville, it had occurred to him to ask *ze Cherman* if he happened to know a young *hausfrau* back there called Petra... but he'd quickly decided against it.)

In the event, Hübel got shot right through his right hand in a firefight one night on the Cambode border, but it wasn't as bad as it looked — though it was still bad enough to get him his return ticket punched, and he de-assed Vietnam, (Republic of), honorably with his "Burble Heart", smelling like a rose. He'd shouted *"Goot pie! Oll off you! I vill miss you!"* when the slick took him off to Nha Trang on his way home, and every-one at Camp Happy Holidays missed him.

Missed him....

That was the second worst thing about combat: missing people. You got attached to guys, in strange, intense but completely non-sexual ways that were inconceivable back home "on the block" — and then suddenly they were gone, either from occasionally being wounded and medevaced, or even more occasionally, killed. But mostly just from end-of-tour rotation. *Boom!* one minute the guy was *there,* and the next minute he was gone. It was emotionally... jarring, though it was never something you'd even acknowledge to yourself — not as such, anyway — much less vocalize to your buddies, those who, like you, remained in-country.

The *first* worst thing about combat, of course, were the occasional, but inevitable, spasms of being terminally shit-scared that you were about to die, or have important — even vital — bits of your body blown away. But those episodes inevitably passed (or if they didn't you either didn't know about it, or else your concerns had moved on to another level), and afterwards you experienced a *fucking hell, I'm still alive!* euphoria that rivaled anything offered by the best drugs or even sex.

But to come back to the "missing people" — the "Missing Those That Were No Longer A Part Of Your Life" thing:

It began, of course, with missing the people (and specifically the girls) who you'd left back home.

But soon, as you got into your Vietnam tour, usually around the second or third week, those fine folks back in The World all receded into a cherished but hazy past, and your emotional attention began to turn to missing the guys who were killed, or wounded, or just rotated back, *right next to you, right here*. It was weird, and unprecedented in these men's emotional histories, (such as they were): specifically, *you had no idea what happened to the guys after they left:*

The dead guys — Where were they now? Some small-town cemetery? Arlington? Heaven? Or disappeared down the Memory Hole?

And the WIAs — Had they died on their way home? Or were they getting better? If so, where? Did they feel bitter? Or were they in too much pain for even that? Or maybe just relieved to be out of it? Would they even maybe be coming back? (Some did....)

And the guys whose tours had merely ended — They'd been as close as biological brothers here at Camp Happy Holidays, but would henceforth revert to being unknown — anonymous — back In The World, back On The Block. Whatever. Wherever. Did they miss us?

It was all so evanescent. (Not that many of them would have been familiar with that word, but its meaning haunted all of them nevertheless.)

One thing was for sure, though: As long as you remained in a combat situation, you missed 'em all — and you found yourself regretting the absence of an ever-increasing number of people... it was like you carried around with you your own personal AWOL/MIA roster that kept, dishearteningly, lengthening. The whole thing was a depressing fucking business, for sure, and you had to be made of tough stuff to function — let alone prevail — in it.

Each one of them would learn what fighting men had learned since armies had existed: That relationships between men in combat were unlike anything else in the whole Human Experience: Sentiment plus black humor plus asperity plus stoicism, all distilled in a simmering soup of impending dismemberment and death — it was quite a heady emotional cocktail.

So as a result, cynicism reigned. It turned out that nothing in the world — no thing — was a more dependable generator of cynicism than combat. In fact, it could be said that the universe that existed under a camo-covered steel pot was the *home* of Cynicism, Inc., pure and simple.

And in addition to the previously-mentioned fireworks that returning combat vets weren't overly crazy about, one could add Halloween. Once you've lived the *real* Halloween, it was hard to get it up for the official one.

+ + + + + + +

One fucking episode in particular would keep recurring to Henderson like a goddamn monstrous fatigue-draped scarecrow rising from some hideous rice paddy-sized open sewer:

It had been about mid-day, early in Henderson's 10th month. He'd been with his radioman, the junior commo specialist, Spec 5 Cleotis Jones, a likably wiseass black electronics whiz-kid from the supremely misnamed "Gold Coast" slums of Detroit who'd enlisted at seventeen — after the Marines had turned him down for being underage. The two of them, Henderson and Jones, had taken a squad of ARVN Ruff-Puffs with them to check out a report they'd received from an old Dak Phuoc papa-*san*, who'd told Hübel (just before he'd de-assed with his holed hand) that they'd seen some NVAs hiding weapons and boxes of ammo in this certain spot by "their" creek, little Song Phuoc.

The patrol had indeed found a cache of about eighty old Soviet SKSs, but only two boxes of 7.62 ammo. *Strange.... Still....* Henderson had photographed all this with his little Instamatic, for whoever'd be replacing Hübel the intel guy, after which he popped a couple of grenades into the pile. He then had the guys dump the twisted remains into the rocky stream, and then they headed back.

They were about four hundred meters from the Happy Holidays perimeter. Henderson was carrying his own PRC-25 radio because Jones was up front, walking point. The kid tripped a line which pulled a Soviet F-1 grenade out of a container that rolled next to his rooted, booted feet. Jones was still staring, bug-eyed, at the thing, when, a half-second later, it went off — ripping off both his legs at the hip. And not clean, like amputations, no, it was more as though some horrendous giant had just *pulled* Jones' legs off, like maybe one would do with an overly-cooked chicken.

By the time Henderson had got to him, Jones had hemorrhaged away about half of all the blood he contained, and Henderson could see immediately that the poor fuck was done for. Henderson lifted Jones' head and cradled in in his arms. Jones, *yo, mah main man!* Jones. There he was, quivering — half man, half chopped sirloin steak. Seeing Henderson, he'd squeaked, in a high, un-Jones-like voice, "Sir, what...."

And that had been the merciful end of Jones. Spec-5 Cleotis Robinson "The Piston" Jones, not-quite 19 years old, blood type O, No Religious Preference. Truth be told, he'd been something of a rising-star hoodlum in some Mau Mau gang or other back in Detroit, and he'd only enlisted half a step ahead of the law. But he'd turned out to be a model soldier, had shown remarkable aptitude at getting field radios to work when others couldn't, had done well in jump school and had somehow managed to bullshit his way into the Special Forces. Anyway, Henderson had liked his cocky steadfastness and had personally chosen him as his RTO. And now the dude was *gone*, and Henderson's ears pounded and banged and his eyes misted, and he puked until he thought he'd puked himself inside out. And then he began to shake.

Some of the ARVN Ruff-Puffs had gone on back to the perimeter to raise the team's acting XO, Master Sergeant Montrose, who'd come out, bringing with him another detail. Together they'd wrapped up Jones, along with whatever bits of his legs — including a boot with a foot still in it — that they could collect, and they'd all humped their way back to Camp Happy Holidays. During all this, Henderson didn't seem to be able to say much. Or even so much as a single word.

Later that night, in the clapped-out rickety little wooden hooch that served as his combination CP and sleeping quarters, Henderson's eyes had actually teared-up, as he shakily sipped from his bottle of Johnny Walker Red — the only time in his entire young life that he'd ever remembered even coming *close* to crying....

The next day Henderson had written to Jones' grandmother in Detroit, the kid's designated Next Of Kin according to the Info Card the S-1 in Nha Trang had on him:

"Ma'am, your grandson was a fine, fine man. He was the best of the best, and he died bravely, in the service of his country. I and the whole team of which he was a cherished and valued member and brother, share your grief and pain. Yours sincerely, J. J. Henderson, 1LT US Army (5th Special Forces Group), Republic of Vietnam".

Jesus Fucked-Up Christ.... Jesus Fucked-Up Christ....

11/ 0940 HOURS

"The deed is all, not the glory."

— EDWARD C. BYERS JR.

Not long after Jones' death, Henderson had received a letter from Robin. Actually, it wasn't even a letter, but one of those engraved wedding announcement cards:

> The Honorable and Madam Thurston B. McPompous,
> The Fourth, Are So Goddamn Ecstatic To Announce
> That They've Finally Managed To Fob Off Their Only
> Daughter The Lovely And Nubile If Unfortunately
> Horse-Faced Arabella Onto The Bewildered And
> Still-Bepimpled Young Master Kevin....

— one of those.

Only Robin (or whoever had sent out the invites) had gotten Henderson's APO number all fucked up, and by the time the wretched thing had reached him she was already three months married, and Henderson just had to laugh. The thought crossed his mind to send Robin and her NEWSWEEK asshole a wedding present — maybe Jonesy's jungle boot with his foot still in it — make an exotic addition to the trendy, eclectic "The New Irony" décor in the newlyweds' new home in (so it said in the invite) Ardsley, NY... if they were still married, that is — it *had* been over three months, after all.... Or maybe treat NEWSWEEK to an anonymous letter: "Dear Sir or Madam: I have it on good authority that one of your hip and with-it young cinema reviewers — the one that was in South America with Dennis Hopper — is secretly in the employ of the Central Intelligence Agency. Yours sincerely, A Friend". *Yeah, talk about your "New Irony"... Ah, but no... none of that... fuck it — just... fuck it... as Jonesy himself used to say, "It don' mean nothin'"....*

Here, the goddamn village of Dak Phuoc had just been "visited" again. Last night, in fact. The Mayor (more accurately, the Chief), an amiable farmer called Nguyen Loan, was found in the morning, dead, with his throat cut. And his wife and four kids — and, it seemed, two other random kids as well — had been abducted. An "officially"-mimeographed notice had been left on the Mayor's table in the main room of his crappy little house, that read, in Viet,

THIS IS THE FATE THAT AWAITS ALL COLLABORATORS WITH THE IMPERIALISTS AND THE PUPPETS.

RALLY TO THE PEOPLE'S LIBERATION ARMED FORCES.

(PRESENT THIS DOCUMENT FOR SAFE PASSAGE)

Or maybe I could send this *to Robin and her dork new husband,* thought Henderson, as he pocketed this NVA-printed missive, to pass on later to Sgt. (three stripe) Reece, Hübel's replacement intel specialist who'd finally pitched up. In any case, *Good for you, Robin... good for NEWS-WEEK.*

+ + + + + + +

After the death of Cleotis Jones, things seemed to go downhill, if you could even use such an expression under the circumstances that pertained at that time in the Vietnam-Cambodia border area of Phuoc Long Province, for Henderson and Team A132-Charlie.

Ironically enough, their particular corner of the conflict had become the focal point for the NVA's "retrenchment" that was the result of the successful Nixon-Abrams Vietnamization campaign, so while things might be winding down in much of the rest of South Vietnam, here in the vicinity of Dak Phuoc the shit was *increasingly* hitting the fan, as the NVA moved back into Cambodia: The Chans and the Ruff-Puff Regional Forces were taking fearful casualties. Now this might be (as Henderson suggested in his periodic Sitreps to the brass in Nha Trang) due to their, the Allies', new-found post-Vietnamization aggressiveness, but nevertheless, the result was that it seemed that whenever they killed an NVA troop, three more, seemingly more dangerously desperate, were in the jungle the next day to take his place.

Moreover, Henderson no longer enjoyed going out on patrols. No, check that — he'd never actually *enjoyed* any of this shit, but... it had seemed right to him, and he knew what he was doing. And, in fact, he did it well. But now he was beginning to dread it. *Fuck me, am I finally beginning to "burn out"? Christ, maybe I am. Hell, it happens to everyone else — why wouldn't it happen to me? I mean, I never claimed to be fuckin' Superman, did I...still, fuckin' hell....*

+ + + + + + +

Things for Henderson finally achieved a kind of grisly, hair-raising and only partly-cathartic critical mass in an absolutely insane episode that occurred not long after the death of Cleotis Jones:

It had been at mid-dawn. (In Vietnam, where over half of all engagements occurred at daybreak, the guys had taken, in their bull sessions and after-action reports and suchlike, to distinguishing between early-dawn, mid-dawn and late-dawn). Henderson had been moving along the paddy-side part of the perimeter, checking that everyone was awake that was supposed to be awake.

At that same time that Henderson was doing that, out over on the other side of the main paddy that abutted Camp Happy Holidays, just inside the tree-line, about two hundred and fifty meters away, one of their LPs was packing up, preparing to head back in to camp. That LP, that night, had consisted of three guys: A132-C's most junior member since Newhouser's death, heavy weapons-expert Spec 5 Tim Conover, from Lumber City Ferry, Wisconsin, and two Ruff-Puffs, a 50-year old part-time farmer and his 17-year old nephew.

Conover was just handing his "Prick-6" radio to the papa-*san* so the old man could alert the gunners on the perimeter wire, in Viet, that they were heading in, and so not to fire — when the three of them were opened up on by half a dozen black-clad NVA sappers who *also* happened to be lurking in that corner of the woods that morning, and who'd decided to pounce on the LP as a target of opportunity.

The crisp, pristine dawn silence had been rent by the horribly unmistakable sound of AK fire, as well as the yells of the Ruff-Puffs and shouts from Conover, which were amplified across the still water of the rice paddy. And Henderson, looking up from exchanging pleasantries with a couple of Chans in their M-60 machine gun position, had just lost it. Just fucking *lost it.*

Spitting out *"Ga-DA-mmit to fucking fuck, already — ga-DA-mmit to fucking SHIT...!"*, he grabbed up the M-60 by the handle and yelled *"Open the fuckin' wire!"*. The Chan machine-gunner pulled on a rope that lay near their position and a small section of the elaborate concertina wire erection slid aside to make a two-foot gap, through which Henderson now crashed — accompanied willy-nilly by the other member of the Chan machine gun team, the one who'd been feeding the ammo. This bewildered but dutiful fellow continued to rather desperately hold the ammo belt into the side of the gun with one hand while carrying a full can of M-60 ammo in the other, as together they splashed into the rice paddy.

The two of them charged through a catty-corner of the paddy, and chundered up towards the beleaguered Conover and his little LP.

As soon as he saw the four near-side black-clad NVA sappers, Henderson opened up, pouring fire into them from behind. Then he turned his gun onto the two far-side other ones, who revealed themselves as they tried to shift *their* fire onto this sudden wild-man apparition. Conover and the two Ruff-Puffs, all three already wounded, had already been prone on the ground by the time Henderson had materialized... from nowhere.

In less than five seconds, it was all over. The six NVAs were dead, with one of them damn near cut in half by Henderson's M-60 — he'd been the last of the six, which was why the Bush Pig could train extra, lingering fire on him.

Conover had taken two AK rounds, one in the shoulder and one in the hip, but would be OK — as would also be the two Ruff-Puffs, who'd each taken a round, one arm and one leg-each.

Master Sergeant Montrose joined them about two minutes later, and set about relieving Henderson (who once again, just as he had been after Jones' death, seemed incapable of speech) of the Chans' machine gun, and then used Conover's radio to urgently summon whatever medic was handy. The veteran Master Sergeant then organized the policing up of the NVA bodies. The wounded Papa-*san*, although bleeding from a leg, kept hopping about, trying to embrace the expressionless Henderson, and was most voluble in his shouted elation:

"Mistah Jelly he Nombah Wan! — he go bookoo dinky-dau, he kaka-dau aw En-Bee-Eh, he best GI, Nombah Wan fa shua, Okay! Okay! I like Mistah Jelly too match!..."

For his part, Henderson, he'd just been... terminally... *pissed off.*

After Master Sergeant Montrose (who was still, at that time, the team's Acting Executive Officer) had written up the incident and sent off the report to Nha Trang, the brass there decided to put Henderson in for a Silver Star. (If Conover hadn't been part of the LP that night, it would have been "just" a Bronze Star with "V", but because an American was among the rescued, it got bumped up.) The Special Forces had, over the years, acquired a certain priority in these matters, and the award came through remarkably quickly — a few days before Henderson's tour was up, in fact. And when the colonel at 5th Group Hqs. announced it to him over the horn, and told him he'd be physically given the medal when he passed through, on his way out — well, that had been the first that Henderson had even heard that he'd been put in for the thing, and his reflexive pleasure at the news was tempered by equal measures of astonishment and bemusement.

+ + + + + + +

And so eventually, ineluctably, Henderson's Vietnam tour came to a spluttering, frustrating, paranoid, nervous — even panicky, and short-tempered... end. And not one goddamn minute too soon.

Enough.

Enough of these fucking incoming 82mm mortar rounds whose hot searing slivers would I swear to God find you even to the center of the earth,

Enough of insane reports on AFVN and in headlines clipped out and included in guys' letters from home about such crazy shit as "Senator Proposes Reparations To North Vietnamese War Widows" — and this is in addition to the guys already being all bummed-out by fuckin' Dear John letters and hearing personal messages on little reel-to-reel tapes and even, now, cassettes that say "I'm sorry but no one supports the war anymore and I'm afraid I don't feel I can see you when you get back or even keep writing to you...",

Enough of the motherfucking jungle which is nobody's friend — nobody's, *you hear me?*

Enough of the damn people, who, in their best *moments are impassive and non-committal lumps of unresponsive shit, and whose default mode is lying, stealing, trickery and, not least, stinking of their fucking* nguoc mam.

(Even the prettiest girls stank of this vile substance. On the other hand, a Saigon-Tea Girl had once told Henderson that "You 'Big Noses' all smell like dead flesh". Well, *"You BeegNose aw sme-oo lahk dead fless!"* is what she'd *actually* said. *Holy jeez. We do?* Henderson had mentioned this to Gallaway, saying "We think they stink, and they think we stink. Ain't that great? And — good news for race relations — she goes on to report that we all stink the same, you brothers and us honkies alike." The ever-wise Captain Gallaway had said, "Yeah, Henderston, we all what we eat. That's why we should all try t'eat nothin' but dandelions and pretty bon-bons. Don't fuckin' worry about it, my, heh, brother.")

Enough of seeing guys' guts and unidentifiable organs hanging out in places they shouldn't be, such as outside their fatigues. Or on the ground. Or even hanging off of fuckin' trees, for fucks' sakes.

Henderson had had enough. How many guys — Americans from Team A132-Charlie — had he lost? *"Happy Holidays" my sweet aching white ass....* Or, come to that, how many Cambodes? How many ARVN Ruff-Puffs?

And this pinko punk cocksucker of a Senator wants to give reparation money to... NVA war widows? *Have they finally gone* totally, *irredeemably fucking nuts back home? Jesus Christ... I mean, seriously — what the* shit?

12/ 1000 HOURS

"Life is black and white after combat — war is Technicolor." — *TUCKER SMALLWOOD*

McElmore's H-34 lumbered on. Henderson dozed through the insanely loud engine drone, a frown on his face. His mind was processing more vaguely recent unpleasantries and turmoil — interrupted by the odd, fleeting flashes of what might have been recalled happiness, spasms of undefined pleasure. But regardless of those last — all in all, this was proving to be a troubled doze:

Henderson had returned to The World (well, California) at the end of the summer of 1971 a gray, pallid — if grease-creased and red-dirt-en-crusted pallid — shadow of his already not-tremendously substantial former self.

Although he *had* acquired a bit of color — at least superficial, *surface* color, that he'd don later, in the form of a whole panoply of "fruit salad": Three full rows of it, once he eventually bought it and got it all pinned on, including the new, unmistakable red-white-and-blue Silver Star ribbon, which would be topped by the all-important saxony-blue-and-silver CIB, and on the other side of his jacket, the navy-blue Presidential Unit Citation ribbon and silver South Vietnamese jump wings. To a civilian, this stuff might appear like a lot of shameless vainglory, but from one service guy to another, a uniform's decorations served as useful, time-saving wearable resumés.

Henderson's sour attitude had only partly de-fused itself by the time that, a mere few weeks after the Listening Post incident, he — again, along with some 300-odd other Gis — boarded the red-striped World Airways DC-8 "freedom bird" at Tan Son Nhut, heading back to Travis AFB. His residual pissed-offedness was definitely one of the competing emotions that clouded this magic, mythical DEROS (Date Estimated Return from Over-Seas) day that had, for a year, dangled, like a carrot in front of a beleaguered donkey, in his subconscious.

Virtually all of Henderson's boisterous fellow passengers were semi-delirious, either at the prospect of "gittin' back to some a mama's sweet apple pie" (if they were white) or "gittin' mah ass back onna block" (if they were black), but all Henderson could do was brood upon the enervating prospect of facing and responding to the questions and disapproval of a whole remembered array of friends, relations and acquaintances whose inability to even *begin* to comprehend his experience of the past year would be, he was absolutely certain, total and utterly beyond remediation.

Their refueling stop in Hawaii had been fittingly surreal. On the way over, a year ago, they'd stopped in Guam and Okinawa, but for some reason, on the return leg, the World Airways itinerary was different, and they pitched up for an hour and a half at Honolulu International.

Those three hundred returning servicemen were all in the clothes they'd been wearing on their last day of duty, i.e., yesterday, which for most of them meant combat fatigues, in various stages of stinky rottenness, and most still were more red than green, from the laterite mud and dust.

They also had very little carry-on luggage, and virtually nothing checked-in. And truth be told, they all, even the REMFs, felt uncomfortable and naked without their weapons.

In short, and taken altogether, they were a spectacularly unappealing mob, and the combined World Airways/Honolulu Airport security people and MP/SP "authorities" were particularly eager to keep them away from the general traveling public. Which in their case meant herding them to the relative Siberia of Gate C-38, the most remote Gate of the whole airport. Here they were penned into a sort of corral affair that, happily, at least contrived to include an "Aloha Bar", from where they could buy, if they had civilian American greenbacks (which most didn't, but in the delirium of the moment, many as did bought for those as didn't) beers — even if it was the local swill called "Primo" — for 75 cents and mixed drinks for $1.50. Since just hours previously they'd been paying 10 and 25 cents respectively in EM, NCO and Officers Clubs dotted throughout Vietnam, Republic Of, this represented a horrifyingly unwelcome "sticker shock" for the men. Guys who were already disoriented by the intoxicating smell of gardenias, frangipani and who-knew-what other flowery aromas that wafted around and reached even their God-forsaken nether corner of the Arrivals Hall, as well as by the snatched glimpses of halter-topped, short-shorted, mini-skirted and even bathing-suited Round-Eye pulchritude they could eyeball from behind their porous enclosure. The airport and military authorities' idea being that the said passing pulchritude should be, please God for all involved, kept as clear of their leers cheers and catcalls as possible:

"Oo baby, don' I know you? I think I know you — "

"Ayayay aloha baby I love you, I give you alla my back pay..."

"Holy crap, I wanna get off here — where do I fuckin' sign?"

Even the semi-honked-off Henderson had been affected — actually discombobulated — by the soft, otherworldly loveliness of this Paul Gauguin-meets-The Beach Boys version of The World that prevailed on that warm evening at Honolulu International....

And then this unexpected vision of heretofore un-glimpsed heaven-on-earth was snatched away as abruptly as it had been sprung on them — as too soon they all had to re-board their Freedom Bird, and a couple of short hours later they were dumped back into the stern and impersonal, if all-too familiar, ministrations of definitely un-fragrant and shambolic Travis AFB.

Here Henderson duly allowed himself to be bounced, pinball-like, through the (shorter) officers' line, repeatedly showing his military ID card and the orders he'd received out of 5th Group Hqs in Nha Trang about a week previous (US troops in Vietnam didn't carry passports).

That done, and once officially recorded as being back in-country, he then proceeded to a special Joint-Branch Paymaster counter where — after a considerably longer wait in line, and after he'd had to volubly and even threateningly insist that the reluctant Spec-4 clerk that he eventually came face-to-face with behind a bullet-proof window fetch the manager, a bald and ill-tempered major, to call his, Henderson's, branch of The Lone Star Bank in Houston to confirm the status of his account — they'd grudgingly agreed to cash one of his personal Lone Star checks for the eye-popping amount of $1,500. During his year in Vietnam, 95% of his lieutenant's salary, plus jump pay, plus hazardous duty pay, had automatically gone into this stateside bank account, making him now, as they said in the trade, fairly liquid. (The other 5% had been paid to him in Vietnam in "MPC", "Military Payment Certificate", a small part of which had gone illicitly on booze and Saigon Tea Girls in-country, and the rest quite licitly on R&Rs in Bangkok and Hong Kong.)

Then, rather than follow the streaming surge of bewildered-but-smiling, jetlagged-but-jubilant troops out and onto a variety of city-bound buses, the now-newly pecunious Henderson peeled off from the others and, hoisting his modest bag, made his way the not-inconsiderable distance on foot to the same Officer's Club he remembered from a year ago.

It was 1145 H, and the place was fairly empty (returning flights from Vietnam arrived in the morning, while departing ones took off in late afternoon). It being thus sparsely populated, unusually for him Henderson eschewed the bar and went to sit at a table-for-two in a corner. There were two reasons for this: One was that he didn't feel like chatting to anyone just now, least of all to a barman, and the second was that he was aware of the red dirt on his threadbare fatigues and general Dak Phuoc funk that he bore about his person like the aura around Pigpen in "Peanuts", and this caused him some unfamiliar and unwelcome self-consciousness.

He opened the small Puma sport bag that he'd bought in Nha Trang for 50 piastres and which constituted the entirety of his luggage. It contained his green "Class A" uniform, his canvas toilet kit, and a camouflaged nylon poncho-liner that he'd for some reason decided at the last minute to cram in, back when he was de-assing Camp Happy Holidays. And also the envelope that contained the "flimsy", the last remaining copy of the Orders he'd originally received from the Sergeant-Major in Nha Trang about a week ago, from which all the copies had since been peeled off by various clerks, and which he fished out now.

He read, for what seemed the hundredth time, that after a period of seven days, not counting travel time, of his arrival back in CONUS (Continental United States), he was to report to something that sounded like someone's idea of a bureaucratic joke: the Office of Special Requirements (OSR) in the South East Asia Current Tactical And Operational Joint Integrated Intelligence Command Task Force (SEACTAOJIICTF), a monstrosity that not even the most seasoned D.C. bureaucrat had been able to force into a workable acronym. An appended NB further informed him that this mysterious bureaucratic entity was apparently located in one of the Pentagon's numerous sub-basements.

Henderson blinked at these instructions in bemusement for the last time, and folded them away. On the face of it, the assignment certainly didn't look too promising, but on the other hand, he still had almost eleven months to go on his three-year enlistment, and what the fuck — a guy had to be *somewhere*, didn't he (as the saying went. In fact Staff Sgt. Vincent X. Rogers had had something to say about this, if Henderson recalled correctly....), so why not this? Whatever it might actually turn out to be....

Meanwhile, there was this seven days' leave to attend to. Did he have to take it? His leave, that was... *Has any GI ever, in recorded history, turned down leave?* And if he did had to take the leave, did he have to take all seven days, or could it be just a few? Henderson had no idea what the regs were on such things, nor even where to go to find out. (He'd asked the Command Sergeant-Major in Nha Trang just this very question when he'd first read the Orders, but that crusty old piece of boot leather had just barked at him, "Thass a fuckin' dumb question, if I may say so, lieutenant, sir. Ain't you learned yet that in this army ya take what they give ya? Sir.")

One thing for sure was that he was in no hurry to go anywhere in particular, just now. In fact, whenever he'd even pondered the question, Chuck Berry's old tune "No particular place to go!" had popped into his brain, and he'd then promptly switch over to other stuff. Indeed, the whole question of where to go once he'd actually DEROS'ed had remained unresolved in his turbulent mind, during his last days at Camp Happy Holidays and on the long flights back — but now was crunch time. And crunch time called for a beer. *Yup, thinking always goes better with Lucky Lager*, and as he rose and went up now to the bar in the good old Travis AFB O Club to fetch one, he also gathered up a few newspapers that were available, next to the basket of mints at the end by the stewards' station and which were going unread for the moment: The San Francisco Chronicle, The New York Times, and The Washington Post. Not that he was in the slightest bit interested in their news *qua* news, but the first person he'd thought to maybe link up with had been Junior, and he thought that if the team he now pitched for, the Angels, were currently home in Anaheim, he might see if... *let's have a look, here, ... nah, fuck,* according to the sports page of the Chronicle, the Angels were up in Detroit at the moment, on what appeared to be an extended road trip... *well, I don't need no fucking De*troit, *that's for sure... sorry 'bout that, Jare Are — but meanwhile, "Get Some" — throw at their fucking heads.*

He was also tremendously fond of his kid sister Geraldine, of course, but in his present state of mind she was the *last* person he felt like hanging out with... *hang out with Geraldine? And her flaky space-cadet friends? –Jeebus H Humphrey....* No, the very notion didn't even *compute* where Geraldine was concerned, not just now, anyway.... And even *less* did anything compute when he thought briefly of either his dad or mom, neither of whose exact locations he would even have been able to pinpoint at the moment anyway — not even if you put a gun to his face. So his immediate family was not any kind of option. *I'll check in with alla them later, when I've got my shit a little more together....*

He'd have *loved* to catch up with fucking Rojo, but he had no idea where to begin with *that* rat-fucker, either... *Alaska?* Fo-geeehdaBAH-did, baby! *–as he'd say.... hmm, what about Gallaway? maybe Gallaway might be a more realistic bet....* He rose and invested 40 cents into the pay phone by the O-Club entrance/weapons-check station to call the number in Greenwood Mississippi that Gallaway'd given him, only to get a courtly lady — either Ma or Granma Gallaway, hard to tell over the phone which — tell him "Mahcellus be in Memphis", and she gave him a number there. And then Henderson had to go to the bar to get more change and plunk in another 40 cents to call Memphis Tennessee. Where he got a machine — *a machine!* — that told him to call again "later". *Fuck it, Gallaway, I gave you two good shots — that'll do.*

So what he *did* do, after he'd had a valedictory Dewars shot with a Lucky Lager chaser, was reluctantly de-ass this most convivial O-Club and walk to the Travis AFB main PX, where he bought a full set of badges, ribbons and decorations for his Class A uniform. Then he went into the not-so-fresh-smelling PX men's room, locked himself into a stall and, sitting on the crapper, carefully pinned and affixed his purchases onto said Class A's, into which he then changed, stuffing his filthy fatigues into the Puma bag. *If I'm gonna take on this latest, current version of the United Snakes of Amerika, I'm damn well gonna do it in full fuckin' regalia, and you better fuckin' believe it.*

He then emerged out onto the kerb and hopped a bus to Oakland Airport, with a view to catching a flight directly to D.C. — only to discover, to his disgusted astonishment once he got to Oakland International, that there *were* no Oakland-to-Washington flights. So, cursing and (metaphorically) spitting blood, he had to take *another* bus to San Francisco Airport. Once there, he wrote a check to Braniff International Airlines, after an absolutely scorching Braniff desk girl with a blinding smile had mollified and disarmed him by charmingly explaining the obtuse magic by which a round-trip ticket to D.C. was actually cheaper than a one-way ("Say what? Say again?" "Oh don't worry your lil ole head about it, it's weird, I know, but just take the round-trip and throw away the second hay-aff!"), which she was even happy to give him for half-price because he was in uniform. He walked away from that Braniff desk actually wishing he could spend his 7-days' leave with *her*....

On board the flight east, while sipping the contents of further graciously-offered teeny bottles of Scotch, he perused the copy of the Washington Post that he'd filched and brought with him from the O-Club, specifically the classified section for studio/efficiency apartments in D.C. and northern Virginia — some kind of atavistic instinct told him he wouldn't *at all* like D.C-adjacent Maryland. None of the names of the specific DC and Virginia residential areas meant anything to him, but he could see right off that, once he'd acquired a set of wheels, he'd be able to find a suitable crash-pad pretty easily. As the Aussie F-4 Phantom pilot he'd met and became drinking buddies with on R&R in Bangkok used to endlessly assure him, "Naow fackin' worries, mite...."

+ + + + + + +

By the time he landed at D.C.'s National Airport, he'd put together something like a short-term plan of action, the first step of which was to rent a car.

Here he was inclined to frugality, and the cheapest rental he could find turned out to be a Chevy Vega from Budget Rent-A-Car, a pathetic excuse for an automobile whose 140 cubic inch lawnmower engine was so underpowered that if there'd been any sort of incline in the greater D.C. area Henderson would have been forced to open the door and push things along with his left foot. But happily he wouldn't be encountering any such inclines, because when he'd asked the very nice girl at the Budget desk (whose niceness fell *just* short of the splendid, fondly-remembered Braniff girl's) where there might be some used car lots reasonably close to the airport, she'd directed him to an apparently developing suburban enclave just a flat mile or two away called Rosslyn, which was where, on a used-car lot (and bowling alley and anonymous CIA building) -lined thoroughfare improbably called Glebe Road, he struck paydirt:

Cruising slowly up and down this Glebe Road, Henderson had originally had it in his mind to find something sporty, to replace his beloved Alpha, (which, he'd recently learned from a p.s. at the bottom of a postcard from Junior, had now been more or less "taken over" by sister Geraldine). But quite by chance, parked in the back of a plastic-flag bedecked emporium called

BIG AL'S CHRYSLER-PLYMOUTH
New & Used, Top Buck$ Paid!

ignored and seemingly written-off, he espied something that stole his heart:

It was a magnificent black 1959 Imperial "Crown" limousine, an only-slightly rusting Royal Barge-like conveyance that had not yet *quite* achieved Stately Old Wreck status, with a functioning glassed-off partition inside it behind which crouched a pair of leather jump-seats that themselves could have served, in another setting, as quite adequate arm-chairs. This thing was not light years removed from the car Kennedy'd been killed in, but it was older and with its flying-buttress-like tail-fins and massive tank-trap-like chrome grille, it was *way* more garish. It certainly still commanded attention, and bordered on the breathtaking. It even had intimations of being actually *inhabitable* — and in some comfort, at that... a notion that definitely had bolstered Henderson's interest.

"This thing run alright?" Henderson asked the skinny oldish guy in white shirtsleeves and gray slacks that he wore damn near up around his armpits who came out to greet him, and who, incidentally, certainly didn't look to Henderson like any kind of a "Big Al".

"Sure, like a yacht. But a hell of a lot cheaper — nine hundred bucks, it's yours. I'll even throw in a set of rear snow tires for ya."

Henderson peeled off $800 from the wad that he'd convinced the tight-fisted Paymaster back at Travis to fork over. "Tell you what, sir, you also throw in the registration-and-plates hassle — and do it pronto — like *yesterday* — and I'll give ya eight for it."

Not-Big-Al snatched the bills and declared "Done! — seein' as yer payin' cash, and seein' as yer a Green Beanie — I got a nephew over there, Marine, crazy kid — c'mon, follow me, I'll need yer name an' perticklers — you can drive it away in a hour..."

Because you couldn't register a car in Virginia without a Virginia address, which Henderson didn't have yet, the regal Imperial got registered to Henderson at his Pentagon "address" that appeared on his orders.

"Wow, fancy-shmancy" Not-Big-Al commented as he filled out the paperwork.

Not-Big-Al had then even gone so far as to press-gang one of his establishment's gofer-mechanics to accompany Henderson to the nearest Budget Rent-A-Car location to turn in the Vega, and bring him back to the lot. Indeed, Not-Big-Al was revealing himself to be a veritable prince among men. As he jiggle-tested the freshly-attached "Virginia Is For Lovers" rear number plate and handed Henderson the keys, he said,

"Remember, that's a 361 Hemihead you got pulling this baby, so leaded hi-test only — enjoy it, son."

The Bush Pig now took command of, and gingerly maneuvered, his just-acquired Cunard Liner-like Imperial a little way down Glebe Road to a Bowl-A-Rama. Not that he had the slightest intention of bowling, but the place did have a lit neon Carling Black Label sign in one of its windows, which suited him fine. It took him a little practice to get the hang of parking the thing, (an operation that was, in truth, more like *mooring* than parking), but at that hour the parking lot wasn't full.

He went to the small bar at the far end of the bowling alley and got himself a Carling and a shot of Dewars, took same to a booth, and spread out the Washington Post that he still had from Travis — the paper was recent enough, and he sure wasn't about to give those VietCong-loving motherfuckers who put out the Post even fifteen cents for a more current copy if he could help it.

He turned to the Apartments For Rent section of the Classifieds. The fact of the matter was that up until that point in his life Henderson had never actually lived alone — he'd never paid rent to anyone before, and no, fraternity dues didn't count. So he was quite new to this game, and wasn't *really* all that sure what he was looking for. But instinctively, he intuited two things: 1/ he was looking for what they called "minimalism", i.e., cheap, small and uncomplicated; and 2/ not in Maryland.

Accordingly, he began with northern Virginia, but except for this Rosslyn, his acquaintanceship with which was less than half a day old, he knew nothing about all these other town names. So he then thought to have a glance at the D.C. listings instead — specifically the North West quadrant, that he remembered being told once by some girl (Robin? Geraldine?) was where Washington's small minority of white people clustered.

There wasn't much that seemed to fit his bill there either — everything looked to be either too big, too expensive or too long-term... except, hang on, hang on, there *was* one entry, here,

"17 & Q; studio, clean, full amen.; short &
med-term; parking; 175 mo.; 2 mo. dep."

that looked conceivably doable.

He had no idea where "17th & Q" might be, but it was enough for him to go to the Bowl-A-Rama's pay phone and call the number in the ad. What sounded like an English-accented male at the other end invited him to "come by and have a look" which is what, after scribbling down some instructions, and hesitatingly guiding the Imperial across the Key Bridge into what he would soon learn was "Georgetown", he'd proceeded to do.

Which was how Henderson came to sign a renewable 3-month lease on an "efficiency" apartment ("efficiency"? That was an amusing euphemism for what was essentially just a glorified room with an attached shower/crapper and a cooking alcove....) with a disarmingly charming old queen of a landlord, whose "English accent" turned out to be just extreme campy theatricality, and who eyed Henderson approvingly.

It had turned out that his new address was nowhere near the trendy, and expensive, Georgetown, but further to the north and east, and, in fact, closer to 17th *and Corcoran Street,* than "17th and Q". But, as his new friend the landlord explained "Saying Q rather than Corcoran saved a few pennies on the classified, they count every letter, you know...". And it seemed that this section of the prominent 17th Street thoroughfare served as a kind of a Checkpoint Charlie-like demarcation line between the white part of NW (specifically the Dupont Circle area that lay just to the west of Corcoran and among whose whites Henderson would learn figured a disproportionately high number of homosexuals), and the black part of NW, directly to the east.

The little pad suited Henderson fine — and its being more or less on the periphery of a pretty much fairy neighborhood didn't faze him in the slightest — in fact, he found the gregarious homos to be generally hilarious and cantankerously entertaining. And the preponderance of blacks across the street, on the other side of 17th, there, hell, they were OK too. In fact, his last two years had so thoroughly racially integrated his consciousness that Henderson would have found any other demographic arrangement to be oddly incomplete — and this setup seemed somehow reassuring and helped to remind him that even if he was now supposed to be playing at living like an ordinary citizen, he was still in the Army — and essentially a tourist in civilian Amerika.

And he *liked* his immediate neighbors, too — just outside his residence's front door, on the right was a Chinaman-owned High's Ice Cream store, and even better, to the left sat the quasi-exotic and black-owned "Cairo Liquor Store", a star customer of which Henderson quickly established himself — particularly for their House Brand of scotch, "Clan Cairo".

And finally, there was ample parking for the Imperial in a dusty lot round back, behind an alley. (That particular little corner of NW was not yet, back in late 1971, over-developed.)

So all in all, Henderson was tolerably well pleased by his new home.

+ + + + + + +

Which was considerably more than could be said for his new job at the Pentagon, the only happy aspect of which seemed to be that driving *to* northern Virginia from D.C. in the mornings, and reversing the process in the afternoons, involved driving *against* the rush-hour flow — which made the commute a relative skate.

This grotesquely-named SEACTAOJIICTF (SouthEast Asia Current Tactical And Operational Joint Integrated Intelligence Command Task Force) that he'd somehow allowed himself to be assigned to, turned out to be a largely anonymous gaggle of Army, Marine Corps and Air Force colonels and Navy captains and their E-4 clerks and civilian secretaries, occupying a veritable tiny village of offices and cubicles in a corner of the SE side of the sub-basement's A ring; a bunch of people who Henderson sincerely hoped knew what they were supposed to be doing, because for the life of him, *he* certainly couldn't figure out what that might be.

Within this labyrinth of suites and unmarked doors he'd eventually found the somewhat separate bureaucratic warren of desks that apparently constituted the "Office of Special Requirements". Here he'd been welcomed by an Air Force colonel, who'd told him he'd been assigned to the "Contingency Desk" — a notional bureaucratic sub-entity that must have been of the then-new "stealth" variety, because other than himself and his assignment *to* it, Henderson never found any actual physical evidence of its existence, and certainly no other member *of* it.

He was given his own desk, but the phone it came with had no outside line. Rather, it was explained to him that this apparatus on his desk was an extension phone with which he could call other numbers in the Pentagon directory, or, by going through a Pentagon operator, he could ask for an outside line.

On his desk he also had, like in a NEW YORKER cartoon, actual "IN" and "OUT" trays, in the first of which memos and other official-looking documents would mysteriously appear, that he was meant to read and initial, and place in the second. These documents seemed either to deal with obscure and imponderable internal office matters, or else outside news items which were often stamped CLASSIFIED or SECRET (but never TOP SECRET) which struck Henderson as ludicrous, inasmuch as they contained nothing more insightful than what you could get on the TV news or in the papers.

Henderson spent much of the ample time that he found he had on his hands observing such of his immediate colleagues as were within his eyeballing range. He even indulged in desultory chit-chat with them, especially with some of the more attractive civilian females, who were plentiful, and who, in turn, seemed quite receptive to the presence of the trim and clearly out-of-place young Special Forces first lieutenant who'd suddenly appeared among them. He even ventured to attempt to socialize with one or two — eventually setting his sights on one in partic-ular, a self-assured, vivaciously cynical red-headed knock-off Ann-Margaret approximation who, upon discreet initial inquiry by Henderson, miraculously appeared to be amorously unattached, called Bev — with surprisingly encouraging results. (And the famous piece of "Life's Wisdom" — the one warning of not eating and shitting in the same place, or whatever was that one which signaled the peril of dating a workmate — be damned).

But Bev the Redhead aside, the main reason that his initial attempts at social interactions (if that's what they even were), with such of the few of his supposed new colleagues that he ever even saw, were halting and tentative... was that Henderson never, psychologically, really considered this assignment to be even a semi-permanent, or, come to that, a remotely serious one:

I mean, what the hell is this place? Hell, it's not a proper "assignment" at all, really — I mean, look at me, what the fuck am I doing here? — what, for that matter, are they doing here...?

Accordingly, after Henderson had judged that he'd wasted just about enough of his and the government's time since his arrival, figuratively –and sometimes even literally — twiddling his thumbs at this Kafka-esque SEACTAOJIICTF, he approached the genial Air Force colonel who'd originally welcomed him,

"Sir, uh, I hope you, or anybody else who might be in charge here, won't take it personally amiss in any way, uh... if I apply for a transfer outta here — I mean, I'm, hah, not actually *doing* anything here and, uh, I was thinking of putting in for maybe an instructor gig down at the JFK School at Bragg."

"No, by all means, nothing personal whatsoever, lieutenant, by all means, go ahead, be my guest. But I'm pretty sure you won't get it."

"Oh really? Why's that, sir?"

"Well... that's just been my experience with you 'Contingency' fellows...."

"Yeah, 'you Contingency fellows' — see, that's another thing, sir, there don't seem to *be* any other 'Contingency fellows'. In fact, this whole so-called 'Contingency Desk' business — that's something I was gonna ask you about — seems, if I may say so, sir, more like the *phantom* 'Contingency Desk', you know?"

"Look, lieutenant, I'm afraid you caught me when I'm running late — but you go ahead with your transfer request, if you want, no problema, go for it — "

Which is what he'd done. He even enlisted the knowledgeable and efficient, not to mention friendly and fragrant, aid of the aforementioned Bev the Redhead, to get the bureaucratic modalities for requesting a transfer exactly right. But, although the exercise did have the happy incidental result of further securing for himself the convivial social companionship of the delightful Bev the Redhead, true to the Air Force colonel's prediction he did not get his transfer. Indeed, his request never even received a *response.* His and Bev's carefully-crafted official appeal had apparently just vanished... *poof!* Gone with the wind... Disappeared into the ether... forever....

13/ 1010 HOURS

"To a combat vet, the civilian world can seem frivolous and dull, with very little at stake and all the wrong people in power."

— SEBASTIAN JUNGER

Speaking of the ether, just at that moment McElmore for some reason made a sharp banking left turn, which briefly caused Henderson to open his eyes onto a cloudless blue sky, out there beyond Sandoval's open door, instead of the normal green.

Annoyed at the disturbance — *c'mon, Mac, you know the fuckin' way — what're you doin', avoiding a fuckin' deer?* — he grimaced, and settled back into his netting... *where was I? Yeah, Bev, the delovely Bev... and that joke of a non-transfer letter... that left me stranded in D.C. ... although I gotta say, my set-up there wasn't all that bad, it was actually semi-OK — maybe not exactly Numbah Wan, but for sure a solid Numbah Three and maybe even a Two....*

It was true, he liked his little "efficiency studio" up on 17ᵗʰ and Corcoran well enough; he *loved* his Imperial; and he was most fond indeed of Bev the Redhead, who at work was the queen of her little coterie of smiling, fellow mini-skirted and a-lot-smarter-than-they-looked typing-and-filing Pentagon drone-ettes. And when she was off-duty she could not have been more... *accommodating*, that was the word for it.

But meanwhile, it was undeniable that Henderson was chafing.

The greater *ambience* of late-1971 "Amerika" (as his "radical" contemporaries — and they were undoubtedly the 24-year old Henderson's contemporaries — called it), or at least what he'd briefly seen of it from his fleeting vantage points so far of Oakland/San Francisco and now in Washington D.C — was not sitting well with him. And as a result, he didn't at *all* "feel good in his skin".

This expression "Feel good in his skin" had been one that had been introduced to him in a Georgetown/M Street bar when a drunken young guy in an exquisitely-cut Cardin suit and a French accent had rudely, belligerently and quite gratuitously invaded his "personal bubble", one evening when Henderson was there after work with Bev and a few of her friends, and demanded,

"*Hé,* you *lieut'nant parachutiste,* 'ave you been to ze Vietnamme?"

"Yes." He should have left it there, but had rashly added "Why?"

"Why? *Why?* Tell me, *lieut'nant parachutiste,* 'ow do you feel een yore skeen? Do you feel goode een yore skeen?"

Henderson had scotched further proceedings by telling the Frog to "Fuck off, you fucking weird person" and, Bev the Redhead in tow, de-assing the bar — but the "in your skin" phrase had stayed with him.

So Henderson was not, to use another phrase that was just becoming popular in those days, a happy camper. Part of him was still tense and sleepless and often mentally back up on the perimeter of Camp Happy Holidays. Another part of him sat in this pointless hive of bureaucratic inscrutability, alternatively trying to sneak idle peeks down secretaries' cleavage and less idly wondering what in the fiddly-fuck he was doing there. And still *another* part of him passed daily, either on foot or in his attention-drawing quasi-Batmobile, through and around half-farcical and half-violent demonstrations against "Amerika" that more often than not featured the prominent waving of Viet Cong and North Vietnamese flags.

They're flying the enemy's flags in my country's capital. What the fuck is that?

So there was no way that *any* of this could be construed as a healthy state of affairs for the Bush Pig.

But through it all, and still and all, the music was great, the girls were nothing if not nubile (or at least *this* one was), and because his needs were minimal, cash was not wanting. And so Henderson, troubled mind notwithstanding, found ways to pass the time with, and in, varying degrees of equanimity, if not actual contentment.

At the top end of Henderson's personal gratification scale was when the splendid Bev the Redhead (in reality, the young lady that he fondly called Bev the Redhead was the well-educated — Bryn Mawr College — and rigorously brought-up daughter of a highly respectable "Mainline" Philly family, the dad a bit of a bigwig in insurance — the Browne family of Gladwyne, to be exact) was available, they'd drive to a thumpingly convivial nightspot called The Bayou, half-hidden down under the Whitehurst Freeway, and consume pitchers of beer and other stimulating potions as the excellent house band knocked out covers of

Creedence, Steppenwolf and The Band, after which they'd repair to his little Corcoran Street hideaway for a night of adult exercises. And the next morning, they'd furtively and a little sheepishly drive in to work together.

But when she was otherwise occupied, Henderson would head out alone, on solo Road Shows, to Baltimore (dangerous), New York (complicated), Rehoboth Beach Delaware (over-hyped) and Philly (unpretentious but pedestrian).

To facilitate this interstate vagrancy, this motorized Gypsying that Chuck Berry once celebrated as "riding along in my automobile, with no particular place to go", he'd introduced a few amenities to his already commodious Imperial which, in truth, more resembled a small ambulant funeral parlor than your basic car *qua* car:

- a toaster-sized .45 record-player that he'd bought for $3.50 at a garage sale on the way to Rehoboth when he'd gone there for the first time. It plugged into the cigar-lighter and worked great — specially when playing Henderson's favorite single record, "A Double Shot Of My Baby's Love".
- his nylon camouflaged poncho-liner from Vietnam which served as the blanket for the luxurious and commodious back seat.
- an Igloo cooler for the beer and odd other stuff (such as, for example, unfinished sandwiches), which he painted black (the cooler, not the beer and unfinished sandwiches) partly to keep with the Imperial's color scheme, and partly to make the receptacle less obvious for if/when cops stopped him and peered inside.
- and he even kept discreetly tucked under the front seat an empty plastic quart-sized Tide detergent container with a handily large aperture, for pissing into on occasions when it was raining or oth-

erwise inclement — or when he was stuck in a traffic jam, and wazzing in the comfort of nature was not an option.

But, again, other than the undoubted, if transient, pleasure he got from his opulent old car, the complaisant Bev, and his impeccably functional if exiguous studio, things were not completely copacetic (another word newly *du jour*) with young lieutenant Henderson, there in Washington D.C., as 1971 prepared to become 1972.

Try as he might — the more he cruised around in the early morning hours, all too often being stopped and harassed by the Virginia State Police (Bev had a small apartment in an Annandale hi-rise, *and while we're on the subject, "Virginia Is For Lovers" my ass!*), the more stupid movies he went to (and all too often stomped disgustedly out of), the more inane parties he was, or they were, invited to and endured, the more idiot TV he watched — the more he realized that he didn't fit in to this current version of... well, of civilian life. *Not for me, man....*

Too often, drunk and angry and especially when he was alone, he'd get into fights, some of which he'd even, to his amazement, actually win (it all turned out to be a matter of who got in the first punch). And the "freakier" or more "radical" the opponent or, more likely, opponents, the better. Not that he went around *looking* for fights, mind you, but... well, here was the problem:

Even though, unless he absolutely *had* to be in uniform, he made it a point to go around, whenever possible, in civvies — he certainly wasn't eager for any repeat of that "een yore skeen" performance — and the *last* thing he'd ever think of doing was to inflict unsolicited "war stories" on anyone, the inescapable fact was that his goddamn pain-in-the-ass Army haircut ineluctably gave him away, in 1971, as what the protesters had taken to calling a "lifer pig". This happened no matter *what* he was wearing, or no matter how inconspicuous he tried to make himself.

And, sorry, but after that year at Dak Phuoc and A132-C and all the concomitant shit blood misery hassle and death that went with it, he fucking well wasn't about to take any obnoxious, gratuitous and impertinent shit off of these left-wing hippie ignoramuses, who seemed to dog his every step and turn up in every venue he was at, like so many malignant spectres in a "Ghost Train" fun-fair ride. Maybe, as Bev would soothingly suggest, he *was* being a little paranoid, but then again they *did* seem to be everywhere. (And no, fuck it anyway, *pace* Bev, he inwardly knew that he *wasn't* being paranoid at all — they *were* fucking everywhere.)

Although he only partly and imperfectly apprehended what was, at the time, happening to him, what in fact *was* going down here was the involuntary and reluctant politicization of young Jerome J. Henderson — he, who'd always considered himself to be happily "apolitical", and certainly no kind of conservative, either with a small or capital C.

Really.

Indeed, throughout his college years and right up until just about his commissioning in the Army, if you'd pressed Henderson, he would have told you that he couldn't be bothered with any of these weird trendy *issues* that were suddenly sprouting up all around him. He would have laughingly told you that he didn't give a rat's patoot if eco-freaks enjoyed intimate congress with their pet whales; or if women's libbers set fire to their bras and smoked 'em; or if left-wing nuns decorated their Christmas trees with their IUDs if they felt like it... Henderson couldn't give a shit.

And the cops? The original "pigs"? *Please. Don't get me fucking start-ed.* Henderson had never been particularly enamored of cops, inasmuch as the overwhelming preponderance of his increasingly frequent inter-action with them (q.v. Virginia State Police) had been to be arbitrarily, it seemed to him, stopped, braced, breathalized, searched and hauled up before sleepy Magistrates of the Peace, where he was forced to pay a seemingly endless and fucking *expensive* succession of speeding and drunk-driving fines. (Back in 1971 it was not yet the case that one got as a matter of course thrown into the calaboose for such infringements, but one *did* have to endure, in addition to pay-now-or-else-fines, a lot of mock-stern and often rambling lectures from bored-yet-irritated magis-trates.)

He'd certainly never been any kind of "right-wing nut". *What? Ah cam-aaan, will ya? Don't start busting my balls with that shit....* He'd nev-er been able to figure out the slightest reason in the world for putting someone in jail for ten years (or even ten minutes) for smoking grass.... And he was all in favor of being able to swim in a river, as he'd frequently done as a kid, without necessarily being toxically or radioactively poi-soned an hour after getting out... And as for "race" — *What? The spooks and beaners and all that* lio? *Look, I'm fine with all those people, so just gitthefuckahtahere with that shit — yeah — go peddle it somewhere else.* Hell, he'd always taken people as he found 'em — if you were a good man you were a good man, and if you were an asshole you were an ass-hole, and color just didn't fuckin' enter into it — and he'd felt that way *long* before he'd ever met Rojo or Gallaway *or any a those jokers....*

So no, Henderson was no "right-winger", much less any kind of Repub-lican. (Although on the other hand, Democrats, in his vague political consciousness, barely counted as Americans at all, anymore). He hadn't even bothered to vote in '68, even though he'd just become old enough to do so. In fact, speaking of voting, he and Junior had once had the following colloquy on the very question. It had been in the fall of '70 and they'd been in a bar somewhere and for once the TV above them was tuned away from sports and onto the news, where they were jabbering about the mid-term elections:

Junior had stopped picking his teeth with the Alpha ignition key and had mused,

"Hey, I jess realized — I could vote if I wanted. Huh, imagine that shit. Yo, Jerome, you registered? You gonna vote in this thing? Like, you know, for Pop's pal Reprefuckingsentative Dingleberry?"

"Peckerhead. The man's name is Peckerhead, get it right."

"I stan' c'rected.

"Anyway, hell no."

"How come?"

"Please." And Henderson drained his beer and seemed prepared to leave it at that. But then he added, "But ah'll tellya what, sparky — I'd vote for *you*, you ever decide ta run fer somethin' — a maniac like you I could get behind. But until then, leave me the fuck out."

"Huh. Don't hold yer breath."

"And there it is. Yo, *jefe*, two more — "

+ + + + + + +

So all in all, surveying the Contemporary Scene made Henderson un-happy, repelled, discombobulated, uncomfortable and generally out of sorts. In short, he was, (eight years before President Jimmeh Cawdah would actually never use the word), a one-man, ambulant case of *malaise*.

But now make no mistake: this was not some kind of Freudio-Dr. Spockian-anal retentive-borderline sociopathic-BF Skinnerite case of un-housebroken cosmic-karmic maladjustment.

No — not, (to use a Rowan and Martin-ism from the boob tube), in your bippy.

It was just, rather, that Henderson was not a goddamn idiot. He knew what he fucking-well knew. And what he fucking-well knew was this:

He knew that whether it was Gloria Emerson in THE NEW YORK TIMES or Seymour Hersh in THE NEW YORKER who were claim-ing it, or a hundred thousand screaming zoned-out hippies waving Viet Cong flags in San Francisco who were loudly insisting on it — if some-one told him that one and one was three, he knew that that was bullshit. Bullshit on stilts.

Man, he *knew*.

He knew, for example, that US policy in Vietnam was not to kill inno-cent civilians — on the contrary, he knew all too painfully that he *him-self* had lost some of *his own guys* because they'd either been told to, or had chosen to, convolute and endanger them*selves* in order to *avoid* kill-ing innocent civilians. And, moreover, he knew that the communists' expressed policy was to do precisely *that*: Indeed, civilians were the com-munists' *real* targets, rather than the Americans (who could, after all, shoot back. And who, anyway, would eventually be leaving Vietnam, dead *or* alive).

He knew other things as well:

He knew that the US was in South Vietnam because North Vietnam had invaded the place — there was no other reason, *pace* all that "Gulf of Tonkin Incident" bullshit, and notwithstanding all that other fucking "civil war" crapola. *"Civil war"? Are you shitting me? With who, the Viet Cong? Give me a fucking break — the Viet Cong are an invention of the fucking KGB, propagated by the fucking NEW YORK TIMES, and by now there are more actual Viet Congs on American college campuses than in all of South Vietnam. "Civil war" my ass — if there's any civil war going on anywhere — if it's "civil war" yer lookin' for — it's goin' down right here, right now, in the goddamn United States....*

But no one, save perhaps for the preternaturally patient and unaccountably indulgent Bev the Redhead, particularly wanted to hear the things that Henderson knew — and even *she*, it had to be said, not all *that* much. Which disinclination, cynic that he'd become, hadn't really surprised him; in fact he'd already intuited that such would be the case, back at Dak Phuoc, when he'd contemplated his impending return to "the world".

So Henderson kept what he knew mostly all bottled up.

Instead, stuck in this phantom No-Show incomprehensibility of a desk un-job at the Kafkaesque joke that someone had apparently thought it a neat idea to call the SEACTAOJIICTF, he contemplated his future. Did he want to re-up for another three years, when the time — not *all* that far off — came? *I mean, fighting a war's all well and good and all, but do I really feel like stomaching the Army during peace-time? Which sooner or later is bound to come? I mean... all the rock-painting and the petty bureaucratic bullshit?* The prospect filled him with a queasy feeling of hostile apathy, which might seem like an emotional contradiction, but trust Henderson to manage it.

His beleaguered, Clan Cairo-sodden mind ventured farther afield — what might he do as a civilian? Well one thing certain: he sure as shit was not about to skulk back to Houston and ask old J.D. to help him supplement the GI Bill and put him through something like law school. *No fuckin' way.* J.D. would've done it, of course, but Henderson would sooner have gone off to Iceland and signed on as an apprentice shepherd — or, for that matter, joined the NVA — than go back to school. *Any kind of school....*

OK, so what else, then? *Hmm...* Back at Bragg, he and a buddy, a 2LT Steve Marshall, had batted around the possibility of one day going part-ners on buying an old stock car track/property that seemed to be per-petually for sale in Covington, Kentucky. Marshall had read about it in one of his many car mags. They'd discussed the idea of alternating car races with rock concerts, and the prospect of smothering to death from all the easy dough and groupies. So one evening up there in his little pad, nestled between the colored folks and the fags at 17th and Corcoran, Henderson had fished out Marshall's number, the zip-code of which ap-peared to be somewhere in Ohio, and called him. But all he'd gotten was a recording telling him that said number had been disconnected. *Jesus, Marshall, you fuckhead, fine partner you'd make — getting busted by the damn phone company... Meanwhile, what is it with these asshole Army pals of mine and the phone company? — first Gallaway, now Marshall....*

Well, so much for all *that*, then…. bye bye Creedence Clearwater Revival… bye bye groupies… bye bye Richard Petty… Bye bye….

+ + + + + + +

So he chafed. He vegetated. He spun his wheels. Bev the Redhead used the expression "faffing around", and Henderson liked it,

"Where'd you get that?"

"We used it at school."

"Well that's what I'm fuckin' doing here, faffing around."

They liked to visit the Washington Zoo up on Connecticut Avenue — one of the few corners of D.C. that seemed relatively free of anti-Vietnam demos and riots. They ate ice cream up there and looked at the monkeys. Once, Henderson had gone up there alone, when Bev was "otherwise engaged" consoling a fellow secretary who was having "boyfriend problems", and he'd found himself staring for longer than he'd planned at a rather mangy and smelly, yet strangely sympathetic, hyena… who, it had to be said, *also* didn't seem to be able to adapt all that well to Vibrant and "Relevant" 1971 Amerika. The two of them, Henderson and the hyena, had actually spent some twenty minutes in each other's company, which might well be a record of sorts, if records are kept of hyena/human-onlooker interactions.

Another time, at "work", the enigmatically tight-lipped Air Force colonel had stopped by his desk one day and asked Henderson if his passport was "up-to-date".

"Huh? Why, is something up, sir? Something you can tell me?"

"No, lieutenant, no particular reason — but we do, in this shop, try to insist on ready mobility — "

"Which shop would that be, exactly, sir?"

"*This* shop, lieutenant — as I was saying, it's policy in this shop that everyone's passports be up-to-date — so see to it. Lieutenant."

Well, what the hell, he had precious little else to do, and his passport, which he'd gotten his sophomore year in college so he could join some fratty brothers on that Easter-break trip to Nassau, was due to expire in a couple of months anyway. So one morning, instead of heading to the Pentagon, he directed himself to the corner of 19th and Pennsylvania Ave., where the imposing Passport Agency building stood.

But once there he found it blocked off by a large contingent of the black-uniformed wannabe storm-troopers of the supremely mis-named Federal "Park Police", and — *why am I not fucking surprised?* — blue-and-red-with-yellow stars VietCong flags adorning some upper-floor windows and the solid red-with-a-yellow-star-in-the-middle North Vietnamese flag fluttering atop the building, against the cirrus-dappled Washingtonian sky.

Wearily — and warily — Henderson approached one of the Park Police troopers. "Hey, officer, what the hell's this? As though I didn't know — I mean, I hesitate even to ask..."

"Passport building's closed, sir, I'm gonna need you to move on."

Henderson produced his Army ID card and Pentagon pass and said "Yeah, well that's as may be, but I need a new passport — I got urgent official business in there — "

"Oh, *urgent official business,* eh? *Weeeell,* that changes *everything —* "
Turned out these Park Police bastards were actually pretty good at sar-
casm when they put their backs into it, "Look, I'm gonna ask you again
to move on, sir."

"Alright, alright, I'll move — but please, what the hell *is* this, anyway?
— who the fuck, pardon my lingo officer, is pullin' this shit? And fl-
yin', holy mother of God, the fuckin', again, pardon the lingo, *En-vee-ay
fuckin' flag on a Fed'ral building?*"

"Well, if you must know, it seems like some SDS kids from Georgetown
and GW — a whole bunch a them went in supposedly for passports, and
then took the place over. Now, I'm gonna really need for you to move
along, sir — "

"Well, yeah, but — why don't you and your..." Henderson gestured to
the many other Park Police troopers around them, some on horseback,
"pals here just go in there and kick 'em... the fuck *out?* — 'stead of keeping the likes of me from renewing my passport — that I need for urgent
official bus — "

*"I'm gonna need for you to move on, sir — now I'm not gonna tell you
again — "*

In the event, when he finally slunk back to his car and made his igno-
minious way back to his basement desk at SEACTAOJIICTF and related his sorry tale, the whole passport-renewal matter was serendipitously
whisked out of his hands, and shortly thereafter the combined bureaucratic skills of Bev the Redhead, the enigmatic Air Force colonel, and
"other channels" mysteriously produced a stiff new passport for what
appeared to be a civilian version of Jerome J. Henderson. For which all

he was now required to do was write out a check for $20, made out to "US Passport Service".

"Be interesting to see, given that goddamn flag, who endorses this fucker — some bank in Hanoi, maybe?" he said as he handed the check over to Bev.

"Just give me that. And by the way, you owe me a dinner for this — and a nice one, this time."

Another time, a Sunday — and this particular fiasco was on Bev, totally — there had been a surreal collective foolishness called "Global Love Day". No shit, that's what they called the thing: one of Bev's girl-pals and fellow SEACTAOJIICTF super-secretaries, a delightful black chick called (for real) Gloriana — the one of the recent "boyfriend problems" — had informed Bev of, and inveigled her to join her at, some horrendous Peace/Love/Flowers "happening" in the Mall, with a huge rock music lineup being headlined by the thunderous black psychedelic band The Chambers Brothers. Henderson had been, not surprisingly, a little skeptical:

"Hey, look, I like the Chambers Brothers fine, but I can't be goin' to any fuckin' 'Global Love Day' with a million stinkin' hippies — I mean even if I wanted to be there, I'll be lynched with this fuckin' GI haircut of mine, they'll think I'm a fuckin' nark...."

But the girls persuasively prevailed upon him — playing to his male vanity: "Look, we'll need you to protect us, come on, don't be a wuss!" And in the end, it turned out he needn't have worried about the "million stinkin' hippies" after all:

Because the whole swarming, milling, roiling shooting-match had gotten almost immediately violently hijacked — before the first half hour was even over, midway through the Ma Chambers' boys belting out "Love, Peace and Happiness" — when a gang of young black kids, hard to tell but they looked to be eleven-to-thirteen years old, emerged from seeming nowhere, grabbing white girls' hand-bags, white guys' backpacks and ripping off hippie neck-wallets.

It was a planned act of organized aggression that quickly provoked widespread fist-fights, inevitably resulting in a heedless, not to say headless, stampede in any direction away from the young black plunderers.

A colossal, if impromptu, fracas that culminated, (the Mall being after all Federal property), in the inevitable and enthusiastic intervention of Henderson's old pals, the friendly and cuddly *gendarmes* of the Federal Park Police, who grabbed, pushed and clubbed with abandon — mostly, it had to be said, the white victims of the robbers, while pretty much missing the young black perps themselves, but this was undoubtedly more due to the numbers of the former and the nimbleness of the latter, than any nefarious design.

And the three of them, Henderson, Bev and Gloriana, had been lucky to extricate themselves from the mini-race-riot, (for there was no other word for the sudden hash-and-acid-fueled contemporary manifestation of Hieronymous Boschian hell), unscathed.

(puff puff) "Fucking hell — you girls alright?" Henderson inquired rather fatuously, as they pulled up to the relative safety of the looming proximity of the Washington Monument.

(pant, cough) Bev: "Jesus Christ — what's *wrong* with these people?"

(cough, pant) Glorianna: "Hey, I'm really sorry guys, this was *not* in the plan!"

"That's alright, sure as hell not *your* fault — holy shit, send me back to Two-Corps...." but Henderson was already scanning the distant buildings for a tell-tale glimpse of neon, "c'mon, I'm dying a thirst, gotta find a bar — they got any bars near this stupid goddamn Mall? Bev? Hey — you girls know everything, you know this town, there a bar near here...?"

+ + + + + + +

And so in this bumpy, uneven fashion Henderson's days became weeks, and even months, and he was no nearer to deciding anything about his future.

But his professional position, his attitude, and, indeed, his very existence, remained jumpy. Temporary. Finely-balanced, perhaps, but... precarious nonetheless.

One morning he came in unusually, for him, late. Though considering how little he had to do at his "Contingency" desk, the notion of punctuality was really only a rather quaint bit of atavistic baggage that he carried with him from his trainee days — like unthinkingly shining his shoes and making his bed.

In any case, that morning they'd deviated his "contraflow" single-lane drive in to the Pentagon for some unexplained road-work, and the Imperial had almost run out of gas in the resulting stop-go-stop-again jam... and he'd had to find a station for *that*....(locating and driving into a gas station when on bumper-to-bumper I-495 during rush-hour when the needle's passed E... *just... don't ... even... fucking... ask.)*

So he was almost an hour late by the time he came sliding into his cubicle, abashed and with his eyes averted from censorious fellow-cubicle-occupant scowls and trained instead onto his well-shined shoes, to find a small envelope stuck in the carriage of the typewriter on his desk, addressed to:

1LT J.J. HENDERSON
CONTINGENCY

14/ 1020 HOURS

"Every time there's a war, the same damned people always show up. The funny thing is you never see them in between."

— *CHRISTOPHER ROBBINS*

Sandoval the Kicker nudged his passenger awake by bumping one of Henderson's outstretched boot-soles, and mimed a cigarette. Just as wordlessly, Henderson fished out a Salem from his few remaining ones in the not-yet-moist-with-sweat pack in his black T-shirt's little breast pocket.

Goddammit, he wake me up for that? *A smoke? Whyn't he bug McElmore for that, he smokes too an' he's awake, at least — least he's supposed to be... Now, where the fuck was I before I was so rudely...? Yeah, that envelope — that fateful fuckin' envelope...*

Inside the envelope stuck in his Smith-Corona that morning had been one of those pink inter-office memo slips. This one said, simply, "See Col. Helios, room B-4780A"

The fuck? Colonel Helios? Who he? Henderson quickly scanned his brain to see if the name rang any ominous bell (Security? CID? MPs?) and came up blank, and then glanced around to see if anyone in his vicinity was smiling at him, in case this was some kind of practical joke, on account of his being late. But no, he couldn't see anyone smiling. He went over to Bev, who'd come in this morning independently of him and whose cubicle had a line-of-sight to his, and waggled the pink slip at her.

"Hey, kiddo — any idea what this might be about? You know a Colonel Helios?" But Bev just smiled and shrugged.

So he took himself the convoluted distance to room B-4780A. Whose door turned out to not to have any name or other signage on it at all, causing Henderson to double-check the pink slip in his hand. No, this was the right door. It occurred to him that its very anonymity had the ironically unintended effect of rendering the damn thing glaringly conspicuous — unless, of course, it turned out to be a broom closet.

He knocked, entered, and found himself inside a room with a small desk off to one side at which sat a uniformed female Spec-4 who notably wore no name tag and looked rather like the homely clerk/typist Miss Blips in the Beetle Bailey cartoon. And further in, by the back wall and facing Henderson, was a somewhat grander desk behind which sat a ferocious-looking, shaved-headed guy in his late 40s wearing a tan civilian suit, white shirt and plain navy blue tie; a get-up that fooled no one. *"Helios"? The guy looks less Grik than I do, fer chrissakes... if anything he looks like a fucking Nazi — in civvies....* And still no signs, name-plates, indentifiers — nothing, anywhere.

Henderson stood there, resisting the instinct to salute, as the guy wasn't in uniform. After a small pause, the other man, presumably Col. Helios, half-rose, stuck out a paw to be shaken, and said,

"So you're Henderson. The latest 'Contingency' body."

"Yes sir. Yes sir to the first, and I guess so to the second." *Latest?*

Hand-shake concluded, Helios re-sat himself. "Silver Star, I understand. That ain't beanbag — good work, son."

"Weeeell, i— "

" 'Well' nothing. *I* don't have one — damn near *none* of us have one. You must've done *some*thing." The tone of his voice wasn't such as to invite further comment.

The fellow now reached into a drawer and, for a moment there Henderson half-expected him to pull out a pistol. But instead he emerged with, of all things, a business card, which he handed over.

"I'm Colonel Helios, take a seat, lieutenant." (He pronounced it "Hell-ios".)

There's wasn't anywhere immediately obvious for Henderson to park his ass, and while Miss Blips procured a black plastic folding chair for him, he looked at the card:

Colonel George Xaire Helios, U.S. Army
Special Forces (Airborne) Command
Special Requirements Division

"Special requirements" for exactly *what* was, needless to say, not only not made clear, but not even hinted at... and anyway seemed rather beside the point, actually, just at the moment.

"Lieutenant, your name, along with your file, has been referred to us — never mind by who — and we've been holding it while we waited for a slot to open up, a slot where we feel you might be able to be of further use to your country." He paused, for no apparent reason other than perhaps an imagined dramatic one. "But first you'd have to sign on for another three years of active duty. On the other hand, you'd be promoted to captain upon re-upping, and I can tell you that the slot in question is a very interesting one."

"Very interesting assignment", eh? And what might that be — PT instructor at WAC School in Fort McLellan? Nah, probably not....

"Whew. OK. Well, sir, first of all, thanks for finally addressing my status — I was really starting to get a little antsy, back there. And... as long as you put it the way you do, I gotta level with you, sir, I don't exactly have any other burning prospects at the moment. So I'll tell you straight-up that I'm pretty inclined towards taking up your offer — but can I at least know what the 'interesting assignment' might be?"

"Sure, that sounds positive enough for me to proceed, and it says here you're already Top Secret-cleared, so yeah — the idea is for you to fill one of the forty slots — used to be thirty, but we got it pushed up to forty — we've got for 'Special Advisors' to the Armed Forces of the Kingdom of Phuland."

"Say again, sir, *Phuland?*"

"Yes, Phuland, Phuland — Kingdom of — goddammit, lieutenant, it also says here you're supposed to be smart."

"Yeah, no, I mean, of course, sir, I know where Phuland *is* — I just didn't know we had active operations going up there. Heard rumors, of course, but those were mostly about Laos.... Cambodia, Phuland, those were even murkier — "

"Well, our show in Phuland is based loosely on the pretty successful one we've had going up in northern Laos, only it's more recent, which is why maybe you've only heard, heh, murky rumors — which is good, by the way, if a... wise guy like you only heard rumors, that's good. Anyway, yeah, like Laos, we're all technically *civilian* in Phuland — civilian clothes, civilian cover, unmarked aircraft, all that — and it's all coordinated by the CIA's paramilitary people, their 'SAD', the Special Activities Division, in conjunction with one of their, uh, airlines, in this case America Tropic — ATAS — the little brother of Air America — they'll be yer link to th' Air Force, in Phuland — "

At this point Helios was interrupted by a beeping sound from his watch. He frowned, pushed something in on his watch, scribbled something on a pad on his desk, and with no word of explanation, continued,

"Now, also like Laos, we're limited by Presidential Directive to how many guys we can have up there, which is why you've been on hold all this time. But now a guy's got WIA up there and been medevaced. Guy called Mann, a good, hah, man — an Agency para. Anyway, he'll live but he's not going back, least not anytime soon, so that makes you good to go — you're in like Flynn, kid. You'll find a pretty familiar mixed bag up there — some ex-, some not-yet-ex-CIA, some Marine Recon, the medic's an Air Force doc I believe, quite a few recent Green Beanies, hell you might even recognize one or two of your guys from 5th Group up there. 'Fact, you oughtta feel pretty much at home — be right up your alley, I should think. Your people. *Our* people."

And with that, Colonel Helios stood up and this time came out from around his desk. Henderson instinctively stood as well, and the two shook hands again. Then, putting an arm around Henderson's shoulder, and pausing to nod in the direction of the still-silent and still-seated Miss Blips, ushered him towards, and out, the door, saying,

"So, the specialist here, she'll be in touch, and she'll work with you over the next few days, tell you what you need to do, where to go, get you all read-in, all that crap, and I'll see you before you ship out. But meanwhile call me if you think you need to, for any reason, the number's on that card." He paused at the door. "Sooo, Lieutenant Henderson, barring something unforeseen, next time I see you you'll be Captain Henderson, and", he actually winked at the Bush Pig, "meanwhile, don't go getting into any trouble between now and then. Welcome to the team, son."

And that was that.

Henderson found himself back out in the corridor again.

And, although he was *pretty* sure he hadn't actually, positively, given his definitive assent to this new life-move, much less signed anything, he guessed it didn't matter — he was, as the colonel said, on the team. Another team. A new team — but by the sound of it, not much different from the old team. *Hah! it's like that Who song, "here's to the new boss — same as the old boss!" And what the fuck — why the hell not? What else was I planning to do? Huh?*

+ + + + + + +

So Henderson found himself with a new lease of life — he was practically re-born. And his new circumstance changed his outlook completely.

Invigorated by a state of exhilaration that he hadn't remembered feeling in a long time, if ever, Henderson got to work with "Miss Blips". Who turned out, incidentally, to be a young lady called Spec-4 Margaret Hagen, an unfortunately rather mousey-looking but otherwise thoroughly admirable pastor's daughter from Edina, Minnesota. Although it would have been difficult to find two more dissimilar souls to pair up for a co-operative project than the newly-promoted Special Forces Captain J.J. Henderson and the unobtrusive-to-near-invisibility Spec-4 "Clerk-Typist" Margaret Hagen, the fact is that the two got along famously. He kidded her, and she unhesitatingly gave it right back to him. She never called him "sir", and not only did he not mind, but he preferred it that way. And for his part, he called her "Dipesto", because he and Bev had recently been to see "Five Easy Pieces" together, and Jack Nicholson's line to the ravishingly cross-eyed Karen Black, *"Dipesto, why don't you take that sign off your tit and you and me go out and have us a real good time"* had embedded itself onto his brain like a limpet.

And like an actor's agent sending her client off on auditions, Margaret/"Dipesto", the former Miss Blips, had him bouncing off from one office to another in the "Greater Federal Area", getting "briefed" at secluded little bureaucratic niches and offshoots of the CIA, the State Department, USAID, some of the more obscure outposts of the Pentagon itself, and finally at the discreet offices of America Tropic Air Services, up on Connecticut Avenue. Henderson joked with Dipesto (and, after hours, with Bev, who was also Top Secret-cleared) that he reckoned that actually *all* the people he was being briefed by were CIA, except for the officious, dorky Suits at the CIA itself, who were probably all KGB/GRU.

So quite quickly, in a number of days that you could count on your fingers, Henderson got "read-in" to the history of the Vathak Dynasty; the Meu-Jong; the politics, sociology and economics of international opium; the current state of the Chinese and Soviet conduits to, and the Phu portions of, the Ho Chi Minh Trail; recent NVA activity inside Phuland; the Neutrality of the Kingdom of Phuland Codicil to the Geneva Laos Accords of 1962; the latest developments in neighboring Laos; and, not least, young King Pom's bio.

To Henderson, this King Pom character actually sounded like a pretty alright, stand-up guy. And much later, in the bar one night at the ATAS compound in Phu-Lama, he, Henderson, would remark to an eclectic group who happened to be doing some after-hour drinking there at the time, that he wouldn't mind going drinking with the King —

"You know, maybe take him to the White Rose, loosen the guy up a little."

He'd been astounded to be told in a friendly but earnest manner by a young Are-PAF officer in their group that perhaps Henderson might consider being a little more circumspect. Apparently it was a punishable offense in Phuland to "speak lightly" of the King.

"Oh come on."

"No, is serious."

"Ah, come on — what better way is there to forget the burdens of king-ship than — how long does a blow-job at the White Rose take? Five minutes? Ten? OK, if you've got a lot on yer mind, say *fifteen* minutes— and done! With a quick five-buck 'special' lube job at the good ol' White

Rose Servicenter. hey, just cause yer King don't mean you don't have... well, you know..."

"*Sssss.* Is disrespect, Mistah Jerry. Talk other things."

But that was all yet to come. At *these* pre-deployment meetings in and around the District of Columbia, Henderson was informed of the ground rules under which he'd be operating — the rules under which the other Operation Roundhouse advisors were already operating:

* Cover: Or rather "cover", because incredibly — no, *insanely* — the cover that had been chosen for Henderson was that of a "crop-duster" for the Department of Agriculture. *Eh? Say again? What's that, now? I thought I heard you say "crop-duster" for the Department of Agriculture.* It had taken Henderson a small while to realize that the guy from the CIA wasn't joking when he'd announced this. And he mentally kept shaking his head in incredulity as he spent a whole day acquiring a laminated ID card, along with some rudimentary backstop documentation, from the Department of Agriculture's "Office Of The Executive Secretariat" in the bowels of their huge building on Jefferson Drive.

* No uniforms. *No problema.* Henderson drove the Imperial out to the Tyson's Corner Sears where he bought a couple of pairs of boot-cut Levis and four black T-shirts, with little breast pockets.

"What about footgear, can I keep my Vietnam jungle boots?"

"Yeah, I'm pretty sure the guys have those, out there," said Spec4 Margaret Hagen/Dipesto, "They'll be OK."

* A different CIA guy, this one less surreal than Crop-Duster Man — a laconic, crease-faced fellow from the Paramilitary Office of their Special

Activities Division ("SAD-SOG"), who in fact looked rather as though *he'd* just returned from Phuland — maybe even that very morning — impressed upon Henderson the "Three Paramount Rules" of paramilitary duty in Phuland, Kingdom of:

1/ Don't get captured.

2/ *Really* don't get captured.

3/ Review Rules 1/ and 2/.

He also counseled Henderson, "And don't go messin' with the Meu-Jong women, it'll jeopardize your mission. Your mission *and* you. Their men are like Mafia guys or Ey-rabs — their women are like private property, and they'll kill ya if you so much as look sideways at 'em — plus, Meu-Jong tail's not that great to begin with, trust me. And anyway, there's *bookoo* Phu broads in Phu-Lama that you can go crazy with. So, no reason at all to go sniffin' 'round the Meu Jong girlies."

"Right. Got it."

* And of course, the press. Or "media" as it had become known, as the Vietnam War had seen TV overtake the traditional press as the world's principal opinion-generator. (Vietnam was not merely the "Rock and Roll War", but it was also America's — and the world's — first "TV War").

Ah yes, the always meddlesome — and virtually always hostile — US and, indeed, global, media: Specifically, how to avoid it if possible, and how to deal with it if necessary.

But for this particular "block of instruction", Henderson had a "teachable moment" of his own to impart, and he did so by interrupting the State Department dilbert who'd just started pontificating to him on this subject. As Henderson related it:

One morning back at Dak Phuoc, not long after he'd taken over Team A132-C from the departed Gallaway, a forty-ish blonde round-eye bimbo clad in some fairy fashion-designer's laughable idea of camo fatigues, had dropped out of the co-pilot's door of a regular resupply Huey from Nha Trang, right there on the pad in the middle of camp. She carried a big black leather (also designer) shoulder bag that contained recording equipment, and she immediately, without the slightest by-your-leave from anyone, set about shoving a mic at whoever she saw, US, ARVN or even Chan, and asking all manner of leading questions, such as (to the Americans) "Do you think you should be in Vietnam? In fact do you know *why* you're in Vietnam?", and (to the non-American troops) "What is your policy towards innocent civilian villagers? Or refugees?".

Henderson first got wind of this exotic intrusion when one of the guys unloading the chopper humped some ammo and dumped it at Henderson's feet, away from the actual landing pad, where he stood, inventorying the new deliveries,

"Yo, El Tee, who's the tang?"

"The what? Where?"

"Go check it out, sir — best fuckin' resupply yet –!"

So Henderson had checked it out. Turned out this undoubtedly good-looking (if you liked 'em a little on the high-mileage side) uninvited chone was one Micheline Gary, a very glamorous, but terribly serious

French "freelance", ex-star at PARIS MATCH, whose most recent international media triumph had been a hagiographic documentary, a lot of which had been filmed in the jungles of Bolivia, on the then-*chic* commie "philosopher" Régis Debray, the pal of the late Che Guevara. She was "sort of married" (her words, in an International Herald Tribune interview: *"plus ou moins mariée"*) to a famous left-wing Franco-Czech film-maker, and most recently they'd both been among the guests at Leonard Bernstein's infamous Park Avenue "Radical Chic" party for the Black Panthers, the one that Tom Wolfe had so deftly skewered.

At the time, Henderson didn't know any of these details of *Mlle.* Gary's background, but he nevertheless instinctively observed her attempts at "interviewing" his men with mounting unease. But he was reluctant at first to intervene because he knew this shit was politically complicated, risky and fraught. So instead he went over to the Huey pilot, a guy he knew from previous runs, and liked — but he still testily asked him,

"Sammy, why the fuck you bring this cunt out here for? You think we need this shit out here?"

"Shit, Pig, we thought you'd *'pre*ciate a little piecea Frog ass in this dump — thought you'd *thank* me — "

"Thanks for shit, dickhead."

Henderson turned and watched the reaction of his men, specially the younger guys, the Spec-5s — as they were approached by the predatory blonde with the mic. He had to admit that, all politics aside, this creature *was* by way of being one sexy-looking piece of ass, and these kids, unlike Warrant Officer "Sammy" the chopper pilot *who really oughtta've known better,* were innocent and ignorant in the wiles of devious leftist propaganda, and as this seductive apparition approached each one, and moved among them, they just thought they'd Died And Gone To Heaven. But Henderson damn well knew better, and he didn't like how this was developing *one bit*. And so he decided to put a stop to it. He finally walked over and confronted *Mlle.* Gary,

"Ma'am, I gotta ask you to desist from troubling my men — you got some credentials to be here?" Henderson had no idea what authority, if any, he had to even "ask for credentials", much less to prevent anyone, specially a journalist, from "being here" — but he was determined to wing it.

Her accent revealed itself to be part French, very *16ème Arrondissement,* and part "posh Sloane" Brit.

"Oh Leftenant, are you in charge here? How fortuitous, as I'd specially like to put some questions to *you* as well — "

"No, sorry ma'am, we're not doin' this today — I'm gonna ask you to get back on that chopper there — " He could see that its unloading was complete, and they'd chucked the outgoing mail-sac into the Huey's open door and the three ambulant Ruff-Puff WIAs and one Chan stretcher case (no US WIAs today) were pretty much all on board.

"But Leftenant, surely you have some views on the illegal bombing of Cahmbodi*a*," (she bizarrely put the accent at the end) "which is after all less than a kilometer from here — "

Now impatient fury overcame Henderson, and he decided to go all-in, and fuck any consequences. First he turned and called out to his men, ordering them to move on,

"OK, guys, show's over, clear on outta here — go! ... and get on with your shit."

And then he re-addressed *Mlle.* Gary and got up right into her face, like a ballplayer having a beef with an umpire:

"Now listen-up, lady. You de-ass yer pro-commie self from my location *raht* now, and get back on that chopper..." he was forcing her to back up towards the Huey, whose engine WO "Sammy", seeing how things had suddenly turned, here on the pad, was cranking up, "... and if I ever see your sorry ass here again I might just arrange for you to experience a, let's just call it, an *unfortunate occurrence* that would look to the 'outside world' very much like the handiwork of your beloved and, may I say, mythical 'Viet Cong' — courtesy of my good friends the Chans, here, who are no fonder of uninvited pro-enemy pests like you than I am — and my friends the Chans're *so* hard to control, you know..." Ms. Gary looked as though she indignantly wanted to interrupt, but Henderson didn't allow her to, and he'd by now just about backed her up to the chopper's open door, "...and you can quote me on all this, *mademoiselle* — that's First Lieutenant Jay Jay Henderson, aich ee enn dee ee are ess oh enn. Now *get on that bird* ... before I lose my temper."

Holy cow. *Quelle scène!* Even Master Sergeant Montrose, who'd emerged from the Command-and-Control hooch to see for himself what all the commotion was about, had been impressed by Henderson's performance at that moment.

Whereas, the dilbert from State, listening to the story, was quite aghast. Horrified, even. In fact, he seriously wondered if Henderson was quite right in the head.

+ + + + + + +

So one way or the other, Henderson took on board pretty much all there was to take on regarding the little Kingdom of Phuland, and the covert US military involvement there. Or at least all one could take on board in air-conditioned briefing rooms in and around Washington D.C.

And then one Tuesday morning, exactly seventeen days after his initial, momentous chat with Colonel Helios, Henderson was ready to move out.

He came to an amicable arrangement with his ever-charming old queen of a landlord, in which they agreed to split the deposit. The guy told Henderson "You're always welcome back here, Jerry, in fact I wish the other tenants were more like you — you've been an absolute *ghost*."

He packed up the rather spartan entirety of his domestic belongings into an Army foot-locker and a large B-4 bag, both of which he'd bought at an Army-Navy Surplus store on M Street (that was mostly frequented by hippies), and had them shipped by the Post Office "slowest/cheapest available" to the Henderson family compound in Sugar Land.

And then, there being no Junior (who was currently laboring in Kansas City) on hand to take ownership of yet another Jerome Henderson automotive legacy, he enlisted the cooperative-to-the-end Specialist Margaret/Dipesto to follow him in her little Datsun Bluebird out to the Glebe Road and back again to "BIG AL'S CHRYSLER-PLYMOUTH, New & Used, Top Buck$ Paid!", to reluctantly unload his beloved, lumbering land-ship.

The skinny old guy in white shirtsleeves and gray slacks up damn near around his armpits had been replaced by a harassed-looking younger guy with slicked-back black hair and a red tie to go with his white short-sleeved shirt, but he'd have to do. Henderson announced to him,

"Hi. Listen, I bought this magnificent mother here some months ago — I love it, but I'm re-deploying overseas and so I need to sell it back to you guys. I paid $800 for it at the time — here, I still got the invoice — and I've added some highly desirable amenities to it, but I'll accept just my original money back."

"This was *ours*?" the guy said in genuine wonder, as he peered into the Imperial's ancient sumptuosity.

"Damn right. The old guy who sold it to me was reluctant to let it go — I had to convince 'im."

"Ed," said the guy, as if that explained everything. He opened and leaned into the trunk, for some reason.

Henderson resumed, "You lookin' for bodies in there? I'm tellin' you, this is a great vehicle — real motorcade material."

The guy slammed the trunk. "If it checks out under the hood, I'll give you two-fifty for it."

"Two-fifty! Hey!, whattabout yer 'Top Buck$ Paid', there? With a dollar sign on "Buck$', even?"

"That's it pal — and I'll probably regret it — not a lotta call for Batmo-biles around here, you wanta know tha truth — OK, ease it onto the rack, there, an' let's have a look."

So that was that, but not before Henderson had salvaged his camou-flaged poncho-liner that he decided to keep for himself, and his little .45 record-player, that he offered to Margaret/Dipesto — but she declined.

"That's very nice of you, but I don't really have... you know, .45 records." *OK, kid, your loss'll be Bev the Redhead's gain.*

Speaking of whom, on P-Day (Phuland Day) Bev the Redhead got per-mission from *her* supervisor at SEACTAOJIICTF to drive Henderson to the then-fairly new Dulles International Airport, for him to catch Pan Am Flight OO2 (the westward version of Pan Am's two daily round-the-world flights, the eastward one being designated Flight OO1), to Bangkok.

She held the trunk open of her little sky-blue Triumph TR-4 as Hender-son, clad in a white dress shirt, old green fraternity tie, and new tan gab-ardine suit from Sears, (that looked not unlike the one Colonel Helios had worn, that only time the two had ever ended up meeting), chucked in his other new B-4 bag, which was about half empty, containing not much more than his old jungle boots, new jeans and black T-shirts, toi-let kit and Junior's old Commanders cap.

As she expertly darted through the traffic on Route 267 on her way to the airport, she asked,

"So how actually long is this gig of yours *for*? When can we — I –again hope for the pleasure of your distinguished company?"

"Well, I've got another eleven months on my enlistment, so I can't see how it can go a lot longer than that...."

"And you expect me to still be available for you, to be waiting for you, when you get back?"

He paused slightly, to measure his words. Finally, "Naaa, not really, I guess not. I mean, no, ac*orse* not."

Now it was she who paused, processing. Then she said, with her usual hint of a smile, "Well, we'll see. You never know, maybe I will be."

"Well that'd be *great*. But don't worry, I'm not expecting it."

"Good."

They were kissing quite warmly and lingeringly in the front seats of the little TR-4, which she'd wedged between the taxis at "Departures", when a female Chantilly city cop on airport duty came by to tap with her baton on the convertible top and break it up inside — "Yo, people, this a unloading zone, not a make-out hot-spot — "

+ + + + + + +

And so, twenty-two hours, one stop (in Fairbanks Alaska, a hiatus which Henderson spent, from the vantage point of a stool at the astonishingly raucus Headwind Bar, scanning patrons and passersby alike in the vain hope of spotting the elusive Rojo) and about eight in-flight Scotches later, a somewhat haggard Henderson arrived at Bangkok's aged and ever-chaotic Don Mueang International Airport.

He asked around for the America Tropic desk, and was told, after some considerable head-scratching and colleague-consulting at the Information Desk, that he'd have to catch a *song thao* jitney bus and "you go cahgo aewia — Ame'ka-Twopic obah deah, in cahgo aewia!"

He did as he was told and sure enough, in a scene eerily reminiscent of the one that had gone down at Tan Son Nhut Airport in Saigon a couple of years previously, he eventually spotted — and made for — a virtually anonymous little corner of a large cargo warehouse, where a small crowd of Southeast Asians of various nationalities waited beside pungent bundles of definitely non-"designer" baggages.

Henderson pulled up at this remote little hive of importuning humanity and managed to corner a furtive round-eye fella in civvies and with a clip-board who admitted, under insistent interrogation, to "being with" America Tropic Air Services, and through whom he, Henderson, eventually secured for himself a much-coveted spot on a packed "civilianized" ATAS C-46, bound for Phu-Lama International Airport.

+ + + + + + +

"Howdy-do, Henderson — I'm Smith, CO of this outfit, Roundhouse, the Customer, whatever you choose to call us — we've been expecting you, come on, I'll give you a quick orientation....",

was what the genial ex-Special Forces colonel who'd become a CIA Special Activities Division poobah and who now posed as the US Defense Attaché in Phuland, where he oversaw the nebulous Combined Logistics Group, had said... when Henderson had found him in the garage-like "CLG-C" (the appended "C" stood for "Contingency" — that word again!) "Annex" building. A building that stood next to the stately colonial-style (it had once been the residence of the British High Commissioner, but the Brits had found it too expensive to keep up and had gladly sold it to the Yanks) US Embassy compound in Phu-Lama.

As he welcomed Mann's replacement, Smith rose and escorted Henderson into a large platoon-sized "squad bay"-type barracks/dorm room in the Annex.

"That's where you bunk," and he indicated a naked metal cot by the wall, with some bedding folded at the foot of the bare springs. "And the latrine is through there, through those doors at the end."

Continuing to another door in this Annex, this one closed, with a prominent cypher lock on it, he said,

"That's our Control and Commo Center, there — the cypher-lock code is ANATNOM, which is Montana spelled backwards, that's where I'm from — if the fuckers ever grab you we'll have to assume they've gotten the code out of you, and then we'll have to change it which'll be a real pain, so that's *another* reason not to get grabbed."

Returning to his own desk in his office, Smith put his hand on Henderson's shoulder and wound things up,

"So welcome on board, kid. Helios tells me he's seen worse than you, which is high praise from him and good enough for me. Now, there's only two main things to remember and you'll have an OK tour here — One, when you're out in the toolies make damn sure you know who you're shooting at before you shoot — because the NVA aside, there are more jokers among the players here than there were in Vietnam. And Two, when you're here in Phu-Lama, make damn sure you know who you're talking to before you talk, because — as I once heard the Russian *attaché*, my KGB counterpart, say at a cocktail reception: 'The air listens.'

"Now then, how's that huckleberry Helios doin', anyway? He didn't by any chance give you any cigars for me, did he?"

Before Henderson could get beyond opening his mouth to respond in the negative, Smith irrepressibly plowed on,

"No? Damn! Well, never mind — so look, son, I'll let Sergeant-Major Hollings there,"

He indicated the human block of granite seemingly studying a bit of paper at a corner desk,

" — issue you your weapons and field gear, and get your paperwork squared-away, and I'll see you at the Club in the Embassy basement at 1800 hours, and introduce you around — some of your fellow Round-houses. Then — oh yeah, I forgot to mention, we share the chow-hall and the Club with the Embassy civilians — it's alright, they're all more or less on our side... And for your information, in case no one's bothered to tell you, we're occasionally known as 'Cons' out here, to others and to ourselves — it's short for 'Contingency'...."*Ah! Hah! And there it is....*

+ + + + + + +

Well, that had now been some three months ago, and, at least down here in this little Southeast Asian mini-Geneva that was Phu-Lama, Henderson was *still not entirely* clear on Who was doing What to Whom, or more to the point, *for* Whom — although he *was* fairly clear on Why.

Everyone in little Phu-Lama — Phu, American and every other nation-ality — was convinced that everyone else was working either for the CIA or the KGB, *or both,* a phenomenon that rendered it a most hilarious place indeed.

And furthermore, due to the series of fatuously optimistic (or naïve) treaties that had supposedly rendered Phuland "neutral", a Round-house "civilian" like Henderson could wander around the dusty streets of Phu-Lama and brush by some sweaty Soviet "tourist" or an actual NVA cadre (occasionally, if they were part of an official "delegation", even in actual uniform) who might have been sniping at him just the day before, or better yet and with a bit of luck, that he might himself catch in an ambush, tomorrow, up in that virtual Other Country, the Pang Phu Meu.

"Weird" didn't even begin to cover it.

Thank God the KGB and NVA fuckers don't, at least that I know of, frequent the White Rose — because that *might semi-seriously blow that joke of a Phuland Codicil to the 1962 Geneva Givemeafuckingbreak Peace Accord all, well and truly, to hell and gone....*

But generally speaking, Henderson understood the set-up. And he accepted it (not that it would've occurred to anyone to ask him, or anyone would've cared in the slightest what he thought if they had). Especially up in the mountains, where, after all, is where it counted. And where, of course, he was heading now....

15/ 1030 HOURS

"A soldier's skill is nine parts judgment."

— *ALLAN MALLINSON*

Sandoval's nudge to Henderson's boot was now almost a small kick, and the upwards nod of his fly-like helmet indicated that they were nearly on-site. Henderson, already all kitted-up, moved to the gaping open door, kneeled and peered down and out.

They were circling the small clearing that served as the actual landing pad at Landing Site-Echo, on a naturally-flattened ridge atop one of thousands of the jagged karst cliff-mountains that made up the Pang Phu Meu, waiting for the troops down there to put out the "E" that was their "OK-to-land" signal. Henderson had overseen the confection of this "E" out of five empty rice sacs and had explained its importance to the illiterate ILFs (Irregular Local Forces). After an exasperating interval, two guys from Captain Che Kak's SMSB (Special Mountain Security Battalion) bestirred their skinny asses to lay it out — and McElmore went in.

As it rapidly rose to meet them, Henderson looked down on what was, in effect, a half civilian and half military camp:

Little kiddie-*sans* and old women-*sans* were scurrying around — the former in excitement, and the latter to secure any loose stuff that might flap away from the incoming chopper's turbulence, and to shoo away intruding chickens, pigs and pye-dogs. ILF soldiers rose from cooking fires or from morning siestas (*?*), or emerged from God-knows where, pulling up their trousers (*??*— *don't ask*). Tents buckled and billowed as the H-34's rotor wash increased. Even the troops in the so-called fighting positions — the discrete, inside-the-wire the mortar pits, and the machine gun bunkers along the ridge-line perimeter — came running over for this Big Event:

The American helicopter was coming, and bringing with it goodies — "gifts" ("*khongkhvans*" in Phu). Everyone felt important, and even a little flattered, when the American helicopter came.

This great incomprehensibly noisy flying thing has been brought all the way from America specially for us — *those North Vietnamese devil-turds might be hard and cruel fighters — they damn well* are *hard and cruel fighters — but they don't have anything remotely comparable: A regular, (well,* fairly *regular), American helicopter for their supplies and wounded, do they.... Mind you, the American helicopter* also *always brings with it an American big-nose officer, most recently this dark little one with the unmistakable green and white hat with a "D" on the front.... now of course we don't have anything particularly* against *this newest American, except that he's just like his predecessors — every time he comes he has a toky-toky palaver with Captain Che Kak and then, after he's flown away, he invariably leaves behind a Captain Che Kak with a noticeably changed attitude — not the Captain Che Kak we know and prefer, the Captain Che Kak who leaves well-enough alone — but rather a Captain Che Kak who behaves quite tetchily for several days, making us clean our weapons, clean up the landing area, pick up and stack loose ammunition and, worst of all, go out on damned patrols — dangerous patrols where we have to try to find where those North Vietnamese devil-turds are camped — all sorts of tiresome shit like that.*

But no matter — that doesn't matter today, because Captain Che Kak is not here — he must not have known the American helicopter was coming, because he is gone down to the village, visiting with, and paying the death dues to, the family of recently-killed Sergeant Dho, whose house is at the bottom of the valley, by the stream. So things might be alright today, and the American's visit may not result in the extra duty that it usually entails... Of course Captain Che Kak will come back, and he will sooner or later get together with the American, but after that it might be too late to organize patrols, and by tomorrow Che Kak may have gone back to having other things on his mind....

Such were the thoughts going through the minds of the Meu-Jong ILF and SMSB troops as they watched McElmore's great clattering, quivering pile of metal noise touch down in the eye of the billowing whirlwind of red dust it had just created.

The rotors, top and aft, were still spinning but oblivious to that, the women, kids and even old men immediately tried to clamber on board, all loaded up with bundles and baskets, pots and rice bowls. All trussed up with the odd live chicken, furled umbrellas, newspaper-wrapped parcels of dried fish, and every manner of myriad shit that might seem mindlessly random to outside observers but which Henderson and his Roundhouse colleagues had come to realize were apparently of vital importance to their Phu and Meu Jong owners.

But Henderson, who'd already been through this drill countless times, managed, with his rifle and radio slung around his neck, to hold them off, while Sandoval began the laborious process of dragging forth the supplies, and literally kicking them out the door. Again, he wasn't called a Kicker for nothing.

In the midst of this mini-scrum at the chopper's open side, Henderson craned his neck around to look back and up at McElmore, who'd left his pilot's seat and was standing on the right front wheel with his out-stretched hands, flashing both once and one once, indicating that, given the air-thinned elevation of LS-Echo, he couldn't take back more than thirteen passengers, with all their kit and clobber.

So now Henderson had to perform the unenviable Solomonic task of picking out those that looked to him to be the most dire of the wound-ed Meu-Jong soldiers. Who had dutifully assembled themselves and were standing, sitting or lying on their backs, on the designated edge of the landing site, but they'd been eclipsed and left behind in the dust by the onrushing surge of clamoring and determined civilian mama-*sans*, kiddie-*sans* and even some papa-*sans*. Normally it was Che Kak's job to decide who'd go back on the American aerial ambulance/"bus", but Henderson couldn't seem to spot him anywhere, just now, and he had no time to go looking for him — a sitting "Imperialist" helicopter atop a karst ridgeline being one of the most inviting targets in this particular part of the world, both Henderson and McElmore were painfully aware of the need not to hang the fuck around needlessly.

So Henderson temporarily forgot about Che Kak and instead helped Sandoval to muscle aboard the three stretcher cases, and then he pointed to those ten walking WIAs who he decided made the cut, who now ei-ther got on board under their own steam, or had to be helped up. There were still some walking wounded troops left on the landing site, so obviously none of the initial mini-wave of civilians could be allowed to stay on board. *Sorry people, maybe next time.* It was a tough call — a tough cull — but as the old Brit hands liked to say back in Phu-Lama, "there was nothing for it". Henderson and Sandoval shoo-ed and shoved the unhappy civilians off.

Finally, re-hoisting his own by-now-askew rig over his shoulders, Henderson clapped his Kicker on the back, and himself hopped down onto the dirt of the landing site.

As he herded the yammering un-wounded civilians back and away from the chopper, he spotted, near him at the front of the disappointed little crowd, a youngish Meu Jong woman holding in her arms a small child who seemed to be wrapped in a mass of bloody rags but whose face nevertheless appeared to be clinging to one of the woman's exposed tits, so the little thing must be alive, at least. From where the blood was located on the rags, Henderson surmised that the kid — baby — had been hit by something in its mid-section, and consequently might not be lasting too long, and certainly not without quick medical intervention. *Right. Fuck it — McElmore can just pedal a little harder....* Henderson grabbed the young mama-*san* and her little baby from behind and hoisted them aboard into Sandoval's grasp, shouting above the din to his kicker to nevermind the numbers and.... *just fuckin' deal with it.*

"Secure 'em somewhere, and make sure they're included when the others're taken to the hospital!" Henderson yelled, and Sandoval nodded.

By now McElmore was back in his pilot's seat and had already started building up torque. The noise, which had never quite abated, increased again.

Henderson, still about two meters from the open side-door, and guarding against any last-second stowaway attempts, moved a bit to his right so as to be in McElmore's line-of-sight from the cockpit, and gave him the thumbs-up. Immediately, the old bird roared, tilted forward onto its great broad nose, and lifted off. Henderson clutched his cap and shielded his eyes from the flying pebbles, dust and odd bits of debris.

Fairly quickly the chopper grew smaller and its clatter faded as, once it moved off the ridgeline and into the void below, it actually initially *lost* altitude.

And as the general uproar and hoo-hah on the landing site subsided, to be replaced by the normal human chatter in staccato Phu and Meu Jong, Henderson switched on his walkie-talkie-style HT-2A radio:

"Yankee Whiskey, Bush Pig."

"Yeah, go Pig."

"Okay, sport — remember, come get me at 1500, right?"

"Copy, will do — see ya then. Out."

16/ 1035 HOURS

"In a counterinsurgency the people are the prize not the playing field."

— *TOM RICKS*

Henderson buckled up his pistol belt, which until then had been hanging loose, and squared himself away. He performed a quick 360°-eyeball of LS-Echo and lit up a Salem from a new pack. (He'd keep the few left in his old pack to hand around to deserving Meu-Jong troopies.)

Another goddamn scorching day — sweating already.... Where the hell is goddamn Che Kak, anyway? The sombitch knew I was coming up this morning — hell, the fucker insisted on it, said he needed the ammo bad, couldn't wait — even made me re-schedule the hop to LS-Papa. Something musta come up with him....

Henderson moved over to some nearby ILFs who were starting to go through the new supplies, sorting and piling the stuff into separate stacks on the scrub edge of the landing site, preparatory to carting it away.

They nodded and smiled at him in greeting, and Henderson grinned back, *"Nyob zoo,* fellas –" Although he *had* picked up the odd word of Meu Jong, he still sure could've used Mekki....

One little oldish guy in ancient shower shoes and an old and appallingly muddy M-1 Carbine slung across his back was engrossed in opening one of the cases of frags. Henderson addressed him,

"Hey chief, grenades for kill Vietnamese, OK? *Bat tua* Viets, hunh? Not for cookee the goddamn rice — *tsis ua noj mov*, hunh? *Tsis* goddamn *tsis*, troop, if *Tus* Che Kak he toky toky me — damn, what's the word, if he... if he... *hais* me that you soldiers, you guys, *nej tuaj*, use the grenades for the cook the rice *noj com mov*, no more have grenades. I no give." He shook his head emphatically in time with his "I no give", " — and if no more grenades, the Viets, *Nyab Lab*, the fucking Viet communists come and *bat tua* the whole fucking bunch of yas — " and he made a dramatic throat-slashing gesture, "Hunh? Understand? *Koj puas?Comprenden, amigos?*"

The effort to dredge forth even the few relevant (he *hoped* relevant) Meu Jong words he thought he knew had actually dizzied Henderson for a second, there, but the little brown ILF and his mates smiled, nodded and giggled their assent.

To Henderson, these grins either meant mindless "Yes, massa-boss" compliance or else it was just a nervous reflex signifying "We haven't got the faintest fucking idea what you're talking about, Big-Nose", and in either case he had no doubt whatever that at the next possible, un-supervised, opportunity, they'd resume their maddening practice of cooking their goddamn rice with the gunpowder from dismantled American M-26 frag grenades.

Where the fuck is Che Kak, anyway?

"*Kov hog* Che Kak?" shouted Henderson, sort of *urbi et orbi.*

The Meu Jong irregulars echoed him, calling out the question to one another until finally, a young trooper wearing sergeant's insignia on a too-large fatigue collar, a guy whose face Henderson remembered but not the name — Che Kak or Mekki would have told him of course but in their absence Henderson didn't want to lose face by asking — came trotting over and said,

"Che Kak *muaj* — Che Kak *mus muaj zos!* — ", and he pointed in the vague direction of the cluster of dwellings down in the valley where the soldiers' families lived. If the little ville even had a name, Henderson didn't know it. He and previous Roundhouse advisors just called it "the *zos*", which meant "village", and it was just over a mile away but, given the terrain, it took about forty-five minutes to hump to.

The young Meu Jong sergeant now embarked upon an elaborate (and, Henderson had to admit, quite skillful) pantomime of a female person — the universal "melon-hands" gesture — crying and behaving all distressed. Rending of hair, chest- beating... it was real standing-o stuff....

"Yeah, OK, Che Kak go pay death penalty in the *zos*, right?" and he pulled out of his ass pocket some of his few greasy old Phu bank notes, the better to make himself understood.

"Aaaaanh..." the young sergeant grinned.

"OK, *compadre,*" said Henderson. "You'll do." (Henderson suddenly missed Gallaway — and just as quickly banished Gallaway from his mind and replaced him with the thought of another, older, character — an ILF NCO-type that Che Kak used as a kind of First Sergeant up here, an efficient little geezer called "Sao" — *Where the fuck is* he? *Ah fuck it, non-communication with him'd be no better than with this kid, here...*

He was about to return the money to his pocket, but hesitated... it seemed somehow crass to do so... The ratty Phu currency was actually worth about thirty US cents, but Henderson reckoned it was worth thousands of bucks' worth of what the D.C. brass amused itself by calling "Civic Action", and so he muttered, as much for his own benefit as anyone else's, "Here, buy some soady-pop for the kiddie-*sans*", and handed it over to the boy-sergeant before him, who accepted it in both cupped hands.

"*Aaaaanh, ua taug, tus!*" ("Aaaaa, thanks, boss!")

"Sure, no sweat, pal."

But still and all — fuck me, here I am with no fucking terp and that irresponsible joker Che Kak not warning me that he'd be off doing his thing down in the valley — hell, he won't be back for at least an hour, probably longer — Jesus Christ, I'm suddenly in danger a looking a little like a fifth-wheel bump-on-a-log with its thumb up its ass, here... Damn, I really shouldna come without little Mekki — yeah, he was out sick, I know, but I shoulda scrounged some other terp — hell, any warm Phoo body woulda done, I coulda got one from Smithy, ... or postponed — naaa, postponing was no good, they fuckin' need the ammo here at Echo....

Performing a bit of theater involving shrugging his shoulders and scrutinizing his watch, he inquired of this kid-sergeant when he thought Che Kak would be getting back, in response to which the fellow pointed to the sun and dragged his finger down to the nearest cliff-top. "Aaaaaanh...."

Great, just great — the fucker'll be gone all day, of course he will — after handing out the Grievin' moolah there'll be the mandatory baçi *with a lotta rice wine, and other ceremonial bullshit involving ancestors and what-*

not — and no doubt that snake Che Kak'll take advantage of the situation to score himself some ripe and vulnerable Meu Jong nookie....

Henderson knew from experience that a fixed, shit-eating grin was the default confidence-inducing expression to adopt in this part of the world, so, pasting one onto his face now, he moved away from the Meu Jong soldiers and the new supplies to... think this thing out.

It was almost a quarter to eleven — and he had to do *something* to fill the time until McElmore returned, at three... Normally, if Mekki and Che Kak had been to hand, he'd have chatted expansively with the ILF and SMSB lieutenants and sergeants, but...

Right — first things first: he found a lonely stack of empty ammo cans on the edge of the landing site, waiting to be taken away if ever a chopper had spare weight/room, and sat on them. He pulled out his note-pad, turned to a dry page, wrote down the date and time, and composed a note to Che Kak. *Wait, what if Che Kak gets back while I'm still here? Well, ...all the better — I'll make sure he keeps what I've already written, as a reminder for when I'm gone:*

"Che Kak, I came this morning like we planned before, on the radio (he had to tailor his English a little towards Che Kak's near-pidgin), **but you had already gone to the village. You *lo-xi*** (asshole) **I think you go there to play with the women! Anyway, this is all the supply I can bring this week. Notice I managed to get some Claymores — MAKE SURE THE GUYS POINT THEM IN THE CORRECT DIRECTION! I hope next week to bring you 1 or maybe 2 of those M-79 grenade-launcher 'poom-poom!' things that you have been asking for, with a few boxes of ammo for them. I'll also try to bring you up a radio like the one I have so**

that bookoo big fuckups like what happened today don't happen **again** (actually giving Che Kak a personal radio was still waiting for Col. Smith's OK, and was not a foregone conclusion — but Che Kak didn't need to know that). **We understand that, although you have the big radio in the CP hooch, you are not there so much and are busy in other places, and that you need a small one to carry around with you. Anyway, I'll see what I can do — I am working on this. Meantime, I sent back 10 and a ½ of your wounded on the chopper — the "½" was a baby-san with a wound in her gut — I don't know the mama's name, but the wounded guys we couldn't take will tell you — and you should tell the mama's people, if they don't know already — or they will worry what happened to her. I will also take as many as I can when I leave in a few hours, and the remainers will also tell you who and how many that was.** (He turned to a fresh page — his fourth already) **NOW: I want you to call me tomorrow at 2000 hours, and I'll need you at that time to give me the latest positions of the NVA units Alpha, Bravo and November that your patrols spotted this last week. (I trust you sent out patrols this last week!!!) — AS YOU KNOW THIS IS THE ONLY WAY WE HAVE TO TELL THE AIR FORCE WHERE TO HIT — This is why it is so important that you always send out patrols and get me the informations — If you don't do this, I don't want to scare you, old buddy, but THE NVA WILL COME AND KILL YOU ALL IN YOUR TENTS.** (He moved to yet another page.) **And speaking of getting me the informations, when we finally talk on the radio again use the goddamn code I gave you last time. That's what it's for — the NVA listen to our radios.** (He could have added, but didn't, that the Communist Phu Istakat allies of the NVA could actually understand Che Kak better when he was on the radio than *his American allies* did.) **Sorry about the 81mm mortars,** but still no can do. I think we have better chance with the M-79s. **BUT FOR FUCKS SAKES STOP YOUR GUYS FROM COOK-ING WITH THE POWDER FROM THE FRAG GRENADES — my bosses at Headquarters get bookoo BOOKOO pissed off with this. So anyway, I am giving this to** (he yelled over to the retreating young sergeant — "Hey, *tubrog!*" {sergeant!} *"Dab tsi?"* {what?}"How do you write your name?" — Henderson mimed writing and pointed at the kid, reckoning this was more diplomatic than actually flat-out asking his name... "Chang Koo! Me Chang Koo!") **Sergeant Chang Koo to give to you. Meanwhile, keep up the good work. Don't forget to call tomorrow night. Your friend, Mr. Jerry.**

He folded what had by now become a semi-bulky wad of pages in half, wrote Che Kak's name on the back, secured it with one of the two rubber bands he always carried around on his wrist, and walked over to the kid who he now knew as Sergeant Chang Koo.

"For Che Kak — not lose, not forget."

"Aaaaanh."

Henderson now embarked on a desultory "inspection" of the defensive perimeter around the landing site's clearing and the attendant shacks clustered around the point where the one-lane dirt track from the valley reached the clearing. He peered into bunkers, most of them manned, but some empty, noting the amount of ready ammo available at each, pulling back the bolts on some of the laterite-encrusted 50-Cal. and M-60 machine guns, to see if they were even capable of firing — they all, rather miraculously, seemed to be. He confirmed fields of fire, but, in truth, all this activity was really pretty rote, as any proper direction these ILF troops would receive would be from Che Kak rather than from him. No, he was just here to confirm "Long Nose" American support — which in reality consisted of three things: a/ Resupply, b/ Medevac, and, from time to time, c/ Hell From On High delivered by the US Air Force.

Throughout this little what passed for an inspection tour he was closely shadowed by a posse of about a dozen giggling, wide-eyed half-naked kiddie-*sans,* who might have shared five torn flip-flops and three pairs of ripped shorts between the lot of them. Aping the immemorial Audie-Murphy-In-Salerno routine, he handed out such C-Ration Chiclets as he could produce from his person, and almost immediately regretted doing so because his supply was so meager that by pleasing a few, he only succeeded in disappointing the many. *Shit.*

"Hey mistah, you gib? You gib? Hey mistah!"

This was all *fucked-up....*

He rejected as impractical, not to mention ethically dubious, the idea of substituting some of his Salems for his insufficient Chiclets, and resolved instead to bring *a whole fucking box* of Chiclets the next time he came up, even if it meant buying 'em in the open "black" market near the airport in Phu-Lama.

Having exhausted the supply of bunkers and machine-gun positions to check out, and now anxious to shake his now-rather disgruntled and even mutinous claque of persistent urchins, it suddenly occurred to him that it might not be a complete waste of his time if he found and paid a visit to the "Civilian Refugee Coordinator", Mr. Kwat. *What the fuck — couldn't hurt. Probably falls under the rubric of "Civic Action" — something like that, anyway.... Not only it can't hurt — it could, in fact, be taken as positively rude* not *to be seen to punch the old guy's ticket while I'm up here....*

This Mr. NOKN ("No Other Known Names") Kwat was a slightly weird-verging-on-the-sinister, and definitely inscrutable, elderly (or at least elderly-*looking)* personage of no fixed address and with no official responsibilities, at least none at LS-Echo that Henderson had ever seen evidence of. The geezer had been, to put it mildly, something of an enigma to Henderson right from his, Henderson's, first visit to Landing Site Echo.

On top of which, the old guy certainly didn't look Meu-Jong, hell, he didn't even look *Phu* — if anything, he looked *Vietnamese,* of all fucking things (but how could that even be?) And he dressed eccentrically, too: while the Meu Jong ILF and SMSB troops were in green, and the Meu Jong civilians were in black, Mr. Kwat wore a set of baggy *grey* canvas-y pajamas, and his wispily be-whiskered face was crowned by a wildly anachronistic black hi-top bowler hat that looked borrowed from James Bond's pal Goldfinger's pal Oddjob. In fact, he always looked to Henderson like a character who'd absent-mindedly wandered over from an adjoining film set.

However, if it was still unclear to Henderson (one of whose jobs it was to know such things) from just where the clearly non-indigenous Mr. Kwat's authority among the locals — to the extent that he *had* any — sprang, one thing he *did* know about the guy was that Kwat was one of the few denizens of LS-Echo, other than Che Kak, who'd actually ever *been* to Phu-lama....

And speaking of Che Kak and Mr. Kwat, the old man had only ever come up once in conversation between Henderson and his RPAF counterpart, an occasion that had taken place back during Henderson's initial on-site orientation:

" 'Civilian Refugee Coordinator', you say? What the fuck does that even mean? There *aren't* any 'civilians refugees' around here — less you count the *entire population* as 'civilian refugees' — sounds maybe like some kinda *boo*-shit to me, Che Kak — "

"Hah hah, maybe. *Aw* peeper want be lefugee from gah-dam commoonits, so yes, can say we *aw* lefugee — and I don' know what he 'caw-aw-di-nate'!, hah hah, I don' know, Mistah Jerry — Mistah Kwat he be heah befo' even I come heah. I think he know peeper in Phu-Lama, impawtant peeper. Anyway, he no bodda nobodies."

"Well OK, sport, if you say so...."

Hmmmm. Landing Site-Echo and its attendant village, with its consensus-elected civilian "Elder/Chief", had an approximate population of some 1,500 to 1,600 Meu Jong souls, none of them, as far as he could tell, "refugees" in any normally-understood sense. This was because first of all, none of the communists in the area, neither the Phu Istakat nor their NVA muscle, controlled *any* population concentrations to speak of, from which people might be expected to flee. And secondly, if there ever *were* any real, proper refugees — in the sense of being an escapee from communist control somewhere — they were flown priority by America Tropic to Phu-Lama for debriefing and eventual resettlement. So the whole "refugee" thing was bogus from pretty much every angle.

Still, Henderson had thought enough of the nagging matter of the odd old "Refugee Coordinator"'s incongruous presence on LS-Echo to bring it up with Col. Smith:

"Che Kak laughs him off, says he's harmless, but I dunno — he weirds me out, a little."

"Ehhh, I reckon Che Kak's right. Look, this is just Echo's lingering version of a cockamamie UN initiative from a couple years ago. GOP ("Government Of Phuland") was given some money to burn — by the UNHCR, the 'refugee' boondoggle people — and so they found slots for some useless bodies with political connections, put 'em on the payroll, and scattered 'em around on various Landing Sites. And so these people come and go, spend half their time back here in Phu-Lama. Don't sweat 'em, kid, they're irrelevant — better you concentrate on getting the ILFs to take their asses outside the wire and do a little patrolling — gotta keep the NVA locations and numbers current...."

So alright, then. Thus having duly expressed a certain Mr. Kwat-skepticism, Henderson had then been happy let the matter drop.

And if we're stuck with the guy, out here, might as well be civil — So after a little searching and asking around, ducking around among the few tents, lean-tos and shacks, Henderson eventually found the enigmatic personage in question squatting in front of one in the group of sheds that clustered around the juncture of the landing site and the dirt track that led down into the valley and to the *zos.*

The hi-top bowler-hatted figure in gray was bent over, a small bamboo contraption that was clearly some ethnic species of pipe sticking out of the side of his face, Popeye-style, and he was doing something to the chain on his new-ish but already battered light-blue "Mobylette" scooter-bike (the only motorized conveyance in all of Landing Site-Echo other than Che Kak's captured Soviet "GAZ" jeep, which was currently with him in the village as he carried out his, ah, humanitarian duties).

"Hey, hah you, Mr. Kwat! *Nyob zoo,* my friend...!"

The old man looked up, then stood up and acknowledged Henderson with a nod and a big gap-yellow toothed rictus grin, "*Aaaahn,* Mistah Jelly, hah hah hah, OK OK, hah hah hah."

The scope for small-talk between them was decidedly limited, and their mutual smiles — their mutually bogus grins — were painful to maintain.

"So, all OK with you, Mister Kwat? All number one?"

"*Aaaahn,* nambah wa— *NGWAI! Ra ngwai! Ra ra ra!, ra ngwai!*"

This last, which Henderson recognized as a kind of pidgin Viet/Meu-Jong rendition of "Fuck off, vamoose!", was directed at the posse of urchins which, like the cloud following "Pig-pen" in the "Peanuts" cartoon, had — despite, or because of, his Chiclets — trailed behind Henderson's saunter around LS-Echo, culminating at Kwat's shed.

Brandishing a replacement chain for his Mobylette, the old man succeeded in dispersing the kid-*sans* with the dyspeptic efficiency of a Phu Archie Bunker. During which Henderson stood there, sadly aware that he had no further pleasantries to send Kwat's way, and again cursing his decision to leave the terp Mekki behind. *Never fucking again, and fuck the chopper's load-weight — next time I'll just kick off the stupid Toys For Tots bin.... 'Cause this stone sucks — without Mekki I'm just a helpless grinning idiot out here, when all's said and done....*

But his conversational problem with Mr. Kwat was just then rendered moot by the abrupt appearance of two old Meu-Jong mama-*sans*, who appeared from stage right with an evident bone to pick with the venerable "Refugee Coordinator".

They just barged in, as though Henderson wasn't even there, and started berating Kwat in the most agitated way, jabbering a mile a minute, and Henderson, taken aback, found himself concentrating on their impenetrable torrent of invective, trying to pick out the odd word he might recognize, which might give him a clue as to what their beef was about....

... when suddenly, out of nowhere and eclipsing all human noise, came a bone-shaking and ear-popping

CRUMP!

Oh fuck! — is it — ? Henderson wheeled around, and saw some smoke behind him, and some falling clumps of dirt in the air.

CRUMP! CRUMP!

Howaly shit! — INCOMING!

17/ 1055 HOURS

"I don't ask you to be unafraid, simply to act unafraid."

— GENERAL CHARLES GEORGE "CHINESE" GORDON

In the mini-second it took Henderson to turn back to face Mr. Kwat, they'd all vanished. All of them — Kwat, the aggrieved mama-*sans*, even the banished kids who'd been still hovering nearby — all *pfffft*, no longer there, disappeared down unseen rabbit-holes, gone to hiding God knows where.

Despite the shock of the sudden attack, Henderson couldn't help marveling at their alacrity... when — *CRUMP!* — he snapped out of it and decided to emulate them — *di-di your ass the fuck outta here!* — *where the fuck is there any cover around here?*

He whirled around — actually a few times, rather pathetically, almost resembling a dog trying to catch his own tail. *Can't use any a those sheds, which are not only flimsy as fucking houses a cards and little more than lean-tos, but they serve as fucking* aiming stakes, *for fuck's sakes... So there* isn't *any goddamn cover — but there's* that, *over there —*

He spotted the open garbage pit — LS-Echo's communal garbage *dump* was actually more like it — behind one of the sheds, a portion of ground that sloped gently down from the little plateau on which the chopper pad sat, and *might* therefore afford him a modicum of safety from flying shrapnel — *CRUMP!* — and towards which Henderson now launched himself — *CRUMP!, fuck!,* that *one just hit the path, there — couldn't be more'n 20 meters from here!* — like an Olympic swimmer in a hands-outstretched dive... into the stinking field of tin cans and chicken bones and banana peels and cardboard boxes and unidentified pigs' organs and God-knows what else. He hung grimly onto his rifle and radio as his ungainly pack knocked him on the back of his head and his web-gear got all twisted around his armpit when he landed. He instinctively shrugged all his equipment more or less back into place before sort of wriggling himself an inch or two down into the fetid detritus in which he lay.

He'd been through similar attacks back in Dak fucking Phuoc — not necessarily cowering in garbage dumps, perhaps, but (as they said in Robin's Noo Yawk City), *from incoming he knew!*

He wiggled himself around and peered up and looked back to more or less where he and Mr. Kwat just a moment ago had been standing, when — *CRUMP! CRUMP! CRUMP! CRUMP!* — and he buried his face back down in the rubbish.

Jesus fuck! — *they're just fucking* walking *this fucking stuff right across the length and breadth of the LS, all the fuck over the tents and those pathetic hooches, there... Sounds like 60mm... yeah, I'm guessing it's 60....*

Again, and reluctantly, he forced his face to raise up and have a look. Just in time to see — *CRUMP! CRUMP!* — two more rounds land about fifty meters in front of him. The first scored a direct hit on a windowless poncho-tin-and-clapboard construction, whose walls and roof were literally blown away and Henderson saw what looked like three, or maybe four (it was hard to be sure) bodies and major parts of bodies — civilians — "coming to rest" on the bits of flimsy wood, fabric and dirt where the hooch had stood.

God almighty, I wonder how many more goddamn rounds of this shit these fuckers can have? *Maaaan…. Meanwhile, yeah, sure, alright, 60MM might not exactly be your BLU-82 15,000 pound "Daisy-Cutter", but it'll do you a right severe fuckin' damage nevertheless, if* — as he was seeing through horrified eyes right now — *it lands in your immediate vicinity. To not even think about if it lands on* top *of you….*

CRUMP! fucking more CRUMP! crashed and the earth (in the form of this garbage pit) shook, and hot shrapnel zinged all around and sliced into anything in its way, some of it seeming to be about a half inch above Henderson's Dallas Commanders-capped head, and he buried his face ever-deeper into this garbage, *his* garbage… this refuse-refuge…. He closed his eyes to keep them from getting stabbed or cut by anything sharp… there was a disintegrated wet paper bag down under his chin area that contained what might be inedible animal parts… he *hoped* they were inedible animal parts, because the alternative didn't bear much thinking about…

Fucking shit!…. *Alright, this can't be allowed to drag on indefinitely….*

Henderson groped down around his right ass-cheek on which his radio was now lying and found the relevant knob, which he turned on. Then, trying not to expose his hands too high above the slight depression that he'd created for himself in the rubbish, he hastily extended its thirty-inch long, rod-like antenna.

"Yankee Whiskey, Yankee Whiskey, this is Bush Pig, how do you copy? Yankee Whiskey for Bush Pig, come in, over — "

Then, faintly, masked by a goodish bit of hissing and crackling, came "Pig, Whiskey. I copy you two-by, how me?"

"Whiskey, Pig. 'Bout same-same. Listen, Mac, we're takin' some — " *CRUMP! CRUMP!* " — fuckin' incoming, as you probly jest heard — I'm pretty sure it's sixty. It seems kinda heavy, could be bad — I seen people go down already — but I can't tell jest now 'zackly *how* bad — " *CRUMP! CRUMP!* " — cause I'm hunkerin' down at the moment with my nose buried in a pile a shit — literally, if you wanna know — " *CRUMP! CRUMP!* " — Plus I got a ti-ti unforeseen problem in that I can't talk to anybody too good up here, just now, Che Kak's not available — but that's neither here nor there..." *CRUMP! CRUMP!* "God-*damn*!— hear that? *Fuck. Me.* Point is, I may be needin' you sooner'n the fifteen-hundred that we'd agreed — gonna be bookoo wounded for sure to get outta here — heh, not to mention *me. On the other hand, I don'* want you comin' *near* this fuckin' place till I give you the green light."

"Roger that."

"Yeah, don' need *you* gettin' busted up on top a everyone else — "

"Weeeell..." McElmore actually gave a little chuckle.

" — *last* fuckin' thing we need."

"No argument there, kid."

"OK, so stand by on the horn for me there, wherever you are — make sure you keep it open, an' I'll let you know when it's a Go for you to come back. Meanwhile, ask a Buzzard if Tango's got any fast-movers available, could maybe suppress these fuckers — if they got some, or even one, tell 'em to stand by, I may get a better idea if there's a partic'lar location to hit after I've had a chance to find one a th' NCOs, here, — maybe one of 'em'll have a notion. Copy?"

"Alpha alpha, lil buddy, and wilco. Keep yer ass down an' soon as you give the word, we'll come haul yer sorry seff out... Hey Pig, you know what? I don' think they pay you guys enough."

"Well, Mac," *CRUMP!* "I believe that's affirmatron. OK, I'll see ya. Out." He reached back and fumbled around a bit before switching off his radio and cramming the antenna back down.

+ + + + + + +

He again raised his face slightly from his Field Of Shit. To have another look at this mess, at least what he could see of it from this supremely undignified vantage point.

It occurred to him that they hadn't taken any rounds for maybe a whole minute, now. *Maybe it's over. Maybe.*

And as each mortar round-less second ticked by, he inevitably became aware of the screams and shouts from all around him that started penetrating his still-stunned consciousness. First, and above the rest, were piercing random shrieks. Then he heard the less shrill ones, the moans and laments, which filled-in the soundscape like a kind of macabre orchestra, welling up in a hideous, layered crescendo.

I really should move my ass out of this stinking dump — though I do gotta 'dmit, given the fucking circs, it's been comfy and damn welcome — and get up and start sorting this shit out. Well... give it a few seconds more.... The fact was, he'd miss this little field of garbage, to which during the past three minutes he'd become physically and even, (in a way only a soldier under fire could understand), emotionally attached.

Then he heard a distinct voice, a male one, seperate from the other human sounds in that it was neither in obvious pain nor a cry of terror. But it certainly was loud — it sounded artificially *amplified* somehow.

NOW what the fuck?

Henderson struggled to his knees, and then to his feet. He did a 180° eyeball of all that was before him. Not much, to be honest — lotta dust in the air, from the explosions, and one of the shacks was on fire. Several black lumps — bodies — over by the junction of the dirt road and the landing site itself. All, of course, accompanied by cries and wails from all sides.

And then he saw the source of that male voice — it was Mr. Kwat. *Why am I not fucking surprised? How the fuck does this guy just* appear *in places? — I've never seen the guy go* anywhere, *like, you know, move from one place or another — in transit — he just...seems to teleport himself and materializes* somewhere.

And so, yup, there he was, wayover to Henderson's right, at the far edge of LS-Echo, right where the karst dropped off precipitously, facing out into the jungle below. And he was standing precariously — *lucky for him there was no wind at the moment* — on an upturned wooden wheelbarrow. From which perch Henderson could clearly make out the old dude's bony ankles which were prominent between the thick black rubber flip-flops and the too-short gray canvas "pajamas". The Oddjob hi-top bowler hat was still firmly atop his grizzled conk (*is the fucking thing glued on?*), and he was holding, under his chin, ready to deploy again, a kind of jerry-built megaphone. *Jesus H. Humphrey, these people are too fucking much, I swear to God.* Actually it was a plastic red-and-white affair that had begun its life as a Phu-Lama traffic cone but now had its base sawn off and a tea-kettle handle duct-taped onto it. And Mr. Kwat was just pausing for breath. Before resuming his loud and clearly urgent and heartfelt declamation, in what sounded to Henderson like Phu but he couldn't be sure — directed into the heavy green triple-canopy below.

Fuck me, would you just look *at the old coot? Fucker looks like Fu Manchu at cheerleader practice. I don't know what the fuck he's yelling, but he's probably pouring out a ration a shit at whoever's down there — NVA but you never know, could be Istakats, who the fuck knows, and does it matter? — guy's gone around the bend, anyway, that's for sure — I gotta go over there an' try'n calm him down, get him ta knock it off 'fore he gets drilled between the eyes by an AK round... not, heh, that that would bother me all that* much, *but... naa, better not go there....*

Henderson almost smiled at the bizarre scene down there at the far edge of what passed for a runway, and then sighed as his gaze reverted to what remained of the shacks and sheds between here and there.

But Henderson the Bush Pig could not have been more mistaken about what Mr. Kwat had been frantically transmitting through his make-shift megaphone — because what he'd been bellowing, and now, having paused for breath, *resumed* bellowing, was this:

"Stop! Stop! Istakat fighters! I beg you to stop the shellings! We have already lost many people, mothers and children! Do not shell us any more! Do not attack us or bomb us or kill us any more! If you stop, we will deliver to you the American imperialist officer who is here amongst us! Come and get him and our soldiers here will not shoot at you! I, the UNO representative, will see to it, I will guarantee it! But you must act quickly! — the regular Royalist commander is not here for the moment, so now is the time to act! Trust me, Istakat soldiers! We have lost too many people and do not wish to fight you and further die! Come and take the American imperialist and leave us alone! Act now before the Royalist commander returns!"

But the distracted and catastrophically oblivious Henderson continued to listen to Kwat's harangue now more in bemusement than anything else. In fact, the Bush Pig was already thinking beyond Mr. Kwat as he stood there in his garbage pit, getting his act together,

Okay, so first calm down Mr. Kwat — then I'll try'n find that kid, Sergeant Chang Koo, and together try to narrow down where the mortar fire came from — then radio Mac the coordinates so he can bring in the Phantoms. And while we wait for them to do their thing, and also while we wait for Che Kak to get his ass the fuck back up here — the fucker's obviously heard this shit go down, here, and he's bound to be on his way back, probably right 'bout now — Give fuckin' Kwat something to do, get him to give a hand in moving the wounded to next to where McElmore'll set down... Then raise ol' Mac again an' we can work out something more definite, de-

pending on how many bodies we got, probly he'll haveta crank up another, second ATAS bird, get us all outta here at the same time.... One way or the other, time to take the situation in hand, here....

He spat out some dirt that he found he still had in his mouth — *better damn well be only dirt*. And took a swig of warm canteen water. His ears were still ringing from the detonations of the mortar rounds.

No matter what. No matter what fucking else, it was always a fucking relief and a pleasant, to put it mildly, experience, not to mention surprise, when the incoming stopped and you found yourself still with all your requisite parts attached and without any fucking new holes in you....

But so OK, back to first things first. Go calm down Mr. fucking No-Other-Name Kwat; things were bad enough without the old shit-for-brains getting such surviving Meu Jong civilians as might hear his caterwauling all in a worse froth than they already no doubt are.

Henderson brushed a bit of what looked undeniably like *real* shit, as well as other shit, off his jeans, rearranged his askew webbing and rucksack, and re-positioned his rifle and radio onto separate shoulders, and finally forced himself to step away from his shithole.

The cries of pain and distress continued all around him, but the first actual casualty he encountered was lying in the red laterite dirt, about thirty meters in from the turn-around end of the landing strip:

As he'd been carrying some crates of ammo away from the Landing Site, young RPAF/ Private Hoa Chik, a nice quiet Meu Jong kid with whom Henderson had worked in the past, had been hit in one shoulder by a large hunk of shrapnel and was now on his back, lying in quiet, teeth-gritted agony, dropped ammo cans scattered around him. The kid's clavicle bone was exposed, much of his pectoral muscle was gone, and, indeed, his whole arm appeared to be still attached only tenuously. His eyes, from which tears streamed, didn't seem to register Henderson, or anything else, for that matter — they just stared off into the middle distance.

Hoa Chik was attended by three apparently unscathed ILF soldiers who were obviously concerned for the kid, but were just as clearly unsure how to proceed. So, for that matter, was Henderson — the wound was too big for a single first-aid bandage to cope with. The only good thing, if that was the right word, was that there didn't seem to be any imme-diate danger of bleeding out. So Henderson mimed to the ILFs the act of taking off Hoa Chik's trousers (what was left of his shirt wouldn't have sufficed) and urged them to use the black pants to wrap the kid up, around the upper body, tight, like a shroud — Henderson ended with a dramatic flourish, jerking his fists apart to emphasize tightness.

Then he moved on. He wasn't sure, but it seemed as though the noises around him were now sounding more like cries of grief and shouts of anger. And, if anything, they were growing louder.

He passed a middle-aged mama-*san* with a badly bleeding cut on the side of her head, above the ear. She seemed dazed but she clung to a baby-*san* in a sling at her breast as she stumbled past Henderson, going in the opposite direction. He unclipped his first-aid pouch and gave her the whole thing, indicating that she should put some iodine from the little bottle therein on the wound, and wrap it up with the bandage also contained therein. But he couldn't hang around to see if she properly understood — he was determined to get to Kwat, who for some reason, (and rather illogically, given all the seemingly more-pressing mayhem around him), had some-how become something of a fixation with the Bush Pig....

18/ 1110 HOURS

"You can't make more than one mistake in war."

— *PETER JONES (UK "Spectator")*

But when Henderson turned away from the woman with the cut head and took the few remaining steps to the edge of the ridge upon which Landing Site-Echo sat — the very spot where, the last time he'd looked, old man Kwat had been standing berating the enemy below through his idiot traffic-cone — the space was empty. The upturned wheelbarrow was still there, *here it is, the stupid thing's right here,* but there was no Kwat. Things were once more bereft of Kwat. Kwat *di-di-mau*-ed. Kwat, he vanished. Split. Gone, Kwat *he dis-pee!,* yet again.

Goddammit, already, what now? — where the fuck has the old loon transmogriphied himself to now...?

Henderson revolved his torso and cupped his hands to his mouth and yelled *"Hey Mr. Kwat! Where you?",* and as he turned back again, reversing his movement, he bumped into the muzzles of two AK-47s, held by two men who'd somehow materialized from thin air and whom Henderson could immediately identify — from dead bodies he'd previously seen (and even searched) — as members of the communist Phu Istakat.

They wore shapeless dark blue pajama-style tops and bottoms — not, in fact, *totally* unlike the gray outfit Mr. Kwat favored — tan North Vietnamese Army combat sneakers, and tan NVA web gear. And on their heads were steel-blue "Mao"-style *casquettes*, with large red plastic stars on the front. One of the two had an American Army canteen hanging from his belt.

Henderson froze, and he felt the blood drain from his face.

Stupidly, reflexively, he opened his mouth to yell "*Hey!*" but immediately realized the fatuity of such a reaction, and as quickly shut up.

God God God God God, Christ almighty, what the fuck is this? — *as though I didn't know — Jerome, this* really *sucks. This can't be real....*

And even as he processed what was happening, his instinct or his training (it was impossible to know which, but he *did* have a nanosecond's flash to that Nepalese hand-to-hand instructor back at Bragg) kicked in and he turned his attention to the two AK muzzles an inch from his sternum. Henderson tensed himself to try to knock the rifles away from him... *shove the two fuckers if not on their asses then at least off-balance, and make a wild dash for it.* He was actually flexing his legs and right arm, poising to erupt — when what felt like four, *four!,* unseen hands grabbed his arms from behind, at the elbow, and brusquely crossed them behind his back. In which position his wrists were tied competently and tightly together.

Jesus Christ, two more of the motherfuckers! God almighty, how the fucking hell have I allowed this to happen? — I mean, it's not even fucking conceivable –!

A feeling of abysmal disgust flooded Henderson's brain.

Caught like this, like a confused clueless fucking pussy E-Nothing train-ee, with his head up his ass....

You just about deserve this, you dumb shit — you know that? Now you better think of a way ta get yer ass outta this shit — and pronto, the sooner the better... time ain't gonna be on yer side, kid....

As this latest catastrophe was befalling him, Henderson could see, lurking about fifteen meters behind the two Istakat fuckers who continued to face him, back there where he'd been hiding among some rusted 50-gallon fuel drums, the wretched Mr. Kwat, his wispy beard fluttering in a breeze that Henderson, where he stood, certainly wasn't feeling. The old man's skinny arms were wrapped around himself and, as it clearly wasn't chilly, could it mean that he was... worried about something?

Hoping to forestall the sudden onset of dread, and attempting to keep nascent panic under control — attempting to... *focus...* on some scrap from his suddenly vanished world of the tangible, the mundane, the... *manageable,* Henderson found himself shouting,

"Kwat! You shit! You miserable fuck! What the fuck d'you think yer — what the fuck did you do?"

But, perhaps not surprisingly, no response came from Mr. Kwat. He just stood there, watching this little self-generated drama unfold. Hugging himself, under his hi-top black bowler hat.

His dark eyes darting, Henderson looked away from fucking Kwat, and away from his captors, and now scanned over to his right, at the chopper pad of LS-Echo itself and then beyond, to the wreckage of the Meu-Jong shacks and hooches. Civilians and soldiers were beginning to show themselves, to emerge from wherever they'd been hunkering, and to even move about a bit. But Henderson noticed that no one, *absolutely no one*, was looking at him — *not even glancing in my general direction*. RPAF/ILF soldiers were now actually bestirring themselves, starting the painful process of digging themselves out of collapsed positions and locating and then securing members of their families, ... *and not one of them is even* accidentally *looking over here!*

He suddenly screamed in the direction of this renewed activity, "HEY, GODDAMMIT, OVER HERE! *TSHAJ NI!*" But he continued to be most pointedly ignored.

And it struck him with a physical wave of nausea that they were selling him out. That in the immediacy of the just-completed devastation, and in the continued absence of their Captain Che Kak, they were opting for the easiest, most painless way out —

— *You stupid fuckers,* flashed through his brain in the matter of a second, *you don't have to do this! All this was was a single — maybe two, max — piddly-shit 60mm Istakat mortar attack — I was about to call in the Air Force* just fuckin' now, *woulda pounded the area around here into fuckin' twigs an' mud in two fuckin' minutes — but no, you assholes couldn't wait — you think yer buyin' yerselves* a single fuckin' thing *by selling me out...?*

Actually, the Meu-Jong of Landing Site-Echo happened to *like* this particular little American, who, in the short time they'd known him, had always tried to be fair and sometimes made them laugh. But the blunt truth was that he was dispensable. He could, and almost certainly would, be replaced — but this deadly rain from the Istakat or Vietnamese, (it didn't matter to them which), cannons was killing them *now*, and it had to stop *now* — and if trading the American achieved that end, so be it. The denizens of LS-Echo each reflexively understood this, without the need for any coordinating palaver between them.

+ + + + + + +

A three foot long, half inch thick bamboo pole was now thrust up between the back of his head and his bound hands, and the bottom end of it shoved in under his belt, up against his coccyx. *Jesus Christ — nothing like overkill....*

Then, two soggy rags that smelled — and tasted — of nothing good were tied over his face, one over his eyes and the other over his mouth, and knotted behind his head. Henderson tried to maintain his mouth closed when the rag was applied to it, hoping thereby to keep the use of his teeth and the possibility of speech at least as theoretical options, but the unseen Istakat dickhead gave the rag a sharp yank, forcing it into his open, gagging mouth. *So here I am, trussed up good and tight — like a fucking goddamn turkey from Weingarten's supermarket. Holy shit.*

While part of Henderson's mind remained laser-sharp, the other part refused to fully register what was happening to him. In fact, part of him no longer felt *quite* like he was occupying his own body, as though he were somehow a spectator to all this. Even worse, and more ominously, he could sense his consciousness trying to, as it were, slink away — trying to vacate the shameful premises — and he had to force himself mentally to fight against this... this incipient abandonment of his mindfulness. One thing for sure: All of this was horrifyingly unprecedented to the Bush Pig.

They spun him around and prodded him down off the edge of LS-Echo's ridge, and immediately Henderson stumbled on the unseen uneven ground, with two guys holding him up by each shoulder. As they set off, the Istakats exchanged some parting, shouted words in Phu with Mr. Kwat, whose quavery response already sounded far away to Henderson.

Kwat, you thrice-fucked fucking fuck, when I eventually but inevitably leave these pricks holding the proverbial bag and if possible with their dicks in their ears and their heads up their asses — and get back up here, your sorry ass better not be around or I swear to God your stinkin' ancestors won't even be able to recognize what's left after I'm through with you, you miserable piece a shit....

Even as he was mentally processing this bit of satisfying, if facile bravado, Henderson was trying to break through the gale-force turmoil in his brain and concede to himself that, at least for the moment — in his present state — escape was pretty much unthinkable. "Non-operative". *Nevah hotchee.* At least for now.

Gotta wait till they take me to where they're taking me — if I try to run off, blind, now, I'll get nowhere and they'll shoot me before I go ten feet. Gotta calm the mind, gotta not panic, gotta think. *Gotta keep lucid, so I can think quick — and react like fucking Superman when the Right Moment comes... and there* will *be a Right Moment....*

Blinded, gagged, and bound in this painfully awkward configuration, with all his equipment still hanging from him and clanking stupidly all about, it took all Henderson's concentration to stay upright as his four (*apparently* four) captors propelled him down into the inter-karst jungle below.

After what must have been about three hundred meters, the ground leveled out and they reached a shallow stream. Some consultation among themselves concluded, the Istakats again prodded Henderson with their rifles, and they all clomped into the rocky wetness, splashing around unsteadily.

At one point, the two Istakats who'd been guiding Henderson by the armpits let go of him as they all slipped on the invisible rocks and he pitched over, sprawling face down into the creek. As he fell, the front sight of his M-16, which the Istakats had strangely, amazingly, not yet bothered to relieve him of, hit him painfully where the back of his head met his neck — between his skull and his first vertebra. *Wow! Fuck! Aghh!* Spitting silent curses and maledictions into his stinking gag, Henderson unsuccessfully tried to blink back the tears of pain that seeped into the blindfold and mixed with stream water. He was yanked up painfully and awkwardly — as a result of all this stumbling and flailing his ammo bandoleers were all tangled and his HT-2A radio had slung around to his front so that it was now banging against his chin. The two guys who'd let him fall grasped him more firmly now, and laughed and commented to each other in Phu about the Imperialist's clumsiness and resulting discomfiture.

"Look at the arrogant one, not so grand now!"

"Hah hah, I'm sure he misses his mother!"

But they kept a tighter rein on him now, as they emerged out the other side of the creek and proceeded further, deeper, into the jungle.

Actually, maybe it was a result of his captors' clearing a path through it, but to Henderson the stuff didn't seem *quite* as thick and impenetrable as the last jungle he'd come up close and personal with, a little over a year ago, now — the one between Camp Happy Holidays A132-C in Dak Phuoc and the Cambodian border.

On the other hand, the ground here appeared to be definitely more uneven than in that little corner of Vietnam and, despite having two enemy pricks holding him, they were guiding him from behind and thus branches thorns and vines still kept grabbing his shoulders and ankles, and thwacking him in the nose, ears and neck. But Henderson didn't notice this too much, because since leaving the landmark stream, the Bush Pig had decided to try to keep track, more or less, of how many steps they'd taken (if you could call his stumbling forward progress "steps"), and in vaguely which general direction they'd been moving. He did this so that when the time came to extricate himself from this fucking shit-show, he'd have some idea of where the stream was, and LS-Echo — to which he had every intention of returning, *and no fucking mistake* — beyond, just uphill from the creek.

As they made their way, and presumably approached whatever passed for their destination/home base, (and as Henderson mentally counted paces), the four Istakats that made up the "snatch party" inevitably loosened up a bit, talking and laughing among themselves. Capturing an Imperialist "advisor" was a *big* deal, and they were anticipating good things... at the very least official approbation, and maybe even some tangible benefits — perhaps an extra ration of chicken to go with the rice, and conceivably an Anti-Imperialist Emulation (1st Class) Medal for each of them. Henderson could hear them laughing.

Laugh you little shits. You'll be laughing out yer asses when the Bush Pig springs the dirty on you, you fucks.... three hundred seventy five, seventy six, seventy seven....

Henderson was hurting badly in his arms, hands and head, and was undeniably scared to hell. He was also endlessly bitter at his betrayal, and unutterably disgusted with himself at his own stupidity. And all this churning mental turmoil produced within him a towering, overwhelming, certainly irrational, and almost tearful... rage. A rage that even the perennially short-fused Henderson had never felt before — and a residual vestige of his beleaguered rationality told him that this was all to the good: He knew that sheer rage was often the one factor that spelled the difference between prevailing in these dire situations and... well, not prevailing. Clarity of thought, speed, and resilience, sure, they were all a part of survival — but anger was the fuel that kept it all in overdrive.

About twenty minutes after they'd staggered across the stream, and by about the point that Henderson had almost reached thirteen hundred paces, he abruptly stopped feeling the jungle buffeting him, and they came to an apparent halt. The unseen Istakat hands let him go. Henderson stood there, breathing hard, now suddenly feeling utterly alone.

19/ 1130 HOURS

"War is nothing but a catalogue of errors."

— DAVID BROOKS

But of course, he wasn't alone. Henderson could sense that they were in some kind of a clearing. He could hear what sounded like about a dozen men talking. They weren't particularly loud, but the murmuring certainly sounded animated and even excited — there was some laughing and even the occasional child-like giggle.

Then a voice barked what was clearly a command, in Phu, and the four hands that had brought him this far re-emerged from the void to push Henderson backwards, against a tree. It felt to him, or at least to his shoulder blades, like a large tree, almost as wide as he was. Leafy twigs and small branches were hacked away. His rucksack, two ammo bandoleers, web-gear, pistol belt holding his holstered 9mm Browning, M-16 rifle and HT-2A radio were finally all yanked off him and dropped in a pile at his feet. The bamboo pole was removed from his back and, with his hands still tied together, positioned in the bend in his back above his ass, he was pressed firmly against the tree-trunk.

As the four hands continued to hold him there, he felt yet other hands wrapping a rope around him and to the tree, beginning with a noose-like arrangement around his neck and spiraling down across his chest, stomach, hips and legs, down to his boots. Feeling this, Henderson glumly noted that however shitty these Istakat "troops" might be at actually fighting, some motherfucker certainly had trained them well enough in the art of tying people up — *Maaaan, I am well and truly, good and* up against *this fucking tree....*

But still his mind struggled against any further slide into panic or despair:

Alright, alright, keep it together, Jerome... we'll just wait and see what pans out here... Something'll develop, it's bound to, it always does... Just cool it for now — as if I have a choice!... but wait and watch... watch for lapses... and weak links... try to pick out a weak guy... just watch... and keep thinking, planning — they're not gonna keep me tied to this tree forever, they're bound to move me again — and then *be ready to do something, be ready to jump....*

+ + + + + +

His blindfold and gag were now removed by the same hands that had deployed the rope. Henderson's first reaction was to spit repeatedly — actually, his mouth was so dry it was hard to properly spit at all, but he tried anyway. And he shook his head violently, like a dog. *FWAH! OOOF! PWEH!*

"Water, please," he croaked, and waggled his tongue out, hoping to mime thirst. Whereupon from somewhere behind him, behind the tree, an arm reached around, holding what looked like a white ceramic soup-

plate with some water in it — which was thrown *splat!* in his face. He used his tongue to catch a few drops as they dripped off his nose and from his upper lip.

He looked around. *Yeah, a clearing, alright. And a fairly big one, for being in the middle of the fuckin' jungle — maybe thirty, thirty-five meters across.* It was even big enough, Henderson noticed, as he glanced upwards, that there was a healthy patch of open sky between the top branches of the triple canopy.

There was a dormant cook-fire in the center, on either side of which lay, each about two meters off, two dismantled WWII-era Soviet RM-39 50mm mortars. *So, 50s, not 60s — but two of the fuckers — no wonder it was such a rapid-fire shit-shower back there at Echo....* And nearby stood crates of ammo for these babies, some open and some still sealed, with Cyrillic writing stenciled on the wood. And there were even more crates of mortar rounds stacked over by the jungle's edge. *Shit, these fucking turkeys are better supplied with mortar ammo than* we *are, up here... thank you* so *much, US Congress....*

Altogether, Henderson counted eleven of the Phu Istakat sons of bitches. One of them, clearly different from the rest, was dressed in black "pajamas". The other ten, who included the four who'd captured Henderson and brought him down here, were clad in blue what could only be described as sackcloth. Except for the dude in black, they all seemed to look pretty young, and Henderson could deduce from their features and yellowness of skin, (as opposed to brown), that they were all ethnic Phu — not a Meu-Jong among 'em. Despite their current jovial demeanor, they looked generally raggedy, dirty and skinny. On the other hand, their weapons — all standard North Vietnamese-issue, which meant all Soviet, except for their machetes, which were ChiCom, seemed to be maintained in good shape. In fact, these two mortars and the men's individual AKs practically *shone.*

Also placed variously throughout the clearing were:

- An abundant supply of NVA rice tubes, olive-brown and five feet long each. There was a stack of filled ones over there, and another pile of empty ones, over there.
- Six small 2-man ChiCom-made NVA pup-tents, standing erect — if a little saggily. A micro-canvas village taking up a whole section of the clearing.
- A stand-alone folding field table on which sat a bakelite box containing a Soviet ТАи-43-P field telephone, attended by two folding chairs. Under the table were, neatly stacked, a supply of cardboard tubes that, Henderson correctly surmised, contained maps.
- By one of the larger trees, also at the edge of the clearing, sat a smallish, 2x2x2-foot safe — What the fuck can be in there? Money for the guys' pay? — flanked by two padlocked wooden footlockers. Even despite his current condition, Henderson would have dearly liked to know what was in those, too.
- A separate stack of wooden crates and cardboard boxes, all of which had red crosses, ONU, UNESCO, and WHO/OMS stenciled on them.
- Off to another side there was a pile of about eight or nine old Soviet bolt-action M-91/30 Mosin-Nagant rifles, next to which were copious stacks of tin-canned 7.62 ammunition that of course could be used for both these old weapons as well as the men's AKs.
- An impressive little pyramid of still-boxed Soviet RGD-33 "potato-masher"-type hand grenades.

- And finally — in a much smaller clearing, no more than three meters in diameter, located right off the main camp, where a path
led off into the jungle, and which was enclosed, appropriately
enough, by rusty chicken-wire — there pecked and clucked some
dozen or so happily oblivious red chickens. From its fllimsiness,
this little jerry-rigged chicken set-up looked rather more transient
than permanent.

Henderson surveyed all this and couldn't help thinking, *Jesus Christ,*
fuck me, would you look *at all this crap? — ol' buddy Che Kak would shit*
himself with envy if he could see all this gear. Fucking hell....

+ + + + + + +

His four captors had now left him to join the other communist soldiers,
standing away from Henderson's tree, and they all checked him out and
commented about him among themselves.

For his part, Henderson stared back at them with seeming impassivity...
although he felt far from impassive. Again, his teeming mind was telling
him to stay sharp — of course he was completely aware that he was in
deep, mortal shit, here, but at the same time he remained somehow convinced that one way or the other he'd extricate himself from this mess.
Above all, he was aware that if he had any hope *at all* of getting free of
this shit, that *bookoo* sharpness by him would be required. And finally,
he was painfully aware that with each passing minute — unless he was
moved again, which might create new opportunities — escape became
more difficult... more problematic... *and up until now, these fucking peo-*
ple haven't made a single slip-up... at least that I've *been able to catch....*

Presently, the one guy that was in black, rather than blue — the one who looked slightly older (maybe in his 30s, while the others seemed to be in their 20s and even late-teens) — approached Henderson's tree, stopping about six feet from it/him. He had two diamond-shaped bits of red felt sewn onto the tips of his collars, which denoted NCO/"junior cadre" in the Phu Istakat; (officers/"senior cadres" wore yellow/"gold" little felt diamonds). He was also different from the others by being short-er than they, and if he hadn't been sort of held together by his brown leather NVA belt and web gear, his black "pajama" get-up would have more resembled a kind of old-fashioned painter's smock than anything recognizable as a proper uniform. (Not, of course, that *Henderson* wore anything recognizable as a proper uniform either, but that was another matter....).

Moreover, this little Istakat NCO in black was bareheaded, and his spiky black hair stuck out in all directions, causing him to look rather as though he were being electrocuted. And finally, adding to his distinctive appearance was the fact that, although he was merely thirty-one years old, his teeth, at least what remained of them, were brown and appeared to be in the process of rotting.

This, then, was Phu Istakat Junior Sergeant Kho Methek. Both his par-ents had been school-teachers in Phu-Lama and his maternal grand-mother, who'd largely brought him up, had been responsible for setting his teeth off on their road to ruin by spoiling the lad with a regular sup-ply of cheap sweets. He'd joined an "underground" Istakat cell while a student at the little National University in Phu-Lama, hoping thereby to acquire what had up till then eluded him, i.e., a "sexually liberated" girlfriend — but all it had ended up getting him had been an assignment to a god-forsaken corner of Xuam Long Province, out in the distant, misbegotten Pang Phu Meu. On the other hand, he had, thanks to his relative literacy, risen to the rank of Junior Sergeant, so he was not entirely without prospects. Moreover, his "senior cadre" up here in this corner of the northern mountains, the young North Vietnamese lieutenant, had mentioned that they had Moscow-trained dentists in Hanoi and that after liberation had been finally achieved, he might sponsor Kho Methek to travel there and have his teeth "looked at". Kho Methek liked to imagine a trip to Hanoi.... where *certainly* there must be plenty of the up-until-now merely mythical "sexually liberated girls"....

But now, in this jungle clearing, he was, at least in the temporary absence of the Vietnamese lieutenant, the senior man present. And his — well, ... *their* — unit's just-completed valiant action had resulted in this unimaginable good fortune, in the form of a captured American.

So now Junior Sergeant Kho Methek duly struck a pose in front of Henderson: legs apart, and hands on hips. And he intoned, in his almost comically pompous, university-acquired cod English,

"Ameh'can impeeyalist! You are spy faw the CIA, and helper of the blood-sucker lackey régime in Phu-Lama! And theah-faw, I declare on behalf of the peeper of liberated Phuland, that you are now the peeper's pris'nah, and you must co-op'rate with us in all thing. As CIA outlaw you are ill-legal and theah-faw, you have no right." He paused, and transferred his hands from his hips to behind his back. "So now tell us, Ameh'can pirate: Who are you?"

Henderson was still pissed-off beyond reason at having allowed himself to be captured, and, despite his better judgment, found himself answering,

"Who am I? Sheeit, you just *said* I was a CIA pirate — so why're you even asking? You know what, little man? Go fuck yourself. That's right, go fuck yourself, you little ass-wipe. Just go and fuck yourself in your ass, you shitbag little commie fuckface. Yeah, whyn't you try that? And meanwhile," Henderson added as a completely reckless afterthought, "if you can't get your shit together, go get somebody who can — because I don't deal with fuckin' amateurs."

No sooner had he unloaded this — even as the words were escaping his mouth — Henderson was regretting allowing himself to adopt a tone of such mad truculence. (Not least because that splash in the face had done nothing for his parched thirst — and *this* kind of talk wasn't likely to be conducive to his getting even a small drink of water anytime soon.) So he was already considering a change in tactic, even before Kho Methek responded.

For his part, the little Istakat sergeant's face was burning. Because of his sepia coloring, he didn't actually redden, but he blushed with shame and anger nevertheless. His quirky version of spoken English might resemble that of Inspector Clouseau's valet Cato, but he *understood* English perfectly well — and he particularly understood the insults that Henderson had hurled at him.

After the American appeared to shut up, Kho Methek stood there for a silent moment, staring back at him. He was doing his best to maintain the appearance of assured command, because he was agonizingly aware that his entire squad, his "section", was observing him with almost as much fascinated interest as they beheld the captured Imperialist.

Sergeant Kho was pretty certain that none of his men understood the insults that the angry little American had hurled at him, which was *some-*

thing, at least, but otherwise he felt far from confident about how to proceed:

They'd never had an American prisoner before, and Kho couldn't remember what — or even if — he'd been told to do in such an eventuality. With captured Meu-Jong, it was simple enough: They either agreed to be enrolled in the labor brigades that carried rice and supplies eastward to the Ho Chi Minh Path, for the North Vietnamese Army, or if they balked in any way, they were shot. But an *American* must be a different proposition, must he not? Surely you couldn't expect a big loud pampered American (not that *this* one appeared all that big or pampered, but still....) to push a bicycle laden with rice and ammunition through the jungle to the Vietnamese DMZ alongside all the other coolies, students and prisoners, could you? Or maybe you could — Sergeant Kho just honestly didn't know.

And worse, not only didn't he know how to proceed, but Kho wasn't even sure what he was expected to *ask* this captured foreign devil, much less what to do if he continued to insult him, and be stubborn and aggressive and insolent. And so far, Kho realized, as he fought back persistent inklings of panic, he hadn't even been able to get the American to *tell him so much as his damn name*, let alone anything else. Somehow, he, Kho, would have to prevail in this unprecedented and fraught situation, not only to maintain his aura of leadership, (not to mention to maintain face), in front of his men, here, but also to win eventual approval and perhaps even praise from the Vietnamese lieutenant.

+ + + + + + +

The Vietnamese lieutenant in question, "Senior" Lieutenant (*Thuong Uy*) Nguyen Be of the People's Army of Vietnam was currently off at the Small Cave, updating the inventory of their medicines. He had just finished helping his section of Phu Istakats to set the aiming sights on the mortars, preparatory to a barrage on the Royalist outpost as had been ordered by Regiment, and then had left the senior NCO, this rather jumpy and fussy fellow, Junior Sergeant Kho Methek, to get on with it. *They'll never learn if you don't let them do it themselves....*

For there were many medicines, newly arrived — this last batch from Sweden, via Hanoi — to check, tally and secure in as cool and dry locations as possible in their makeshift "medical depot" halfway up a karst protrusion, known among themselves as The Small Cave. He'd expected to absent himself for some time, but he was confident that Sergeant Kho could cope — he was, after all, (and if nothing else), among his own people.

+ + + + + + +

Back at the clearing, Sgt. Kho forced himself to re-address the defiant little scowling American, tied to the tree:

"You. You are typical impudent, arrogant, and woman-and-chierdren-killing Ameh'can impeeyalist waw-mongah pig. I strongly urge you to adopt a civil tone."

What? What did this weird little fucker just call me? An 'imperialist warmonger pig'? Who the fuck talks like this? Henderson flashed back to that surreal scene with Leah, the Maryland Congressional "staffer" with the big tits who'd had a cow when she'd seen his Vietnam Zippo, back at that Georgetown party, back in the "World" — *Shit,* she'd *called him that... she'd "talked like that"....*

Even in his mental turmoil, Henderson managed a burst of exasperation as he blotted out all that past idiocy, and re-focused on *this,* current, idiocy. Like Kho Methek, he *also* needed to mull how best to proceed, what tactic to use, and so now he merely replied, barely audibly,

"If you say so, pal. Sure. Why not."

Kho resumed. He desperately needed to break through, here,

"The Phu Peepers' Istakat Liberation Fawces hab no tolerance faw impeeyalist mercenary criminals. You are an impeeyalist mercenary criminal, and theah-faw it is correct faw you to suffah Peepers' Justice. Of *caws* you will make full confession. But first, yaw name. Yaw *name,* Ameh'can mahderer, *what is it?*"

Henderson now rather frantically considered whether it was wise, or unwise, to divulge his name. Advisable? Or not? It was *probably* OK, no? — "Name rank and serial number", yes? no? That was allowed, wasn't it? *No! I mean, yeah, "name" OK, but no, no "rank and serial number" — I need to fucking remember who the fuck I am, here — or rather, who the fuck I'm* not.... Henderson now thought back on that fucking farce of a Department of Agriculture ID card, that he hadn't carried with him for fear of.... for fear of *what,* exactly? *Fucking thing would sure come in handy* now — *for fucks sakes... maaan, I laughed at that piece a shit when they gave it to me back in DC, but I sure ain't laughin' now....* So now he wasn't sure... he might regret this, later on, but for now it seemed like the least bad option:

"My name is Henderson. I'm an employee of the American Department of Agriculture. I'm a, uh, crop-duster."

Sergeant Kho took a little time to digest this, while blinking furiously, many times.

"What are you saying? Depahtment of Agri-cutchah? Depahtment of... *Agri-cutchah?*"

"That's right." And he added, utterly lamely, "Crop-duster."

"Depahtment of Agri-cutchah, Depahtment of Agri-cutcha...." the Istakat sergeant repeated it as he stepped over and picked up Henderson's M-16 from the pile of gear at the foot of Henderson's tree and brandished it up and down. "And this is a tool of yaw *'agri-cutcha'* I suppose?"

In his newly-adopted policy of reticence, Henderson was at first reluctant to respond to this at all. Instead he looked over the Istakat sergeant's head at the other men, standing in a rough semi-circle, behind him. His eyes fell on a slightly older-seeming guy, who he hadn't noticed before — in fact, the *only* one of the black-clad Istakats who, Henderson now noticed, didn't seem to be in possession of a firearm of any kind. Perhaps he was a senior coolie — perhaps even an unwilling, embittered civilian who'd pissed someone off, maybe been denounced, and been impressed into rice-humping duty — it might be a bit of a stretch, but the guy *did* appear to be unarmed.... *Hmm... OK, it's a long shot, but he might conceivably prove to be an ally, in the right circumstances... Keep an eye on him, Pig... Gonna haveta come up with something soon... Meanwhile, this little lunatic is still yammering at me, still waggling my fucking rifle at me....*

"Eh? What is *this,* impeeyalist pig — a hoe? A rake? A spade?"

"I need it for self-defense. This is a war zone. As you, huh, well know."

"Seoff-defense. Seoff-defense!" Kho threw the still-armed and loaded M-16 to one of the nearest Istakat soldiers, who, amazingly, managed to catch it on the fly, the extruding 30-round magazine just missing his face.

Kho now bent down and extracted Henderson's Browning 9mm pistol from its holster, and he pretended to inspect it. He heard one of the men behind him whisper something to another, which subconsciously caused him to attempt to physically puff himself up. He even felt — and hoped he looked — a bit like an *officer,* holding a pistol like this. Impulsively, he fired a round in the air, "for effect", and then pointed it at Henderson's mid-section.

Up in the Small Cave, NVA Senior Lieutenant Nguyen Be heard the echoing pistol shot coming from the clearing, and stopped counting the individual boxes of Swiss penicillin. *Aie!, this can't be any good — I'd better di-di back over there and see what the hell's happened... Cứt!Đù!Al-ways there is something!* And he snatched up his AKM, re-donned his pith helmet, and went running back through the jungle to rejoin his charges.

Meanwhile, the Browning in his hand still faintly smoking, Sergeant Kho had resumed,

"... and this, this pistaw, must be *awso* faw seoff-defense, I suppose — Hmmm, it seems to me, Ameh'can impeeyalist, that you hab *sooo* many tools faw seoff-defense, faw a fahmah. I nevah befaw see a fahmah hab *so many* fahming tools that shoot 5.56 cariber and 9 em-em lounds —

no, I think you work for that wawld-famous agri-cutchah organ'sation...
cawd the CIA —"

At which point he was interrupted by, of all things, Henderson's HT-2A radio — which must have at some stage turned itself on. Perhaps the power switch had been inadvertently activated when Henderson had stumbled while crossing the creek and all his equipment had gotten discombobulated... or maybe when the Istakats had taken it off him and thrown it to the ground... or maybe he hadn't even properly switched it off back in his garbage pit — who the fuck knew? In any case, it suddenly hissed loudly and.... *started to talk!* (The HT-2A radio had a "push-to-talk" button on it that was necessary to press in order to transmit, as well as a separate "squelch"/"mute" button, but otherwise, when the radio was simply switched on, it could and would receive transmissions, unaided.)

So suddenly, bouncing off the trees of the otherwise silent jungle, came the whiskey-cured bass tones of America Tropic Air Services Captain McElmore... except that to Henderson's ears, McElmore now sounded like he'd never sounded before: McElmore had always previously been supremely laconic — but he sure wasn't laconic now:

> *"Bush Pig, Bush Pig, Bush Pig — Yankee Whiskey. OK, so I last tried to raise you 'bout fifteen-twenty minutes ago, but it was all negatron. Tryin' again now, li'l buddy, an' I gotta tellya I'm gettin' a li'l spooked about what's happenin' out there with you. Now, if for some reason you cain't talk but can copy me, listen up: I'm on my way back to your location and my TOT is about three five, an' I'm bringin' with me a Cobra, a Spooky and*

two A1s, all from Tango, and they've all been well instructed by your man Smith — who I've been dealin' with direct, by the way, them an' the Buzzards — an' those   good people are gonna blow away everything to shit around Echo. An' I mean they're gonna come in heavy, a total three-sixty, an' a half-click deep. Now, soon's they're done with that, I'll be settin' down on Echo again, at which time I'll be expectin' for you to haul your skinny ass aboard bookoo ASAP — I kidnapped the Embassy Doc and have him with me, here, 'case you need a li'l help.

So if you copy, just hunker down, pucker up and stand-by. The Seventh fuckin' Cav is on the way and not to worry, son, we'll get your ass outta there. See ya soon, kid. Out."

The hissing sound came back on, loudly, for a second or so, and then it, too, disappeared. Then, silence.

To Henderson, McElmore's words had been electrifying.

Previous to those words, previous to this crazy radio deciding on its own to come to life (like something out of an early Disney cartoon, or a good dope trip) the alarming fact had been that Henderson had found himself no longer fighting incipient panic, but rather the opposite: he'd been starting to battle a creeping — and quite lethal — inclination to "turn off", to tune out, to just somehow *will* this whole terrible, impossible scene away — a feeling that, when added to his crushing thirst, was making him light-headed, dizzy and even physically numb....

But now!

Listening to McElmore's words, spoken in a more urgent version of his familiar and reassuring voice, Henderson seemed to suddenly forget his present predicament, *tied up to this fucking tree like a pathetic fucking Thanksgiving turkey....* He stared at his suddenly magical HT-2A radio on the ground at his feet, as though it were a living creature. *Goddamn McElmore — what a pisser! — what a fucking pisser, right? Goddamn Seventh Cav, man! — I mean, too much, man, the guy's fuckin' bringin' it! McElfuckingmore, I love you, man!*

It even fleetingly occurred to Henderson's revived kaleidoscope of a mind to speculate on how it would be when he and McElmore were back — *Soon!* — *the wheels are in motion now!* — at the O-Club bar back at the "Combined Logistics Group" compound in Phu-lama — *how many double Wild Turkeys is the old fart gonna extort outta me for pulling my 'skinny ass' outta this?* Henderson actually, physically, laughed at this mental picture; (at least, he'd *meant* to laugh — in *fact* what came out was a barely audible, croaky little snicker).

McElmore's voice on the radio, however, had, ominously, a distinctly different and definitely more alarming effect on the handful of Istakat soldiers, who heard it, all agog. In a word, they were spooked. *Seriously* spooked. They hadn't understood the words, of course, but they knew that it was an American voice, an American Air Pirate voice from the sky, probably the pilot of one of those horrible Death Planes — and those words obviously had to do with this American Imperialist prisoner that they'd taken. *What would happen now? Certainly nothing good.* They shuffled around nervously, their eyes wide with apprehension.

But their reaction to this Radio Transmission Of Probable Impending Doom was as nothing compared to Sergeant Kho Methek's — for whom this whole prisoner-episode had, with dizzying speed, somehow become a complete and irretrievable nightmare:

The penny in Kho Methek's brain clacked, or clicked — or slipped — or did whatever pennies did in brains... the *point*, for Kho, was that it all suddenly, instantly, became crystal-clear:

IT WAS A TRAP! Of course, a trap! No wonder *the little American Imperialist showed no fear, and had insulted him — and now even* laughed *at him! That treacherous old "UN Civilian Refugee" grandfather, Kwap or Kwat or whatever his name was, and this little Imperialist "adviser" — had planned this all from the beginning! They'd* planned *for the American to be taken by his men.... And there had clearly been one of those devilish American radio-beacon devices somewhere on the American's person, or somewhere in his equipment — maybe even in that radio itself — which would guide their forever-damned Air Force right to their position,* right here, *bombing them and killing them all! The radio had just confirmed this! That was the helicopter pilot, boasting of their impending incineration! The Americans had planned to fool him, to humiliate him, and catch him and his exposed men, out of their caves, and roast them alive and destroy them!....*

Kho Methek had heard of such things happening before, to other Liberation units....

Well it's not going to happen to me! *It's not going to happen* here! — *they will not succeed, NOT THIS TIME! —*

Sweating heavily from his scalp, upper lip and even his palms, Kho re-gripped Henderson's Browning 9MM, with which he'd just fired a shot into the air, now in a two-handed grasp, re-pointed it at Henderson's body-mass, and fired off another round. This one crashed into Henderson's mid-section, a little above and to the left of his navel.

Henderson didn't really properly mentally scan any of this; all he felt was a sledgehammer — sledgehammer, hell, more like *atomic* — blow to the stomach, immediately following which his whole body felt like it had turned to ice... and then, (as though as a mocking reminder that he was still alive), he had the searing sensation that someone had stuck a fiery poker up his ass.

As he tried to mentally come to grips with these new, disparate and competing bodily traumas, he realized that on top of everything else, his eyesight was turning cloudy. *HOLY SHIT, I'M SERIOUSLY STARTING TO LOSE IT, HERE* — He shook his head, hoping to uncloud his vision, but no dice — *SHIT SHIT SHIT, KEEP IT TOGETHER, MAN, KEEP IT TOGETHER....*

Kho Methek fired again, this time missing Henderson completely — hell, he even missed the tree.

Some reflexive, deeply atavistic reaction now caused Henderson to shake his head with increasing violence, from left to right, from side to side — was he instinctively trying to present a moving target? (His head was, after all, the only part of his body, other than his fingers, that he could move.)

Henderson thought he was yelling — *screaming* — but in fact no sound came out of his open mouth.

His last thought was an inchoate *"HEY! WAIT A MINUTE...!"*

A now-utterly frantic, desperate Kho Methek re-tightened his two-handed grip on the Browning, tried to aim properly, fired again — and this time hit Henderson right above the left eye. The dark red hole that suddenly appeared on Henderson's forehead was merely dime-sized, but much of the back of his head splattered into the bark of the tree behind him.

The Bush Pig was now, just like that, as dead as it's possible for a Bush Pig to be.

Dại úy Henderson *caca-dow.*

Mistah Jerry bookoo fini.

"Sorry 'bout that, GI."

20/ 1145 HOURS

"Wars of subversion and counter subversion are fought, in the last resort, in the minds of the people."

— *FRANK KITSON*

Sergeant Kho Methek was by now emptying out the remains of the Browning's magazine into the offending HT-2A radio — which responded to the fusillade by bouncing up and down in the dirt — when NVA Senior Lieutenant Nguyen Be burst into the clearing. The young Viet quickly took in the scene, and before the lowest branches of the trees behind him had even stopped swinging, he'd gotten a pretty good idea what had transpired here.

Nguyen Be had already been in an irritated mood, and it had been exacerbated by the first shot — the one that Kho'd fired in the air. Counting out all those damned hundreds of individual portions of penicillin from the UN or the World Health Organization or wherever... was an annoying-enough task as it was, and now he'd have to start all over — *when* he eventually got back to it.... But then there'd been three *more* shots, and that could only mean that things had somehow gotten terribly, totally out of hand.

What the devil is it now? he'd thought as he'd rushed back *I leave that ass-kissing flunky Kho Methek to carry out a simple harrassment-by-fire mission against the Imperialist landing strip at the Royalist outpost, surely a task not even beyond* his *modest abilities... But no, now there's this firing from* inside *the camp — my camp! And by the way, that sure as hell was not our own AK fire, either –đụ má muy!, these Phu so-called soldiers really* are *like children* — foolish *children — worse even than the pathetic Pathet Lao — though not, at least, as bad as those berserk Khmer Rouges — please, don't remind me of* that *amok episode....*

He took in the *tableau* with an expert's eye: An American prisoner — *an American prisoner!* — tied to a tree. The fellow was obviously dead: Although securely-tied, his body sagged and buckled at the knees, his head hung down, and in addition to the man's camouflaged tunic and black T-shirt steadily soaking in blood, there was a big mess of bone and brain on the tree behind the head.

Nguyen Be's gaze moved to the pile of personal American military gear piled at the dead man's feet, and then to midway between that stuff and the cooking fire in the center, where stood the quivering figure of Sergeant Kho Methek, still clutching the now downward-pointing Browning, from which *still* rose tiny wisps of gun-smoke.

The stupid, stupid *fool!*

Nguyen Be had always thought Kho Methek too vain (though what he had to be vain about with those awful teeth of his was a mystery — insecure, bordering on the neurotic would be more accurate) and too easily given to irrationality to be in command of a section. Or rather, a glorified squad, which is what months of jungle attrition, Royalist ambushes and the Imperialist air force had reduced it to. But when he'd brought the matter of his sergeant's inadequacy up with Major Ho An Cau at their last Senior-Cadre "Criticism And Emulation" session, the major had pointedly corrected him,

"Comrade Lieutenant, sometimes you expect too much of our little Istakat brothers. Remember that they have not been forged by many years of Party discipline and patriotic combat as we have. So better to be patient. Kho Methek is well-educated. Also, his family has useful connections within the Royalist bureaucracy. We should not remove him merely because you think him vain. Now, if he should show weakness under stress, or ideological deviance, let me know of it. But otherwise, unless you have a better candidate for command to propose, you should continue to use him."

Bah! Although he'd never breathe such a subversive thought to *anyone,* Nguyen Be had thought at the time that that had been a mistaken load of complacent hubris on the part of the major.

And so now, as a result of this official foolishness by senior cadre, the first American Imperialist that they'd managed to capture *in all of Phuland* had been stupidly and wastefully killed. A total waste. *Come to think of it, isn't that the very term that the barbarous Imperialist GIs use for killing — "waste"?* The ironic aptness was not, er... wasted on Nguyen Be. *Stupid stupid stupid.* Criminally *stupid.* To Nguyen Be, who came from the fishing village of Bãi biển Xuân Hội, near Vinh, Kho Methek's had been an act of counterproductive mindlessness akin to the foolish fisherman who, overcome with aggravation and blinded by frustration over a paltry catch, throws it back into the sea.

Nguyen Be saw right away that there were three courses of action open to him: He could:

- Openly castigate and shame Kho Methek in front of his men, causing him to lose face;
- Demote him — say, to rice-carrying coolie — on the spot;

or

- Execute *him,* in turn.

But whatever he decided to do, Nguyen Be knew that he'd have to do it immediately. All eyes (including Kho Methek's) were on him.

Well, Senior Lieutenant Nguyen Be of the People's Army of Vietnam was nothing if not decisive.

+ + + + + + +

(Nguyen Be was only 26 years old, but he'd already been fully engaged in the Great Anti-Imperialist Struggle for over eight years, and it was for good reasons that he'd been elevated to one of the youngest Senior Lieutenant-Political Officers in all of the PAVN. He'd almost lost his life in the retreat from Hué in 1968; he'd gotten pounded almost to mud in the A Shau Valley in 1969; he'd directed logistics under the rain of B-52s in northern Laos in 1970, and he'd commanded a battalion of Cambodian KPC "insurgents" in Kompong Som in Cambodia in 1971. As a result of all of which harrowing service he'd harvested one Vietnam Liberation Order Badge, three quaintly-named Defeat American Aggression Badges, and the Ho Chi Minh Order - Second Class.

And now he was assigned to Phuland.

He was not, to put it mildly, an unmotivated young man.)

+ + + + + + +

As he surveyed the rock-still Istakat soldiers arrayed behind their sergeant, Nguyen Be knew, without the slightest doubt or hesitation, how
to handle this troublesome... no, not troublesome, worse than that, *unnecessary*... situation. His lower lip trembled in barely-suppressed rage:

"Comrade sergeant! Did you shoot the American?"

"Yes, comrade! Our mortar fire was so accurate and devastating that the
Phu elder up there, the UNO Refugee grandfather, seemed to offer him
to us in return for our ceasing fire. So I sent a team, and we successfully
captured him. But then, as I was waiting for your return, we heard over
the Imperialist's radio, here, his pilot, his Pirate pilot, explaining to him,
the American so-called adviser, the details of their plan to attack us, and
to rescue him. So, immediately realizing their plot, I executed the Imperialist and — " he pointed with the Browning over to the obliterated
HT-2A, "— destroyed the homing device which was in the radio."

Even considering the source — *"the man is just unsatisfactory, a blunder
waiting to happen"*, *I* told *the damn major* — Nguyen Be was amazed at
such an imbecilic story, and he almost even smiled at it. Almost.

"Comrade Kho, you have acted very foolishly. If you were an actual
Imperialist agent yourself, you could not have done more harm to the
Struggle than you have just done here."

His blood draining from his hands and face, Kho Methek listened, open-
mouthed and horrified, and couldn't help noticing that the imperious
young Vietnamese lieutenant did not seem to even be addressing *him*, so
much as the other men.

And still, Lieutenant Nguyen Be was not finished.

"You know very well, Comrade Kho, or you *should* know, that prisoners — *especially* American ones — are among the most useful and valuable weapons the People have in their Struggle. Executing an American prisoner is as if you rolled a live grenade down the barrel of one of our heavy mortars... the same, only even worse, since even heavy mortars are easier to come by than American prisoners. Comrade Kho, if you saw one of your men sabotaging one of our heavy mortars, you — I am sure! — would not hesitate to mete out People's Justice, am I not right?. *Well, Comrade sergeant?*" Acid on "sergeant".

No answer came from Kho Methek, whose eyes were now bowed. Or rather, in lieu of an answer, he simply dropped Henderson's pistol down into the red dirt. *How could such rare good fortune as capturing an American Imperialist so quickly and comprehensively turn to crushing shame and public excoriation? HOW?*

Now! Nguyen Be thought, *Now! An enduring lesson for these men!* Senior Lieutenant Nguyen Be knew nothing if it was not the art of Teaching People Lessons.

Eschewing the Soviet Makarov 9mm holstered at his hip, Nguyen Be smoothly slipped his AKM off his back, flipping off the safety as he did so, and, stepping to his right a few meters to avoid hitting the other Istakats, he fired off six quick single rounds into Kho Methek.

Every round impacted and, because the sergeant had begun to turn when he saw the lieutenant go for his rifle, (trying to flee? perhaps hide?), the six rounds ended up tracing a diagonal path from Kho's left shoulder down to his right hip bone. *Heh,* thought Nguyen Be in some professional satisfaction, *a bloody ceremonial sash.*

Kho Methek fell where he'd stood, with one arm, fittingly enough, flopping onto Henderson's shattered radio.

Re-slinging his rifle, Nguyen Be now stepped to the center of the clearing, beside Kho's inert body, to address his remaining men. Who, throughout the shocking just-completed little drama, had neither so much as said a word or even moved an inch.

+ + + + + + +

Nguyen Be knew them. He knew how to handle them. He knew that they liked, respected and, above all, feared him. When their determination to fight would flag, when they grew fearful of dying and tired of hardship and suffering, when they grew homesick and discouraged — he, Nguyen Be, their Political Officer and, yes, Spiritual Leader, would console, cajole, shame, entreat and inspire them. With uplifting talk of proud ancestors, wives, children, sweethearts, parents, grandparents, uncles, glorious traditions and ceremonies... not to mention Imperialist War Crimes and World Struggle. And he would speak glowingly to them of New Systems and even New Worlds to come. And then he'd somberly point out to them that even if they were forced to make The Ultimate Sacrifice *now,* untold prosperity, dignity, pride, honor and National Identity would be handed down to their descendants, as their just and hard-won heritage.

In short, the usual Leninist catechism, though carefully crafted to fit local Phu conditions. And one which Nguyen Be had to from time to time admit to himself that his ragged Phu Istakat elements didn't always *fully* understand and take on board, certainly not with each and every *dialectical detail* and *deterministic nuance* fully and satisfactorily digested. But even on those occasions when he sensed that he might be in danger of losing the focus of his men, Nguyen Be would redouble his passion and crank up his eloquence, and he'd invariably prevail. Because Nguyen Be was an excellent orator. And he knew it.

And furthermore, he had the advantage of *fervently believing this stuff himself.* Truly, Nguyen Be was a True Believer.

And finally, and rather more prosaically, he'd been doing this thing for a *long* time, now. *Yes indeed — the Imperialists might have "chaplains", and something they call the "USO", and Red Cross "donut dollies", AFVN radio and even — imagine! — television, or any number of other decadent follies and fripperies — but the Forces of Liberation have leaders such as me, Senior Lieutenant Nguyen Be, Political Officer of the PAVN... and I'm* more *than a match for those rotten Imperialist Pigs.*

Even as a boy, back in that seemingly ages-ago fishing village on the seashore near Vinh, young Be had displayed the mark of leadership. Never a shred of self-doubt. When buffeted around like a spray-drenched ragdoll and even stabbed by gaffe-hooks and other implements during bad weather at sea, he'd seemed impervious to pain, both physical and mental. Many — certainly many Westerners — might have considered him a dangerously obsessed maniac... what the colonial French right here in Annam might have called *un obsédé* and the colonial British of Phuland "a bloody nutter". No matter, because to his men, whether Vietnamese, Lao, Kampuchean and now Phu, Nguyen Be had always been, and certainly was now, a man to be followed and obeyed.

+ + + + + + +

So that was why Lieutenant Nguyen Be could face these ten Istakat soldiers, having just murdered their commanding sergeant, with serene confidence. These men hadn't been Kho Methek's — they were his.

"Brothers! Comrades! Sergeant Kho Methek committed an unpardonable crime, a crime against the People's Struggle, tantamount to sabotaging our efforts here in what the Royalists call the Pang Phu Meu but what we know as the Liberated Zone. We undergo enough difficulties as it is without having to endure the gratuitous and selfish aberrations of an erratic, hysterical neurotic. Panic under pressure, catastrophically bad judgment and total misunderstanding of the Party's Basic Line on the part of those who would purport to lead us, is intolerable. So, as you see, we have not tolerated it. You know, I know, and Kho Methek knew... the penalty. And now he has paid that penalty."

With his foot Nguyen Be gently nudged one of Kho's legs. "We can forget him now."

His words, in impeccable Phu, rang out with clear authority. Like so many other participants in the Phuland war, (to include, of course, the late J.J. "Bush Pig" Henderson), Senior Lieutenant Nguyen Be's tan PAVN uniform bore no national insignia. But he looked healthier, and certainly less disheveled and bedraggled, than the Istakat soldiers before him here in this jungle clearing, and he radiated command.

He motioned to two of the Istakats, younger even than the others — couldn't be older than mid-teen — standing together at one end of the semi-circle,

"You two, bury the sergeant. Use the spades that are over there under the table."

The two dragged Kho Methek's body off into the bush.

Nguyen Be now surveyed the remaining eight faces, and quickly decided upon one: Private Hak Sip. Having started as an adolescent rice bicycle-pusher, Hak Sip was still well in his teens and not yet quite sophisticated enough politically, but he was certainly courageous and had proved himself resourceful under fire — Nguyen Be had recently seen him rallying and organizing his terrified mates under an Air Pirate attack. Nguyen Be was confident that the requisite political instruction would be administered soon enough — he'd see to that — but for now,

"Hak Sip. You are now the acting Section Leader. You are now acting Corporal Hak Sip. If you perform well, you will receive confirmation of your promotion from Istakat Liberation Headquarters in Hanoi."

Nguyen Be strode over to one of the foot-lockers on the edge of the clearing, rummaged around in there and returned with two bits of diamond-shaped red felt, which he pressed into Hak Sip's cupped hands.

"Here, sew these on as soon as you get a chance. You know how to sew?"

"Yes, comrade."

"Good. Good man."

Now came the important part: The Lesson To Be Learned. Always, always, there was The Lesson To Be Learned.

"Now listen carefully to me, comrades. *An American Imperialist prisoner is never to be killed.* Under no circumstances. Well, at least not here, and certainly not by you. In fact, your job is not only not to kill them, but to even defend their lives with yours, if such a dire exigency arises. And you know why. Because our comrade leaders of the Great Anti-Imperialist Struggle use Imperialist prisoners to exert political pressure on the Imperialist leaders — or rather, on the populations of the Imperialist countries, particularly the women, the young and the black ones, who will clamor against their leaders — to withdraw their forces and cease their aggression. The Imperialist civilian society is weak, decadent and sentimental, and they behave childishly and irrationally when one of their sons is taken prisoner. Indeed, I can tell you frankly that one live American prisoner is worth more than *three* dead Americans. If not more. So it is of paramount importance that when an Imperialist is captured, you control all your completely understandable feelings of anger and revenge. I know, I know, it gives a great feeling of pleasure to kill American so-called 'advisor' pigs, and fallen American Air Pirates. But if they can be taken alive, that is the prize of prizes, and it is of the utmost political importance to endeavor to do so. And the political, after all, is the most important thing — the political aspect of *anything* is more important even than the military."

Nguyen Be now paced around a bit, giving them time to digest this mouthful. He could have easily gone on without pausing, but he had an innate sense of the dramatic, and how to use it. Presently he resumed,

"Now then. It is important that you concentrate, and understand, what I will first tell you, and then what I will do. Kho Methek committed a very bad mistake and duly paid the price for it. But. *But.* There is something *always*," he dragged out the word "always", so that it came out in Phu *saheeeeemi*, "to be learned from even the most costly mistake. By remaining clever and always keeping in mind the psychological and cultural weaknesses of the decadent Imperialist enemy, we can still derive some valuable advantage — even global, strategic advantage — from this American Imperialist's death. You have heard me teach you of such things in the political classes that we've had in the past, but now you will see some of those principles put into practical action. Hak Sip, fetch me the camera from my canvas case, there, behind the table...."

And with that, Nguyen Be put his impromptu Political Lesson into practical action:

Grasping this Asahi Pentax camera that he'd "liberated" out of the rucksack of a dead Imperialist Marine back before he and his fellows had been driven out of Hué, he turned it upside down, inserted a roll of 400 ISO film (for use in dark places, which their camp undoubtedly was), and went to work.

Motioning that Hak Sip should come with him, the two approached Henderson, still hanging from his tree. Nguyen Be unclipped Henderson's K-Bar knife and its sheath from his pistol belt, and gave it to Hak Sip.

"Here, this is now yours. And you can start becoming acquainted with it by cutting down the Imperialist."

Once they had Henderson laid out — pretty much where Kho Methek had recently lain — Nguyen Be started photographing. With the practiced proficiency of a Vietnamese Larry Burrows or Sean Flynn, he took Henderson from every angle, including close-ups of his face — and even, clinically, of the mess that was the back of his head.

He also included shots of all of Henderson's equipment, preparatory to bundling it up and sending it by truck to a special Ministry of Defense warehouse in the Ba Đình district in Hanoi. Except for the K-Bar knife that he'd given to Hak Sip, and which the boy held out also to be photographed, Nguyen Be had *not* bestowed Henderson's firearms, the M-16 and Browning 9mm, upon the Istakats, here, or even appropriated them unto himself. This was partly because of the incompatibility of the Americans' ammo — ammunition re-supply was enough of a headache as it was. But mostly because of the small detail that those unsmiling sticklers, back at PAVN Hqs. in the Hanoi Citadel, maintained that whole department dedicated to the collection and judicious re-use of captured US weaponry and gear, and not sending "war-prize" stuff back to them was a punishable offense.

But even though he assiduously photographed even such personal items as Junior's green Dallas Commanders baseball cap and the contents of Henderson's rucksack, the NVA lieutenant had been disappointed by not being able to come up with any indication of Henderson's proper identification — Nguyen Be hadn't been present when Henderson had given up his name and mentioned the "Department of Agriculture" business to the late Sergeant Kho, and the surviving Istakats, who hadn't understood word-one in any case, were hopeless. But then, finally, Nguyen Be had hit unlikely paydirt when he took off Henderson's old leather-and green-canvas Vietnam jungle boots:

While the weapons and equipment had to be sent back to Headquarters, there were no strictures against re-using a dead enemy's clothing, and that included watches and footgear. So after pocketing Henderson's Timex, Nguyen Be set about inspecting Henderson's scuffed-but-still-serviceable boots to see if they could be worn by one of his guys, when he noticed — *what is this?* — that written in black magic-marker over a background of typewriter "white-out" fluid, on the tops of the inside of each boot, was:

1 LT J.J. HENDERSON
078-38-2761

Aha! A couple of years' worth of mud, rain and, above all, friction and sweat had darkened the white background and somewhat smudged the black letters, and Henderson had obviously overlooked these old labels when so carefully "sanitizing" himself, back in his Roundhouse hooch in Phu-Lama. But it was all certainly still legible enough, and Nguyen Be photographed this crucial bit of information with particular care.

When he'd photographed every conceivable bit of Hendersoniana — indeed, exhausting the entire roll — he extracted the film, pocketed it, and addressed his men again:

"Our Intelligence people will ensure that copies of these photographs will be sent first to ideologically convivial news organs in Asia, and then to more globally influential ones in America and European countries. Although basically capitalist, the press and television in America is also at the same time greedy, corrupt and most importantly — and perhaps surprisingly — unpatriotic, and we in the People's Republic of Vietnam have long-since cultivated many useful, influential contacts in what they call their 'media'. Thus, these photographs will undoubtedly be published and widely disseminated by them, and a great outcry will predictably emanate from amongst the many millions of Americans who are, thanks in no small part to our and our many friends' efforts, increasingly militating against the foreign aggression policy of their Imperialist government."

The men watched and listened to him intently. They rather wistfully remembered their own homes, which, in their proletarian functionality, were largely decorated precisely with pictures cut our of popular magazines — so press photographs were something they could readily-enough understand.

"Right. Now then. There is another thing we can do. Not perhaps as important as manipulating the Imperialist press, but still important — certainly important to us here. Corporal Hak Sip, bring back your new knife."

"Yes, Comrade Lieutenant." Hak Sip approached, K-Bar again in hand.

"Hak Sip, I want you to use that knife to cut off the Imperialist's head. Go on, get down there and saw it off — with his own knife, which will certainly be poetic People's Justice."

Hak Sip looked down at Henderson, and gulped. *Cut off a head? Me? With a knife?* He half-seriously considered questioning the order, but quickly decided not to.

In the clearing's now-complete silence, Hak Sip bent to his task. This heavy-duty K-Bar knife was undoubtedly as sharp as anyone could want, but even *it* soon proved not up to the job, and presently his sawing bogged down. Strenuous as his youthful efforts were, he just couldn't seem to get through the cartilage and bone. *Shit, what a shitty business....*

Observing the lad's increasing discomfiture, Nguyen Be walked to another foot-locker, extracted and returned with a brand-new, olive green Chinese "Red Harvest"-brand machete, which he handed to his acting Section Leader.

"Here. End this."

A few brisk whacks, *thok! thok! thok!*, and Henderson's head now rolled free, if that was the right word.

"There, Comrade Lieutenant." Hak Sip handed the machete back to Nguyen Be, and resumed his place with his mates in the semi-circle.

The Vietnamese lieutenant now used the machete to hack down and prune a largish bamboo plant, ending up with a sturdy pole about ten or even eleven feet long. He sharpened both ends and forcefully stabbed one tip into the bloody neck at the base of Henderson's head.

In fact, what remained of poor old Henderson's head was beginning by now to no longer resemble anything obviously human, but neverthe-less... Nguyen Be went over a few feet, policed up Junior's green Dallas Commanders baseball cap and jammed it onto the ex-Bush Pig's now-pulpy cranium. And then hoisted the whole hideous, bloody mess aloft, like a trophy. Which it undoubtedly was.

The men watched all this with eyes transfixed with an astonishment that even approached, in a few of them, horror. Nguyen Be nodded at one of the physically stronger ones,

"You! Phek! Take one of your mates with you and both of you carry this carefully — if the head falls off just jam it back on — to the stream at the ford where your raiding party just crossed it, and find the pocket of calm water near there where the Royalist soldiers and their families go to wash and fetch water. You know where. And plant this firmly on their side of the stream bank, at that gathering spot. Remember — on *their* side."

Soldier Phek stepped forward, grabbed the pole, and, with one of his buddies in tow, went scurrying off back into the jungle, on this *ad hoc* mission of Advanced Psychological Warfare.

Nguyen Be wiped his hands on his tan uniform pants, and, nodding at the spot in the bush where Phek and his pal had disappeared, resumed The Lesson:

"Yes. It is always important to remind the local people here, these Meu-Jongs, that although the Imperialists have great and cruel airplanes and bombers, they are ultimately weak, and un-resourceful, and utterly without Socialist Morality, and, like everyone else, they are completely susceptible to People's Justice."

He pondered the headless corpse at his feet, and wondered if he was missing anything... Had he thought of everything?... *No, yes! There is something else! Just a small personal consideration from me, Senior Lieutenant and Political Officer Nguyen Be of the People's Army of Vietnam, to the "great" American War Machine....*

"Corporal Hak Sip, hand me your knife yet again — we're not quite finished with it yet. Thanks — " he took it and once again addressed his men.

"The final political lesson for us to learn from today's opportunity will take the form of a small joke between us, the Forces of Liberated Phu-land, and the American Imperialist Expeditionary Force in Phu-Lama." He smiled broadly at them. "Maybe this man's, this 'advisor''s replacement — if there is to be one — will think twice before being foolish enough to follow his late colleague out here."

Nguyen Be went once again to the foot-locker from which he'd previously fetched Hak Sip's red felt diamond bits, and returned now with a resealable plastic bag, the kind the Americans called "Ziploc", that had somehow found its way from an American PX to the Pang Phu Meu and which he normally used for loose ammunition rounds.

Plastic bag in hand, he squatted down by Henderson and undid the corpse's Levis. With surprisingly deft (alarming to the watching Istakat soldiers: *Has the lieutenant done such a thing before?*) slices, he cut off Henderson's penis and testicles. He put this bloody "package" into the plastic bag, and went with it to the folding field table, at which he now sat. He ripped off a page from a Japanese child's notebook (which had unicorns and rainbows on the cover) and carefully printed out the following, in his best English:

> SIR:
>
> THIS IS ALL THE REMAIN OF 1LT J.J. HENDERSON 078-38-2761.
>
> MAYBE YOU WISH TO PASS ALONG THE ENCLOSED TO HIS FAMILY IN AMERICA.
>
> WE VERY ENJOY TO HAVE 1LT HENDERSON VISIT WITH US IN THE LIBERATED ZONE OF PHULAND.
>
> THANK YOU AND PLEASE SEND US MORE SUCH PIGEONS.

UNTIL WE MEET AGAIN, SINCERELY YOURS,

THE ISTAKAT PEOPLE'S ARMED FORCES

OF LIBERATED PHULAND.

He read a Phu translation of this to the men, who nodded and mumbled *"aaannnhhh"*, before folding the sheet of paper and putting it into a square airmail envelope that he had, there, in his modest stationery cache in his foot-locker, writing on the front:

EMBASSY OF U.S.A.

PHU-LAMA

(PERSONAL)

He carefully placed this envelope, the roll of film that he pulled out of his pocket, and the ghastly mess sealed inside the plastic bag into a separate pocket of his rucksack, which he specially cleared of other odds and ends for this precious cargo.

Right, that's done.

Nguyen Be changed mental gears, and addressed his new Section Leader,

"Hak Sip — Corporal Hak Sip — when the Imperialist Air Pirate spoke on the radio, what exactly did he say? Or if not exactly, were you able to get a sense of his words? What was this affair of a bombing plot, this nonsense that Kho Methek was babbling about?"

"I really can't say, Comrade Lieutenant, I couldn't understand any of it. And you must realize, we were all... a little frightened. It was a highly confusing moment. Sergeant Kho, who *did* understand some English, was certainly frightened by the radio's words — in fact they drove him a little bit crazy. Which is why, I think, he killed the American. So I think the words from the radio were a warning or threat of some kind."

"Hmm, no doubt." Nguyen Be was glad he'd elevated this youth, Hak Sip, who clearly could think on his feet. The Vietnamese lieutenant now addressed them all,

"Well, probably sooner than later, as it becomes clear that they will have no response from this end," and Nguyen Be nodded to the remnants of Henderson's radio, "the Imperialist bosses will realize what has befallen their man, here, and the Air Pirates will react with their usual cruelty. Meanwhile, it is of utmost urgency that I take all this — " he pointed to his rucksack by the table, " — to Regiment. So I will go now, and be gone for, oh, I would say, at least three days, maybe four. While I am gone," he walked over and put a hand on Hak Sip's shoulder, "Hak Sip is in charge, and you will obey his instructions as though they were mine." He paused and looked at each of the soldiers individually, in his face. Then he dropped his hand from the lad's shoulder and resumed, more briskly, almost businesslike, "Now I want you to gather up what you need from here, and hide the rest well, and then go and rest in the caves until I return. Before you go, take the Imperialist body off somewhere for the carrion — you needn't bother to bury it, I don't want any more time lost. You men fired well today, and you did *excellently* to capture the Imperialist pig — while I am at Regiment I will recommend an Emulation Citation for this whole section which, if accepted, will result in an augmentation of the Basic Ration. Understood?"

"Yes, Comrade Lieutenant, sir!" they answered in unison.

Although it was *slightly,* just barely, noticeable — their collective response was a *tiny bit* less loud and enthusiastic than such responses usually were. For the fact was that Nguyen Be's shooting of Kho Methek and the mutilation of Henderson's body had left them, well, slightly... queasy. Nguyen Be had detected, and noted, the subtle nuance in their reaction, but he didn't worry about it. The men would get over it — he Knew Them.

+ + + + + + +

So it was that twenty minutes later, the clearing was empty of men and visible equipment. Only fresh human blood gleaming and seeping here and there into the red dirt suggested any evidence of recent occupation by Man.

Indeed, by the time the Huey Cobra gunship, and the C-47 Spooky "Puff The Magic Dragon" virtual "flying machine-gun", and the two propeller-driven A1 "Spad" Skyraiders — all out of the US Air Force's 6232nd Combat Support Group (CSG) in Udorn Thani AFB in northern Thailand — that McElmore had had the Buzzards urgently call up and that he now guided into the AO... finished performing their maxi-efficient pulverization number — 360° around LS-Echo and a couple of hundred meters deep — the only actual human body they ended up hitting was, ironically enough, that of what remained of Jerry Henderson.

+ + + + + + +

And at Landing Site-Echo itself, when McElmore finally set down his old H-34, desperately intent on extracting his Bush Pig, he was, of course, met with what he soon realized was a complete catastrophe.

By now RPAF Captain Che Kak had regained the Landing Site, back from his truncated mission down in the village, and was jabbering to a small knot of RPAF soldiers. But he broke off and ran to the front of the helicopter as it landed.

McElmore, who powered down and put his craft in the helicopter version of neutral so that their shouted conversation could be understood, had never seen the normally competent and unflappable Meu-Jong officer in such an agitated — even distraught — state.

As Sandoval struggled not entirely successfully to limit the shambolic surge of both wounded civilians and ILFs to board and drag even more seriously injured behind them, McElmore emerged from his pilot's perch and stood on the right front tire, from where he yelled at Che Kak,

"Where's Mister Jerry?"

"Mistah Mac!, Mistah Mac! They take him — Istakat come and take Mistah Jerry!"

"WHAT? FUCK! Fuuu-UCK! How the fuck did that happen?"

"I not shua! — I down in village when mawtah attack hit, but peeper heah tell me that Mistah Kwat, the old UNO guy, he tell to Istakat come and take Mistah Jerry — and my men too busy with mawtah damage and dead family, many injah, bookoo dead bookoo injah — they don't pay attention, they thinking othah thing, they only thinking dead and injah family — and so they, Istakat, come to take Mistah Jerry!"

McElmore was only vaguely familiar with "Mr. Kwat", the "old UNO guy" — such people and their functions were not a daily concern of his as an ATAS pilot — and he now demanded, lamely and in obvious frustration,

"Where the fuck is this UNO guy, this Kwak guy, now?"

"I don' know — he dis'pee! — I think he hide, I think he see you come and he ron 'way an' hide! He scare!"

This was fucking *terrible. Unthinkable.* But on the other hand, above all else McElmore knew that he couldn't sit around idling endlessly on this chopper pad. It wasn't doing squat for the poor fucking Bush Pig, that much was now horribly clear, and it wasn't all that healthy for *himself*, either....

"OK, listen, Che Kak, I'm afraid there's nothing I can do about this shit now — an' I gotta get outta here. You wanna come back with me to Phu-Lama? We'll make room — "

"No, bettah not — If I stay, peeper still hab hope that they will still get suppawt from Phu-Lama, from Ameh'ca. But if I go, I scare these men, my men, will not stay, they will give up fight, and go home, or ron 'way, go to othah village — and I scare we lose Echo compretery. So, no — mo' bettah I stay heah, faw now."

"OK, well you hang in here — don't worry, I'll be back, and I'm sure they'll for shit-sure send a replacement for Mister Jerry."

With that, McElmore threw a worried glance at the human bedlam that his cargo space had become, yelled at Sandoval to *"Close the fucking door now! — Che Kak, help him! — or we'll never fucking lift off!"*, regained his pilot's seat, throttled up to the absolute max, and clattered hastily, if unsteadily off. As soon as he was airborne he got most urgently on the horn,

"Roundhouse Six, Roundhouse Six, this is Yankee Whiskey, over."

"Yankee Whiskey this is Roundhouse Six, go."

"Roundhouse Six, Yankee Whiskey — OK, you gotta get me your Actual, and I mean el pronto — we got some bad shit here at Echo, *terrible* shit, the *worst* — the Bush Pig got took. I say again, the Bush Pig got took. Bad guys got 'im. So get me the Actual. Over."

21/ THE NEXT HOURS AND DAYS

" 'Those observing war from the safety of their living rooms' have become the most important political force engaged today in modern warfare."

— DANIEL HENNINGER

As it happened, Senior Lieutenant/Political Officer Nguyen Be of the People's Army of Vietnam had known *exactly* what he was doing. Comprehensively-trained as he was, he understood The Bigger Picture as well as he understood his handful of Phu Istakat irregulars in the Pang Phu Meu.

What he had referred to as "Regiment" to his men was in fact the "Istakat Division" of the Political Department of "B-6 Front (Liberation) Headquarters" a large, sprawling secret PAVN semi-permanent encampment of hangar-like buildings by the Black River (*"Sông Đà"*), about a hundred klicks northwest of Dien Bien Phu, *just* on the Lao side of the unmarked spot in the mountainous jungle where the borders of North Vietnam, Laos and Phuland, at least theoretically, met.

And it was there that Nguyen Be — after a tortuous walk to the nearest Phu artery of the Ho Chi Minh Trail, followed by a hopped ride on a passing NVA Russian GAZ truck — had expeditiously handed over his disgusting packet of Henderson's private dingalings, with accompanying envelope.

These the political muckamucks at the B-6 Front (Liberation) Headquarters then hand-courier-ed, via yet another Russian truck, to Hanoi, where, at the "108" Military Central Hospital on Trần Hưng Đạo Street, the "package" and accompanying envelope were transferred to the trusted care of a friendly (i.e., co-opted) French doctor who was officially part of France's "*Coopération*" aid program.

This doctor, a member of the French Communist Party and a paid intel asset of the North Vietnamese version of the KGB, (an outfit euphemistically known as the "Liaison Directorate" — *Nha Liên Lạc*), then flew with the package, that was now labeled "medical tissue", and its accompanying envelope on a quick Aeroflot hop to Phu-Lama, where he borrowed one of the local *Coopération*'s Peugeot 404s and, later that night, simply heaved the bundle, to which the envelope was now taped, out the car's window as he drove past the heavily-guarded US Embassy in the early morning hours. Whereupon package and envelope were, a few minutes later, gingerly recuperated by the Marine Guards and, after the envelope's contents were read and the package carefully prodded and tested for booby-traps, opened.

Both Nguyen Be's note and the by-now thoroughly putrid plastic sack were waiting on his desk for Col. Smith when he arrived at his Defense Attaché office in the Embassy later that morning — and by noon of that same day, the package-plus-note were flying back to Washington D.C. in a hastily-prepared Diplomatic Pouch, addressed to Col. Helios. And an exceedingly grim Smith was on a scrambled phone-line, rudely rousing his colleague Helios in the latter's McLean, Virginia, bedroom:

"Sorry to wake you, George, but we suddenly got us a *biiiiig* problem, here...."

+ + + + + + +

Back at "B-6 Front (Liberation) Headquarters" Nguyen Be's roll of exposed film — which was much more strategically important than poor Henderson's privates — was handled quite differently:

Nguyen Be delivered the film, along with yet another explanatory note, to a Soviet GRU colonel (Soviet Military Intelligence, although in civilian clothes), attached to the "B-6 Front", who, after he'd read the note and listened to the sweaty Vietnamese lieutenant's explanation of the context behind the contents of the roll of film, drove both it and himself to Hanoi in his GAZ jeep.

There, in the GRU's extensive annex attached to the Vietnamese Communist Party Logistics Complex near the airport, the film was developed, and the prints and negatives, along with Nguyen Be's note, were put on the first-available Aeroflot flight to Moscow, where the GRU immediately passed it on to the "Active Measures Division" of the KGB's 1st Chief Directorate.

There, the string-pullers in the требования ("Requirements") Bureau of Active Measures' Research Department in a sub-basement at #2 Dzerzhinsky Square went into high gear: They activated "Agent Subway".

Agent Subway (the KGB already had another agent called "Metro") was in fact a by-now middle-aged, still-unmarried American woman who the KGB had recruited some years previously, when she'd still been a student "activist" at New York's Hunter College. She currently lived in

Washington D.C. and worked as a staff assistant to a certain Democratic Congressman from New York City.

And now the KGB's Active Measures Bureau cranked up Agent Subway's case officer at the Soviet Embassy on Wisconsin Avenue in D.C. Whereupon this man, "Sergeï", transmitted Henderson's name and serial number to Agent Subway by dead-drop, with instructions to produce "all available documentation".

This "documentation" turned out to consist of a microfiche-ed copy of Henderson's Department of Defense "201" (Personal) File, which Ms. Agent Subway had obtained by calling in a favor from a friend of hers — a member, of all things, of her monthly book club — who happened to work as a senior clerk at the Pentagon. Agent Subway could have instead just filled out and submitted a standard Form GS-311-A "Congressional Privileged Records Request", but that would have taken some considerable bureaucratic time and her Russian "boyfriend" Sergeï had stipulated that Moscow required the info on Henderson rather *"viery viery queeklië"* so she'd just asked her book-club chum instead.

And on the 6th of May, 1972, the senior receptionist at TIME Magazine's editorial offices in New York City signed for a registered, thickish, manila envelope from a P.O. Box address in Rome, which turned out to contain a color print *with* corresponding negative (yes, the generous KGB had even made copies of the negatives) of every photograph of the dead Henderson, and his equipment, that Nguyen Be had taken, a mere few days previously. All of them, that is, *except* for the ones of Henderson's severed head on the bamboo pole — the KGB wanted to anger Americans against their fellow Americans who'd sent the "Advisor" *to* Phuland, but certainly not anger them against whoever *in* Phuland had, in fact, cut the unfortunate guy's head off.

And accompanying this *photomontage* was an anonymous typewritten note (which the CIA would eventually determine, long after the story had ceased being sensational and they'd managed to pry the documents from TIME's recalcitrant mitts, was written on a Swedish "Facit" typewriter), which read:

> *These photos, of the late US Army (Special Forces)*
>
> *Captain Jerome J. Henderson, serial number 078-38-2761, of Houston, Texas, were taken on the 27ʰ of April, 1972, in the Liberated Zone of north-eastern Phuland. We thought you in the American press might be interested in seeing some on-the-spot reportage from America's latest War of Imperialist Aggression. A war about which, we are confident, the American People have known, up until now, precious little.*

Rather surprisingly, given the inflamed and one-sided ideological tenor of the times, especially in the "adversarial press", there had then actually ensued a heated debate, during a late-night meeting of TIME's Editorial Board in their own "Time-Life Building" on New York's Sixth Avenue, about the "propriety" of publishing the pictures of dead Henderson, particularly the more grisly ones — and as a cover story, yet.

But after a marathon exchange of impressively bitchy acrimony spiced with specifically recriminatory accusations of bad faith, cowardice, pandering and ideological betrayal, it had eventually been "collectively" decided to overrule such ultimately quaint considerations of national security and good taste, in favor, ostensibly, of the all-conquering "right to know" — though in *fact* the real motivation was to satisfy the imperative of "raising awareness"....

And so... in the very next issue of TIME, there was the visage of the murdered Jerry Henderson on the cover, cropped from the shoulders-up, in full color, the bullet hole in his forehead three inches below the bottom of the "I" in TIME. The cover also featured a diagonal "banner" that managed to cram in all of the following:

PHULAND: THE BRUTAL SLAYING OF A US "ADVISOR"
Our Secret Involvement In Our Newest SE Asian Adventure:
How Much, And Since When?

+ + + + + + +

As soon as he could after his somber conversation with Colonel Smith, Colonel Helios had prevailed upon the Department of Agriculture's Office of Personnel's Department of Special Projects to "notify" the Henderson family of the Bush Pig's "disappearance"; neither the Department of Defense nor the Department of Agriculture could very well declare him "MIA" because of course there hadn't officially been meant to *be* any "A" involved by the U.S. Government in Phuland to begin with.

This "notification" procedure — the first step of which was a personal visit by an anonymous, if decorous, Ag Department flunky, and then followed-up by an official letter from the Ag Secretary — had been thrown for a considerable loop right from the get-go, because Henderson, back when Miss Blips/Margaret Hagen had given him all that paperwork to fill out prior to deploying, had entered his sister Geraldine as his "Next of Kin"; (his first choice had actually been Junior, but he'd ended up not using him, considerately thinking of the peripatetic nature of his brother's professional schedule). And not surprisingly, poor Geraldine had not handled the "notification of disappearance" all that well. Indeed, it's no exaggeration to state that the stunned girl had, in the new parlance of the time, freaked out.

In short, brooded Colonel Helios, the execution of the whole "notification" thing, first with the distraught sister, and then with the impossible-to-reach parents, had been far from ideal... *far* from ideal... And that had been *before* this monstrosity of a TIME cover story....!

But *now.... Jesus Christ on a crutch....*

Colonel Helios realized in depressed resignation that he'd now have to go down to Houston himself — though, in fact, now that he thought it through a little more, making himself suddenly scarce in Washington wouldn't exactly be the *worst* move in the world, at the moment....

He asked Beverly Browne to step into his office. Poor Bev the Redhead was *also* in a state of semi-shock, but at least she seemed to be holding her shit together a little better than sister Geraldine had managed to do.

"Listen, Miss Browne, Beverly, I'm afraid you knew the kid, sorry, I mean Captain Henderson, better than any one of us here did — nah, that's alright, you don't have to explain, we knew all about you and him, it's no problem, believe me — but tell me, did you ever manage to learn anything about his, uh, family situation that might be useful to us now, at this tragic... and, ah, frankly, *difficult* moment? *Any*thing?"

(*sniff*) "Well... I suppose if he was close to anyone — other than, I guess, me — it was to his kid brother, the baseball player...."

+ + + + + + +

Up in their upscale four-bedroom colonial in Westchester County, Robin's husband collected the Saturday morning post from the mailbox embedded in the pillar down at the end of their considerable front drive. Although he was still with NEWSWEEK — in fact, more prominently than ever — he made it a point to keep up with the competition, and was particularly taken aback when he saw this week's TIME cover: *Hey, isn't this....? Don't I — Don't we....?* He looked inside the mag and saw the name.... *Yeah, I remember now, I knew it — this guy was on Robin's list of wedding invites, she said he was an old friend of a friend from school when I asked her who the fuck he was — she even showed me a picture of them at Coney Island... well I'll be damned....*

As he flopped the magazine onto their kitchen table, he said to Robin,

"Hey Robbie, you may wanna be sitting down when you see this week's TIME — "

Robin, who'd been making herself her first coffee, froze when she saw it. Literally — her blood went cold; (the cliché, as they usually are, was very accurate.)

"Huh," Mr. Robin continued, with deliberate insouciance, as he, in turn, approached the complicated Italian coffee machine, "you know, in that picture, your buddy looks a lot like that famous shot of the dead Che Guevara, you know? Except your guy doesn't have a beard, here — otherwise, the whole layout, it's just like ol' Che when the CIA nailed him in Bolivia, back, what, in '67, I think... Remember?"

What? Yes, no, I don't remember ... or maybe I do ... what? What're you talking about? Che Guevara? what? no, no... no... just... no. For God's sakes, this is Jerry Henderson, *for God's sakes... what? ... no ... what? What did*

you say? How on earth did this ... what was he doing? ... wait, where? what?

Robin just couldn't even *begin* to register any of this....

+ + + + + + +

It is, from today's vantage point, redundant, painful and, above all, unnecessary to rehash in *too* much detail the whole panoply of shameful national horripilation that followed the public revelation of Henderson's death:

American newspapers screamed bloody murder — at their own government. Apoplectic front-page editorials, the works.

American senators, congressmen and congresswomen, unanimously on the Democrat side but including many Republicans as well, pontificated, bloviated, hyperventilated, huffed and puffed, and generally had simulations of fits.

American TV "anchors", "commentators" and talk show "hosts" flapped and frowned and touchingly enacted Great Moral Outrage. Again, at their own government.

American hippies freaked out over "American Imperialist Aggression in Phuland, man", and, in fully-deployed Protest Mode, flopped themselves out and pitched indignant camp over ever-expanding public spaces.

American "disadvantaged youths", in heartwarming displays of "solidarity" with Phu Istakat "freedom-fighters", rampaged and looted liquor, sporting goods and appliance stores throughout their urban enclaves, most notably in Los Angeles, Newark, St. Louis, Detroit and Cleveland.

American Catholic, Protestant and Jewish clerics of all ranks, and from all sub-denominations, signed and issued cringingly embarrassing *pronunciamentos* of a scolding and hectoring nature, and even staged "symbolic" (mercifully for all involved, *only* symbolic) "immolations", to protest this latest US Government act of perfidious immorality.

Near-apoplectic "Ad Hoc Committees" of Scientists, Psychiatrists, Doctors and, above all, College Professors issued Ringing Denunciations.

A near-totality of "Hollywood", with the conspicuously lonely exceptions of John Wayne, Jimmy Stewart, Ward Bond and Bob Hope, signed outraged petitions and generally made a great spectacle of itself, in ostentatious support of, inevitably, "Phu Liberation".

Ordinary American students — of *course*, ordinary American students, both college and high school — "struck". (I.e., stayed home and goofed off.)

And, not least, the Georgetown University franchise of the SDS (Students for a Democratic Society) mounted a "guerrilla" raiding party on old Dr. Ho Tou Fat's little Phu Embassy/Residence up on Massachusetts Ave. in D.C., where they threw what they claimed was pig's blood across the front door and adjacent windows. Although in reality it was only red paint — *Hey, where we gonna get our hands on real* buckets of pigs' blood *in D.C.? You shitting me, man? That's a bitch, man, ain't no such shit lyin' around in no city, man, forget it, that don't exist, man....*

In short, the nation — or at least that portion of the nation that was deemed by those who decided these things to "matter" — convulsed.

+ + + + + + +

Back on Landing Site-Echo, about a month after Henderson's abduction and murder, Che Kak himself narrowly survived an assassination attempt. He'd been out on the perimeter, checking the supply of, and where necessary issuing fresh, ammo to his handful of ILF irregular troops, when a sniper round, fired by a newly-Nguyen Be-trained Istakat sharpshooter, neatly took off almost all of his left ear. Two inches to the right and his head would've been pulverized.

Despite being rendered partly unconscious, he'd managed to raise Roundhouse-6 on his finally-supplied "Henderson-type" radio, and the next-available ATAS chopper had come and hauled the shaken Che Kak's ass back to Phu-Lama for medical attention. After which Colonel Smith and some of the more senior of Henderson's remaining Roundhouse colleagues had brought him in and they'd huddled with the doughty RPAF Captain, whose head was still all freshly bandaged-up.

"Hey, Che Kak, you look like a mummy!"

"Mummy of who? My mummy dead, long time befo'."

"OK, forget it — "

They'd discussed the matter of diminishing assets and morale. The poor Meu-Jong civilians on Landing Site-Echo had not yet recovered from the devastation of the mortar attack, and, over a lunch of tea, White Horse scotch and sticky-rice, Smith, the senior Roundhouse guys and Che Kak had agreed to close down LS-Echo. Just shut the whole damn thing down, lock-stock. ATAS would re-locate its fifteen-hundred-or-so Meu-Jong civilians to the larger, and more defensible LS-Kilo, a couple of klicks to the southwest, and Che Kak and his small cohort of a couple of hundred troops would merge with, and reinforce, those already at Kilo.

It was a setback, there was no denying that, but one good thing that came out of this decision was that it afforded them the opportunity to solve "The Mr. Kwat Problem": Thus, the old traitor was told that he was being sent back to his UN Headquarters in Phu-Lama (which he was), and that a special ATAS helicopter was being sent just for him (which it was). However, unfortunately for him, on that flight, on which only the ATAS pilot, an ex-Army Military Intelligence 1LT-turned-CIA case officer called Phil Aderman who was Henderson's replacement, and a Thai member of their special Paramilitary Police (PARU) who was disguised as the kicker, were on board, Mr. Kwat suffered a fatal fall out of the Huey's open door into the karst cliffs, some three thousand feet below. It was a terrible, shocking tragedy, of course, and the Operation Roundhouse advisors in Col Smith's Combined Logistics Group shop had with grief-stricken enthusiasm rolled dice to see who'd be the one who got to officially notify the UN.

+ + + + + + +

Young King Pom Matak of Phuland would be less lucky than Che Kak. The King was assassinated on 17 July 1972:

Two kilos of Soviet PW5-A *plastique* had been stuffed by a Buddhist monk, a secret member of the Phu Istakat, into a huge basket of flowers which the monk's *wat*, "The Great Wat", had prepared as a welcome gift to the King during a much-publicized Royal visit in which His Majesty was to come there and pray for the nation. The basket had been entrusted to an utterly unsuspecting, and impossibly winsome little 10-year old Phu girl, who had smilingly hefted it over into His Majesty's welcoming arms. At which point, *boom!*

In addition to the King and the little girl, twelve others, including two government ministers and one Reuters stringer, had been killed outright, and forty-five bystanding well-wishers had been wounded. And when the word "wounded" is used here, it is not "cuts and bruises" that are being referred to, but rather charming dismemberment *à la* Cleotis Robinson ("The Piston") Jones.

In America, two days after the King's assassination, CBS Evening News would breathlessly report an "Exclusive": That there was "speculation" among "seasoned Southeast Asia hands" that the regicide atrocity in Phu-Lama "might" have been committed, or "commissioned", by the CIA, who, in the words of the stern and authoritative-sounding CBS "anchor", "...might have had reasons of its own to want to replace the King with someone more 'compliant'. There is, of course, ample precedent for such an occurrence, as was most recently seen in the 1963 CIA-engineered assassination of President Ngo Dinh Diem of South Vietnam."

This particular bit of CBS "speculation" had begun its meandering virtual-life as a "news" item in the leftist Cypriot newspaper "πάλη" ("Struggle"). Which "news" item had been wholly fabricated by the busy and creative boys in the KGB's Directorate-Д ("*Dezinformatsiya*"). It had then beaten a rapid bureaucratic path into the hands of the KGB-chauffeur of the Russian Embassy in Nicosia, who had hand-delivered it to a Cypriot KGB-agent cut-out (a garrulous tomato wholesaler, as it happened), who had, in turn, himself dropped it off into the mailbox of the "Struggle" newspaper. Then the item, which appeared in "Struggle" the next day, had been "picked up" by the AP's Mediterranean Desk, and CBS had gotten it from the AP.

Not, in fairness to CBS, that they had any reason to know of the KGB origin of their "Exclusive"... but the question lingers: Would CBS have been deterred from running it if it *had* known of the story's Soviet provenance? One likes to *think* so, of course, but in those parlous times, that was by no means a certainty.

+ + + + + + +

And... in a deserted spot near a clearing in a jungle valley in the Pang Phu Meu, an old he-tiger happened across the semi-decomposed remnants of something. The tiger, although certainly experienced in such matters, was at a loss to identify the creature-thing from which this meat came, partly because it had been dead for, by jungle standards, rather a long time — and partly because it had no head. But the tiger ate it anyway.

THE END